UNLUCKY LIKE US

BOOK 12 IN THE LIKE US SERIES

KRISTA & BECCA
RITCHIE

CHARACTER LIST

Not all characters in this list will make an appearance in the book, but most will be mentioned. Ages represent the age of the character at the beginning of the book. Some characters will be older when they're introduced, depending on their birthday.

The Hales

Loren Hale & Lily Calloway

Maximoff – 25

Luna – 20

Xander – 17

Kinney – 15

Ripley (grandchild) – 20 months

The Cobalts

Richard Connor Cobalt & Rose Calloway

Jane – 25

Charlie – 22

Beckett – 22

Eliot – 21

Tom – 20

Ben – 18

Audrey – 15

The Meadows

Ryke Meadows & Daisy Calloway

Sullivan – 22

Winona – 16

The Abbeys

Garrison Abbey & Willow Hale

Vada – 16

The Security Team

These are the bodyguards that protect the Hales, Cobalts, and Meadows.

KITSUWON SECURITIES INC.
SECURITY FORCE OMEGA

Akara Kitsuwon (boss) – 28

Thatcher Moretti (lead) – 30

Banks Moretti – 30

Farrow Hale – 30

Oscar Highland-Oliveira – 33

Paul Donnelly – 29

Quinn Oliveira – 23

Gabe Montgomery – 23

Kannika "Frog" Kitsuwon – 18

PRICE KEPLER'S TRIPLE SHIELD SERVICES
SECURITY FORCE EPSILON

Jon Sinclair (lead) – 40s

O'Malley – 29

Ian Wreath – 30s

Vance Wreath – 20s

Chris Novak – 30s

Ryan Cruz Jr. – 20s

…and more

SECURITY FORCE ALPHA

Price Kepler (lead) – 40s

Tony Ramella – 30

Bruno Bandoni – 50s

Monroe – 30s

…and more

A NOTE FROM THE AUTHORS

Unlucky Like Us is the twelfth book in the Like Us Series. Even though the series changes POVs throughout, to understand events that take place in the previous novels, the series should be read in its order of publication.

Unlucky Like Us should be read after *Misfits Like Us*.

A NOTE FROM LUNA HALE

Dear Unearthly Reader,

And so, this is a new part of my journey, which we call *life* here on Earth. I wasn't sure I should continue, not after all that's happened, but he's a big reason why I'm not stopping. If you ever find this, you should know there are good people on Earth. He's worth knowing. He's worth remembering. And when the world has decayed and all I've ever known has disappeared in time, you should know the very best of humankind is him.

Read this. (I hope you understand my language.) He might be long gone with me, but I hope he's immortalized in this text. Please, keep him alive.

It's always been easier to believe in you than anything else, and I do hope you exist. I still hope this finds you well. Keep it safe, wherever your voyage takes you.

Somewhere far, far away,
Luna Hale

PART ONE

"The will to win and the power of war are given by the dark side—or, as dawn throws back the night...they are given by the light!"

- Tales of the Jedi: Knights of the Old Republic (Ulic Qel-Droma and the Beast Wars of Onderon #1)

1

Luna Hale

IF I COULD STAY ON the shingled roof for another lightyear, I would. I'd never unplant my butt from this very spot. I'd just wait here until my dad changes his mind and gives Donnelly permission to date me.

I think I have a better chance of rotting away on the roof.

Donnelly has disappeared into the dark of my parents' backyard. After fighting to see the last outline of his body, he's just…gone. Instead of glancing up at the twinkling stars, I gaze down at the sketch he just drew for me.

Black pen bleeds into the ripped paper: him and me kissing among whirling planets and stars, all fancifully drawn in one continuous line. Like we're forever connected to the galaxy of our dreams. I clutch the sketch protectively. It's the embodiment of us. Of what we could be.

Of what I *hope* we will be.

I hate that it still feels so out of reach. Like this *happily ever after* version of us lives in another timeline. But I know what Donnelly would say. I can practically feel the warmth of him beside me, murmuring the loving words against the pit of my ear.

"Believe with me."

I whisper in the night, "I want to." *Oh, how I want to.* The cynical pieces of me struggle to cling on to that light. Reality is darker. Sadder. Bleaker.

I try to take a breath. The savory smell of meatloaf wafts through my open window. Joining a family dinner is the last thing I feel like doing. An ache has blossomed in my chest, and I don't know how to temper the pain other than to transplant it with anger.

We didn't need my dad's permission to date. Not really.

Donnelly and I are both adults. We're not stuck in some medieval romance where he has to beg the king to wed the princess. It's not like that at all. Though, here on this planet, I am considered an American princess. Fame and media are usually the bigger considerations when dating anyone.

How much privacy will they lose?

How much media attention will I gain dating so-and-so?

Will the public hate them or love them?

We haven't even breached that stage of deliberation. We're trapped in the beginning.

I do understand that Donnelly wants this to be easier for both of us, and that means having my dad on our side. It's a rational plan. A *good* plan.

Especially if my dad's hatred of Donnelly somehow becomes a headline: *Loren Hale Disapproves of Daughter's New Boyfriend!* I could see the press eating up the rivalry like it's a seven-course meal.

I just hate this shitty outcome where my dad told Donnelly to live in purgatory until his family is no longer a threat. Tears prick my eyes. Because I know, deep down, that Donnelly's family might *always* be a threat. And what then?

We'll never be together.

"Luna?!" my sister calls out. "Mom told me to come get you for dinner!"

With the sketch in my fingers, I hug my knees to my chest and blink repeatedly to keep the waterworks at bay. My throat swells too much to talk.

"Luna?!" Kinney's voice grows louder. I imagine she's walking deeper into my room. "Are you on the roof? You're not trying to get beamed up again, are you?"

There's a sharpness to her voice like she thinks the idea is completely absurd.

Some of my very first trips to my roof were in pursuit of being taken away by extraterrestrial life. By you, unearthly reader. Not only to see a new planet. New galaxy. But I felt like the only way to escape my problems was to leave *this* planet. The idea of being kidnapped and swept away somewhere better had this dark allure.

I guess it doesn't seem as cool now.

Donnelly probably wouldn't be beamed up with me, and I don't really want to live on a planet where he's not there.

"Luna, did you hear me?" Kinney steps closer to my window and sticks half her body outside.

I turn my head a fraction, and her narrowed green eyes fix on mine. Dyed black hair is chopped at her collarbones, bangs shading her brows.

"The aliens aren't coming for you," she deadpans. "But if you fall off the roof, you *will* turn into a ghost."

She sounds so much like our dad. It just enlarges a rock in my esophagus. Words are lodged.

"I'll be down in a sec," I say so quietly. I'm unsure if she hears.

Her black-painted lips draw into a thin line, and her vexed expression is riddled with blistering concern. Kinney wears worry like a dress made of razor blades. Unapproachable, untouchable. It's as hard for me to near her as it'd be for any enemy.

We continue to lock eyes in a game of chicken, unmoving and unspeaking and waiting for the other to spew their thoughts. I've never been a great competitor at anything, but breaking contact first sounds as exhausting as spilling my heart.

So I just stare at my sister.

She's sixteen now, but her gangly frame and youthful face shave years off her age. Like me and our mom, she could pass for several years younger, and even though she's firmly a teenager, I still feel the five whole years that separate us like boulders we can't push.

Years don't always create caverns and mountains between siblings.

Sulli and Winona are secret-handshake, hip-bump close, but for some reason, Kinney and I never reached that tip in the sister pyramid.

I think it's because she'll always be closer to Xander, the way that I'm closer to Moffy. Maybe she's contemplating this too because she finally blurts out, "I'll go get Moffy."

"No," I say hurriedly. "I'm fine. I promise." I make a move towards the window to demonstrate just how fine I am. While I step through the threshold, my sneaker catches on the windowsill, and I awkwardly splat on my fuzzy rug in a belly flop.

Oof. Beached flounder has become me.

She blinks. "Super graceful."

I burrito-roll onto my back. While I take a heavy breath, she's extending a hand to me. I clasp her palm, and she helps me rise to my feet. The sketch is still in my possession. Carefully, I slip the paper underneath my bed pillow.

I remember Donnelly's words as he called up to me. *"That's what I imagine in the end. You and me and our galaxy. And maybe I don't want you to forget it."*

"I never will," I told him.

I never will.

It's this tiny, delicate ember of hope that I'm trying to cradle close.

Kinney watches me hide my sketch as if it's a diary. "What's that?"

"A drawing." *Just a future not yet written.* But I hear Donnelly again, telling me it's in the stars. It's already written.

I'm trying to believe.

My ribs constrict, and gradually, I face my sister.

Kinney crosses her arms, her sheer black sleeves complementing the dress-overalls she wears. Dark shadowy makeup further boldens her green eyes. "I'm not a fool, you know. I saw Donnelly talking to Dad. Then he came up here, and next thing you know, he's sliding down your drainpipe to leave."

Red heat bathes my cheeks. "You were watching from a window?" How else did she get that visual?

"Xander and I were." She examines me, up and down, as though she can exhume every buried secret. But even with all my secrets, I'm almost positive who knows what.

The "good head" experiment is only known by my penthouse roommates and Oscar (Donnelly's best friend/Charlie's bodyguard).

Most of those roommates see Donnelly and me as close friends with inside jokes and flirty inclinations. If they have their suspicions about a secret relationship, they haven't shared them with me.

Only Farrow and Maximoff really suspect we're more than we were since Halloween, a week ago. The night of our first kiss.

No one knows Donnelly is StaleBread89.

No one knows for sure that Donnelly and I had sex.

So Xander and Kinney are among the ones that have zero idea that I've had any romantic involvement with Donnelly. In their eyes, we're *just friends.*

And now she's starting to Nancy Drew this like it's The Case of Her Big Sister's Strange Love Life. I guess Donnelly visiting my bedroom is fishy—even if I could blame it on a friendly encounter.

"Okay," I breathe, my eyes raw. My heart has already floated out of my body. I think I truly did give it to Donnelly before he left.

"Okay?" She sounds harsh, but her frown deepens. "Are you upset about him or are you upset about your leaked fics?"

The leaked fics happened at 2 a.m.—last night or this morning, depending on your viewpoint of 2 a.m.—and it feels as fresh as Donnelly just leaving my parents' house. My Fictitious account is deactivated. Gone. My stories like *Human Him, Cosmic Her* are no longer on the web for people to disparage, but screenshots are forever.

The internet is forever.

I haven't looked again to see what people are saying. I'm scared.

Really scared.

An overwhelming pressure tries to crush my chest, and I intake a tighter breath.

"I don't know," I mutter.

"You don't know?" she snaps like that's impossible.

How could I not know what's troubling me? *I do know.* I know it's everything. I know it's easier to just shut down. To switch an *off* button.

Staring far away at the floorboards, I lift my hoodie's hood over my head, and I imagine I'm disintegrating after a Thanos snap. I'm fluttering pieces of dust, drifting into the air. No one feels pain after they dust. They're just gone.

Invisible.

Not present for the bad days, the awful months, and then they reemerge years later as time has passed without them. Without me.

"Luna," Kinney says shakily.

I'm not looking at my sister. My life—it's changed in ways I didn't imagine. In ways I didn't want. With my fics. With Donnelly.

We can't be together.

Not yet.

Maybe never.

Pain flares again, and I try to go numb.

"*Luna*," Kinney forces out my name.

"What do you want me to do?" I whisper.

"Something! Don't just stand there looking dead!" It's then that I hear her panic, and I avoid her gaze while I skim the bookshelves in my childhood bedroom and the star embroidered fabric tapestries billowing from the ceiling.

What would Kinney do if her heart was broken?

Destroy.

Everything.

Breath stuck in my throat, I bolt to my desk and sweep my arms across the surface. A metal lamp, Marvel comic books, and Funko Pops crash against the floor. I don't stop to revel in the destruction. I just create more like a wild creature has body-snatched me. Blood pumping hot, I rip at the hanging fabrics. Dark blue tapestries tear from their thumbtacks in the ceiling.

"Oh...kay, *okay*...this is good," Kinney says, more to herself. Louder, she tells me, "Let it out, Luna. Go for the pillows!"

I fling some bed pillows, my off-kilter pulse ringing in my ears. "The bookcase!"

Quickly, I charge for the bookcase, I throw *Star Wars* novels on the ground. One by one, books I reread and reread, their spines lovingly worn—they meet the floorboards with a loud *thump*. Oxygen is hard to reach, caged inside me with an unfamiliar beast.

I chuck volumes of *New Mutants* my mom bought me when I was twelve, and they slam against the walls. Hot tears burn but don't escape. A feral growl rumbles through my heaving body, and I hurl an armful of *Dawn of X* comics on the floor in a heavy heap.

"Keep going!" Kinney encourages.

I grip the dark brown bookcase and pull. I want the entire thing off its hinges, out of the wall. I want every single item on this shelf to meet a new distorted and battered position, to feel exactly how I feel.

I scream and rattle the bookcase, possessed with the rawest rage and pain. It hurts. It's been hurting, and now it's erupting outside of me.

With strength—strength I didn't realize I have—the wide bookcase lets out a sudden creak and shifts forward. Collectibles and paperbacks begin to slide at me.

"Luna, not that!" Kinney shouts. "Push it back!"

I don't.

I want this.

Comics pelt my head from the top shelves. A ceramic Spider-Man mug shatters at my bare feet.

"LUNA!" Kinney is standing further away, safe from the avalanche.

The bookcase weighs a million times more than I can brace, and as the entire wooden structure teeters forward, I want it to bury me. I want to live underneath the rubble of my childhood. Maybe it'll be where you find me.

In this single solitary moment, I'm not scared of being crushed.

That should scare me, I think.

"LUNA!" Kinney shrieks in pure terror. Her voice jolts me. *She's watching.* I try to push at the bookcase and support the weight for my sister. My arms tremble, tendons screaming in my forearms and shoulders.

It's too heavy.

It's coming down.

I am the creator of my own doom.

"Kin—" I start, but her name is torn out of my throat as someone barrels towards me.

Mom.

Her wide panicked eyes are on this impending demise, and quickly, she clutches the frame of the bookcase—the bookcase that's at least three arm-spans wide. The bookcase that nearly swallows my entire wall. The bookcase that's seconds from crushing me.

She tries to heave the thing upright.

"Go, Luna! Leave!" Mom yells at me. I've never heard her yell like that—with so much urgency and distress.

She can't support the weight on her own either, so I stay and try to dig my feet in. Kinney is suddenly on my other side, using her back and shoulder blades to thrust the bookcase to its original position.

It's at a fifty-degree angle.

It's bearing on all three of us.

"We can't," I mutter, breath knotted inside me.

"We can," our mom says through gritted teeth, trying her mightiest to upright what I've dislodged. Guilt nips at me. "On the count of three, we all push our hardest, okay? One, two, *three.*"

We push. My arms vibrate, and I hate the little voice in the back of my head, whispering that we can't, telling me to just end it.

Give.

Up.

Luna.

I don't want to. I don't want to. I don't ever want to be that person.

Tears burn my eyes. I hate how exhausted I already feel. I hate how I want to erase two nights in a row.

But then, I don't.

I never want to erase Donnelly.

"Is it moving?" Kinney questions.

"Yeah," Mom nods profusely, sweat beading her forehead. "It's almost there."

It hasn't budged.

"Again," Mom decrees. "One, two, *three*."

We heave. I start to lose my grip and my feet slide. No, no! "Mom!" I shout as the bookcase groans and tips forward on us. *This is all my fault.*

"Okay, we need reinforcements," Mom realizes in a quick, panting breath. "Lo! *Lo! LOREN HALE GET YOUR BUTT UP HERE!!*" Her panicked words in a scream do the trick.

Footsteps pound harder than my heart, and more than just my dad appears.

"*Jesus*, Lily," Dad says, fear encasing my mom's name. He's already racing into my bedroom, along with my brothers and Farrow.

They all ram the bookcase against the wall. Xander uses his shoulder like Kinney had been. The structure *thunks* against the plaster and then stays eerily motionless.

As the dust silently settles and I'm still here among broken mugs and thrown books—I'm not invisible; I haven't dusted yet—their eyes veer around the destruction and onto me.

The source.

I'm…ashamed.

I've never shown my pain like Kinney, and it's too loud and exposed.

"I'll get a broom," Mom says with a hearty nod, beelining for the door. "Everything's going to be okay, Luna!" She shouts super quickly on her way into the hall. Moffy follows in a jog and says something about Ripley being in his highchair.

I blink repeatedly like I'll finally inherit teleportation. My mom says it could've skipped several generations, and we truly don't know whether Great Grandma Pearl had superpowers or not. She died before I was born, but Dad always disputed the idea and said the woman never left Palm Beach.

To which, Mom replied, *that we know of.*

I like my mom's imaginative version of Great Grandma Pearl—a superpowered woman who explored the world without anyone ever suspecting. I picture happy wrinkles around her wide smile while she's riding a moped in Florence with a hot Italian hunk. In the next hour, she's sipping tea in London by her awesome self, then she's exploring the Pyramids in Cairo with her sister Margot and ferrying along the Golden Horn in Istanbul.

Charlie said it's one of his favorite ferry rides, and I'm still surprised he answered me when I asked him about the best ferries in the world.

So in this moment of my life, I am blinking and blinking and hoping Great Grandma Pearl's teleportation existed and that it finally transfers to me.

Please.

I don't know how to recover from destroying my childhood room. My parents could've turned this space into another office or gym. Instead, they preserved it for me.

That's how good they are.

How kind.

And how dumb I am—to ruin it. Over what? Throwing my books isn't going to bring him back!

"What the hell happened?" my dad asks, out of breath. The sharpness of his gaze cuts from me to my sister.

Kinney is waiting for me to explain. To share what I never shared with her: *the details.*

I bring the collar of my hoodie up to my eyes. My chest is being crushed with a weight heavier than the bookcase. Turning away from them, I go towards my bed and trip over the comics I'd thrown.

My knees hit the floor.

Farrow bends down, his arms around me while I crumple. A gnarled sound I've never heard myself make suddenly ruptures out of my lungs, and I choke on a scream.

The scream morphs into me crying into my hoodie.

I hate this feeling that claws at me. I hate it so much.

Knelt behind me, Farrow has a calming hand on my neck. He might be my brother's husband, but he's been a friend to me—and it's nice… it is *really* nice having him here. Once he whispers for me to breathe deep breaths, my cries die like a wounded bird going motionless, and I try to take a lungful of air.

I rub at my splotchy, hot cheeks and fight the urge to hide in my hoodie.

"It has to be her fics, right?" Xander asks softly. "It's going to be okay, Luna."

My dad looks distraught seeing me in this much pain, but I'm avoiding his daggered eyes more than anyone. I just can't…

It's going to be okay, Luna.

I shake my head slowly.

"I know…" Xander stammers for the words. "I know it feels like it never will be."

I lift my anguished gaze to my seventeen-year-old brother. Xander Hale isn't a supernova in my sky. He's not Eliot or Tom or even Moffy. He's my little brother who was stuck inside a decrepit, often dusty and darkened castle, and if anyone knows the roadmap out of that awful place, it'd be him.

Chunky red headphones rest around his neck, and pieces of his shaggy brown hair touch the lashes of his expressive amber eyes. It's hard to look away.

"I know you don't want to be here…" Xander tells me. "But you have to ignore that voice. Not forever. Just ignore it this minute, this shitty second."

This minute.

This second.

I inhale slowly.

"Small hurdles, you know?" Xander says quietly. "You can do that. I know you can, sis. You're way stronger than me."

Hot tears fall in a blink because I don't think I ever have been. I think sometimes I'm the weakest of the entire Hale family. Or maybe, I'm just the hardest on myself, but how can I even be certain that's true?

"It's *Donnelly*," Kinney says with bite. "He hurt her."

No.

The word is lost inside my swollen throat. I start to shake my head, and Farrow looks out at Kinney like she's so wrong. *Thank you!*

"He'd never hurt Luna," Farrow says like it's unfathomable.

She humphs, arms still crossed.

His brows rise. "He'd sooner hurt *himself*, Kinney."

She snaps, "You're just saying that because he's your friend."

"No, I'm saying that because I know my friend."

"But you don't know what he did!" Kinney charges forward, and our dad puts a hand on her bony shoulder, stopping her in place. "He was in her room! And then he left, and she looked…she was…" She lets out a frustrated, upset huff. "We don't know what he did, okay? He could've broken her heart or made some kind of *unconsented* move on her."

"Whoa," Farrow cuts in with arched brows. "Let's take a giant step back here."

"I'm not talking to you. You're *biased*. Dad." She rotates to our dad, who has been gazing out the ajar window like Donnelly might still be on the roof. It'd be too much to hope he's wishing for Donnelly's peaceful existence. It's more likely he's hoping he can drag him back inside and grill him.

"Luna and Donnelly are friends," Xander pipes in before our dad can. "I'm with Farrow—he wouldn't hurt her. This is probably about her fics."

"You're biased too." Kinney turns on him. "Donnelly is your *bodyguard*. Dad is the only rational one here."

Xander groans. "You're always going to take Dad's side."

Kinney glares. "No, I'm taking *Luna's* side. Our sister. I know a broken heart when I see one because mine has been *pulverized*. What has yours been? Fully intact. Never toyed with. No signs of scar tissue. Nothing."

Xander stares deeper into Kinney. "So what?"

"So you would think this has to do with her fics because the media is your horror, but heartbreak is *hell*. And to quote one of your fictional favorites, 'You. Know. *Nothing*.'"

Xander's chest collapses.

The *Game of Thrones* reference lingers tensely in the air.

"Kinney," Dad says a quiet reprimand, his hand still on her shoulder.

"What?" She twists her head to him. "It's true, Dad. She has to be upset about Donnelly. I just know something happened, and we're just going to do nothing?! Let's hunt him down." *No.* "Threaten his stupid mortal life and the lives of his future ugly children." *No.* "That's the least we could do—"

No! I splinter open. "He didn't do anything except want to be with me!" I shout with everything inside my heart, my throat searing and scratched.

"What?" Kinney squeaks out, jaw unhinged.

Xander goes motionless, his hands on the headphones at his neck.

Mom with her broom and Maximoff with his son are in the doorway. Not sure how long they've been here, but Baby Ripley is perched on my brother's waist. The one-year-old is totally quiet looking from Farrow to Moffy, as though his dads have the answer to the strangeness of tonight.

My cheeks feel warm again, and I imagine they're beet-red and tear-splotched. But I pick myself off the ground, Farrow right behind me. All this time, I've felt protective over Donnelly. Over us. Over what we share together.

And I can't let *anyone* in my family think the worst of him.

I just can't.

I'd rather they know the painful truth. "He didn't do anything except want to be with me," I tell them more clearly.

"And you didn't want to be with him?" Kinney asks with confusion. She glances to Dad. "We still might need to hunt him down."

"What?" our mom's eyes widen at our dad like the witch hunt was erected in her absence. And I guess it kinda was, but not by him. "There are no hunts of people. This isn't *The Hunger Games*."

"Thank you, Lily," Farrow says.

"But it could be," Kinney notes.

"Oh my God," Farrow mutters and then looks at Moffy like, *your sister, man.*

Maximoff scrunches his brows. "Why would we hunt down Donnelly? He's a good person."

Kinney glowers at him. "You've been absent for half the conversation. So don't come in here thinking you know what's going on."

"Jesus, Kinney. I'm just trying to understand."

"And I'm just trying to protect Luna!" She throws up her hands. "What are you all doing?! Dad is with me at least. *Dad.*" She turns to him again.

"Shelve the pitchforks, Kinney," he says gently and more quietly than softly, but then again, my dad's voice is almost never soft.

"Not pitchforks. A *sharpened* knife."

He squeezes her shoulder. "Shelve the knives, battleaxes, all weapons. We're not pointing them at Paul Donnelly."

It takes me aback. The certainty of his voice. Is he really not against Donnelly anymore?

Kinney frowns. She's searching for an adversary of my broken heart. In the battle of good and evil, Kinney needs the villain of all villains to attack. "But Dad—"

"If you want to point a blade at someone, it's going to be me—not him."

Kinney jolts backwards like our dad electrocuted her. Her breathing heavies. "You didn't do anything bad. You couldn't...you wouldn't?"

He wears a half-smile. "Me? Do something bad? I'd never." His sarcasm and way of cheering up Kinney lands lifeless in the tense room.

"*Dad,*" she says, sounding scared. "What'd you do?"

He lets out a breath, glances at our mom for support, and then holds out a reassuring hand. "I meant that if you go after Paul, you're going to have to go *through* me. I'm standing in front of him, and just so everyone in the room knows"—he spins around to lock eyes with each of us, staying on me for an extended beat—"I haven't been *easy* on him. I might've even been hell for him." He cringes into another dry smile. "So…it's complicated." He claps his hands together. "Class dismissed. Let's clean this up. Help your sister—"

"Wait a minute," Xander interjects. "That's it? You're leaving out like half the fucking story."

"Yeah," Kinney says. "This doesn't make *sense*. Why are you protecting Donnelly? And from what? And what does that even have to do with Luna?"

Mom sweeps the shattered ceramic mug into a dust bin. It's the only sound outside of our dogs whining behind the closed door.

Either my dad is struggling to unleash the full truth out of respect for me and Donnelly, or because he's not sure how much Kinney and Xander should know.

I decide to just tell them. It's better than lying, and they're not accepting any vague picture anymore.

"Donnelly came here tonight to ask Dad for permission to date me," I explain. "Of what Donnelly told me, Dad said, *not yet*." I turn to him for confirmation.

He nods once, his neck taut and muscles flexed. "Yep. That happened."

Maximoff and Farrow exchange an unreadable look.

"You like him?" Kinney asks with a deeper frown, and I wonder if she's baffled on how she missed this rare, strange occurrence. Me falling for Xander's bodyguard.

I just nod, words feeling too tender and fragile to share.

Xander stares at the floorboards, unblinking.

"Why not yet?" Kinney asks our dad. "If they both like each other, what's the big deal?"

"His family," Dad starts to say, just as Xander suddenly bolts out of the room.

"Summers!" Maximoff calls after our brother, but Xander is gone. He leaves, hopefully just for his bedroom. Our parents share a quick glance, and I think they're deciding on who stays for me and who goes for him, but Maximoff makes things easy.

He passes Baby Ripley to Farrow and says, "I'll go check on him." Quickly, Moffy runs after our brother, his footsteps echoing down the hallway. "Xander!" I hear the slam of a bedroom door. The opening of it. The close of it again.

Xander's not so great reaction to knowing I'm falling for his bodyguard—and that Donnelly has attempted to be with me—is sitting like curdled milk in my stomach.

"Why is he this upset?" my dad questions Farrow, his ass now in the hot seat.

My temples start pounding from the mental detours.

"You're asking me?" Farrow adjusts his son on his hip.

"You do know *Paul* the best of everyone here."

Ouch.

But I guess that's probably true. Farrow knows Donnelly in ways that I might never learn or come to discover. That sucks—the idea that I can't even voyage deeper into Donnelly's mind, his heart. That the exploration has limitations and borders, and I'm standing at the *No Entry* sign.

Farrow tips his head. "That's definitely debatable."

"Debatable, okay." Dad nods a lot and paces a short distance back and forth. "You know what? I have a *serious* problem with *you* right now and it's not even funny."

Oh no.

2

Luna Hale

"ME?" FARROW SAYS.

"Yeah, *you*," my dad retorts. "I want to laugh. I would really goddamn love to, but this has to stop." He raises his hands in a way like he'd love to strangle his son-in-law.

Farrow looks stumped. "I don't follow, Lo."

"You. Donnelly. Acting like you're nothing more than two hallway acquaintances." He stakes a glare on him. "Do you know how annoying that is? Do you know how different things would've been if you'd just been upfront with me?"

Visceral heat radiates off Farrow's brown eyes. He could give Cyclops a good run. "I've *been* upfront with you, Lo. I told you exactly the kind of person Donnelly is, and you still chose not to listen to me."

"You never said you met him when he was seventeen."

Farrow's face screws up. "What difference would that've made?"

"Papa?" Ripley blubbers up at Farrow.

He takes a breath. "It's okay, little man." He kisses his son's cheek. "Lily, do you mind…?"

After my mom ditches the broom and fills the dustpan, she gladly lifts her grandchild in her arms. She bops his nose, and Ripley lets out the cutest giggle. I'm a little jealous of the baby cuddles. I just hug my arms around my body.

Farrow faces my dad head-on. "And?"

"You were teenagers."

"Okay, but what does that change? I told you that he has no bad bone in his body. I told you that he'd give you the last shirt he owns. Right off his back. Shit, I told you he's been *kind* towards the women he's been with, and he would let Luna rule his world if she wanted to. I told you he'd *be there* for her. I told you they'd be good together. So what the hell does us meeting as teenagers have to do with *shit?*"

"I wish I knew what he meant to you from *you* or even *him.* Not from Luna. Not from Moffy. Instead, you just kept telling me who he is."

Farrow keeps shaking his head.

"You left out an important part."

Farrow breathes angrier, shaking his head harder. "I didn't."

"You forgot to tell me he's like your brother."

It knocks Farrow one step backward. He rotates his head away from my dad.

"That's the thing, Farrow. I had no goddamn idea the depth of how close you were to him. I didn't know what he *meant* to you." My dad cringes into a wincing smile. "And that's the *other* thing, I should've known. It was right there in my face." Guilt knits his brows. "He was your best man, but for some goddamn reason, I thought you were just college buddies. Crossed paths later and decided to become bodyguards around the same time. But you aren't just college friends. Right?"

Farrow takes the longest second to recoup from this bombshell. I haven't seen him this frazzled before. Not much ever seems to unsettle him.

My dad crushes the silence first. "I learned that he followed you to Yale when he was a teenager. I did some digging after that *nonchalant* comment from *Paul,* and I learned from 'sources' that he stayed with you for most of your adult life. I learned that you do know him better than anyone else on this fucked planet, so you can stop acting like you don't."

Farrow's eyes are reddened as they meet my dad again. "It shouldn't have mattered. I gave you enough."

"I didn't know how *deeply* you knew him. So when you vouched for him, I would've liked to know it was coming from the closest thing he has to a fucking brother."

Farrow looks tortured. He combs a rough hand through his hair.

Dad sees. He blinks a lot, like he's reassessing what he's saying to Maximoff's husband. "I'm not trying to blame you, Farrow. I should've asked more questions. I should've realized sooner. I'm not saying you're at fault—"

"You're saying it would've made a difference," Farrow says through clenched teeth. "I don't advertise my relationships like they're commercials on a fucking TV screen for other people to consume. They just exist. They *are*."

"I guess I missed it," my dad says, bitterness to his words. "Maybe I didn't even want to see it. Maybe I was afraid of what it'd mean. You and him. He'd be *inescapable*." Skin pleats between his cinched brows. "It would've been easier to be slapped in the face with the truth. But that never happened." My dad shrugs at Farrow. "Why do you both undercut what you are to each other? You more than him? I don't get it. Honestly. What's the point?"

"We don't undercut shit," Farrow says quietly, almost under his breath. "We know what we mean to each other, and that's all that's ever mattered. This is the first time it's ever been a point of contention with anyone."

"I would've liked to know," my dad says just as quietly. "It would've meant something to me."

"We didn't grow up together," Farrow reminds him.

"Neither did me and my brother. I met Ryke the day I turned twenty-one."

Realizations wash over me about the same time that Farrow's expression changes shape. I think we're both understanding just how much this would've *meant something* to my dad. He loves Ryke to his deepest, rawest core, and I wonder if he's reevaluated everything Farrow has ever said about Donnelly.

I wonder if that's ultimately a big reason why his heart has shifted.

I imagine he's thinking if Farrow has seen good in Donnelly for years, if Farrow loves Donnelly to his deepest, rawest core, then maybe Donnelly isn't a bad influence or a bad guy. Maybe he's a man worthy enough to be with his daughter.

To be with me.

I don't even care that it might've taken Farrow to change my dad's perspective.

I don't care that it wasn't me who could've done it.

I'm just glad it's happening.

It's shifting.

Hope glimmers, and I wonder if Donnelly saw this tiny spark before he left the house. I wonder if this is partly what he was trying to leave me with too.

My dad holds Farrow's gaze. "Christ, you were *younger* than even me and my brother when you two met."

Farrow is unblinking, stunned silent.

"*I would've liked to know,*" my dad says strongly. "It would've mattered. And I don't know why it is, but the bonds we make matter to other people. I know that Ryke and Rose's friendship *matters* to me. Connor and Daisy *matter* to me. Willow and Daisy *matter*. Garrison and Lily *matter*. Just like you and Donnelly are going to matter to me. Hell, you both may even annoy me." He grimaces but stares deeper into Farrow. "But these relationships mean something to the people who love you. And I love you like a son, and I'm…I'm *sorry* I didn't take your word beforehand. I'm sorry I'm an ass. I've been an ass. You deserved a father-in-law who listened, and I didn't. But I promise, I'm going to try from now on."

Mom smiles a soft, proud smile over at Dad, but like me, she's on pins and needles looking back at Farrow.

His eyes are bloodshot, and his nose flares from emotion. "I'm going to hate knowing that's all it would've taken for you to believe me earlier, because I would've done *anything*, Lo. I would've done anything for him." His Adam's apple bobs against his neck tattoos, and he scrapes another hand through his hair. "There is something that I thought would've made a difference—but it was never that."

"Yeah?" my dad frowns.

"Yeah." Farrow takes a beat. "I've been wishing I could give you the slam-dunk: the reason you'd actually feel like *shit* for ever hating Donnelly, but I couldn't. Because I love that motherfucker, and when he tells me not to say shit to you, I don't say shit to you, but you need to ask him. At some point. You need him to tell you everything he's done."

I assume this has to do with the adoption and Ripley. All my penthouse roommates know Scottie only let Farrow and Maximoff adopt Ripley after a deal that Donnelly made. He's been giving Scottie his paycheck, and as far as I know, my dad has no clue Donnelly has been broke for Moffy's son.

"I'll ask him," he says.

I take a small step forward. "You don't hate Donnelly anymore?"

Dad locks eyes with me. I've been pretty quiet, and my voice sounds raspy and hurt still. I can see him trying to soften his gaze for me, but honestly, it's making him look constipated. "I'm getting to know him. Let's start there, okay?"

I nod, knowing it's a beginning at least. He's never really tried before.

"But you need to put the brakes on this, Queen of Thebula."

"Dad—"

"You and him. *Brakes.* Can you do that?" Severity sharpens his gaze.

Pain flares again. "But—"

"His family is dangerous, Luna. There are no *buts*. I'm handling this with Donnelly. It's the team-up no one saw coming, especially me." He touches his chest. "It's Cyclops and Peepers."

"Peepers?" I cringe at the worst X-Men villain *ever*. He did not just refer to Donnelly as *Peepers*. His enlarged eyes and bald head make him look like a toad.

Like my dad is eating glass, he slowly amends, "Cyclops and whoever you choose."

I don't know if Donnelly reminds me of anyone but himself, but I'd never cast him as a villain.

"Peter Parker," I say softly. I think about Peter's tragic backstory and light-heartedness amidst adversity as he swings between buildings with a joke and a laugh. He's also one of my favorites. "Spider-Man."

Dad makes another cringey face. "*Fine.* Cyclops and Spider-Man."

A team-up. It is a strange reality, but one that feels better than them being at odds.

Dad looks at me with more seriousness. "And in the meantime, just use some patience." He glances over at Mom. "Does anyone in this family have any?"

Mom raises her hand. "Me."

He smiles lovingly. "Yes, you do, love." He swings his head back to me. "Your mom will share some patience with you."

"*All* the patience," Mom says to me, like we'll get through this together. I'm not alone. It tries to swell inside me. It tries to banish cynicism and dark tides. But negative voices creep up and whisper, *you have to do this alone. You shouldn't need her aid.*

"I'll help." Kinney begins to smile. "Let's take down the Donnelly family."

Dad turns to her. "This is a solo slaughtering, little Slytherin."

She gapes. "But you just said Donnelly is helping!"

"How exactly is he helping?" Farrow questions, more ire in his stance.

"We're working on it. If you want to join, I *might* accept your membership. We'll see."

Kinney looks peeved that she's not being included.

"Might," Dad assures her.

She rolls her eyes. "Whatever."

Farrow runs a finger over his lip piercing. "You said you're going to protect him, Lo. So if your fucking plan is to send him back to South Philly to speak to his father, you *better* not hang him out to dry. Or else I'll have a problem with you."

Dad wears another half-smile. "Spoken like a true brother."

"I'm serious."

"As am I." He shifts his weight, his sarcasm replaced with real gravity. "I'm going to protect him. I promise you that."

My teeny tiny ember of hope sparks to life again. Maybe, possibly, taking down the Donnelly family is a priority to my dad. Maybe it's not something impossible.

Maybe it's right around the corner.

At what cost, though? The concern all over Farrow is verging on *fear*, and I know how heinous the Donnelly family is. They went after Beckett on Halloween, and in turn, they assaulted Beckett's bodyguard. But I've never really met anyone related to Donnelly. All I have is my overactive imagination.

I start to picture Donnelly drifting in the dark. I picture him opening a door and drowning in a sea of vipers. My pulse races, and my deepest desire is to run right after him. I think of all the times he's run after me, and I don't want him to be alone.

But we're not together, so how does this even work?

3

Luna Hale

THE PIT IN MY STOMACH destroys my hunger, and Xander still hasn't emerged from his bedroom. Dad goes to talk to him, and even though I'm worried a comet just tore through my relationship with my brother, I think the best path is the one where I give him space to digest everything.

Right now, I really want to see Donnelly, to know he's still in my orbit and hasn't rocketed to another solar system.

I tell my parents I'm thinking of just heading home for the penthouse in Center City. To my surprise, my mom offers to drive me. I thought she'd stay behind for Xander, and I try not to feel guilty knowing I'm taking her from him.

My mom is behind the wheel of her black Aston Martin. The fancy SUV was an anniversary gift from my dad several years ago. My parents rarely flaunt their wealth. Uncle Connor and Aunt Rose are the ones who love designer brands, jewelry in the six-figure mark, and rare bottles of wine.

At some point, my parents' feelings changed on cars.

Dad bought a Bugatti, and Mom reluctantly loved it more than her old BMW. I remember she said she felt like she was cheating on an archaic thing for the newer model and it felt wrong.

Cars aren't people, love. They don't have feelings. You're cheating on nothing. That's what my dad said.

After that, I wrote a sci-fi story on Fictitious about sentient cars with feelings in a futuristic society. They're not exactly people, but they have a consciousness. Kinda like *Herbie* and *Transformers*, but with a *Battlestar Galactica* feel.

Readers seemed to like that one…

But it's off Fictitious now. Deleted with my account. Though, it's printed and buried in my closet, pages stapled together.

I frown and watch my mom smoothly switch lanes, comfortable in the leather seat. She really does love the Aston Martin. If it does have feelings, it'd be purring in content.

The headlights illuminate the Philly roads. Our bodyguards follow in their own vehicle behind us, and I wonder if Frog is bored out of her mind with the company of Security Force Alpha.

I glance down at my phone.

Too afraid to unlock the screen and see social media, I just stare at the time and a pic of me and Donnelly in our shared bathroom. A mirror selfie: his inked arm is resting on my head while I show off my green tongue piercing. He's flashing his silver nipple ring.

It could be innocent to those who know us.

To strangers it's flirty and spicy enough to elicit intrigue. Comments. Suspicion.

I captured the photo a couple days after our first (and only time) having sex, which was a week ago. We've mostly fooled around after that, but his cock has only been inside me the night he made my bounty hunter/alien queen fantasy come true. Then, we dated in our bedrooms for the week. When he came home from protecting Xander, we would binge TV, eat Tastykakes, smoke a little. I wrote on my laptop some nights, and he drew in his sketchbook.

It never moved out of our rooms. Never became something more. But I guess I thought he was on the road to being my boyfriend, so I made the photo my lock screen.

"I guess I need to delete it," I mutter aloud.

"Delete what?" my mom asks, barely glancing over. Her green eyes maintain contact with the street and nighttime traffic.

"A picture of me and Donnelly." I like how happy we look. *Radiant* isn't a word I'd use in my fics to describe characters that are like me, but I start believing we look radiant together. Apart, do we seem gloomy? Miserable?

I don't want to be miserable without him, but moving on from him isn't an option I desire or could even take. I've tried to get over Donnelly already, and that didn't work.

"It's your lock screen?" Mom asks.

"Yeah."

"Don't delete it," she says fast like I'm already on the verge, but I haven't even unlocked the phone yet. "Just change the lock screen to something else while this thing is going on."

This thing is the vague stand-in for *dealing with the Donnellys*.

She flicks on the wipers as light drizzle pelts the windshield. "What's the pic anyway?"

"I'm showing off my tongue ring. Donnelly is flashing his nipple piercing." I already feel defensive, so I add quicky, "He's cool."

Cool?

That's the best I could come up with? Sure, he's inked and pierced, and he's spent part of his life as a tattooist, but that's the very surface of Donnelly. It's not even underneath the skin. He deserves *more*, maybe more than I can give, but I'm going to try.

I sit up straighter in the passenger seat. "That's not why I like him. It's not because he's cool."

She's just listening with a tiny smile. It encourages me to go ahead.

Very quietly, I ask, "Do you remember the slumber party at Jeffra's house? When I was little?"

Her round face blotches with red marks. I think in anger—though, my mom is rarely furious. Her brows bunch together. "The one where the girls played a prank on you?"

"Yeah, that one."

They wrote *Weirdo* on my forehead while I'd been sleeping, and my dad came and picked me up with Uncle Ryke.

I watch the streetlamps fly past us like floating orbs in the darkened sky. "Dad told me that it's okay if I never had friends. He said that I'm the queen of my own galaxy, and after so many years, I've realized there are people in the universe who make you feel at home. Donnelly has made me feel like my galaxy is the happiest, most exhilarating place to be, even if I'm the only one there." I drop my head and gaze back at our photo. "He treats me like I'm his moon. His stars. Like I'm the person who makes him glad it's today and there'll be a tomorrow, and I don't know if I've ever been that for anyone who's not my family."

I'm important to someone.

I'm not a failure. I'm not a fuck-up or future screw-up to Donnelly.

I'm someone *worth* something. And he's worth *everything* to me.

I hear my mom's hitched breath before I turn to look.

Tears have flooded her reddened gaze. "That's all I've ever wanted for you, Luna." She smiles tearfully over at me but quickly focuses on driving. "You know, it makes sense then." She wipes at the corners of her eyes with her sleeve.

"What does?"

"Why he's trying to protect his moon, his stars."

My heart fills, but it's a little cracked, leaking. "I want to protect him too."

"Then this is the best way." She nods resolutely and adjusts her grip on the wheel, her lanky arms a bit constricted. "Everything will work out how it's supposed to. Yep."

I don't even know what *this* really entails. Am I on a break with Donnelly? Can we be friends-with-benefits in private? We didn't have long to work out the details on the roof, and I'm aching for a certain kind of clarity that only we can give one another.

I squint at the window as flash bulbs suddenly explode in the night like glaring headlights, right near my mom's side. *Paparazzi.* They're snapping photos of my mom from their car.

We go quiet, until she says, "I'm gonna call our bodyguards." She phones our security tail while paparazzi hug us too close. My mom is one of the best drivers, so I'm not too scared. While they're talking about switching lanes, I go into my settings and change my lock screen.

I remove the pic of Donnelly and replace him with one of me from the Halloween Hellfire Gala. I'm outfitted in the green bell-cut dress as Polaris, and I'm holding Baby Ripley in his Lockheed purple dragon costume.

Moffy took the pic for me. It's a cute one, and I try not to overanalyze how I literally just erased Donnelly off my phone.

He's still here.

He's not gone.

Should I text him? Just to hear from him?

No, no. I'm about to go see him. I try to channel patience, and my finger hovers over a social media app. Maybe the uproar over my leaked fics has died down. Maybe checking the temperature of the social media waters will make me feel better.

I click into Twitter.

My feed is a hot mess, and my stomach instantly nose-dives at a tweet.

Luna Hale writing alien porn 100% proves that she's a sex addict. You all are living in a fucking fantasy if you think differently.

The tweet has over 10k likes. A student from Penn that I follow retweeted it. Great. I slump down in the passenger seat.

Returning to a college campus after this public blow-up sounds not fun at all, but I also hate the idea of hiding away forever. Everything just majorly sucks right now.

"You okay, Luna?" my mom asks, and I realize she's off her phone and staring down at mine.

"Uh-huh." I shut off my cellphone and try to hoist my sinking body. "Just…social media."

My fics.

The unsaid thing floats in the air.

She's quiet for a long, long while. She chews on her bottom lip, but eventually, she asks, "Do you want to talk about it?"

I shrug. *They think I'm just like you.* It's not going to make her feel better. It's making me feel really awful. "It's just people online. I know I'm not supposed to listen to any of them." I bite at the cuticle on my thumb.

"You could talk to your therapist. Have you seen Dr. Raven in a while?"

"Not really." My voice sounds smaller. "I just don't feel like talking much." I glance over at my mom. "How is this going to affect Hale Co.? My leaked fics, I mean."

"It'll be fine. You shouldn't worry about the companies. They've been through worse—not that this is bad." She catches herself quickly. "You should call your aunt. Rose was ranting on the phone for over an hour about the types of people trying to ridicule your writing. She called them pigs. Or swine. Maybe both."

I realize I haven't even talked with Eliot and Tom yet. I only sent a thumbs up emoji in reply to their texts from last night.

"And she's right," my mom says with another nod. "They're not good people, and you did nothing wrong. You know that? *You did nothing wrong.*" She emphasizes it with her entire being, her whole core, and God, I want to believe in that as powerfully as she does.

I try to cradle her words, but she hasn't read any of the NC-17 level fics: the graphic smutty ones. She's in my corner because she's my mom…and I am grateful she's in my corner at all. I think of Donnelly again, and I wonder how many people will really be in his.

4

Paul Donnelly

EVERYTHING IS ALL backwards and shit.

Can't date Luna.

Now I'm texting my dad.

I'd say Mercury is in retrograde—but Luna told me that it already happened back in October. So I can't really blame this strange turn of events on any planet.

Just on myself, maybe.

Maybe not. Is there really any explanation for why things go bad? Other than bad luck? The only way to get out of it is to move, so I'm not doing nothing. I'm doing somethin'.

I stare at the string of texts on my phone. I'm the one who opened the door I'd padlocked with a single text.

Wanna meet up for a bite Sunday?

My dad responded in less than five minutes.

Sure. Unless you meant to text someone else. — **Dad**

Nah. I know it's you. Just thought it's time to talk.

Past time. And tomorrow is better for me. — **Dad**

Tomorrow then.

So there's that. But I'm not reaching out to him to bond over hoagies and cigarettes. I might as well be a piece of raw meat thrown into an ocean.

Shark bait. That's me.

And I'm not fooling myself thinking I'm anything else. Xander's dad wants more info about my family, and I figure this is the only way to really get it. What he'll do with it—I'm not a hundred percent sure. To make my family a non-threat, it'd take loads of money, bribery, maybe even murder. And there's still a part of me that thinks Papa Hale has a hitman on retainer.

Anyway, my family has always been a threat. Anything else feels like a dream.

I can't even dream tonight, not when I'm having trouble sleeping. I keep thinking about Luna. The Hales. The family and dinner I walked away from. The world I'm not allowed to be a part of.

In a way, I don't even belong here at this penthouse. I've been crashing in the vacant room next to Luna's thanks to Farrow's generosity and all. Being in that guest room makes me think of her too much, so I find myself on the rooftop with the best views of my favorite city on Earth.

I smoke a cigarette and sit on the ledge of the roof, legs dangling. There's a lot still going for me. A career, best friends, a pillow to lay my head on, enough money to buy my next meal. Still living in the great state of PA. All these things would've calmed my nerves and made me excited for tomorrow.

But none of that stuff really matters without her.

Cigarette between my lips, I open my daily planner and scribble down a new goal.

Today's Focus: show Luna I still love her, even if I can't date her.

I reread that sentence, anger surfacing underneath the hurt. *Can't date her.* Slamming the planner closed, I take a long drag of my cigarette. My phone buzzes in my pocket, and I slip it out and see it's Farrow.

I frown. He should be having dinner tonight with the Hales. I pick up the call.

"Donnelly?"

"Shouldn't you be eating meatloaf right about now?" I ask, unfamiliar salt to my voice. A million times in my life I could've been jealous of Farrow. Never have been.

Not until now.

I hate the bitter feeling gnawing me inside-out, and I pinch the cigarette harder between my fingers, glaring at my reflection in the phone.

Farrow skirts over my question. "You okay? I just heard what happened with Lo."

He knows I've been rejected then. I'm quiet, knowing if I open my mouth I'll just lie to appease his worries.

I wait for him to say, *Man, why'd you go and ask him if you could date her?*

It's the question I've been asking myself all night. The one I have too many answers for.

I wanted easy for her.

I didn't want to come between her and her family.

I thought maybe I'd get lucky for once in my life and he'd say yes.

It's not the question Farrow poses though. Instead, he asks, "You going to answer me or just breathe heavy on the phone?"

"Must be getting me confused with Oliveira. He's the mouth breather," I whisper.

"At least he answers my questions," Farrow refutes. "You okay?"

"Fine," I lie. "How's she?"

"She's not doing fine," Farrow says diplomatically like he knows I'm full of shit and he's full of truths.

My grip tightens on the phone, emotions starting to pummel me. *Can't even be there for her.* Not tonight. "Her fics?"

"Pretty sure this is about you."

I don't want to cause her pain. I do the stupid thing and glance down at the drop. Not scared of heights, but my head goes woozy and I swing my leg over the edge, straddling the low brick wall.

"I'm not planning on leaving her or anything. We're still friends."

"I know," Farrow breathes out.

"She knows that?" Maybe I need to reassure her more. Maybe I didn't do a good job on the Hale's roof. Can't even remember all the things I said. Everything is a fucking blur. My vision gets hazy as tears invade, and I wipe them away roughly.

"It wouldn't hurt to tell her again," Farrow says.

I nod strongly. "Yeah. Tomorrow." I blow out smoke.

"She's coming home tonight. Lily is driving her to the penthouse."

I say the first thing I think. "I ruined Hale Family Dinner."

"Loren ruined Hale Family Dinner," Farrow refutes roughly. "Man, that's not on you."

Okay.

Okay.

I shed that weight as fast as it fell on me. Then after snuffing out my cigarette, I say a quick goodnight to Farrow, silently thanking him for the heads up. I'm already practically sprinting back into the penthouse.

Everyone else is asleep, but a few of the night owl cats roam the halls in their nocturnal state. Earlier, I said goodnight to Orion. Luna's black furred Newfie usually sleeps on her bed.

As I reach the wide hallway, the front door not even in view, I skid to a sudden stop. Mostly because of my pole-vaulting pulse. I try to catch my breath, and I glance down. A tuxedo cat is blocking my next move.

Toodles stares me down like we're in a western.

I should be a *hero* to Jane and Thatcher's cats. I held some of them after the townhouse fire. Saved them from singed tails. But most treat me like I'm an empty can of tuna. With nothing to offer, nothing to give.

It hasn't bothered me before, but tonight, it tightens my chest.

"You gonna move?" I ask him.

He doesn't blink.

"Shoo." I swat a hand in the air.

He doesn't budge.

"I'm just trying to get to the elevator." I want to greet her as soon as she arrives, and if I'm honest with myself, I know it's not Toodles the fucking chunk monster barring me from stepping forward. I could easily outmaneuver this pudgy cat.

It's my pulse.

Racing at uncertain speeds. Is this the right thing to do? Waiting here for her to return? I don't have that answer, but my feet, glued to the floorboards, are making the decision for me.

I can't tear away from this cat. Toodles is the lazy one, but he bends low like he's stalking a rat.

"I'm not easy prey," I warn him.

He slowly extends a white paw, creeping towards me.

"I'm not."

I'm not.

He's gonna pounce.

I let out a gnarled groan. "You know, pussies and I have a longstanding history, and they usually *love* me." My voice rises.

He hisses.

"What? You don't like being called a pussy? It's what you are, man. A pussy cat. Look in the mirror."

The *click* of the front door lock startles Toodles. He jolts like he's struck by lightning and dashes into the kitchen, his paws scraping against the hardwood.

She's here.

I back up into the living room. What the fuck's wrong with me? I rake a hand against the back of my hot neck, and I realize I'm nervous.

But I don't leave. Farrow said she wasn't doing all right, and there's nothing more I want than to be there for Luna when she's hurting.

Especially if it's because of me.

I rest my ass on the back of the blue couch. Hearing footsteps and whispers, I try not to tense. Then Luna's mom emerges first. Lily is a smidge shorter than her daughter, and she's carrying two Tupperware containers.

"Oh, Donnelly." Surprise jumps her eyebrows, not expecting me to be right here.

"Hey," I greet with the tilt of my head. I have no clue what her mom thinks of me. Being on Lo's shitlist, I can handle, but if I'm on Lily's, I dunno...I think I'd still go fling myself off this planet and sob.

Tension contracts my muscles, and I find myself avoiding Lily. Not a second passes before Luna sidesteps around her mom. "Donnelly?"

My heart jumps higher when I see her, and I scan Luna rapidly.

A duffel bag is slung over her shoulder. It'd been an overnight bag in case she wanted to spend the night at her parents' house. Her splotchy round face and swollen eyes drive pain through my chest. Sleeves of her *Thrashers* hoodie are rolled to her forearms, and I see the lyrics I tattooed on her skin from years ago.

It takes all my energy not to hug her. Instead, I reach out for the duffel.

She lets me carry the luggage for her. As I slide the strap on my shoulder, her amber eyes search me for answers. Don't know if I have the ones she's scavenging for, but we do need to talk. I'm dying to give her what she needs.

She's the only girl who wants, truly wants, what I can give, and how *unjust* is it that I have to wait to give her all of me? Fuck me, right?

Always, fuck me.

"I heard you were coming back," I say. "Just wanted to wait up for you."

She nods slowly, her breath hitching. The strain between us isn't natural.

"Meatloaf for you both," Lily interjects, and I almost forgot her mom is still here. Lily extends the Tupperware to me.

I take it and look to Luna. "You didn't eat?" I skim her again, my chest caving. I wouldn't have left her—if I knew she was this broken up—I wouldn't have left as fast as I did.

"I wasn't that hungry." Her voice is small, almost a whisper. She frowns at the floor, and I try to catch her gaze again, seeing something's bothering her. What the hell happened? She gives her mom a quick glance. "I'm gonna check on Orion. Thanks for the ride, Mom." She hugs her mom, then slips away, tugging her sleeves down.

Both Lily and I watch her disappear down another hall.

I crave to chase after Luna, but I can't be rude to her mom. Might not be a gold-star student when it comes to pleasing parents, but I've got some manners.

"Thanks for the food," I say.

Lily nods, turning to me with a tiny smile. "You like meatloaf?"

"Haven't met a meatloaf I disliked." I try to smile back, but I'm glancing at the spot where Luna disappeared.

"Did your mom ever make it for you?"

"Nah, she didn't cook much." Talk about my mom heavies my head. I can't even reach that place when Luna is consuming everything inside me. "I won't let anything hurt her." I just say it.

I believe it.

I'd rather be bait and roadkill than let a single soul harm Luna Hale. And I plan to prove it.

"Just don't give up on each other," Lily suddenly says, and I realize she's gazing at the last sight of Luna too. "Even if it's hard to wait it out. It'll be worth it in the end." Before I can reply, she gives me a warm smile. "Night, Donnelly."

She leaves.

I'd almost think I dreamt it if it wasn't for the meatloaf in my hands.

After a kitchen pitstop, grabbing two forks, some napkins, I'm at her bedroom. Door cracked, I kick it gently open and find Luna hovering over a fishbowl.

She feeds Moondragon fish flakes and whispers softly to the glass. Her *Thrashers* hoodie is tied around her hips, and the white Planet Hoth tee looks self-cropped, scissored in jagged lines. It's also see-through.

I'm drawn down to her metallic gold bra.

Shouldn't be looking at her tits when she's been crying. I sorta feel like dogshit for doing it, but I'm attracted to this girl, and how do I turn that off right now? Images of me kissing Luna, of running my hands along the bareness of her body, of slipping inside her warm, tight pussy suddenly race through my head.

Sex and Luna.

Emotions and Luna.

Life and Luna.

It's all fucking me up.

But God, I don't want to fuck her up too. So I gotta sort through this with her somehow. Using my shoulder blades, I lean back and shut her door.

She's quiet, and I try not to startle her. "Luna?"

Her gaze descends to her feet. "Hi."

"Hey." I walk farther inside and set the meatloaf and utensils on her dresser. "You wanna talk about it?"

She tucks a strand of light brown hair behind her ear. "About us?"

"About us and whatever's bothering you…" I come forward and try to catch her amber eyes again, but they're running away from me. "What happened? After I left?"

I'm an inch from Luna, so close that I hear her uneven breath and feel the warmth radiating off her body.

She works her jaw to keep waterworks at bay, I think. "I'm disappointed in myself." She blinks and finally looks up at me. "I had a…kinda meltdown. In front of my whole family." Her cheeks flush.

For someone so unashamed most of the time, I hate seeing her filled with regret.

I dip my head down to be closer to her. "Couldn't have been a bigger scene than the time I streaked through a Yale quidditch match."

She almost smiles. "Yale has quidditch?" Her tiny, fragile voice is killing me.

I nod. "Got a lot of *stiff wand* jokes tossed at me. Caught 'em all."

"Did you eat them?"

"All of 'em. Tasted like magic."

"You probably levitated."

"All the way home." We haven't broken eye contact, and somehow, I feel like I'm cradling her in my arms and holding her against my chest. Though, I know, an unbearable space is between us.

She whispers, "Um, I pulled my bookcase off the wall. It almost came down on me...and my mom and sister. And that's...that's after I trashed my room." Her eyes well up. "I think Kinney thought it'd make me feel better, but it made me feel worse."

"Yeah, I learned early on that throwing things around just makes everything harder to clean up."

"I'm about to be twenty-one," she says softly. "And tonight, I just feel like...a kid who can't control their emotions. A problem child that should've matured out of being a problem."

I instinctively clasp her hand, encasing mine around hers. "You were upset. Being emotional doesn't mean you're immature. I think you're just not used to it."

"To what?" she murmurs.

"Showing people your emotions. At least the sad and dark ones."

Luna responds so quietly that I almost mishear her say, "It's been easier with you."

Yeah. "I feel that too," I breathe, but a knot twists in my lungs.

She lets go of my hand first. She steps forward and then steps back like an invisible wall is separating us. She wraps her arms around her bare waist, hugging herself.

It's a struggle just watching her.

I want to give her a real hug, but the wall exists for me too. Tension thickens in our silence, and I do my best not to dig for my cigarettes.

Her nipples have hardened, budding up against her metallic bra. My cock stirs, blood heating as I watch her gaze stroke my body and the angles of my jaw. I try not imagining lifting Luna and burying my face in her pussy.

I just follow the route of her eyes as they explore me.

She seems sad. Like she's trying to find pieces of me that've been locked away.

"I know you said we're written in the stars," Luna whispers, her eyes on mine again. "But what does that mean for right now? The more I try to understand, the more confused I get. Like we're just *us* but less than us, than what we were yesterday?"

That hurts.

Everywhere.

I grip the edge of her desk where the fishbowl rests, steadying myself. "We're not less," I say. "We'll never be less." I'm not sure if it's the truth or if I'm just hoping.

"Then *what* are we?" Her brows bunch together. "We can't be boyfriend and girlfriend. But we're more than friends, right?"

My muscles flex. Breath shortens.

"No," I say, even if every word pains me. "We're not more than friends."

Luna blinks, and her face cinches like she's been stabbed. "Oh…"

My throat swells. "*Not yet*," I remind her. "We can be more than friends after I take care of my family situation. But I made a promise to your dad to wait for you, and I am *very* shit at keeping my promises to him. But this one, I want to keep. I need to keep."

She inches backwards, creating more excruciating distance between us. "I'm going to make it easy for you."

Don't.

My eyes burn. "Don't make it easy."

"I don't want to be a reason you break a promise," she says more quietly.

"You won't be." I skate a hand through my hair. "I just don't want *avoidance* to be a thing here."

I don't want to lose you, Luna.

I don't want her to fall in love with someone else. I don't want her to leave me.

She thinks. "Just friends?"

"Friends," I nod.

"Only friends." She nods over and over like she can cement the status of us in place, like she can be okay with it, and I've fallen so deep for her, I can't even crawl out of the hole I'm in.

I just want to live there with her.

She says, "And we're the kind of friends that don't fuck each other."

I laugh. "Girl, that's ninety-nine percent of my friendships." I tilt my head. "The one percent was always just you." She was the only friend I've ever fucked.

Luna finally smiles, her lips slowly rising, and it shines down on my whole world. "So it shouldn't be that difficult?" She crouches to pet Orion, her eyes still up on me. Everything about Luna effortlessly draws me into her stratosphere. Fuck, I'd take her on the rug right now if I could. The way she's looking at me, I know she'd want me to.

I can't.

Made promises and all.

"Nah, it's gonna be very difficult to keep my hands off you, space babe."

She nods, like she gets it. "Same."

Same.

It does feel like we're the same at times.

And I know better than to linger in her room for longer than ten minutes. Even with our invisible wall, I'm not sure how long it'll hold. "You wanna eat?" I wonder.

"Tomorrow. My stomach feels kinda messed up."

"I'll put yours back in the fridge." I go to her dresser and collect the Tupperware meatloaf I left behind.

"Thanks." Her face has fallen a bit. She stays knelt beside her dog. "Xander knows. All of my siblings know."

I solidify in place. "Know what?"

"Why you were at my house. How we like one another and my dad said we can't date yet."

Like is an understatement to what I feel for Luna, but I've already told her that I'm in love with her the night of our first kiss. She expressed *love* back, so I'm thinking maybe she's just protecting the depth of her feelings.

"What'd Xander say?" I ask.

"He just *ran*."

Concern slams against me, and I nearly bolt towards my room for my radio. "Where?"

"To his bedroom—he's okay," she adds fast. "Or, maybe not, but he's at least with my parents. Moffy talked to him a ton."

I grimace. "He didn't take it well then."

"Yeah, but I didn't really talk to him, so I can only guess why he's upset."

I'm trying not to drum up bad theories. It's better if I just talk to my little elf and see what's wrong. I sigh out, then nod. "Well, my boss hasn't called me and said I'm being transferred, so it can't be that bad if your brother still wants me to protect him."

Though, that could change at any point. The fact that it hasn't tonight is the positive I'm pocketing like a Lucky Charm. Gonna ride the marshmallow to a pot of gold, hopefully.

She hugs an arm around Orion. "I think the rumor Delilah Avalon spread about Xander yesterday is being overshadowed by my leaked fics. It probably won't gain any steam, so that's good at least for him."

Xander had been pretty anxious about the lie spreading online. The one where Delilah said he had sex with her after homecoming.

I wouldn't call Luna being blasted in tabloids "good" but I'm not gonna squash her fledgling positivity, so I let it linger.

"He'll be alright," I breathe.

She nods, quiet again.

I'm about to go soon.

I don't really want to, but at least I won't be far.

She swallows hard, her throat bobbing. "I understand why we can't be together."

I turn back to her. "Yeah?"

"I'm not living in a delusion. Your family could try to hurt me like they tried to hurt Beckett, right?"

I stiffen. Go cold.

She winces. "I don't want to dig out things you don't want to share. I really don't—"

"You're not," I say softly, the words ache inside my throat. "You're not, Luna."

She intakes a bigger breath. "I know you've told me a bit about your past, but I just want to know more about your family. And I'm not your girlfriend. I get that I'm only a friend now who's waiting for you…for us. Maybe I haven't earned anything more."

"You don't have to earn it," I say, then stare at Moondragon swimming happily in the fishbowl. It's easier looking away, not seeing her reaction. "But I dunno. It's not like you can meet my parents. These pieces of my life aren't touching you. I'm making sure of that."

"It doesn't mean I don't want to know…and there are pieces of my life that I've never shared with you. Things I don't even think could have been spread through the bodyguard rumor mill."

I know that.

I look at her, and there's a heaviness in her eyes. Sex addiction, media, past hookups that've hit tabloid headlines—those are things she hasn't wanted to talk about. There's been more, definitely. I've always known she's more than the rumors I've heard.

She's told me some stories of being bullied, but to what extent, I can't be so sure either. Luna guards a lot of memories like I do.

Do I want to know more? Yeah, I want to know every last detail of her life. Of who she is. It's a hunger. An urge, and she must be craving the same from me.

We're the same.

But we're different too. Our differences are like unopened books *begging* to be consumed. As far as I go, I've never been read front-to-back by anyone, but I'd check out a library card just to read all of her. She's the writer, though. I'm sure her insides are a whole lot more eloquent than whatever's living in me.

"I want to know more about you too," I cement. "Whatever you want to give me, especially if it's everything."

"Will you give me everything?" she asks.

Yes, is the first gut reaction. *I'll give you my world.*

Except there are dark parts of my world that I'd rather she never really see.

So I end up saying, "I'm gonna try."

"Same."

"Ditto," I grin and flash the *I love you* hand gesture. Then I glance at her neon clock on the end table. It's late. Too late. "Alright, I probably shouldn't overstay my welcome tonight." Her perked nipples are driving me insane, and I smell her floral scent all over me, even though I only held her hand.

She nods like she gets it. "Just friends."

"Only friends. Who happen to share a bathroom, but this isn't to be used and abused for secret rendezvous and whatnot. Gotta keep it rated G for the lava lamp and company."

Am I delusional or what?

With the meatloaf containers in my hand, she watches me go towards the door. "Donnelly?"

I have a hand on the knob. God, I still don't want to leave.

"Yeah?" I ask.

She has a hand on Orion's furry belly, and she gives me the saddest smile I've ever seen. "I'm really glad we're still friends."

I hate this so much.

"Me too, sad alien."

DONNELLY'S DAILY PLANNER
Thursday, Nov 8th

Today's Focus: be the predator. You are a hungry hungry hippo (not literally hungry, thank you late night meatloaf and Momma Lily). Important: make sure Luna knows she's still loved. Try not to fuck your favorite friend. Don't jump her bones (seriously).

To Do:

- Morning tat.

- Gonna go see Dad. Suck it up. Inform Xander's dad first (you've gotta do it).

- Return in time to go on X's detail after school. See what's up with him (smooth things over *pray hands*)

Notes: Could barely sleep after leaving Luna's room. Running on energy drinks and the good ole Ripped Fuel today.

yeehaw and high kicks. Haven't seen her yet. She's prob still sleeping. wonder if I'll get a chance to talk to her before I leave for South Philly???

Meals: cheerios for brekky. Need some *cheer* in my morning. I am the king of the jungle. Gotta get that pep in my predatory step. Gonna eat lunch with Dad. Eat dinner with Luna? Friendship dinner. Might have to invite another friend too?

Water: don't be a thirsty bitch (except when it comes to your girl). ~~Is she mine?~~ chug H20 all day.

Question of the Day ~~Can I take Luna to the Fanaticon Convention in December? Is a butterfly kiss considered a real kiss?~~ Is Ryke Meadows' secretly Loren Hale's hit man?

5

Paul Donnelly

EARLY MORNING IN the penthouse is quiet. I've flicked on the bright lights in the kitchen, the cupboards a warm forest-green, and butcher block counters smell like lemon and Lysol. Though, someone left a half-eaten box of sprinkled donuts near the coffee pot, and the remnants of chocolate turtles lie on a paper napkin beside the sink.

Must be Sulli and Jane.

They're both pregnant. Jane, majorly so, but that's not why there's a trail of sweets. Most of the girls are messy. Sulli's husbands clean up behind her, and I've seen Thatcher do the same for Jane.

Would it be bad if I did that for Luna?

I blink away the thought, considering her mess isn't that bad and doesn't always strike me as something needing cleaned. Most of the time I just wanna live in it with her.

Guest.

I'm a guest here sleeping in the guest room, and I'm trying to remind myself of that. Can't get too comfortable. Can't love it too much, or else it'll be harder when I'm evicted. Told to go.

Babies are coming, not just from Sulli and Jane. Farrow and Maximoff are having a daughter. Still thinking maybe a boy will pop out instead. Their surrogate Millie Kay has a December due date, and that's *three* new kids. I'm fully expecting someone to need the guest room, even if they said they won't.

It's fine, though. I can just move back into the Rookie Room.

Ignoring the tightness in my chest, I listen to a familiar *buzz*. At the breakfast table in the kitchen, only two soggy cheerios left are swimming in a bowl of milk, and my slim can of Lightning Bolt! is beside a glass of water. I don't reach for either.

With black gloved hands, I ink myself using my tattoo machine. Sitting, my leg is stretched out, foot perched on another chair, and I work on a cover-up.

The needle pierces the flesh of my ankle, and I draw lines off the letters, connecting them to form an abstract shape.

Xander

Beckett

Tom

Their names disappear into a swirled design. Been thinking, eventually, it'll be a planet, but I don't have much time right now. It just needs to be unrecognizable.

I'm seeing my dad today, and I'm not making the same mistake twice. When I visited my cousin Colin at his row house, he spotted the tattoo and assumed I'm friends with all these names, and I'm not putting anyone else in danger.

My phone vibrates on the table. I stop shading the line between the *r* in *Xander* and the first *t* in *Beckett*. Peeking over, my stomach flip-flops.

Loren Hale is texting me. I've already sent him a message letting him know I'm meeting with my dad for lunch. I snap off one glove, just to tap into the text.

Meet me at Connor's house first. As soon as you can.
– Xander's Dad

My pulse is racing. I'm going to Papa Cobalt's house. Which is commonly referred to as the Cobalt Estate. Connor Cobalt is going to be there—I'd bet money that I don't have on it.

I tap out a short response.

K. See you.

I snap on a new glove and move faster on inking my ankle. Not my best work, but I'll fix it later. Once I'm done, I clean up, sanitize my equipment, and apply a medical-grade waterproof bandage to the fresh ink. Without the *buzzing*, my ears catch noises throughout the penthouse.

The shut and open of doors. Footsteps pad around, sounding more human than cat or dog.

Is Luna awake?

I shouldn't stick around to see. Seven other people live here, not including Baby Ripley. It's better if I just slip out unseen. My radio is already attached to my waistband, and my gun is holstered.

I'm washing out my cereal bowl when the footsteps grow louder. They're heavy. Can't be Luna. Sounds like multiple pairs of feet.

Gotta go.

Gotta go.

I practically chuck the bowl and spoon in the dishwasher. Kicking the thing closed, I whirl around to see Akara in crisp black slacks. He's quickly tucking in his white button-down with one hand. The other is clutching his phone. Like me, he seems in a hurry.

Alarm bells are ringing in my head.

I'm not dumb.

But I try to play it off. "Nice pants, boss." I nod to him while heading towards the exit. "You going to a fancy Thursday brunch?" I'm hoping those exist.

"Don't go anywhere," Akara says fast. "Donnelly."

I catch myself midstride and swing back around to the kitchen. "Yeah?"

"I just got off the phone with Connor."

Fuck. I figured, but it still dick-kicks me. My boss has been looped in on whatever Papa Cobalt is devising this morning. Akara is in charge of Omega. He runs Omega. But I never wanted this to extend to security. I want this to be a *me and Loren Hale* thing.

It's better that way. Keep it small. Confined.

Private.

I walk slowly back to the kitchen cupboards. "What'd he want?" As soon as I ask, a six-foot-seven Moretti arrives. Toothpick between his lips, gray sweatpants low on his waist, he whispers to Akara.

That's Banks.

For me, it's too easy to tell the Moretti brothers apart, especially with how Akara unwinds more around Banks, and those two interact like they share a secret world.

They do share a wife, and I suppose they share each other too. I think they're lucky to have found love that's worth pushing through all havoc.

Love that endures together is the toughest love. The strongest.

I want that.

I want love that survives with me. 'Cause I know I'm gonna survive in the end. No matter what.

Akara whispers back to Banks, and I wonder if I can sneak out. But if Akara is leaving for the Cobalt Estate with me, then what's the point? I could make small talk. Ask how Kicking It With Kitsulletti workouts are going at Studio 9. They've been filming with Sulli for their fitness app.

I could ask when they plan to make the big "we're married and expecting" announcement so I can finally share the love on Twitter.

I could say a lot, but the way Banks is eyeing me, up and down, stops me from opening my mouth.

He bites on the toothpick. "You going to see Connor Cobalt like that?"

Like a million bucks? I look classy.

I'm wearing a black band tee and ripped jeans. I even put on a watch. "Papa Cobalt hates AC/DC or what?" I ask.

Akara tells Banks, "I haven't told him about the call yet."

"He looks fine." Thatcher has arrived, dressed in his Sunday best: charcoal button-down, black slacks. It's the fall. He should be popping out the flannels.

"All your flannels in the wash?" I quip, my pulse on another ascent.

He can't come with me too. I don't even want my boss as a tagalong, really.

Thatcher curls a strand of longish hair behind his ear, just so he can fit in the comms piece. "I'm going to the Cobalt Estate with you."

No.

"Again, I haven't told him what's going on," Akara says, checking the time on his watch. "We need to head out. Where's Farrow?"

Farrow?

Like demon magic, my best friend suddenly appears. He's wearing his usual black V-neck tucked into belted black pants. His hair is cut short, and the color is ash brown, his natural hue. The dyed strands were fried, so he's starting anew.

Shouldn't be fixated on his hair, but I'm not too happy right now. It's the only thing cooling me down.

"Connor is going over the strategy for this afternoon," Akara starts explaining to me.

I'm looking between the four of them across the kitchen. "For this afternoon?" How much do they actually know?

"You're meeting with your dad," Akara says.

"For lunch," Thatcher adds.

What the fuck?!

I scrape a hand through my hair, avoiding their gazes. It's dawning on me just how involved they're getting, and I don't just dislike it.

I hate it.

Fuck Xander's dad. For expanding this team-up to include not only his friend (Connor), but my friends too. We could've done this without anyone else knowing.

Akara continues, "Connor wants to ensure we're all on the same page. Especially if you need back-up."

"Nice and all, but I don't need back-up." I look straight at Farrow. He knows why. He'd ask for the same thing.

He says nothing. Just holds my gaze.

"Your family has become a *security* issue," Thatcher forces, his voice ten times more severe than Akara's friendly business tone. "If you're a part of an op, your lead and your boss need to be completely informed."

An op?

I thought I was just getting more info out of my dad. Lo said he wanted "leverage" to hold over my family, but then again, he's probably been talking to Connor, lawyers, and private investigators more than he's talking to me.

"Then what's Farrow doing here?" I gesture to my best friend.

"I'm not leaving you, man." His gaze drills into me with this familiarity. Years of being there. Of never truly leaving. And it's a comfort that I shouldn't need.

I know I can survive without it.

"I can do this myself," I tell him. "I'm gonna do this myself." I look between them. "Appreciation, really, but you all should kick back and have a happy Thursday. I'll give you a detailed report on what went down. Cool?"

"No," Akara says with crinkled brows, like I've hopped in Luna's spaceship and flown away. *I wish.* "It's not cool. It's actually uncool."

"Akara—"

"This isn't up for debate. Connor called. He wants us there. We're going. And just so you know, I would've *fought* to go if he said we couldn't. You're my man, Donnelly. I'm not letting you handle this alone."

It sinks in slowly.

Feels good to be protected, to have some line of defense behind me, but just talking about my family with Lo has been a challenge— doing that in front of SFO isn't something I'd volunteer to do unless it was *completely* necessary.

But most importantly, they're in a different stage of their lives. I'm over here fighting for the opportunity to even have a girlfriend. They have more to lose if they're twisted in this shit. And they. Weren't. Supposed. To. Be. Pulled. *In.*

I run a hand down my face.

"What's wrong here?" Akara asks with genuine concern, pocketing his phone. "Help me out, because I don't understand why you have a problem."

"This was supposed to be just me and Lo and *maybe* Connor. No one else."

"You should've gone to Akara first," Thatcher says like I broke a sacred rule, and I did jump the hierarchy. Just didn't know it'd evolve into this.

"Sorry, boss," I tell Akara. "Next time I'll write you a *sympathy* card."

Thatcher glares.

Akara sighs.

At least Banks is grinning.

Farrow raises his brows at Thatcher and says, "You really want to smack him with the rulebook right now?"

Thatcher lets out a rough, deep noise. "I'm not just saying it as his lead." He turns to me. "Why trust Connor and Lo over us? Over Farrow and Oscar? Akara could've helped. I could've helped. We all could've helped *sooner*. Involving the parents first complicates everything."

"You would've just gone to them yourself," I refute.

"Hey, you don't know that," Akara says with a frown. "We've all been through crap together that they won't ever understand. SFO is my family. My priority."

He's building another family. He's got Sulli and Banks and a baby on board.

But SFO is my *only* family, and maybe I should've gone to them first like Thatcher is saying. Maybe it wouldn't be this messy or tense.

Except it doesn't change what I did. And I think I'd do it the same way again.

I glance at the exit. "Can't you take a backseat on this one though? You all need to take a backseat." My heart rate is out of control, and I try to steady my breath.

"Why?" Akara asks.

"You're all about to be dads!" I shout and look to Farrow. "Fuck, you're about to have a second baby. Your job should be protecting clients and your newborns. Not me. I've got this covered, so just take a backseat. *Please.*"

It's my last solid plea.

Akara looks sympathetic but firm. Thatcher just looks pissy, but that's his normal face.

"Come on," I say. "Just think about it."

"We don't have time to think about it," Akara says. "Look, as your friend, I get it. You want less people dealing with your family, but we're going."

I blink slowly. "What about the rookies? You inviting them too?"

"No, we need the other bodyguards on-duty. They'll be with whichever clients need security today, so Quinn, Frog, and Gabe are being shifted around. Banks, you're on the highest risk client."

"Right on," Banks says. He's kicked back against the wall, arms threaded loosely over his bare chest. "And what about Oscar?"

"He's in Amsterdam," Thatcher says.

Knew Oscar has been MIA on comms, but I didn't know where his client Charlie ran off to. There are too many places on a map to guess.

So it's just Thatcher, Akara, and Farrow joining me, and whatever Triple Shield bodyguards are in attendance.

"We're good to go?" Thatcher asks.

Akara nods. "We leave now."

I'm trying to collect myself, but it feels like an animal is wrestling inside my chest. *Fuck me.*

Farrow tells them, "We'll be right behind you."

They say they'll see us in the parking garage. I lean on the cupboards, and Farrow rounds the kitchen island. He rests against the butcher block.

We say nothing at first.

Then again, it feels like we say everything. So when I finally utter the words, it's like he's already heard them. "I don't wanna do this with this many people."

"I know," Farrow breathes. "You can do this on your own. You can."

"Why didn't you tell Akara that?" I ask quietly.

He looks to the left, gathering his thoughts, then comes back to me. "We can do everything alone, you and me. Because we have done everything alone, Donnelly. See, I always thought our independence was a strength." He pauses. "But it's not always one. We've just learned how to live without the things we really need."

It strikes me hard.

"A parent who *cares*," he says. "Someone who makes you dinner at night. Who knows if you didn't come home."

My eyes burn, and his words flow through me like a visceral truth I never saw. One that might've always existed. I intake a sharp breath.

"And man, you need someone looking out for you if you're getting swept into this mess," he says. "I know you wanted it to just be one or two people, but with the restraining orders against your two cousins—"

"Ryan and Patrick." I name them.

He nods. "Both security firms know your family was behind the attack against Beckett now. They want to take down those fuckers as much as the parents do, and it's personal for Triple Shield."

Because O'Malley, an Epsilon bodyguard, was beat to shit and landed in the hospital on Halloween. It was barely a week ago.

I begin nodding, accepting this, finally, but I ask in a short breath, "Do they know anything about Luna? About me asking Lo to date her?"

"No. I don't think Lo wants that getting out, not even within security."

"That's good." Less people who know, the better.

Even trying to be with Luna has a lot of complications, but actually being with her could cause waves too, I know that. It'd mean that over 50% of Kitsuwon Securities 24/7 bodyguards are romantically involved with clients. A number that won't be favorable to any of us, most especially Akara.

I don't know the kind of impact it'd have, so telling him I'm even in love with Luna isn't high on my to-do list. He's already done too much for me.

"You ready?" Farrow asks.

"Yeah." I straighten off the cupboards. "There's only now."

6

Paul Donnelly

"YOU WERE RIGHT," Lo tells me at the Cobalt Estate. "The best shot we have at taking down the Donnellys is through you."

Feels like all of Alpha and Epsilon have swarmed Papa Cobalt's office, plus some faces I've never seen. Must be lawyers or private investigators. They cram around me like I'm a lightweight fighter in this afternoon's pay-per-view match.

Donnelly vs. Donnelly.

Akara, Thatcher, and Farrow are the only ones that I know are *truly* hoping I end up on two feet. This would've been so much worse if they didn't push to be here. Thank God my friends have brains and that shiny five-star perseverance.

Price and Akara are talking quietly while an Alpha bodyguard pops open a black hard-shell case, but my head swings back to Papa Cobalt as he speaks.

"In order to present a strong case against your family for the assault or other crimes they might've committed, we need them to incriminate themselves." Connor pauses in front of me, his perfectly fitted navy-blue suit making him look like the billions he's worth. "That's where you come in."

I see the fancy mic and electronic gadgets in the black case.

Shit. "I can't wear a wire."

"Why not?" Price, the owner of Triple Shield, asks first.

Eyes drill into me from every direction. "They'll check," I say. "I'm not someone they trust."

"Will they check today?" Connor questions. "You'll be in public."

"Maybe not," I mutter, avoiding Epsilon. SFE looks at me like I'm the scum of the earth, and I hate feeling like a worm.

Akara asks, "You could use today as a stepping-stone to gaining your dad's trust?" He poses it to me like a question. "Maybe later, once he trusts you, no one will check for a wire."

"Yeah. Might work," I tell him.

He nods to me with a friendly half-smile. His eyes dart to Epsilon. Their snide glances are apparent from the corner, and I watch my boss go to Price. Few seconds later, Price is ordering his men to *stop*.

That's all he says.

"Stop."

It's only enough for Epsilon to shift their gazes off me, but the heat and ridicule still exists.

I'm used to it, but not exactly in this setting. Not with Lo and Connor and their lawyers present. Not as the focal point of the day.

"Take your shirt off," someone tells me.

Think it's Price. Can't be sure. My head is whirling.

Akara nods to me.

I peel my shirt off over my head. Chest bare, I have Thatcher and Bruno (Lo's 24/7 Alpha bodyguard) taping a wire to my skin. The high-tech gadget has no bulky battery pack. Just the thin wire and a tiny mic.

My muscles burn. I stand so still and try not to breathe too heavy.

Gazes bore into me and trail over my scattered tattoos and my nipple piercings. If Connor and Lo weren't here, I have no doubt SFE would've already said something about 'em.

"You'll wear your normal radio, but your comms mic will be off," Thatcher says. "Your earpiece is connected to this other mic and recorder."

The one taped to me.

Got it.

My bodyguard radio is basically a dummy. Unusable. There for show.

Thatcher continues, "You'll be on a designated frequency for this op, and the mic is going to be hot. We'll be able to hear everything, but he won't know that."

I force myself to focus and not go into a daze.

Akara is close to me as he says, "If your dad asks, you'll tell him the earpiece is just comms for your client. No one can hear you unless you click the mic."

I nod, understanding.

I'm supposed to rat out my dad. They want me to catch him or a cousin or someone spilling their foul deeds so it's recorded and admissible in court.

Only problem, I can't see them confessing anything to me. Not unless they strip me down and hose me off like Colin did. But Akara is right, this lunch could be a stepping-stone, a building block, a path towards *trust*. It's gonna have to be.

Because this set-up might be the only shot I have.

Once the wire is attached, I tug my shirt back over my head.

"Let's clear the room," Connor says to someone. "I only want Price, Akara, and our bodyguards present. The rest can wait in the library."

"Uh-uh, you're not going anywhere," Lo says to another person, and it takes me a second to find him in the crowd. He's speaking to Farrow. "You. Stay."

Everyone begins to filter out of the office, but Connor also calls out, "Thatcher." He motions the unshaven, stoic bodyguard to return to the room, and the door shuts.

It's clear they called back their sons-in-law.

They've got special privileges, and Triple Shield is not gonna love that. But I'm not penciling in *caring about their feelings* in my daily planner.

Right now, the room has quieted. Tension still stretches in the air. I don't know what's next.

"Take a seat, Donnelly," Connor says. A chair is already waiting for me. I didn't see him pull it over.

This is my first time in his personal office.

I know, it surprises me too, considering I used to be an honorary Cobalt.

Self-proclaimed, but I figured I was meant for the lion's den. Not whatever animal hidey-hole the Hales are living in. My feelings have shifted so much, I have vertigo—dizzy at the realization that I couldn't care less about being here.

I just wanna be with her.

This is what it's going to take. And I need to keep everyone safe. I have to.

"Yeah, sure." I walk towards the leather armchair. With fewer people around, I have a better view of the space.

Gotta admit, his office is different than I've imagined. Less modern. Less sleek. Robust wooden bookshelves line the deep blue walls, and a gas fireplace crackles in the corner where leather club chairs remain empty.

Everyone else is standing.

I take a seat, my muscles more strained than I like.

His wooden desk presides over the homey office. It reminds me of Yale's library. Collegiate and warm. Outside the window, leaves of an oak tree have turned golden orange, like flames licking the glass panes.

Connor has a tablet in hand. "Our PIs can't gain us access to your family the way that you can."

I expect someone else to sit, but my ass is the only one in a seat. Am I on trial? I've tried not to think long about Connor's feelings towards me after all this shit has transpired. Shit that I created, really.

His second-born son came way too close to being assaulted. I'm at fault. He should hate me.

But sitting here, I can't really read his expression. Not as well as I can Loren Hale's. Lo just looks aggravated while he's scrolling through his own tablet.

"Whatever you need me to do," I say, opening a floodgate I can't close.

"Before you go to lunch, we need to verify some of the information we have," Connor says.

Lo lowers the tablet. "When the hell did his family tree get updated? And why is it on an infinite scroll?"

"The PIs missed two of his grandfather's brothers," Connor says. "They've been fired."

Damn.

"You fired my uncles?" I joke.

Connor skips over my weak shot at humor. *Tough crowd.* "You call them uncles?"

I shift forward on the chair. It squeaks. "They're my dad's uncles."

"That's not what I asked," Connor says casually, calmly.

I scan him, waiting for the dark signs of hatred to appear. "Uh, yeah. I call them my uncles." I watch Lo join Connor near the desk, facing me, but he checks Connor's electronic tablet, making sure they're on the same page, probably.

Connor looks to Akara and Price. "You both should have the updated report."

"Got it," Akara says, on his phone.

Price nods, using his cell too. He's in a black designer suit, so I'm realizing why Akara dressed to impress and stand on par with the Triple Shield owner.

Thatcher and Farrow hang back near the fireplace with Connor and Lo's bodyguards on Alpha: Tony Ramella and Bruno Bandoni. Do not want Alpha here, but at least Epsilon—like the Wreath brothers and Novak—aren't around anymore snickering in the corner.

O'Malley is recuperating from his injuries, and I'm glad I don't have to see his bruised and battered face this morning. Counting my few lucky stars, thank you and all that gratitude.

"How many *great* uncles, that you apparently just call uncles, do you have?" Connor asks. I must hesitate too long because he reminds me, "We're verifying our information is accurate."

I nod. "My great-grandpop had six sons." *So that's five great uncles and my grandpop.* But I don't say that part out loud. I figure Connor can do mental math.

"No daughters?" Lo makes a face like it's odd.

I didn't think much of it when I was younger. "You're gonna struggle to find a lot of girls by blood in the older generations. The ones that I do know of, they died pretty tragically, but that's not what you're asking, so…" I trail off.

Connor meets my gaze, and I don't shrink beneath his penetrating stare. "Whatever you think is pertinent, please share."

"I don't know what could be pertinent," I admit.

"Anything you can share," he amends. "We'll start broadly."

I nod again, but a knot twists tighter in my chest. Alright, gonna have to spell out the math then. "One of the six sons is my grandpop Bobby—*was* Bobby. He's dead. Died when I was a baby. I was told by pneumonia, but I don't know if that's true. Bobby's brothers are my dad's uncles, so I have five uncles—*great* uncles, technically."

My family history is even murky to me at times, but my great uncles were mentioned so frequently it'd be hard to forget that branch of the crooked tree.

The (Great) Uncles:

Marty, the firstborn. *Dead.*

Bobby, the favorite child. *Dead.*

Paddy, the troublemaker. *Alive. Incarcerated.* He's Colin's grandpop.

Kerry, the free-spirit. *Dead.*

Finley, the follower. *Alive. Incarcerated?*

Raff, the baby brother. *Alive. Incarcerated??*

"I don't care about technicalities in this instance," Connor says swiftly. "*Good* PIs can give me that. We need what can't be found in records."

I try to breathe. "Which two uncles were missing from the report?"

"Rafferty and Patrick," Lo says.

"They go by Raff and Paddy." *Makes sense why the tree grew.* "Uncle Paddy had ten boys, and those boys have countless kids of their own. I don't know most of 'em." I scratch the back of my head. "Paddy, I think is still in prison. Raff, I dunno."

"He's been recently let out," Connor confirms.

I stare off. "Yeah, I didn't know that."

"What's that look?" Lo asks me, his frown deepening. It causes bodyguards to step around my chair and examine my face. I can tell Thatcher follows Tony like he's keeping a close eye on him.

The *only* person behind me is Farrow.

Heat gathers under my AC/DC shirt, but I force myself not to tug the collar. "I don't like him."

"Why not?" Connor questions.

"I don't like most of my family," I say, my pulse racing in unnatural ways.

"Do you feel like Rafferty could be more involved with the assault?" Connor asks.

"Maybe. It's not impossible." Gears click strangely in my head. "How'd you even miss Uncle Raff?"

"Why do you ask?" Connor studies me.

I've dreamed about Papa Cobalt looking me over like I'm a legend. Now I'm just associated with criminals.

Now I'm just a rat.

Loyalty has been a strength of mine, but to be loyal to the people I care about, I need to betray my whole family. A family who'd sell me out so fast—I'm more than aware of that.

"Ryan Donnelly, Patrick Donnelly—the ones with the restraining orders for trying to attack Beckett," I say. "Those are Raff's grandsons."

Lo slowly trains his glare at the ceiling. "Jesus Christ, how'd we screw up this jigsaw puzzle?"

"I didn't," Connor says, his voice carrying little inflection. "My PI did." He swivels the tablet to me, showing a photo of dark-haired and chin-dimpled Ryan and Patrick.

Same picture I saw when I came across their restraining orders. They're in their early twenties and broad-chested. There wasn't enough evidence to convict them of assault. Which is why a wire is now taped above my heart.

"These are your Uncle Finley's grandsons?" Connor asks.

"Nah, none of Uncle Finn's kids have dark hair like that. Most are scrawny too. Those are definitely Raff's grandkids." Before he asks, I say, "I don't know how many *Patrick Donnellys* and *Ryan Donnellys* there are. Probably a lot. I wouldn't be surprised if there's another Paul."

Lo pinches his eyes, then drops his hand. "What now, Connor?" he asks, his tone biting. "We start from scratch?"

"Akara, email Donnelly the family tree," Connor says, but to me, he adds, "in your free time, look through this and correct all inaccuracies. Fill in any blanks."

I nod a couple times.

Connor addresses the rest of security, "If any of you have questions, feel free."

"What about your mom's family?" Price asks me now.

"Um..." I go rigid and shake my head. "Never met them."

"Why not?" he wonders.

"They sorta disowned my mom, from what my grandmom told me. My mom never liked talking about it." I look to my right.

Why do I wish Luna was here?

"What'd your mom do wrong?" Tony asks.

I rub the back of my skull. "She had me."

I drop my hand, then stand up. Needing air, needing...out? Standing was an instinct, a gut reaction, and now that I'm out of the chair, I don't sit back down. I just walk over to Farrow and turn my back on the small audience.

"You have a smoke?" I whisper, digging in my pocket. Empty. They're empty except for my lighter.

He's digging in his. "Breathe."

"I'm breathing."

"You're sweating."

"I'm doing that too."

Concern tightens his eyes on me. "How's your pulse?" he whispers.

"Racing away from me," I murmur. "You wanna catch it, Dr. Hale?"

He twists his head over his shoulder, but I can't see who he's looking at. I'm focusing on the pack of Lucky Strikes that he puts in my hand. I smack the package against my palm.

"Who do you want out of the room?" Lo suddenly asks me.

I flinch in surprise.

"And you can't say *everyone*," he snaps.

I take a breath. "Triple Shield can go."

Tony lets out a short laugh. "Seriously? Is anyone else slightly concerned that he's *breaking* now? He hasn't even been put in front of his dad yet."

"I'm not breaking," I refute.

"You look like you're tweaking," he retorts. "You know what, I take it back. Maybe he will fit right in with his family."

"Shut the fuck up," Farrow snaps.

"Tony," Price reprimands.

"Get out," Connor says more authoritatively. He points at his door.

Tony sighs heavily. "Yes, sir." He exits.

Akara pockets his phone. "My guys and I will leave with Triple Shield."

Price nods tightly, but he seems perturbed, looking between Thatcher, Farrow, and Akara. Those three aren't just bodyguards. Being married into the famous families means they have a lot more reasons to stay than Price does.

Akara is probably smart to play fair and squash rising animosity.

Quickly, the bodyguards filter out of the office. Connor tells them he'll call them back inside in ten or so minutes.

Ten minutes alone with Connor and Lo.

I'm not breaking. I got this.

The door clicks closed.

"You can't smoke in here," Connor says immediately. "I have a wife who'd already love to rip your head off your ugly shoulders and feed your testicles to piranha."

"Her exact words," Lo informs me with a dry smile.

Rose hates me.

The fact is cold and uglier than my shoulders.

Lo adds, "Don't cross the demon or you'll get clawed."

Connor tips his head to Lo. "You know how that feels best of all, darling."

Lo touches his heart.

"I wasn't planning on smoking in here," I say quietly and slip a cigarette behind my ear. "I know Rose hates it." *I know Lo does too.* I pocket the cigarettes. "They're just for later." I look between them. "So why hasn't Rose castrated me yet?"

"Her sister," Connor says. "Lily told Rose not to confront you."

My brows jump. Luna's mom is saving my testicles and future progeny?

It's a strange thought, considering I've never wanted kids, and now I'm thinking about Luna having babies. I run my fingers through my hair.

"To make this very clear," Connor continues, "I also wouldn't have stopped Rose if it weren't for Lo. He said he put you through enough, and Rose didn't need to do extra damage."

Lo wears another half-smile. "What can I say? I was feeling *charitable*."

"I'm happy to be your favorite charity case," I say lightly.

"Did I call you my favorite?" He feigns confusion.

"Inferred it." I'm feeling better now, breathing easier, and I walk a little closer, back towards the chair. Looking at Connor, the words I wanted to say earlier reach my tongue. "I'm sorry."

"For what?" he asks calmly. He definitely knows the origins of my apology.

Feels like a Cobalt test.

I just let it out. "For Beckett."

Connor stares straight through me. Like he can see every organ and blood cell inside my body. No way that's possible, but if someone had X-ray vision, guess I'd say it'd be him.

He knows I've tattooed his son.

He knows I've been Beckett's friend.

He knows we were friends.

He's never put up a stink about it like I'm a bad influence. Never scolded me. Never condemned me. And now, his wife hates me, and he's still looking straight *through me.*

Connor never blinks. "Next time you have pertinent information regarding my children's safety and you don't tell me until it's too late, Rose will be the least of your worries. Understood? Or do you need synonyms for *pertinent*?"

"I know what it means," I breathe. "I'm going to make things right."

"You were talking about your mom's family." Connor places me back where I left off. "They disowned her."

"Because she had you?" Lo says.

"Yeah." Still standing, I bow forward, resting my forearms on the chair. I sift through the cigarette pack. "My parents were teenagers when they had me. Mom was fourteen. Dad was also fourteen. Her family didn't like that she got pregnant so young. They just abandoned her."

"Where'd she live?" Lo asks, his frown crinkling his brows.

"With my dad. His parents took her in." I stand up straighter. "She's in prison, so I'd rather just leave her out of this, if that's okay?"

"It's fine," Connor says, swiping through the tablet.

Lo is searching me, and I'm avoiding.

"We ready?" I wonder and check the time on my cheap black watch.

"Why don't you like your Uncle Raff?" Lo questions, back to that.

"I didn't say he was special or anything."

"Call it a *hunch*." Lo is trying to hold my gaze, and I'm still looking away. Staring at nothing in particular.

"My memories of him are foggy." I take a beat, and both Connor and Lo are quiet, letting me try to unearth the past. "Of what I know, Uncle Raff didn't like his older brother Bobby much. I've heard Bobby was hard on Raff. Maybe picked on him, bullied him. Bobby only had two kids—Sean, who's my dad, and then Scottie, and once Bobby died…"

I see my dad cowering. He's a teenager. I hear a loud clattering noise, but I blink into focus, just as Lo speaks.

"Raff bullied your dad and Scottie?"

"Nah, not Scottie. He was too little. He's only three years older than me," I remind them. "With Bobby gone, my dad became the man of the house. He dropped out of high school. Got a full-time job at the Quickie-Mart. I think he might've sold pot on the side. Meth came later, but it ate away their money. It didn't make them richer."

Connor runs a finger against his temple. "If Raff dislikes Sean, and Sean is the ringleader, then is it likely Raff isn't a part of the stolen Jeep or the assault or anything to do with our families?"

"I'm not sure. I don't know if my dad's even the ringleader or not," I tell them. "He's the one who mostly cooked meth, and like I told Lo, it's mostly for themselves. They weren't big on dealing to outsiders when I was around."

"But they needed money?" Connor asks.

I nod again. "I wasn't involved in that though."

"What about Oliver—or Ollie?" Lo wonders. I remember bringing up my dad's cousin before. "Do you still think he's close to your dad and involved?"

"I'd have to ask my dad." I pocket the cigarettes. "I'll fix him on the family chart thing."

"Is he related to Raff?" Connor wonders.

"No, he's Paddy's oldest son."

Lo rolls his eyes, and I make my way to the door.

I ask, "Ready now?" I'm itching to go and rip this Band-Aid.

"Yeah," Lo says, digging out his car keys. "I'm driving you."

"You can't drive him." Connor rests his electronic tablet on the desk. "We've been over this, Lo."

They have?

"Great, so you heard me last time when I said, *I don't care if I'm spotted.* He's my son's bodyguard. It's not that weird for me to drive him to South Philly."

"Lo—"

"For Christ's sake, Connor, he's going in *my* car. I'm dropping him off. I'm picking him up. If you have a problem with that, take it to your god, whoever that may be. And if it's yourself, there's ten *billion* mirrors in your mansion, have fun."

I'm too surprised to laugh.

"Let's go," Lo says to me, trying to usher me out of the office.

I hesitate and look to Connor.

"He's going to have his way," Connor says simply. "So go with him, but just know, this isn't a good choice. If you're to gain his trust, Sean shouldn't think you're close to any of us."

"He won't," Lo assures. "I'm dropping off my son's bodyguard. He's not a friend. He's not family. He's a *bodyguard*. That's it, Connor."

Why does he want to drive me so badly?

It's a question I don't ask now. Not when it looks like we'll have a whole car ride alone together.

7

Paul Donnelly

LOREN HALE'S CAR isn't exactly *his* car.

He ditched his red Bugatti. Too ostentatious, and paparazzi have an easier time tracking him. So we're in the car Lo and Lily gifted Kinney in October. A black Mini Cooper. It's the car that Kinney told Xander she loved, but she figured her parents would want her to drive their mom's old BMW until she's older.

They surprised Kinney on her 16th birthday. Xander was the one who made sure they knew which car she had her eye on.

Thinking about Xander right now isn't good for the soul. I can't help but think I should be on-duty. Protecting him. He's at school with the Delilah rumors circulating. His senior year is a time he won't forget for *bad* reasons now.

And I don't even know how angry he is at me for trying to date his sister.

Last I heard, Gabe is the one floating over to my position. Being replaced doesn't make me feel great. Not even for a day. An hour. It's just gonna make it easier to replace me for real.

The Mini Coop is snug, and I watch Lo navigate the roads to South Philly in silence. Security is split in two other vehicles. One tails us, and the other is coming from another direction, trying to be more unseen.

Lo told me to "relax" when we got in the car.

Doing this thing called listening to Loren Hale is as comfortable as wet socks, but I can't say he's thrown me to the wolves yet, not when he's sitting beside me in the driver's seat.

I give him another once-over. The fourth one since we left the Cobalt Estate.

"If you want to keep staring at me, we can make a pitstop and get you a magazine," he says, hands tight on the steering wheel. "Pretty sure I'm in at least two at the grocery store checkout."

"Figured you'd be used to staring." I rotate back to the windshield.

"Being used to it doesn't mean I like it."

My mind is stirring up dust. "What'd you want—to chaperone me? Keep an eye on me? Look out for me?" I turn to him again. "Why drive me?"

"All of the above, Paul." He flashes a half-smile.

I lean back, trying to accept that as an answer, even if it doesn't feel like one. "Alright, Xander's dad."

He makes a noise, sounding like a trapped laugh. And then he takes a sharp right turn. We're nearing my old neighborhood. I picked a neutral spot for lunch. Not one of my favorites. I don't need my dad ruining the greats. It's just a deli with a couple benches outside.

My nerves start getting the better of me, and Connor is right—it's better if my dad doesn't spot Lo. "Stop here, I can walk the rest." I unbuckle my seatbelt.

"No. I'm dropping you off."

I don't listen. I open the door of the moving car.

"Jesus Christ." Lo slams on the brakes, slowing down immediately, but I'm already hopping out, my feet catching the pavement with ease.

"See ya." I shut the door.

Lo rolls down the window, glaring at me like a screw is loose. "*Never* do that again."

I flash him the *rock on* gesture, not lingering.

He mutters something before driving away. He'll likely do a loop, then find parking near the Acme. He'll know when I'm done with lunch because of the wire.

He'll be listening.

So will Connor Cobalt and security.

I wonder if they can hear my heart hammering. The only thing keeping me cool and calm is Luna. I picture her licking out a pudding cup and laughing. I picture her dancing to *The Who* with me. I picture her twirling a lightsaber and pretending to save Orion from invisible aliens.

I picture her lying in bed next to me. Gazing up at stars projected on her ceiling.

Memories aren't all bad. Some comfort me. These ones also guide me.

She's why I'm here.

I push back the brewing nerves while I stroll along the cracked sidewalk. Old brick shops line both sides of the street, apartments above them. I spot The Deli up ahead. That's what it's called by the way.

Just *The Deli*.

Like they couldn't think of an adjective or a creative word. Hell, name it after a person and it'd have my stamp of approval.

My pace is leisurely, and I wonder if I'll beat my dad here. But then I see him. He's sitting on a wooden bench outside The Deli. Sleeves of a black flannel are rolled to his elbows, a gray tee underneath. He's older than the last time I saw him.

Can't be certain if the wrinkles at the edges of his eyes are from age or from the meth. He's only forty-three.

His chestnut hair is a darker shade than mine, and his goatee hasn't grayed. He's still scrawny looking, and there were a few times growing up that I thought I could take him.

He taught me that some people look like easy prey, but they're anything but.

I close the distance. And then he swings his head, and we make eye contact. He straightens his spine, and I let out a rough breath. Every step towards my dad feels weighted by quicksand.

I don't want to be here.

I don't want to do this.

I'd do anything to be with her.

It's my last thought before I'm face-to-face with my dad. His blue eyes cradle mine for an obscenely long time. How many years has it been? I never visited him in prison.

I didn't want to.

He tried calling plenty, and I mostly let him talk to Farrow.

I skim him again to shy away from his eyes. I showed Luna his picture—sometime last week after we had sex. She asked what he looked like. I had one photo in my phone. I'd taken a picture of a picture that I had of me and him. I was just a kid, and he had me on his shoulders.

Luna told me he looked like Ethan Hawke. Seeing him now, I can't get that image outta my head.

I take a seat beside him.

He peers beyond me. "Who dropped you off?"

I'm not surprised it's the first thing he asks. He might've even seen Lo as he drove past, so I can't lie.

"The dad of the kid I protect," I say.

"Loren Hale?" His brows shoot up.

"Don't get so excited." I rest an arm on the back of the bench and stare out at the street. "I think he did it to fuck with me. Get in my head or something. I'm pretty sure he hates me."

He makes a *hmm* noise.

"What?"

"I don't know how you lucked out with that gig." He eyes my earpiece and the mic cord that fishes down to my radio. "You're not related to *model* citizens."

"That's 'cause it wasn't luck."

"Right, it was your friend." He doesn't name Farrow. "Pays to have connections, doesn't it?" My dad looks to me like he doesn't know me. "I have a lot of questions for you. Like why you chose *The Deli* for lunch. This place is shit." He grimaces at the crusty sign in the window.

Exactly.

"It's gotten better," I lie. The November chill nips my bare arms. Forgot to bring a jacket.

He snorts. "No, we're going to Heavens' Hoagies." He's already walking, not letting me have a say. I follow his swift gait to the other side of the street. We easily cross through traffic like this part of the city is ours.

I wonder if he believes I have a tail and he's intentionally trying to separate us from security.

The bell dings as we enter the hoagie shop.

"Grab a table," my dad says while he approaches the counter.

My pulse is skyrocketing and nose-diving.

At least security can't speak through this comms piece. At least Papa Cobalt isn't talking to me. That might change with other tech they give me and more time to prepare, but for today, I can rest easy knowing there aren't a million voices in my head.

I pick a gray vinyl booth in the back corner, thinking it's what he'd choose. I haven't been to this place since I was a kid. It'd been my dad's favorite, maybe mine too at one point, but no matter how good the hoagie, I never felt like coming back.

Wawa is better anyway.

I pull out my cigarettes and stick one between my lips.

"Ay!" An older man behind the counter waves a hand at me. "No smokin' in here."

I'm about to put them away when my dad yells, "Since when, Mike? I just saw two guys lighting up in here yesterday."

Mike spins to him, recognition sparking before confusion overtakes him. "Sean, you going to bat for this guy?"

"That guy is my kid."

"Paul?" Mike swings his head to me. "I thought he died."

"Back from the grave," my dad says without a beat. "Two roast beefs."

My unlit cigarette hangs from my lips—too stunned to light it when he sits down with our hoagies and two sodas.

My dad gives me a look. "Go ahead and smoke. Mike just gives people shit."

I pull out my lighter, silently hating I'm just falling into what he says to do.

He slides me my hoagie and takes a bite from his, lettuce falling out of the soft bread.

"How much I owe you?" I reach into my back pocket for my wallet.

"It's on me." He's not meeting my gaze, just chewing his food and swallowing.

I wouldn't normally take the hand-out, one that probably comes with a stipulation, but if I want him to trust me, then I gotta act like I trust him.

"Thanks." I light the cigarette and blow out smoke. "You told people I died?"

"People assumed. You weren't around. No one heard about you going to prison. Death seemed more likely." He swigs from the soda. "Some don't even realize *you're* the Ass-Kicker, the same Donnelly who's become somethin' of a celebrity, protecting the rich and famous." He picks out the tomato. "So there's Paul, my son, and then there's Donnelly, the celebrity. Who's here today?"

I take another drag to calm my nerves. "Who do you want here?" I ask him.

"I don't know this Donnelly. I just know the little shit who used to tie bedsheets to the banister and swing around like he was George of the Jungle." He laughs, his smile faraway at the good memory, but the smile gradually fades like time. "You left."

"Why would I stay?" I breathe. "You and Mom were in prison."

"Your grandmom. She died and you were fuck-knows where."

"She didn't even know I left. Once you and Scottie were sentenced, she just checked out—*she* was gone."

I had no one.

Uncles and cousins took and took. They never gave me anything.

He works his jaw, glaring at the hoagie wrapper. "You could've been there for her...done something for her."

"I was thinking about myself," I tell him honestly. "I wasn't thinking about her."

Regret touches his eyes. He looks away from me. "She did more for your mom and you than you can imagine. She didn't deserve to die alone."

I don't feel badly for my grandmom. I don't even feel *sorry* that I didn't stick around. Being selfish is the only piece of myself that's kept me alive, and it might be one of the few traits I share with my dad.

Because I know if he weren't in prison, he would've been too high to even notice his own mother. He usually was.

I don't reply to him.

It's not like he was asking a question.

I tap ash and pick up my hoagie with one hand. Careful not to rustle the mic taped against my chest. I've been warned several times of sound inference, but leaving a hoagie untouched is suspicious and sacrilege.

He watches me eat. "Why meet with me now?"

I swallow a bite of roast beef. "Things aren't good at work. I'm close to being canned, and I've been wondering how you're doing." There are more truths than lies in there.

"Well, I'm good. Been out for a while now. Mistakes were made. Things are better now." He gives me a warm, charming smile that reminds me of *before*. Before he started using regularly. Before prison. I almost fall into it. Almost believe it.

"You're not using?" I ask.

Things are better now.

How many times have I heard it? Hundreds? Thousands? Every day of my adolescent life?

He sniffs hard, looks around. "Maybe once since I've been back, but it's different this time. I wanna help your mom when she gets out. I'm staying clean."

He can't look me in the eyes and say it.

I see him at twenty-two bent down to my eight-year-old height while I'm crying about Mom screaming an ear-splitting scream in the bedroom. She was hallucinating. Hadn't slept in days. She sounded like she was being murdered.

"She's fine," he said. "She's okay, buddy. Hey, look at me. Don't cry." He wiped my tears. "Are you a strong boy? Huh? Don't cry. You're a *Donnelly*. You remember that." He messed my hair and smiled, one that faded of light the older I grew. "Let's go get ice cream."

He never took me to get ice cream. He got distracted at a cousin's place and he accidentally left me there for two days. My mom cried about it.

And they both promised they'd quit using.

I'm clean now.

Things are better now.

It's just a little bit.

Just one time.

Once more.

Tomorrow I'll quit.

I have this under control.

Believe me.

At the booth, I say nothing to him until he focuses on me.

"What?" he snaps, then leans forward. "You don't believe me? Honestly, do I look like I'm using? You should be able to tell." He motions down his body and across his face like he's John fucking Cena with the wrestling catchphrase *you can't see me.*

It almost makes me laugh, and I do get a good look at him. His face is clear of pock marks, just some old scars. Like the one beside his temple. His usual tick—scratching at his temple—isn't apparent yet. Though, I've seen recovering meth addicts still have the same ticks. The repercussions of using can be long-lasting and permanent.

"You want to see bad? Go visit your cousin Kieran," he says. "He can't even remember what he ate yesterday. He stumbles over every other word, and that's *not* what I want to see for your mom. We've been sober in prison. We still have time to beat this." He lets out a strangled breath, thinking something over. "Meth, man…" He laughs a little like it's a love-hate relationship, and for him, it probably is. "Better than sex. But you know that."

I go rigid, the mic hot on my chest.

Did not want security to hear about me using meth.

"Nah, I don't know what that's like," I say casually enough, and I pick up the soda with my cigarette hand.

My dad frowns.

"I was a virgin when you gave me meth, you know. Couldn't exactly compare the two."

His face contorts, and he shakes his head a thousand times. "I never gave you meth."

I don't want to do this with him. I'm looking at the exit.

"*Paul,*" he forces. "I *never* gave you meth. What the fuck are you talking about?" His South Philly lilt is as thick as mine. He sounds like my dad.

"It was Mom, alright. You know it was her."

"What?" He seems genuinely shocked, but I don't see how.

"You were in the same room," I almost shout. "Vanessa was next to me. She's Mom's best friend—"

"I know who Vanessa is. She's the fucking reason your mom broke her parole." He's fuming.

"Mom was on the other side of me," I tell him. "And she..." I'm not describing what happened while I'm on a mic. Could it add more time onto my mom's sentence? Is that possible? I dunno. I was a minor. I was her kid.

Maybe she's not someone worth protecting, but I can't be a reason she's locked away for longer. It happened forever ago.

"It doesn't matter," I mutter.

"I'll talk to Bridget." He names my mom, and he's staring far away at the wall.

"You didn't know?"

"I didn't know!" he shouts, pissed off. "I thought you took it yourself." He exhales and destroys the hoagie, angrily picking out strips of roast beef.

I want to believe him. If he is lying, just to pull me closer, he missed his calling. Shoulda been an actor.

I down another gulp of soda, the bubbles scratching my throat.

"You shouldn't be talking to Colin," he suddenly says.

It jolts me like being doused with ice. I wonder if security flinched too. "Why not?" I ask him.

"Colin is a little bitch." He wipes his greasy fingers on a napkin. "And you shouldn't have made that dumbass deal with my brother. I don't know what you were thinking."

Cold pricks my spine.

Lo knows *nothing* about me giving my paycheck to Scottie.

My throat closes, and my instinct is to say jack-shit. But I know that won't help draw more out of my dad.

"I'm helping Farrow," I tell him.

"Farrow?" He gives me an unamused look. "The guy who was *loaded* and then married into *billions*. If my shithead brother wanted money, you should've let him get it from your friend. Instead, you're letting him take how much from you? All of it?" He shakes his head with an eye-roll. "Stupid."

I glare. "If you cared that much about me, then why not tell Scottie to back off?"

"I did tell him it's dumb. But once he gets an idea in his head, he's *obsessive*. He was gonna get the money from someone or keep his rights to that kid. There was no in-between. I just didn't think you'd be the first one to cave."

I grind my teeth, avoiding his gaze.

Lo knows now.

Sickness churns in my stomach. I didn't want him to know what I did. Even if it's seen as something good. It's another tally under "why didn't you tell us earlier?" and "why didn't you come to us first?"— and I don't need more of those.

"You should've let Farrow pay Scottie."

"I got that," I say tensely.

He sighs and exhales deeper. "How's my nephew doing anyway? Ripley, right?"

I imagine Lo is freaking the fuck out right now. "He's not your nephew," I say. "He's Farrow and Maximoff's son."

"Whatever. You know what I mean."

"He's fine. Cute."

My dad tries to smile. Remnants of joy are shattered in his eyes. Meth is a pleasure-killer. He thinks it's the greatest euphoria, but all it really does is annihilate the ability to reach happiness after the high is gone.

I suck on the cigarette and blow smoke up in the air. "If things are so good, then why are you stealing Sullivan Meadows' Jeep and junking it for parts?"

His face sobers. "I didn't have anything to do with that."

"Beckett?" I wonder, an untampered rage brewing in my lungs. "You have anything to do with him?"

"With the mugging?"

"You know it wasn't a mugging." I look him dead in the eye.

He grips my gaze tighter than before. "I heard about it in passing. Like I said, stop talking to your cousin Colin. And his dad Roark. He's a little bitch too."

I lean back in the booth. "Who should I be talking to then?"

He gives me a deadpan look. "Who do you think?"

"You?"

"I'm the only one you should trust at the end of the day." He tries to flash a warmer smile. "It's nice. Talking to you. God, I remember when you were little and you *loved* this place. You'd spend thirty minutes flipping through the jukebox pages, and some old lady always came in and gave you a quarter." He looks around. "Hasn't changed much, has it?"

It's different.

Older.

More dilapidated and worn.

I'm different.

Stronger.

"Maybe not," I breathe.

He scrutinizes me. "You hard up for cash?"

"Scottie takes my whole paycheck, but I tattoo on the side," I tell him. "It's enough to eat." It's a lie, considering Akara gave me a raise and my uncle doesn't know about it. "Are you?"

He laughs. "I bartend at the Rhino, what do you think?"

"Thought the Rhino closed down years ago." It's an old musty biker bar.

"It's surviving. Barely." He's quiet. "You know, if you're hurting, you should use what you have. It's right there."

My stomach lurches. "What do you mean?" I have to get him to say *words*. Not just imply criminal acts and bad deeds, like using my connection to the Hales, Meadows, and Cobalts for profit.

"You know what I mean," he says. "You're not a stupid kid. Hell, you might be the smartest one out of all of us." He pauses, skimming me. "The Ass-Kicker. You know people love the shit outta you online?" He grins like a proud dad. "You haven't started an OnlyFans, have you? You'd make a killing."

"Can't," I tell him. "It'd break my contract with private security."

"Just create an anonymous account. They won't know."

"Then I wouldn't be able to capitalize on my notoriety and whatnot." I'm irritated, but I just snuff out the cigarette.

"Start somewhere. If you're gonna shoot a load, you might as well get paid for it. And you have experience doing it."

I die inside.

It's like being sucker-punched, knowing that what he just said... Luna's dad just heard.

"Don't get weird about it," he says quietly. "No shame in the game."

I just nod, unable to speak.

He stands up, and I follow suit, gathering my half-eaten hoagie. Gonna take it to-go, even though my appetite has died too. My throat feels thick from the soda and conversation, so I buy a bottle of water from Mike. I pocket my wallet and take a few swigs.

My head is on a tilt-a-whirl.

I didn't get him to admit to any wrongdoings, but I didn't think he'd confess or implicate anyone in one sitting. As he goes to the jukebox, I ask, "You want to hang out again?"

He smiles over at me, surprise in his eyes. "Yeah. I'd like that." He fishes in a quarter and punches the buttons. "See you around, Paul."

It's chilling hearing my name from his lips, but no more so than hearing the song he plays. The same one I always picked when an old lady gave me a quarter. "Winds of Change" by Scorpions.

I waver for a second. I shouldn't want to return for any other reason than to rat him out. I shouldn't like him, and I'm afraid I'm gonna fall into a trap where I do.

MY HEAD IS STILL FLOATING ABOVE ME AS I LEAVE

and find my way to the Mini Cooper. Lo picks me up further down the street. Hopefully no one notices.

I climb into the car.

Lo's expression volleys between emotions I don't try to read. It'd mean staring at his face for longer than a second, and it's not a place I'm excited to reside.

He just learned I have experience getting paid for sex. He doesn't know the details of what I did, and I'm sure his brain has been rolling through creative scenarios.

Mine would.

"You gonna drive?"

"You okay?" he asks sharply.

"I'm alive, so yeah." I reach beneath my shirt, shut off the recorder, and unplug the mic like Thatcher showed me.

The hum of the air conditioning is all I hear as Lo charts a course for Center City.

He breaks the silence. "Thank you."

"Don't thank—"

"For Ripley," he cuts me off, and I look over. His eyes are bloodshot, reddened like he's restraining the most stinging emotion. "You didn't want me to know." It's not a question.

"I didn't do it for you." I lift my foot to the seat. He says nothing about my boot on the cushion. Elbow to my knee, I stare out the window, watching South Philly disappear behind us.

"What happens if you stop paying that prick?" Lo asks me.

"I don't know. It's why I haven't stopped."

His jaw sharpens. "I'll pay him in the meantime."

"No—"

"You realize I make more money than Connor Cobalt?" He makes a face at me like I hit my head on the curb. "Whatever you're giving Scottie is chump change to me. I'm paying. He'll still think it's coming from you, and he won't ask for more."

I'm still uneasy.

"I'm doing this for my grandson and for Moffy and Farrow. I'm not doing this for you."

It's now that I relent. "Alright. Go ahead."

"Great." After a quiet moment, he groans like he's fighting himself. He cracks his neck and grimaces. "I'm going to ask."

"You don't have to." I try not to tense, knowing this has to be about sex. "You can let it go. Pretend you never heard it."

He lets out a laugh. "God, I wish. *If only*. But my daughter unfortunately likes you."

I smile. "Think she more-than-likes me."

Lo glares, but coming back from seeing my dad, his glare is a welcomed sight. There is no bullshit beneath, and I'm not wondering if he's lying to me. "We're not friends," he reminds me.

"I was just stating a fact, Xander's dad."

"Does Luna know?" His eyes ping to me, then back to the road. He's still glaring.

"I'm pretty positive she knows she loves me."

His eyes lacerate me.

I try not to laugh and piss him off more. "It was a joke."

"Your jokes aren't funny."

I shrug. "Still plan on making them." I'm not gushing about the details of my past, so if he wants answers, he's going to have to ask me outright.

I'm hoping he just drops it.

His jaw clenches, his fists readjusting around the wheel. "The 'shooting the load for money' thing that your dad said—does Luna know about *that*?"

My ribs contract around my lungs. I scratch the back of my head. "I haven't told her outright, no. But it was a long time ago. I don't do that anymore."

"What exactly have you done? Were you alone or with someone who paid you?"

"With someone who paid." I'm baking in this car seat. Put in the oven to roast. I'm not ashamed as much as I am nervous. "I don't like thinking about it," I say.

He contemplates this, and I'm surprised when he doesn't pry harder. He flicks his blinker and turns down another street.

I run a hand across my head. "I've been tested, by the way." My heart rate spikes. "No STDs. I'm negative."

If looks could kill, Lo is definitely trying to murder me. "Is this your way of telling me you're thinking of having sex with my daughter? Because A. Did not want to know that because now I want to throw you out of my car, and B. She should be the most chaste person in your fucking head. You're supposed to be *waiting*. And if it were up to me, you'd be waiting for eternity."

I already fucked your daughter.

This fact, or secret, I'm sheltering is the least of my worries, and I'm not sinking into another worry today. I made it out of the lunch. I'm on the road to seeing Xander.

"Noted," I say lightly.

Maybe too lightly. He shakes his head a few times. "You're something else."

"Something hot." I put it out there.

He touches his chest. "Do I look like your girlfriend?"

"Nah, 'cause I don't have one."

"Music to my ears."

"Knew we didn't have the same music taste."

Lo begins to smile, and so do I.

It's fleeting. His phone rings, and he puts the call through the car's speakers. Connor immediately opens with a gut-punch.

"Donnelly might've been caught getting in your car."

"By who?" Lo asks.

"My dad?" I question.

"No, by Colin. He was in the area. Akara saw him."

"*Great,*" Lo says with a heavy exhale. "Go ahead and say it, Connor. *I told you so.*"

"I have a solution, or a way to mitigate the repercussions. We're going to feed out a headline to the media."

I stiffen.

"What kind of headline?" Lo asks.

"Rumors about you hating Donnelly. It's a feud the press will want to see, and it'll drive Donnelly towards Sean and away from you."

"That's fine," Lo says tightly. "As long as there's no mention of Luna."

"Of course not. I'll send you the draft before it goes live today."

Again, my head is rotating. I didn't imagine my strained relationship with Lo would become media fodder—especially not on purpose.

"Is this really a good idea?" I ask him.

"I don't know," Lo says honestly. "But if we do nothing, it might be harder for Sean to trust you."

I take out my phone. "Is it okay if I call Luna and tell her? I don't want her thinking it's real."

Lo nods to me. "Make it quick."

"Alright." I dial Luna and cup the phone against my ear.

She answers on the first ring. "Hi…is everything okay?"

Luna was still asleep when I left the penthouse, but I shot her a text on my way to the Cobalt Estate.

> Meeting with my dad for lunch. Catch up later, space babe 🤟

I didn't want Maximoff, Jane, or Sulli looping Luna in before me, not when today was about *me* and my family. Didn't want her thinking I'm distancing myself from her emotionally…even if Lo probably hopes I would.

"Sorta. I'm in the car with your dad."

She pauses. "He didn't throw you out of the car?"

"Still a passenger. He actually picked me up."

Lo is listening to my side of the conversation, his serious face like serrated metal edges.

"Whoa…" Her voice trails off, and I take the opportunity to dish out the shit sandwich.

"So I've got some bad news, Luna." In so few words, I explain the headline that'll hit the internet soon and the need to publicly distance myself from her dad.

"But it's fake? You're still in the car with him?"

"Yeah, he's right here." I hoist the phone towards her dad. "You wanna say *hi*?"

Lo glances at the phone. "It's for his own good."

"The world won't ever let this go, Dad," Luna says quietly. "They'll always think you two hate each other."

"Give me the phone." Lo is already reaching for my cell. He holds it against his ear, and I just hear him tell his daughter, "We're taking this week by week. Day by day. You don't need to stress about the future. No one, and I mean *no one*, can predict what's going to happen a year, three years, a *decade* from now. Not even your genius aunt and uncle. Okay?"

"Okay," she says quietly, and I wanna exterminate all doubt in her head—but I stay silent this time, worried if I speak up I'll just be lying to her and myself.

FANATICON

DIRECT MESSAGES

Nov 15th

1:02 p.m.

StaleBread89: bought Fanaticon Convention tickets before they sold out 🤘

Illyana_Dallas222: you still want to go with me?

StaleBread89 read at 1:03 p.m.

Illyana_Dallas222: is that a no?

8

Luna Hale

FIFTEEN MINUTES AFTER I sent the DM to Donnelly, he *still* hasn't responded.

It's fine, I try to tell my anxious heart. He's not in the penthouse, or else I'd knock on his door and chat with him in person.

"He's probably just busy doing security things," I mutter out loud, not to my fish or my puppy. This time, I'm speaking to a living breathing human being.

A squishy, baby-cheeked Ripley Hale is beside me eating strawberries, swinging his little legs on the couch and watching superhero cartoons on the penthouse's living room TV.

I stare at the DMs on my phone, my stomach somersaulting. Besides this blip in communication, I'm just hoping today isn't the day the media decides to run the article about the *fake* feud between my dad and Donnelly.

Maybe I should check, but digging into the internet sounds about as fun as swallowing a sword right now.

"For every step forward, Donnelly and I are taking a giant leap back into a dumpster fire," I tell Ripley. "You know Gamora and Star-Lord had an easier romance. And they're different species!" I fall further back against the couch cushion.

"Wow," Ripley says to me like I'm going through a whole lot.

I let out a breath. "I appreciate the concern," I say softly into a nod. "Truth be told, I'm no Avenger or Guardian of any Galaxy, but Donnelly could be one. He really could."

Ripley chews on a strawberry, staring intently at me.

He's a good listener, just like his dads.

"He's in leagues with the heroes of *all* earthly and galactic realms," I profess strongly.

Ripley gasps in astonishment. "Really?"

"Really, really." I stare off in thought. "Except, *media* is a different kinda enemy." I glance back at my phone. "One that I would've never knowingly created."

My dad and Donnelly finally beginning to mend their hostile relationship? Great. The cannons have been stowed away.

My dad and Donnelly about to be sensationalized in the press for hating one another? Awful. New cannons have been brought on board, and these ones are powered by media and *fans*.

"What's worse," I say aloud, "is Donnelly might have zero chance. My dad, your grandpa, has years upon years of being *beloved*."

For standing devotedly at my mom's side.

For his sobriety.

For raising four children—the oldest of which is treated like a national treasure.

Donnelly is known for his thirst trap videos on social media, which…yeah, they're *hot*. So hot I might've watched them to death and used them for writing inspo, but him lip-syncing to hit songs while shirtless isn't the kinda coverage that'll win over the world. And I hate that they'll likely be pitted against one another to begin with. I hate that people will take sides and there'll be a crusade against Donnelly, just to uplift my dad.

It's not real.

"It's not real," I mutter, more to myself this time.

Normally, I love fantasies. Other realities.

But this alternate reality we're living in is the absolute worst. I want to shut the cover and return it to the library.

And I feel partly to blame. He wouldn't have to do any of this if he didn't want to be with me. I hate that there's nothing *I* can do. Which feels eons worse. I want to help. I want to be a part of the schemes. I can scheme!

I sigh out, "I don't even know the depth of *what* he's doing with his dad." He hasn't explained the security situation. Maybe because I haven't asked outright yet. It's just felt like a tender subject, and I'm a little afraid of detonating a bomb that'll crack a crater between us.

He said he'd tell me everything. Or at least, he'd try. Then why am I so timid about asking?

The same reason why I'm nervous he won't reply to my DM. What if things have changed so much that it's uncomfortable between us now?

I reread his DM. "He wouldn't have bought tickets if he didn't want me to join, right?"

"Nope," Ripley says.

My gut drops. "You think he'll take someone else?"

"Nope."

Definitive signs that I shouldn't be taking advice from an almost-two-year-old, but Ripley is too cute to just ignore. "Is that your new favorite word?" I ask and tickle beneath his armpit.

He giggles, then nods profusely. More baby giggles, until he settles down and munches into the fruit. "I love strawberries, Awnie Loonie."

I eat a goldfish cracker. "What else do you love?"

"Cars!" He makes a *vroom* noise. "Doggies." He wipes his mouth with his hand. "Daddy. Papa. *You.*" He suddenly flings his soft arms around my waist, and my clenched heart untwists.

I hug my baby nephew back. "I love you too." Ripley is the perfect distraction to my mopey afternoon blues, and soon, we find ourselves on the floor. He's leap-frogging with me from one side of the living room to the other.

"Jump!" he says, preparing for the biggest jump of his life. His tiny feet barely lift off the ground, but I make sure I jump the same short distance.

"Jump!" we say together.

He catapults a half inch.

"Whoaaaa, you jumped so far!" I high-five him.

Ripley beams. "Again! Jump!" Just as we hop another step, Donnelly enters the living room, and my heart has leapt another five yards without the rest of me.

He seems to be absorbing the image of me playing with the baby. Car keys looped on his finger, his gun and radio are holstered like he's on-duty, but no one trails behind him. He's all alone.

"Hi," I say, breathless.

"Hi to you." He scratches at the back of his head, his breath just as trapped as mine. Our eyes only shift when Ripley races over to a bucket of Hot Wheels. Ripley doesn't have a bad habit of putting smaller toys in his mouth, so he's allowed Hot Wheels *with supervision* only. "You babysitting?" Donnelly asks, coming closer.

I pick myself off the floor. "Kinda. It's not really a big babysitting gig. Moffy and Farrow just stepped out for a sec." I point at the ceiling. "They're on the rooftop if you're looking for them. I think I saw Oscar and Charlie go up there too."

Donnelly slips his fingers through his tousled hair. "I actually wanted to talk to you." He ends up gripping the back of the couch. The mod blue piece of furniture separates me from him, but how he's sweeping me, I get the distinct notion that he'd love to catapult it if he could.

He wants to talk to me.

I really hope this isn't a bad news talk. I'm *almost* on edge. I say *almost* because something about sharing oxygen with Donnelly always makes me floaty inside. Like I'm a few seconds from an exhilarating takeoff.

"Okay, yeah," I nod. "I'm all ears, even the ones that haven't fully grown in yet."

He starts to grin. "You've got ears on the back of your head?"

"The tops of my feet. Better to hear you with from down below."

"Lemme talk to your foot. Gimme." He motions to me, and I high-kick my bare foot at him. Donnelly clasps my ankle, and my smile is effervescent inside me, keeping me warm.

"Hale?" He talks to my toes. "You hear me?"

"Loud and crackly," I say, then accidentally wobble out of his hold. Losing balance, he tries to keep me from doing a painful split by reaching for my hips, but as he scales the couch, I splat onto the cushions—and he falls on top of me.

Holy shit.

His strong build is melded against mine. Our chests rising and falling together, his hand is on the cushion near my cheek. He's just as surprised he landed here. "Fuck. Sorry." He lifts himself off me quickly. Standing, he's raking his hands through his hair and readjusting his untucked black tee.

My face is roasting.

We both check Ripley, but my nephew is busy racing a yellow Mustang against a green Jeep on the floorboards.

I sit up, trying not to remember the epic, most unforgettable time Donnelly and I had sex. The memories blaze my body in a needy swelter. "What'd you want to talk about?" I ask. "My DMs?"

His brows twitch. "Your DMs?" He digs in his pocket, confused.

"I thought you read it." It says he did with a timestamp.

He skims his phone. "Shit, no. I must've clicked into it, but I never saw it. Your dad"—he jabs a thumb behind him—"called me when I was on the elevator."

"The team-up?" I'm guessing.

"Yeah." Donnelly reads the DM in full, then looks deeper into me. "It's never a *no*. Of course I wanna still go with you. Who else will be Team Callie with me?" He motions to me. "We'll hit up all the Bass panels together. It'll be dope."

Except there's the new underlying fact that we're going *as friends*.

I try to fly-swat away the encroaching disappointment and hang on to the positives. We can still have an awesome time in San Francisco as *just friends*. It's only a month away. Not so long from now, and maybe… maybe everything will be resolved by then. Maybe we *could* actually attend as a couple.

Not so fast, Luna.

I am a greedy bean. Probably too impatient as well. I just want all of him. Now.

"Yeah, it'll be fun," I nod, trying to accept whatever I can get. "I can pay you back. How much was the ticket?" I open my cash app.

"Don't worry about it."

I frown. "Fan conventions aren't that cheap. I can pay—"

"I got it," he says again like it's nothing. Yet, he hasn't taken a seat. He's standing and looking around the room, giving a great deal of attention to a copper lamp and then Ripley's Hot Wheels race.

"We aren't together though," I say so quietly, I doubt he hears. But then his gaze meets mine, and by his saddened expression alone, I'm certain he has heard.

"It's just…it's something I'm doing for a friend," he rationalizes. "I bought your ticket. I also got your bodyguard's ticket and an extra."

I freeze. "An extra?"

"Just in case someone else wants to go."

Oh. "Like Joana?" I throw out there, regrettably.

His face twists in hurt. "I'm not inviting my best friend's little sister. I'm not inviting *any* other girl." He pauses. "Except Frog, but she has to go if you go."

"Who's the extra for then?" I wonder.

"Whoever you want to bring, bring 'em," Donnelly says earnestly. "I just thought it'd be better if more people go with us."

Easier.

A group setting. It's where our friendship started and lingered *forever.* We weren't "share alone time together" kinda friends, because feelings *did* exist and Donnelly didn't want to mix signals when he couldn't act on them. Now, I'm reading this signal pretty well.

Just friends.

Only friends.

"You bought the extra," I say. "You should give it to someone. It doesn't feel right me giving it away."

"Think of it as an early birthday present," he says. "It's yours."

He's giving me way more control over our trip by leaving the extra ticket up to me. I can choose one of my friends instead of his.

I nod, "Yeah, okay."

He brushes another hand through his hair. "I don't wanna tell you who to bring, but if you bring a date—"

"I wouldn't," I cut in fast.

He exhales.

"Lookie! Lookie!" Ripley rushes over to Donnelly, trying to show him a red Hot Wheels truck.

"Watcha got there?" Donnelly crouches to the baby, but he's casting a deeper glance back at me. Seeing him interact with a baby is adorable, but more than that, *this* baby has Donnelly's eyes—they look so much more alike than I realized.

Ripley's cheeks redden, timid all of a sudden. "My truck." He grows more reserved at times and definitely when more people are around. It's not just Donnelly.

"Your truck? You can *drive*?"

Ripley nods.

Donnelly whistles. "Look at you. You're already *way* cooler than your papa. You tell him Uncle Donnelly said so, yeah?"

Ripley nods a ton, acting *very* serious.

He's good around babies. A fact I've known for a while after he made Ripley break into a giggling fit. At dinner one night, he did a magic trick with a disappearing grape. When Donnelly popped it out of his nose, Ripley doubled over giggling in his highchair.

"You like kids?" I wonder.

"When they're not crying." Donnelly stands up while Ripley returns the truck to his bucket. "Baby cries are a nail gun to the heart though. I hate 'em."

"Me too," I say just as Charlie Cobalt struts into our convo.

"Says the two people about to live with *three* newborns," Charlie tells us like we're insane. His suit jacket is thrown over his shoulder like he's either on a Parisian stroll or about to make a quick exit. Considering we aren't in Paris, I think I know which.

"This is a big place," I tell him. "We might not even hear them cry all that much."

He swings around. "They're not guppies in a tank. They'll be in communal spaces *crying*. It's what babies do."

Stop scaring Donnelly out of the penthouse! I want to shout at Charlie, but as I look over at Donnelly, he seems to share the same concern. That I'm about to rocket off to another place, another city, without him. He's married to wherever his client resides, and Xander has a lot of his senior year left.

"I dunno," Donnelly tells Charlie, "babies might come out celestial. Could be a house of three little angels."

"Yep," I nod. "This is heaven."

"Your heaven is my hell," Charlie notes, eyeing the doorway but he lingers. "Move to New York." At first I think he's telling Donnelly.

"Me?" I point to my heart.

Donnelly shifts uneasily.

"No, the wall behind you," Charlie deadpans. "Yes, you, Luna. It's honestly shocking you're still here."

Is it?

I haven't wanted to close this monumental chapter on living with my brother, Sulli, and Jane. Now that they're having kids, I get to be a cool aunt and create memories with their babies too.

"I'm taking classes at Penn," I remind him.

"Have you been on campus since your fics leaked?" He knows the answer.

"No."

"Drop out."

"Or you could stay," Donnelly interjects. "Just putting it out there."

Charlie checks his phone, then the door. Like he needs to go. I'm more surprised he's not bolting.

"You really think I should move to New York?" I ask Charlie.

"I think you'd be happier there, but what do I know? I'm just your cousin." He makes it seem like that title holds *zero* weight, but Charlie has meaning to my life. Even though he's not editing any of my fics right now, I already miss picking his brain and trying to see how he views the world.

I turn to Donnelly. "What do you think?"

"I think…" He's watching Charlie, who's starting to watch us. *Uh-oh.* I forgot how perceptive Charlie can be. Donnelly continues, "You'd be happiest wherever there's a Wawa 'cause it's the best place on Earth."

Charlie pockets his phone. "Sounds more like you."

I say, "Maybe I'm happiest wherever Donnelly is."

Donnelly does a double-take towards me, his lips parting, but nothing escapes.

My words are supposed to be *casual.* A throwaway statement! Yet, I sounded defensive and my face has betrayed me. Heat burns my cheeks, especially at the intensity to which Charlie is staring into me, then into Donnelly.

Donnelly combs a *casual* hand through his hair. He is much better at deception than me, and typically, I think I'm pretty damn good too.

"Because Wawa," I lie. "It's all about Wawa."

"Stamp." Donnelly waves a limp *rock on* gesture. He sees that Charlie is onto us, and he's not so excited about that fact. Neither am I. Charlie can't know I like Donnelly before my best friends—Charlie's brothers—find out. It feels wrong.

Charlie splays his suit jacket on the couch. He makes no move to leave.

Not even as Maximoff joins us.

"Daddy!" Ripley bounds for my older brother on unbalanced little legs. My nephew hoists his arms up at his dad.

Moffy lifts his son high against his chest, perching him up so he's eye-level. "I missed you, little guy."

"Me tooph, Daddy," Ripley tries to enunciate slowly.

"You hungry?"

"Nope." He shakes his head, still bashful at the full room. "I-I ate stwabewwies." He nestles into the crook of Moffy's neck.

I'd think it's super cute, but I'm in an internal panic. Time to go. "Farewell, all earthly dwellers." I flash a Vulcan salute, about to make a quick exit to my room.

"Wait," Donnelly catches my wrist, stopping me.

My heart flip-flops, and the warmth of his hand tingles my flesh. His touch still sparks electric currents through my body. It still overwhelms me, and I'm so glad that hasn't changed with our relationship status.

"I came here to talk to you," he breathes.

Oh right. I stay put.

He checks the time on his black wristwatch. More in a hurry. "Xander hasn't really left the house."

A sad fact. He's been majorly avoiding Donnelly...and me, to an extent. Since my brother hasn't needed a bodyguard, Donnelly hasn't had much of a chance to even speak to him. *Give him space* seems to be our motto, but I'm not sure how much it's helping.

Donnelly continues, "He's planning on working out at home with Thatcher and Banks, so I'm being shifted to Jane's detail, and Thatch said she's in wedding planner mode. She's supposedly checking out a venue for a bride." Why does he seem nervous? He stuffs his hands in his pockets. "I just wanted to know if you'd like to come with me."

I blink. "To hang out on Jane's detail?"

"That's not strange at all," Charlie says with pinched brows.

Donnelly ignores him. "I dunno what you're up to today, but if you're free, I could use the company."

He wants to be in my company, unearthly reader. He is seeking me out, even though we're not supposed to be intimately together.

"I'm free all day." Excitement bubbles. "Let me just get my wallet and stuff—"

"Are you asking her out on a date?" Charlie asks him accusingly.

"Nah, just a casual friend thing." He's still very cool about it.

Charlie inspects him, then Moffy, then me. Back to Moffy. "You really think it's wise for your sister to go out with *him*?"

That stings.

Maximoff adjusts Ripley in his arms. "It's fine, Charlie. Just let them be."

Just let them be. I never really thought Moffy would be *this* supportive of me and Donnelly, and I can't calm my mushrooming smile.

"Fine?" Charlie is wide-eyed. "He's attached to people who *attacked* my twin brother, probably because they believed he's fucking Beckett. What do you think they'll do to Luna if they see he'd rather fuck her?"

"Jesus Christ, Charlie," Moffy cringes. "Can you *not* talk like that around my kid? And me."

"For *fuck's sake*," Charlie doubles down. "The least of the laundry-list of problems here is me talking about your sister having sex with a bodyguard."

Donnelly jumps in, "We're *not* together." He pries out those words from his core, and pain blooms inside me.

We're not together.

Why does that feel final? Permanent?

I frown.

Charlie motions to me, as though my dejection is an admittance. I recover quickly and say, "We're not having sex." *Anymore.* It's a half-truth.

"And I'm a virgin," Charlie says as though it's obviously a *lie.*

Our attraction can't be that apparent. No one else has really sniffed us out, have they?

Maximoff rests a calming hand on his son's back. "No one publicly thinks they're together, Charlie. And Jane will be there."

Charlie's jaw tenses. "Where's the overprotective and self-righteously *ragey* Maximoff Hale?"

Moffy scrunches his face. "I thought you hated that part of me."

"I do, but there are times where it's *necessary*," Charlie sneers between his teeth. "Don't make me fill that role. *Please.*"

Just now, Farrow walks into the strained living room with raised brows. "What the fuck did I miss?" He stops beside his husband and son and flashes a puzzled expression to Donnelly.

"I asked Luna to come out with me," Donnelly confesses. "It's *not* a date, and no one's gonna think it is when I'm on-duty. She's been safe with me, always."

That's the truth.

Charlie looks conflicted about the whole ordeal.

Ripley tries to pry the aviators off the top of Farrow's head. Farrow gives his son the sunglasses, and as adorable as the oversized shades look on the baby, the tension has not vacated the room.

"I'll be fine," I assure everyone. "It's more like an outing with Jane."

"Just be careful," Moffy says.

Charlie flings his suit jacket back over his shoulder. "And I'll tell you what your brother is too afraid to say, *Don't fuck Donnelly.*"

"Whoa," Farrow head-snaps to Charlie and glares.

My pulse accelerates.

Charlie doesn't stop. "He's *contaminated.* Disease-ridden—"

"*Charlie,*" Farrow warns.

Before Donnelly shifts his gaze away, I catch his anger and his hurt. He loves the Cobalts.

"—you fuck him, you die," Charlie tells me. "You understand that; I know you do." Because Charlie has read most of my smut, including the ones with my favorite trope. "Now *isn't* the time to fall for him."

Too late.

"You want to make a point like that again," Farrow says heatedly to Charlie, "don't be surprised when you meet an ending you won't like."

Charlie opens his stance. "Go ahead. Hit me."

Farrow speaks into his comms mic instead. "Oliveira, come collect your baggage."

Now *that* hurt Charlie. His cheek muscle twitches. Then he gets in Farrow's face.

My eyes grow.

"Hey, hey!" Moffy sets Ripley on the floor.

"What is it, Daddy?" Ripley asks, unable to see with the sunglasses.

I'm about to scoop up my nephew. But Donnelly is faster than Maximoff to intervene. He's pulling Farrow several feet back, who's physically ten-times more built than Charlie's tall, lean stature.

"What in the ever-loving…" Oscar is here, racing in from the bathroom.

It's organized chaos. Less unruly than what Eliot incites. Possibly because Farrow, Donnelly, and Oscar are bodyguards, three men with a whole lotta restraint.

Farrow still hasn't given into Charlie or his own anger, and inside this palpable messiness, I lock eyes with Donnelly, a painful longing burrowing back in my lungs.

Fuck him and die.

I'd rather be living on the other side of this trope.

Fuck him and survive.

Why can't that be my reality?

9

Paul Donnelly

I'M WAITING FOR LUNA in the penthouse elevator with Oscar and Charlie. I'm containing gnarled *anger* I'd usually expel in an insult or shit-talk or at times, a fist to a face.

Lashing out at a Cobalt? Can't do it, not even if they insulted my pride and joys of Philly. Breathing, though, feels tougher sharing space with Charlie. I'm not gonna be able to keep my mouth shut for much longer.

My Cobalt brethren called me *contaminated*—like I'm toxic waste. But that's not even what's got me hot.

I finally speak. "I know you might not be mindful of babies and whatnot," I tell Charlie. "But you gotta be when you're around them, and you should *never* provoke Farrow or anyone in front of their kids like that."

Charlie has on dark shades. Can't see his eyes. "He wasn't going to hit me."

"You wanted him to," Oscar points out.

"No, if I *really* wanted to be punched, I would've gone for Moffy, but I didn't."

Oscar is shaking his head repeatedly, unable to look at Charlie right now.

Charlie's frown deepens.

"You stepped into Farrow's face," I tell him. "Don't think you were asking him for a kiss on the cheek, unless you were."

Charlie is unamused.

"Just sayin'," I add.

He drops his head a fraction, then turns to me. "I'll be more conscious if their son is around. It didn't cross my mind in that particular moment, honestly."

I nod, hoping to cool off.

Luna arrives, a small backpack on her shoulder. Slipping into the elevator, she waves but senses the tension and says nothing. Oscar hits the lobby button, and I press *30* so Luna and I can stop at the Rookie Room and get Frog.

Descending, she whispers, "You okay?"

"Getting there," I whisper back. "You see Farrow?"

Her gaze falls. "Yeah." She edges closer. "He seemed really upset. I could tell he wanted to be alone with Moffy."

Farrow was only defending me, but he ended up trapped in a place that I know he would never want to be.

When we're alone on the 30th floor, Oscar and Charlie are gone. Walking down the hall together, Luna says, "I didn't think Farrow would be that upset. It's not like he took Charlie's bait."

"Me and him have *high* bars on what fathers should be." I glance over at her. "Because we haven't had great ones, and I doubt he wanted Ripley to see or hear that at all."

Luna looks saddened. "He's such an awesome dad. Ripley *loves* him. He's always trying to imitate Farrow."

I think back to Ripley's adoption. How I got Scottie to terminate his parental rights, knowing that the baby would be raised by my best friend. *Wouldn't have chosen anyone else.* Ripley deserves to be raised in a household with unwavering love, and that place is with Maximoff and Farrow.

I've never questioned that.

I never will.

Luna suddenly says, "I don't think you're diseased. Everything Charlie said about you was wrong."

"I know," I nod once. "I'm not bent out of shape over it. He can call me a landfill, a walking STD—doesn't mean I am one."

"Even though it's a Cobalt who said it?" She knows how much I respect the Cobalt Empire, and being shit on by one of them isn't giving me heart eyes.

"He was just looking out for you," I say. "Can't fault him for that." I lived up in New York with him and Beckett. Charlie's always been *direct*. Blunt. He shoots shotgun shells at close range, so you have to pay attention, but someone usually gets hurt. Gun was aimed for me this time, but I just feel like he took out my best friend instead.

I slow our pace, not ready for Frog to splice into my time alone with Luna.

She's in deep thought. "Sometimes I think Charlie wants to feel a kinda pain that he can't reach, and he targets people who he believes can take it and give it back."

"Like your brother?" I realize.

"Yeah, like Moffy." She shrugs. "It's just a theory." She adjusts her backpack. "Considering he doesn't go after me *at all* and just tried to warn me against you, he probably thinks of me as a sheep." Luna *baaahs* like a lamb.

I smile over and *baaah* right back. "I called you *hot* if you didn't get that."

She grins, cheeks flushed. "Understood it, since I called you a *hot lambchop*. Guess we're still speaking the same language."

"Guess so." God, I'd love to fling my arm over her shoulders. *Can't.* Feels intimate. So was calling her *hot*, but fuck me, I see a clear path to her, it's more unnatural to swerve into traffic. "Joke's on Charlie though 'cause you're definitely not a sheep, but I'm fucking glad he thinks you are."

"Why?"

"Because if he went at you, I'd be in *his* face."

Can't even imagine how Farrow has felt watching a guy *repeatedly* go at the love of his life. I'd lose my mind.

November sunshine beats down on a fancy garden, complete with marble fountains, white rose bushes, and autumn flowers. Never been to this place. It's outside Philly with no city noises. If I strain my ears enough, I can hear chipmunks rustling beneath manicured hedges of a maze we're currently navigating.

Feels like I stepped into *Alice in Wonderland*, and I'm not particularly fond of mazes. They're harder to escape, and I'm mentally trying to file every twist and turn we're taking.

Comms are quiet in my ear.

Jane and Luna are several feet ahead of us, which makes me uneasy. Frog and I should be out front, not strolling behind 'em at a leisurely walk-in-the-park pace, but Jane was adamant that she chart the course.

"I'm trying to find the *best* spot for cocktail hour between the ceremony and reception," she said.

It's hard to deny Jane.

Hell, it's hard for me to say *no* to most girls.

"You're not missing much at the apartment," Frog chats with me while we walk and watch our clients from a distance. "Unless you count the inescapable sounds of Quinn screwing his girlfriend. I swear they're even louder than her crying gerbil."

"I remember those days where Quinnie got laid." I try not to study Luna more than Jane, who I'm supposed to be protecting. "Didn't think he was that loud though."

"It sounded like furniture got knocked over."

Never heard anything that aggressive through his door. "You sure they were having sex?"

Frog peels her gaze off Luna, just to side-eye me. "It doesn't take having sex to know what sex sounds like."

"I didn't ask 'cause you're a virgin." I hold her gaze for a half beat.

Her face flushes. "Sorry." She sighs, then touches her radio. "*The others* are making me touchier and more defensive."

The others are Epsilon bodyguards. Something we both have in common: SFE loves to jab us with hot pokers. They'll mostly antagonize Frog when none of us on Omega are around, but we've caught 'em enough. Banks went off on Novak not long ago, calling him a fucking coward, but us fighting Frog's battles isn't gonna help her with these pricks in the long run.

It might just make it worse.

They'll say some shit about how she can't even defend herself without backup, so how is she gonna protect a client? I've heard it all before.

Only it was said to me.

Add in the fact that Frog is only turning nineteen in December, a girl, and the boss's little cousin, she has more tender spots they'll poke at than me.

Just as I open my mouth to respond to her, my phone beeps.

Gut dropping, I dig my cell out of my pocket and glance at the text.

Wanna grab a bite to eat tonight? — Dad

My stomach churns. Normally I wouldn't reply. I'm on-duty, but talking to my dad is now classified as a *security* operation. So I quickly send a message.

I'm working now. I'll let you know if I get off later.

He's fast to reply.

Yeah, yeah, I see how it is. I'd choose to be chummy with Loren Hale over me too. — Dad

Shit.

I text back with one hand, telling him it's not that. Just doing my job so I don't get fired. I'll talk to him later. And I pocket my phone.

My dad won't divulge *anything* incriminating if he thinks I'm personally close to Xander's dad and the famous ones. There's just no way. He's too careful.

That article about Lo hating me—it needs to run.

Lo is the one hesitating. It's why it hasn't hit the press yet. He said he hated the first draft of the article. Well, he's probably been through ten rounds of edits by now.

Feels like he's stalling. For what? I dunno. I thought he'd love an opportunity to paint me as a cockroach online.

"Gabe eats like five pounds of tuna salad a day," Frog continues talking about my old roommates. "Who eats that much tuna?"

"Maybe he's a cat," I say, mentally distracted and trying to focus. *Focus.*

"Our resident cat lady would know," Frog smiles over at Jane, who's happily chatting Luna's ear off about the cocktail hour.

Jane switches her sequined pumpkin purse from her left hip to her right for the fifth time. She's been doing that all afternoon. *Must be uncomfortable.* Being that pregnant can't be comfy. Her belly is swelled beneath a fuzzy Dalmatian print sweater and a peachy tulle skirt, and she perches her hand on her lower back like the heavy front load is bearing on her spine.

"Oh! What if we have the caterers serve different hors d'oeuvres in every dead-end of the maze?" Jane says excitedly, stopping to jot a note on her phone. "We can even have little tables along the pathways with petit fours."

"The lost people get satiated too," Luna muses.

"Precisely." Jane types away, but takes time to adjust her purse again.

I approach. "Want me to hold your pumpkin?"

She's confused. "My...? Oh," she realizes. "Yes, that's sweet. Merci beaucoup." She hands me the purse.

I slip the gold chain strap on my shoulder. Pumpkin at my side. "Accentuates my ensemble," I joke, gesturing to my plain fit today.

"Very glam," Frog compliments me.

"What do you think, Luna?" I ask as a friend to a friend. *Just friends here.* Gotta remember that.

She skims me but mostly stays on my eyes. "I never saw you as a pumpkin kinda guy, but it could work."

"Artichoke is more my style?" I watch Jane out of my peripheral.

She's on the move, and I casually spin towards her and everyone follows after me.

"Uh-uh," Luna shakes her head. "Maybe a zucchini since it pairs well with your eggplant."

My cock.

I grin. "Stop making so much sense. It's…" *Turning me on.* Don't fucking say that. I intake a tight breath, unsure of whether we're making this harder for ourselves or easier.

Luna looks just as uncertain. Her smile flips upside-down. Pain knives my side, especially when she catches up to Jane and leaves me behind.

"You should know something," Frog says very quietly, very seriously.

I stiffen. "About Luna?"

She nods. "I can't break Luna's trust in me—I *won't*, so don't ask me to tell you everything."

"Why tell me anything at all then?"

"Because you're my friend too."

Never thought I'd be friends with another girl, to be honest. Probably should be more like a big brother and mentor to Frog, less so like a friend, but being the responsible bodyguard camp counselor might not always be in me, even if I want it to be.

Then Frog adds, "I really don't want to see your heart get broken."

It slams into me.

Luna's seeing another guy already.

She's been out at a club kissing someone else.

She's secretly hooking up with O'Malley.

That last thought—makes no sense. But it douses me with gasoline and sets me on fire.

"Alright," I breathe. "What is it?"

"At the Fanaticon Convention, she's planning to meet up with another guy."

My nose flares and stomach overturns. "Who?"

"I don't know his name, but I call him Wonder Bread."

"'Cause he's a basic white boy?"

"No, it's because his username is StaleBread89."

Pure fucking relief.

I end up laughing. *Shouldn't have doubted Luna.* I feel badly about that, but in this second, I could literally walk on the moon.

Frog scrunches her face at me. "What? It's not *funny.*" She comes in closer and whisper-hisses, "I thought you *like* her. I know I assumed it, but I'm usually not that far off. And she's awesome. You should *love* her, actually. She's that amazing, and she's way better than you, honestly. Fuck you—"

"Frog," I laugh, touching my chest. "I'm Wonder Bread."

Her mouth drops. "Shut up."

"I'm not basic though." I can't even explain anything else yet—my laugh fades and smile vanishes. "They turned left." For the briefest second, I don't have my eyes on Jane or Luna, and before I kick myself too hard, we turn and they're in view.

They're alright.

I breathe out.

Frog surveys the new lush surroundings and our clients.

We're in the center of the maze.

Ivy spindles down trellises, and stone benches surround a sculptural fountain, one of a goddess with a bow and arrow. Water trickles out of her palm, splashing in the pool.

Jane is meandering around, taking notes, and Frog does a good job scouting potential exits. I watch Luna sniff a rich orange flower—what I think are mums. She slips a tiny glance my way. It swells inside my chest. I pull my eyes off her to inspect the pathway we just left—but I look back, just as she does too.

As we walk around the center of the maze, the fountain between us, we steal glimpses of one another. Our eyes catch in quiet, tender seconds, and I almost hear music. I like thinking that moments carry melodies, and being with Luna is like listening to the exultant hum of my soul.

I'll never get tired of the sound.

She begins to smile, but the heartache and longing inside it is tearing through me.

Can't be together.

I'm working on it.

Then I look to the exit, to Frog, back to Jane. She hasn't said anything in the past five minutes or so. For someone so chatty, it's like red skies overhead, warning of a storm. She's also starting to pace.

Luna sees. "Jane? Everything okay?"

"I think this'll work…for the cocktail…party," Jane says, red-cheeked and wincing a little. She's on her phone. "I mean, *hour*. Cocktail…hour."

"You want to sit down?" I ask, my concern suddenly spiking. She's two weeks from her due date, and to take extra precaution, she had a doctor appointment yesterday just to clear her for this garden--outing.

"I passed with flying colors," Jane told me with a wide grin like she aced an exam. She patted her round bump like the baby was also an honorary grade-A student.

So I try not to think the worst. Though it wasn't Farrow checking on her yesterday, and he's the only guy with an MD that I trust. I run a hand through my hair, and watch Jane's face contort into a more pained wince. Not good. So not good.

Frog whispers to me, "Is she going into labor?"

Holy shit, I hope not. I swing my head back to one of the seven hedged archways, only knowing the path we came from. What if she can't walk? I could carry her. Is it safe to carry a woman *in* labor? Probably not, I'm thinking.

I run another tensed hand through my hair. *It's not labor.* There are a million other things it *could* be. But any way I toss it, *pain* isn't a good sign for a pregnant woman.

"Yeah, here, sit," Luna tries to guide Jane to a bench, but Jane just plops down on the nearest perch: the fountain's ledge.

She's tapping at her phone screen, more distressed. "Does anyone have cell service?"

We all take out our phones.

Luna shakes her head to me.

Frog frowns too.

I've got nothing. Why are the satellite gods fucking with me today of all days?

"No? Yes?" Jane asks through her teeth, clearly in pain.

My nose flares, and I pocket my phone while I try comms, but the connection is poor too. "I had signal earlier. Back further in the maze." *I received and sent texts.* "I can go back—"

"Call Thatcher," Jane grits out, then screams, buckling forward with her hands on her belly.

Noooooo. I jolt towards her but there's nothing I can do for *pain.* I'm not even carrying a damn Tylenol on me. Gonna start doing that from now on.

Luna kneels in front of her. "We're here. It's okay. We'll get Thatcher." She rests a hand on Jane's arm, and I'm glad she's here to be a comforting force to her cousin.

"Donnelly," Frog says, alarmed and wiggling her earpiece. "I can't hear anything."

I'm messing with the radio frequency. Static crackles in my ear, which is better than no sound. I might be able to get *something* through comms.

"You remember how to get back to the start of the maze?" I ask Frog.

"I think so, yeah."

"Take Luna. As soon as you two get cell service, call 911, then the med team. Meet the paramedics at the entrance," I instruct. Luna hears and comes over to us. "You're gonna need to lead them here, to the center. There's no time for anyone to get lost."

"Okay, okay," Frog nods repeatedly. "I can do that. Luna?"

"I'm ready. Let's go." She's about to jog away, but she wavers, just to ask very quietly, "Do you know how to deliver a baby?"

Baby.

B.A.B.Y.

Even spelling it in my head doesn't make it seem real. My pulse is trying to go haywire. "Only if watching *Grey's Anatomy* counts. You?"

"*Roswell*," she names another TV show. "Think you have more experience since this is a human baby, not an alien."

I don't know if I can do this, I want to tell her. But like most things in my life, I try to believe I can. "I've got it," I nod to her. "Stay with Frog."

She nods back, then races off with her young bodyguard.

Returning to Jane, I squat beside the mom-to-be, fiddling with the radio while I talk. "How bad's the pain?"

She breathes through her teeth. "It's...*dreadfu—*" Her gritted scream cuts off the word. She's white-knuckling the fountain on either side of her thighs. A knot lodges in my throat.

Come on, comms. Come on. I click the mic at my collar. "Donnelly to SFO, anyone hear me?" Nothing. "Donnelly to SFO, am I coming in clear?" I keep my voice even-tempered. Unpanicked. Even if I feel like that meme where I'm sitting in a house burning on fire.

Jane blows out a staggered breath, tears wetting the creases of her eyes.

"You think it's false labor?" I ask in desperate hope. She's had some scares before and raced to the hospital. Maybe that's why she kept her pain undercover, thinking they're false contractions.

Plus, she's early.

It could just be more of the same. A giant false alarm.

Please, God.

"No...*this* feels different...it's pushing lower..." She looks at me with pure fear, silent tears dripping down her cheeks. "I'm going to have this baby." Her voice shakes. "I'm so scared."

Pure adrenaline suddenly rushes through me.

I don't like how she's sitting on the fountain, so I help her off the stone. She lies down on the soft dirt, her knees bent and legs naturally spread. She's trying to shimmy off her panties, but more tears invade her eyes and the contractions painfully grip her limbs.

Being helpful and all, I reach beneath her skirt and pull her underwear off for her. They're wet. Maybe her water already broke. *Fuck*. This is happening, isn't it? *Fuckfuck*.

"It's okay if I look?" I ask still trying to be calm even if I'm silently screaming *I can't believe this is fucking happening*.

"*Yes*," she says into another scream. "Hurry!"

On one knee, I quickly peer between her legs. No baby's head is breaching through Jane. Good signs? I have no clue, but I can one-hundred percent tell she's dilated. A lot. And that definitely means labor. Meredith Grey would be so proud of me, I think.

She might need to push, but I can't be sure. That uncertainty wedges a knife in my ribcage. I hate not knowing. Hate not being the *best* person for this job. Because I know that's Farrow. But I'm gonna do my best. "Take big breaths," I tell her. "Everything seems fine. No baby yet." *Facts*. Sticking to those sweet facts.

"Are you sure?" She groans into another anguished noise, which only causes me to move faster. I'm unhooking my radio, twisting the knob that changes frequencies.

"Pretty sure," I tell her. "As sure as I can be." Again, I stay calm for Jane. "Ambulance is on its way. You'll get out of here in no time. Then you can laugh about how you almost had a garden baby."

Jane focuses on my voice and her breathing.

"You can call her Olive Garden Moretti."

She almost laughs, the noise caught in her throat. "Thatcher… hates that restaurant."

I know. "I don't know what he's got against it. Their breadsticks are dope."

Jane fights through another contraction, and I check between her legs. No head, but she's *extremely* dilated and she seems to be resisting the natural urge to push. *This baby is coming.*

Am I about to deliver a baby?

Jane and Thatcher's baby, to be exact.

My pulse is so loud I'm surprised that I hear slight chatter in my ear. But that chatter—it's a gift from the heavens themself. I lift my mic to my lips. "Donnelly to SFO? Can you hear me?" *Please.*

"I...you're coming in...clear," Akara responds.

Thank fucking God.

I don't jostle the radio in case it messes the signal. "Get Farrow on the line. Jane's going into labor, and I need some instructions. I have no cell service, and I can *barely* hear you." Where's Web MD when you need it most?

Akara tells everyone else to stay off comms, leaving the channel open for Farrow.

"Here," Farrow says, a little crackly but audible. "How far apart are her contractions?"

"I think every minute or so." I peer back underneath her skirt. *Oh shit.* I speak softly into the mic. "I can see the start of a head." My stomach knots, and I almost think of asking Farrow about maternal mortality rates. Like what are the odds of everything going okay with me delivering a garden baby. But I'm not about to ask those questions in front of Jane.

I can't bring myself to let them into the air.

"Jane needs to push, now," Farrow says. Just like that all ill thoughts drive away. I'm focused in.

I touch her knee. "It's time to push, Jane."

She's crying again and muttering, *no, no, no,* then intakes a sharp breath. "I don't want to do this without him. I don't want to." She wants her husband. She wants Thatcher, and she's sobbing. My heart splits open because I know I'm not a good stand-in for the love of her life.

I wouldn't want this either.

In my mic, I say, "Farrow, give me a run-down of what to do as fast as you can." He does. I listen. It's scaring the fuck outta me, really, because he adds, *in case this happens, you need to do this*—and I'm hoping and praying she won't land in a worst case scenario. "Alright. Now get Thatcher on the line."

Thatcher is in my ear in a millisecond. "Donnelly—"

"You're gonna talk to your wife through comms. I won't be able to hear you, but she can." So carefully and quickly, I detach the radio and pry out my earpiece. I tell Jane, "You won't be able to respond to him, but Thatcher is gonna walk you through this. He's right here."

Jane sniffs, then shuts her eyes, battling another contraction. I reach over her and nestle the earpiece into her ear, then lie the radio beside her.

Please tell me the signal is still clear. "Can you hear him?" I ask Jane.

She nods, her body easing like her husband is a morphine drip. Before I draw back, she catches my hand to squeeze it in appreciation. Relief spills tears out of the corner of her eyes. "Thank you."

Don't thank me yet. I push fabric of her peachy tulle skirt out of the way. "You've gotta push, Jane." I peel off my black T-shirt hurriedly, and with Thatcher in her ear, she begins to push.

Gritting down on her teeth again, her scream this time is one of full-blown strength and anguish.

I tune out the sound and focus on the baby.

"Almost there, one more push," I tell Jane, cupping the baby's shoulders, and as Jane pushes, I ease this fragile being out into the world. My pulse is racing again. 'Cause she's covered in membranes and I hear nothing but Jane's exhausted pants.

"Is she okay?" Jane asks, her voice pitching. "She's not crying. Donnelly?"

Please cry. Cradling her baby girl in my arms, I rub my fingers along her nose to ease out mucus and I warm her back with my shirt. This is what Farrow instructed in the event the umbilical cord wrapped around her neck, but the cord isn't cutting off her oxygen. Still, she's not breathing.

And she kind of looks like an alien. And I wonder if Luna might have done a better job.

I wonder if I wasn't the right person for this at all.

My throat swells.

Please. Please. Please.

I know some people think I'm this toxic thing, infecting everything I touch. But I can't be the reason this baby doesn't take her first breath.

I can't.

I can't.

"Donnelly," Jane starts sitting up more.

Another swipe along her nose, and the baby suddenly stretches an arm and cries out to the world. It pummels me backward, and I let out a strained exhale. All the tension I'd been caging rushes out of me. Jane breaks into happier, more overwhelmed tears.

As I place the newborn in Jane's arms, the waterworks hit me too, seeing Jane embrace her baby, kiss her soft cheek, instantly love her. Life is strange and beautiful, and moments like these, I'm grateful to be alive.

I help Jane take off her sweater so the baby can lie on her chest, skin-to-skin. Without pulling the earpiece out of Jane's ear, I click the mic and say, "Congratulations, Papa Moretti. You've got a beautiful baby girl." I lower the mic to the newborn who lets out softer cries.

Thatcher can hear his daughter.

Jane laughs into more tears. When I release the mic, Thatcher can respond back. After their moment together, Jane sniffs and tells me, "They're asking for you."

So I collect the radio, earpiece. Comms are back with me. "Donnelly here."

"Check Jane," Thatcher orders.

"Get Farrow back on," I say, chest tighter, and my cool-as-a-cucumber doctor friend walks me through assessing Jane. Once I make a guess that Jane isn't bleeding too much, I undo my shoelaces and take out a knife in my back pocket. Gotta cut the umbilical cord.

Everything goes smoothly, but it's not like TV. It's messier, more frightening because she still really needs a doctor and I'm not it. Thankfully, the paramedics arrive about four minutes after I cut the cord. Frog and Luna rush in beside them.

The girls all comfort Jane and grow teary-eyed seeing her newborn. I hang back a bit and let the professionals do what they're good at.

While they put Jane on a stretcher with the baby and start taking vitals, I rub my palms together, trying to wipe off the blood.

"Here." Luna digs in her backpack and passes me a few Kleenex.

"Thanks." I smile over at her, not wanting to take my eyes off Luna. I do my best to clean my hands, but this is a job for soap and water. Balling up the dirtied Kleenex, I stuff the tissue in my pocket.

As we stare out, watching the precious moments before they'll wheel Jane to the ambulance, I feel Luna's hand slip into mine. Softly, quietly…secretly. Even though my palm isn't clean, even though she knows we shouldn't—she's still holding my hand.

I encase mine around hers.

For a moment.

Before we have to let go.

10

Paul Donnelly

HEALTHY BABY. Healthy mom. I hear the news before I personally go back to the hospital. It's been a long day. Showered at the penthouse, squeaky clean now. Jane and Thatcher have big extended families, and I want to give the Cobalts and Morettis this time together. Don't need to intrude, but Jane personally calls me and says, "Can you come here?"

It's so late at night, the birth center looks like a ghost town. No other visitors, but I hear the teeny tiny baby cries. Once I find her room, I knock on the door, and Thatcher answers, towering four inches above me.

I smirk. "Good thing your baby didn't come out six-foot and thirty-pounds." She's only five pounds, two ounces.

Thatcher widens the door, but he hasn't shifted enough to let me inside the labor and delivery room.

My smile fades at the emotional look in his eyes. "Did something happen?"

"Yeah," he nods. "You delivered my daughter. You helped Jane."

It tunnels into me, but I'm not used to barring so much tender emotion in front of people. So I'm staring down the hallway, left and right. "She did all the work. I just cracked Olive Garden jokes."

Jane laughs inside the room. *She heard me.*

My lips rise, and Thatcher just nods to me, "I should've said it earlier—"

"Nah, man, you just had a baby. You only needed to think about her and Jane." I know what he's about to say. The gratitude is penned in the shiny browns of his eyes.

Still, Thatcher produces the words, "Thank you, Donnelly."

I lift my shoulders. "Happy to be there." I mean it. Being able to witness a new life coming into the world has reminded me why I love existing.

Plus, I've always loved being in positions where people depend on me and rely on me. It's why I'm a bodyguard.

Thatcher ushers me further into the room. Jane is propped against the hospital bed, her baby cocooned in a swaddle and sleeping contently in her arms.

Jane is glowing, her smile brighter than last I saw. "You want to hold her again?" she asks me.

"Sure," I breathe, and at Jane's bedside, she passes over her little bundle of joy. I cradle her against my arm. The baby smacks her lips in a tiny yawn, and a wave of uneasy emotion crashes through me, clenching my stomach.

I have a dark childhood.

Probably worse than anything Thatcher even went through, and I have nothing against babies—but sometimes I do feel like they shouldn't touch me.

I try to push past that. "She's so small," I murmur and start to smile when her thimble nose crinkles. "What are you gonna call her?" I ask since they've been flip-flopping on the name for months. "Olive is still on the table, you know. I've never known a single bad Olive, except for that moldy jar of kalamatas."

Jane grins. "Olive is unfortunately off the proverbial table. We've already chosen a name."

Thatcher nods. "Took long enough."

"Oui." Jane scoots higher on the bed, smiling over at her daughter. "We wanted to go with the letter *M*, preferably something Italian. Like Martina."

"Martina Moretti," I nod. "I dig it."

"That's not her name," Jane says. "After what happened, after what you did for me"—I'm shaking my head, but tears are already flooding her eyes—"you *did* help me, Donnelly. You made sure Thatcher was there with me."

Anyone would've done that, but I don't argue. "What'd you name her?" is all I ask.

"Maeve. It's Irish," Jane says. "It means *she who rules*. And in Irish mythology, she's a goddess."

Irish.

Because of me. My gaze clouds with more emotion, and I look down at Maeve Moretti. A baby goddess is the perfect addition to the Cobalt Empire—and to Jane and Thatcher's new family.

I sniff hard to keep tears at bay. "I think she's already living up to the name." Carefully, I hand her back to her mom. "It's beautiful, Jane."

Except my stomach has sufficiently twisted into a pretzel. A bad feeling bites at my heels, and it has nothing to do with the new parents. Everything to do with my situation.

It's a me thing.

I make a smooth, unsuspecting exit, letting them have their calm, happy night with Maeve.

Once I manage to sneak past the camped paparazzi in the parking lot, I find the security vehicle and drive back to the penthouse. "Call Xander's Dad," I tell the car.

"*Calling Xander's Dad*," the automated voice responds.

It rings a handful of times.

"Wake up, Lo," I mutter.

Finally, the line clicks. "Why the hell are you calling me at two a.m.?" His groggy voice floods the car, and I detect slight worry from him. *Slight.* Maybe I'm hallucinating it.

"You gotta run the article. Today or tomorrow, as soon as possible."

"What?" he snaps, still sounding half asleep. "We'll talk about this another day. Shouldn't you be sleeping? In bed? Tucked away? You just delivered a *baby*."

Not just any baby.

A Cobalt baby. I could ask Oscar's husband Jack about how this will shift public perception, but I know fandoms. I know *this* fandom, and once they hear I delivered Jane's daughter, it'll do the inverse of what we've been trying to accomplish.

"I had to cancel dinner with my dad tonight," I remind him. "For *this*. He's not dumb. He's gonna think I'm like Thatcher or Farrow to your family. Like I'm more than a no-named, replaceable bodyguard, and I have to be no one."

Lo is quiet.

My dad won't trust me if he thinks I'm more loyal to the famous ones than to my own flesh and blood.

"*Please,*" I'm begging here.

I'm scared of being caught in this lie.

Terrified, really. 'Cause they won't take me snitching on them *kindly.*

"I'll think about it," Lo says.

I scrape a hand through my hair before returning it to the wheel. "What's the hold up, Xander's dad?" I ask, trying to keep my voice leveled. "Who cares if it has typos?"

"It's not about the typos, and you know that," Lo says with a deep, irritated sigh.

"It's about Luna," I'm guessing, since she'll need to endure this fake feud between her dad and me, the guy she loves. I get it, but if her enemy is the media or my family, I'm going to steer her away from my family—every damn time.

He doesn't deny that Luna is the center of everything. "I'll call my publicist at 8 a.m. and we'll go from there."

It's the best I'm going to get.

FANATICON FORUM

We Are Calloway

Posted by @CobaltsNeverDie

Is Paul Donnelly considered an honorary Cobalt after delivering Jane's baby?

Dude did the MOST to ensure baby Maeve arrived. The Cobalt Empire needs to knight him. Thoughts? And I will accept nothing less than Donnelly becoming royalty through these legendary acts in chaotic times.

@ReedJenkins41: the fact that no one was there with Jane and he was alone = GOAT status. Which def makes him a Cobalt imo.

@banks_and_beautiful: But are we sure that Donnelly was alone? The family's press release said nothing about how or where Jane gave birth. Just that Maeve Rose Moretti and mom were healthy.

@DaughterofRoses: There are literal pictures on GBA News where we see Jane holding the baby on the stretcher in the garden. Not to mention, the freaking EMT told the reporter that Donnelly delivered the baby alone. No. One. Else. Was. There.

@LionsTigers_andHales: Connor should crown him.

@Iluvcharliecobalt: idk about Donnelly but it's horrible that Thatcher missed the birth of his baby. I feel so bad for Jane and him.

@SodaPoporDie: Thatcher is a cheater tho. Who cares if he didn't see his baby? Karmic justice.

@WAC77Lover: Donnelly is the greatest. New favorite. I stan.

@GirlsinPink: Everyone should go watch Donnelly's videos! He's SO HOT. And he's single!!! But not for long bc he's mine, ya'll. I'm claiming him.

FANATICON

DIRECT MESSAGES

Nov 16th

7:21 a.m.

StaleBread89: had to leave early and didn't want to wake you. Grabbing coffee with my dad, then I'm told I *might* be shifted to Xander later today. Something about him going to the arcade with Easton? Wish me luck 😝

8:46 a.m.

Illyana_Dallas222: Good luck, fellow Planet Partner! I'm crossing my many fingers for your safe travels. Let me know how it goes with my brother 🖤

9:32 a.m.

StaleBread89: I'll relay everything. Stay sparkly, space babe ✨

11

Luna Hale

WHILE I SCROLL THROUGH Fanaticon and my most recent DMs on my bed, I reread the messages he sent me and smile a little. I still can't believe Donnelly had to deliver Jane's baby yesterday. He'd been so quick-thinking and composed in the hottest pressure cooker.

I envy him in a way. To have that particular skillset could come in handy. But while we were in the epicenter of the garden maze, I could see it affected him somehow.

So in the car following the ambulance, I asked him if he was okay.

"Yeah," he breathed, "but that's only because I don't have to live in the other reality."

"Which one?" I asked.

"The one where her baby didn't make it. The one where Jane didn't. And it was my fault." He swallowed hard, then shrugged tensely, one hand on the steering wheel.

Frog was in the passenger seat and said, "No one would've blamed you."

The world might've. As cruel and sad as that may be, people online would've tried to burn him at the stake.

I almost told him, *that is an awful reality. I'm happy you're in mine.* But maybe he needed to hear Frog's encouragements. So I stayed quiet.

I'd almost forgotten she'd been in the car with us. For those brief seconds, I thought it was just me and him. Which feels like such a rarity outside the penthouse.

Donnelly changed topics, asking Frog if she liked Bon Jovi. I sunk back into my seat and let them talk the rest of the ride.

I caught him checking on me through the rearview mirror, but I busied myself coloring the galaxy tattoo on my thigh with neon highlighters.

When Jane went into labor, I wish I could've done more in the moment. Been *there* in greater ways. For him. For Jane.

I guess finding cell service and flagging down the paramedics was *something*, but as I replay the whole event, I see myself on the periphery. Like they're inside a flurrying snow globe and I'm stuck on the outside trying to get in.

Maybe I'm just being harder on myself since Donnelly is doing all the legwork for us to be together. He's reconnecting with his dad *for* me. What's my contribution? I'm here. In my bedroom. Relegated to waiting...and writing. Mostly to you, unearthly reader.

I haven't returned to *Human Him, Cosmic Her* in the past week. Not since my fics leaked. It feels too raw, so the Thebulan saga is on hold.

"I'm not useless," I tell Orion while he sleeps at the foot of the bed. My Newfie barely perks up, but I add, "I am *useful*." I try to let the words settle better in my stomach and not fall flat.

Right as I set aside my phone, the screen lights up with the name: *TOM.*

An extra spoonful of guilt pummels me. I haven't told Tom or Eliot about Donnelly, and now that my siblings know the truth and with Charlie onto us, it feels so wrong to shelter this from my best friends. Maybe I can solve this portion of my guilt.

I click into the call quickly.

"Hey, I need your help," he whispers, sounding rushed. "Eliot's going off the deep end."

The deep end could be a myriad of things, but I don't need details.

"I'm on my way." Like he lit up the sky with a bat signal, I jump off the bed in a dash and grab my hoodie from a chair. I pretend it's my superhero disguise, and maybe I can *pretend* to be worthy of grand, earthly heroics.

Maybe I can fool myself for an afternoon. Or maybe…maybe I am in leagues with the likes of the Avengers, with the Seasons, and the Nerd Stars too.

Is that possible?

Are people heroes for themselves first? And then they can be heroes for others? I'm not sure I've completed the first task—just partially check-marked it. But that's me, isn't it? Half-finish things, never fully commit.

I'm not 100% enrolled in college. I've only completed eight courses in two years. I still haven't declared a major.

My fics are offline in limbo and only printed out in my closet.

I can't even manage to fully commit to being Donnelly's girlfriend.

That's not your fault.

I give myself a tiny pep talk, but the self-criticism is very strong today. I'm happy for a good distraction.

"I'll drop you a pin," Tom says before muffled voices steal his attention. "Shit. See you soon, Luna." He hangs up on me.

Racing out of my bedroom, I'm too fast and slam right into a Moretti brother. I don't see which, but when I hear, "Oof, Luna?" I recognize Thatcher's gruff tone.

Shouldn't he be at the hospital?

I take a quick step back, rubbing my forehead that made impact with his hard chest. "Sorrysorry," I say hurriedly, noticing Jane's pastel pink travel bag slung on his shoulder. He must be here to collect more of her things while she's recuperating in the hospital room. "I'm just heading out," I add and start walking backwards and flash the Vulcan salute.

Thatcher narrows his eyes skeptically. "You late for something?"

"Kind of," I say, cagey.

I'm unsure of the trouble Eliot is in, and I don't want to disclose too much information, especially to the Omega lead.

Okay, I know he's Jane's husband and father of her child and not *just* a bodyguard, but honestly that makes it worse. He's a Cobalt by

Marriage. A CBM as Eliot put it, and there are certain things that Cobalts by Blood don't even know about Tom and Eliot. Things I've been sworn to take to my grave.

Thatcher waits for me to say more, but I spin on my heels and sprint to the elevator.

"Where are you headed?" Thatcher calls out, needing to keep tabs on me, and this is when I *know* he's talking to me as a bodyguard and not my cousin's husband or a roommate. Being a new dad clearly hasn't affected his concern for my safety.

Quickly, I yell, "I'll be back soon! Have a good day! Tell Baby Maeve and Jane I said howdy ho!" Sprinting away, I'm high on adrenaline as I enter the elevator. I realize I might not be useful to Donnelly right now, but I can be useful somewhere else and it feels good.

Only problem: I don't want to involve Frog.

I haven't wanted any bodyguard on my detail lately.

Venturing in the city without security isn't new to me either. Tom, Eliot, and I aren't like our older siblings. Paparazzi aren't always lurking around every corner. They aren't always riding the bumpers of our cars. And I'm aware that my stories leaked only a week ago, but with Maeve Moretti entering the world, the spotlight has shifted. And if there's a lightbulb still directed my way, that's what my hoodie (aka superhero disguise) is for.

I draw the black hood over my head, and I make myself small. Discreet.

A while ago, I asked Charlie how he takes rideshares in Center City and Manhattan without being spotted. He told me he has an account with a fake name. The next day, I set one up for myself.

Maybe I *am* my own hero, after all.

I smile, confidence reemerging bit by bit. I pop open the rideshare app on my phone under my alter-ego Illyana Dallas and request a ride. My phone beeps.

You going out? Thatcher called and told me you were leaving the penthouse. — Frog

Guilt blooms like a freshly plucked flower. This one is my own fault. If I ignore Frog entirely, then she can't be blamed. It'll be on me instead, and I'll just be one of the difficult clients to work with.

Like Charlie.

And yeah, some in my family might say I shouldn't be taking pointers from *that* cousin of all my cousins. But I'm not Moffy. I don't make the right decisions all the time, and maybe I understand Charlie more in that instance.

I guess this means I'm less in leagues with the Captain Americas. More in leagues with the anti-heroes of the world. The Lokis, the Deadpools, and the Magnetos.

I wonder if Frog knew she was protecting a sometimes-villain.

My heart pangs as I think of her in the past tense. Frog is a *good* person, and she's been an amazing bodyguard…a *friend*. After Beckett's bodyguard was hospitalized last week, I just keep picturing Frog with two black eyes and broken bones. It's easier sneaking around alone, and I don't want to see anyone on my detail get hurt.

I leave Frog on read just as my ride arrives.

With little traffic, it's not long before I'm dropped off in another part of Center City, an intimidating six-story brick building in view.

THE PHILADELPHIA HEADQUARTERS FOR CALLOWAY

Couture. Garments are designed, tailored, and shipped to retailers and the famous CC boutiques from this building.

It's not a shock Tom pinned this location. Aunt Rose designed a special line of men's suits for the spring, and all five of her sons agreed to model the clothes for a fashion ad. Each suit is even named after them. *The Charlie, The Beckett, The Ben.* Eliot and Tom were able to approve some of the design elements to their suits too, and I remember they needed to schedule a fitting.

Which must be today.

I'm already out of the rideshare and standing on the curb. *Still unrecognized.* It's an intoxicating feeling, and I let it carry me to my best friends. Once I've passed through front door security, flashing my ID, they give me directions to the Cobalt brothers.

Less than three minutes later, I push into the cozy-sized fitting room and drop my hood off my head.

Ohhhh no.

My eyes widen at the sad mannequins lying supine on the carpet with scissors and pushpins, the frilly-edged drapes hanging lopsided on the window like a body smacked into them, and two antique chairs are tipped haphazardly on their sides.

Eliot is currently *standing* on a squeaky couch cushion, wearing nothing but blue boxer-briefs. Panting like he's been chased around the tiny fitting room, he hoists his phone over his head.

"Eliot," Beckett says as calmly as he can, jumping on the couch and attempting to grab the phone, but Eliot is six-four and Beckett is only six-one.

Eliot easily stretches his arm upward and out of Beckett's reach.

Beckett remains even-tempered. He's shirtless, his floral tattoos spindling up his arm, and since he's in sweatpants, I doubt he's seen the tailor yet. "I'm not playing around. Give me the phone."

"You think I'm playing?" Unkempt *rage* brews in Eliot's blue eyes. "I'm not giving you or *anyone* the phone. You'll have to take it from me."

Beckett sucks in a tight breath. "Eliot, please. I'm not fighting you for the fucking phone."

"Come on, man," Ben says from several feet away. He's the only one wearing suit pants, likely *The Ben*. The dark blue fabric is unbuttoned and unzipped—maybe it doesn't even have a fly yet. "You don't want to do this."

"You're wrong, baby brother. I know *exactly* what I want to do," Eliot sneers.

"Fuuuck," Tom mutters, his hands on his head like he doesn't know how to stop this car crash.

Confusion whirls my head. What the hell is going on?

"Luna?" That voice belongs to one of the *four* other people in the room. I barely noticed the Epsilon bodyguards.

I hate that they're wallpaper to me, but I do remember their full names, even if some just go by last names only. They're all in between their early-thirties and late-twenties, and right now, the Wreath brothers, Chris Novak, and Ryan Cruz Jr. are posted near an ornate full-length mirror, watching the Cobalt brothers self-implode.

Of the three, Ian Wreath is the most senior at maybe thirty-three, thirty-four-years-old? He's already taking a step towards me, the authority clear.

The distraction is enough for Eliot to swing his head to me. "Luna?"

Beckett takes the moment to steal Eliot's phone.

"Wait!" Eliot lunges, but Beckett is quicker and nimble, able to jump from the couch and add distance.

"*Luna,*" Ian Wreath calls out again, seriousness coating his voice. "Where's your bodyguard?"

"She's outside waiting in a car," I lie with utter ease. Teleportation might not run in the family, but I know lying does. I could've inherited this power from my parents.

Ian stares me down. He's what the security team calls a "buddy-guard" and I've been around him enough to recognize that this stare-down is weird. Way too odd for comfort. In the past four years as Tom's bodyguard, he's been super hands-off. Like chill to the max.

Right now, he is anything but chill.

Ian folds his arms over his chest. "All it takes is one radio in to see if that's true." He calls my bluff. "So I'll ask you again, where's your bodyguard?"

"You didn't bring your bodyguard here?" Beckett suddenly asks, his concern tripling as he approaches.

How did this turn on me? Am I a magnet for attention? I'm supposed to be helping Eliot! I want to scream. But Tom is catching Eliot by the arm, and they're whispering heatedly, pulling one another into the corner of the room.

Away from me.

Was I not supposed to even be here?

I feel like floating away. Teleportation is way more useful than the ability to lie. Unfortunately, I'm stuck here.

"Luna?" Beckett waves a hand in front of my face, drawing my attention. Said hand also contains Eliot's phone. "Where's Frog?"

I focus on him. Beckett is earnest and worried, and the intention wasn't to cause him alarm, so I just come clean. "She doesn't know where I am. But I got here fine."

"Fucking Omega," Ian curses under his breath, then presses the mic at his collar.

"Wait," I call out, my heartbeat quickening. "I'm really fine. I can just stick around Eliot and Tom today. This is my fault. I don't want to involve anyone else."

Ian's hand freezes at his collar, and severity I've never seen before sobers his eyes. "We're in different times, Luna. I can't be doing this." *Doing this*. He means bending rules. He's bent a lot for Eliot, Tom, and me over the years.

"Different times," I say the two words out loud, and I regret when I do.

Ian's gaze flashes to Beckett.

He's rigid beside me, trauma like shards of glass behind his yellow-green eyes, glazing them in a strange way I've never seen. He watched his bodyguard take down multiple men and be beaten in the process. It's also unlocked a new fear for me.

Hence, no Frog today.

"Ian's right," Beckett says, his voice as smooth as idle water. "You can't be ditching your bodyguard." The next words come hushed. "Especially since you're friends with Donnelly."

Do you regret that friendship? I want to ask him, but I'm scared of the answer. Because if it's *yes*, my heart will shatter for Donnelly.

I study him for another beat, wondering if Charlie told him that Donnelly and I have not so chaste feelings for one another. Beckett has never struck me as manipulative or cunning—he would've outright said *since you love him* if he knew more. My best guess: he thinks we've always been in the friendship zone.

Mixed feelings roil in my stomach, and I don't have time to make sense of them.

"Beckett!" Eliot storms over to us.

Uh-oh. "Eliot," I start, but he's fixated on the phone in Beckett's fist, and Tom curses loudly, distraught since his talking points must've landed flat and he's nowhere near as strong as Eliot. I've seen Eliot lift more than *Beckett* in the gym, and Tom said Beckett's ballet schedule includes gym time *every* day.

He's on a war path towards Beckett. "Give me my fucking phone—"

"Stop!" Ben cuts him off midstride, thrusting a palm at his chest.

Eliot glares beyond him and tries to bulldoze Ben, but Ben isn't thin or scrawny. These two are more evenly matched, seeing as how Ben is considered the jock of the Cobalt Empire. And he's six-five.

Ben just pushes Eliot harder. He barely stumbles.

"This isn't worth it!" Ben yells.

"This isn't worth it?!" Eliot shouts back like Ben just stabbed him in the heart. "So when it's something *you* care about, your *anger* is worth it—"

"That's not what I meant." Frustration grates his voice.

"Then what the fuck did you mean?" Eliot asks painfully, eyes flashing hot.

"It'll make things worse!" Ben rages.

"Things couldn't get much worse!" He shoves his brother.

Ben shoves back. Eliot can't escape the towering wall that is Ben Cobalt, not without a fight, and they begin grappling more forcefully, more furiously—but they're not even furious at each other, not really.

"Shit, shit, shit," Tom breathes, jogging over but staying a foot out of the brawl. "You're an uncle now, dude! This isn't good uncle behavior!!"

Ben has Eliot on the ground, trying to pin him. Eliot is wrestling Ben back, their faces reddened with visceral anger.

Eliot vs. Ben.

This isn't the strangest sight to witness. I've seen it before at the Key West rental house, back during my brother's bachelor party. Ben was trying to restrain Eliot, and Eliot was on a dark voyage, headed for revenge—but I don't even know if *revenge* is the source of his wrath now.

And back then, Moffy was there.

My older brother was the one who put Eliot in an MMA hold. He was the one to end the entire heated moment, and without him present, I can't see how this'll go.

Tom catches Ben at the waist to pull him off Eliot.

"No, Tom," Beckett warns.

I go do my part to help calm down Eliot. Squatting, I put a hand to his broad shoulder, and his elbow juts backwards and jabs my mouth.

Ah...the sting *radiates*. My palm flies to my mouth. Stumbling away, I taste the bitter iron of blood. My lip throbs.

Eliot doesn't even notice me. Didn't even see me or feel the elbow-to-the-mouth. Have my powers of invisibility really kicked in?

"Luna, Luna," Beckett says quickly, seizing my arm and drawing me away from his brothers.

Not invisible.

"I'm fine," I mumble against my hand. I wish Donnelly were here. The other bodyguards know not to intervene in family disputes, but maybe Donnelly would've been the one beside me. Or is that just a fantasy too?

Eliot is still wrestling Ben, and Tom is wedging himself too much between them. Limbs are being tangled and caught, and suddenly, Tom lets out a sharp wince.

"Fuck, *fuck*." He grits between his teeth, shooting to a stance and clutching his wrist.

Beckett comes forward, his hand on his forehead like someone shielding the sun. "Enough," he says too quietly and then shouts, "ENOUGH!"

It stills the room.

I don't think I've ever heard him yell that caustically. He sweeps his brothers and the mess strewn around them. His breath is uneven. "Enough."

I go to my best friend. "Tom?"

He has his back to everyone, even me.

"Did he...?" Ben pants hard, everyone going eerily still. "I-I didn't...did I?" He looks to Eliot.

"No, it was me," Eliot murmurs, concern darkening his features.

"I twisted an arm...I-I thought it was your arm," Ben stammers, eyes glassing.

"Tom?" I mumble behind my hand.

"Hmm." He winces, then says tightly to the room, "I'm okay."

Eliot stands in haste, but his focus isn't glued to the phone. He extends a hand to help Ben to his feet, but Ben is too dazed to take it, watching Tom in pain. So he rises on his own.

"I can call Farrow?" I whisper. He can check Tom's wrist, see if it's just sprained.

Tom shakes his head. "I'm okay, really." He whirls around to us—but then hurriedly gathers his leather jacket off the floor. Once the jacket is on, he stuffs his hands in his pockets, not letting anyone see the damage.

He needs his hand in prime condition to play the guitar.

To his brothers, he forces out, "*I'm okay.*" He frowns at me. "What's with the hand over your mouth?"

"New fad," I mumble.

Eliot beelines for me. He catches my wrist and lowers my palm. "Oh, *fuck.*" More concern rips at his face.

"Is it that bad?"

Tom cringes. "Your lip is busted."

Must be a Hale ramification. Same thing happened to Moffy when he pinned Eliot. A mouth full of blood. Kinda makes me feel more like my big brother, like I did something *good* in a strange way.

Eliot pinches the bridge of his nose. "I'm sorry."

"I'm okay too," I tell him. All things considered, this could've ended a lot worse. Sharp pushpins are littered across the carpet. Ben or Eliot could've rolled onto them, but they managed to avoid needles.

Ben scrapes a hand through his hair, eyes welling up. He says nothing as he gathers his collegiate shirt off the floor and jeans.

"What's wrong, dude?" Tom asks him.

"It didn't have to get that far. *This* didn't have to happen. I'm tired of seeing everyone get hurt—"

"We're not hurt. I'm not hurt!" Tom shouts. "You should be more upset over the fact that you split your pants, dude."

Ben tries to look backwards at his ass, and sure enough, there is a four-inch rip right down the middle, showing off his gray boxer-briefs.

Eliot stifles a laugh. "You tore the ass of *The Ben*."

"Way to go," Tom banters. "Mom will love that bare-assed fashion statement."

Ben's chest caves, his throat bobbing. He drops their humor like a fragile egg cracking on pavement.

Tom's face falls. "Ben. I was joking. Mom won't care."

Beckett walks over to console their youngest brother, but Ben is quick. He's already gathered the rest of his things, and he leaves. One of the bodyguards follows.

Tom exhales as the door shuts. "God, I never know what to say to him sometimes."

"He'll be okay," Beckett says, bending down and collecting the pushpins. He still has Eliot's phone.

I upright a mannequin and ignore the pain swelling in my mouth.

"Why'd you bring Luna into this?" Eliot asks Tom. "This isn't about her."

"This is *all* about her," Tom says with heat. "And she wouldn't want you to burn everything to the ground in her name."

"I'm right here," I remind them. "Right. Here."

Eliot spins to me. "Then you should know that I'm burning everything down in *my* name." He points a finger at his chest. "Mine."

"What's going on?" I ask both of them.

"Show her the video," Tom tells Beckett, and after short consideration, Beckett rises and sets aside the pushpin cup to play the video for me. He lets me hold the phone, trusting me with that much.

It's a five-minute video recording. Muted. Eliot wields a bottle of whiskey in one hand, and he's shirtless, sculpted abs on display, as he talks to the camera with clear unadulterated rage.

"This isn't role rehearsal, is it?" I whisper. He's currently Hamlet in *Hamlet*, a mega-big role for the fall, but if this has to do with me, he can't be acting a part.

"It's not," Beckett answers.

"He wants to post this on social media," Tom explains. "It's a five-minute unhinged rant as he curses out his troupe."

"They're dead to me," Eliot says.

Beckett catches my eyes. "Delete it, Luna."

Delete it?

I've already deleted enough, haven't I?

I can't help but think if Charlie were here, he'd tell me to post it. Charlie and Eliot are alike in some ways—it's the Loki in them, the destructive, mischief-wielding power they cradle and toss like bombs. But they're also so vastly different.

My mind is whirling. "Why are you cursing them out, Eliot?" *And what does this have to do with me?* But an outward dread starts thundering down.

You know, Luna.

You know.

Please…no.

Eliot shakes his head, and he's glowering at Tom again. "I cannot believe you called her to use her as your bargaining chip. She's our *best* friend."

Tom glares. "And she has more sense than you right now, dude. Just chill out."

"Chill out?" Eliot's eyes redden with more hurt. "Chill out? How would it feel if someone were to take your vocal cords and rip them out—"

"*Eliot.*" Beckett gives him a classic *what the fuck* look.

I wince. "Can we not talk about those hypotheticals?" I tell them.

Eliot and Tom have a brutal staring contest. "This is on you, brother," Eliot says. "You're the one about to cause her pain. Just remember that."

"Then maybe I know her better than you." Tom stands his ground. "Because she'd want to know."

I might be a Hale, but I'm not slow.

I'm not an idiot.

I've figured it out, okay.

"They fired you?" I ask Eliot. "Your troupe fired you after hearing about my stories?"

Eliot shakes his head once. "No, they're too spineless for that." He glares at the ceiling. "They gave me an ultimatum. Either I leave the company or I stop associating with someone that would do damage to their family-friendly brand." The fury in his gaze doesn't subside when he looks to me. "First thing I told them was, *you realize my parents have a porn tape out in the world?* Apparently, past indiscretions don't matter as much."

So he quit.

For me.

Because of me.

And here I thought my parents' companies were the ones going to take a hit. Not my best friend's career. This hurts worse than any elbow to the mouth.

"There are other theatre companies," Beckett tells Eliot. "Fuck the one that would make you take an ultimatum. You don't want to be with them anyway, but you also shouldn't torch the bridges you've built to get there. You don't know who's friends with who behind-the-scenes. The art world is small."

I'm cold.

"It's the point of the matter," Eliot says. "The world should know what kind of people they are."

"Let our family's publicist put out a statement then," Beckett says diplomatically.

"Beckett's right," I say. "If you post a rant video, you're just going to get more shit too."

"I'm not afraid," Eliot decrees. "Fuck everyone who thinks you wrote something gross or obscene. Fuck the *fans* who want me and Tom to stop being your friends." Hot tears invade his eyes, like those last comments have punctured raw pieces of him. I haven't dived too deep or long into the internet this week, and I'm starting to guess he has.

Tom crosses his arms over his chest. He looks to me. "We'll always be your friend, Luna."

I know.

I'm lost for words though. Every piece of information hollows me out more and more. My mistakes have grown like thorny vines, twisting around the people I love. Guilt has become heavier like a weighted blanket impossible to throw off.

Eliot watches me, his ire almost dissipating into more concern. "It's not your fault, Luna."

It is my fault.

It'll never *not* be my fault.

I stare at the phone. *Delete it, Luna.* This time, I pull the trigger and delete the video.

Eliot runs two angry hands through his hair and releases a guttural noise like he just lost his very voice. Did I rip out his vocal cords?

I blink back a worse feeling, but no decision I made was going to have a happy ending. Eliot wants to unleash his rage in a manner for everyone to hear, but I've watched my older brother slam enough fists in public to see the consequences.

I don't want that for Eliot.

"Oh...shit..." Tom curses, staring at his phone screen. The confounded look on his face only somersaults my stomach. I don't need another car crash. Another blindside.

12

Luna Hale

"WHAT IS IT?" I near him the same time Beckett and Eliot do. Tom reveals the screen, a trending news article staring back at us. The headline:

Loren Hale Enraged at Son's Bodyguard

Enraged? My family's publicist couldn't use a milder word like... not happy? It's slowly dawning on me that the fake article is no longer a far-fetched idea that could've been shelved. It's been executed.

It's real.

My pulse ascends as I skim some of the text.

An inside source close to the family says that Loren Hale has become increasingly irate towards Paul Donnelly, the personal bodyguard of his seventeen-year-old son Xander Hale. No one has been able to identify exactly why, but our trusted source has confirmed that termination is on the horizon.

Paul Donnelly, a former tattooist, has tattooed multiple of the Hale children, including the firstborn Maximoff Hale. Our source says that Loren Hale has never approved of Donnelly, and the tattoos have only exacerbated his dislike—but it's not why Loren is planning to fire the Security Force Omega bodyguard.

> We've been told that Donnelly has trouble following
> Loren Hale's house rules, and Loren might not want him
> around his youngest son as he becomes a legal adult.
> Xander Hale turns eighteen on Christmas Day, and it's
> hinted that Donnelly will be axed by then.
>
> "He's a bad influence," our inside source said. "It's
> been a long time coming."

I knew this article might drop, and yet, it still hurts. *I'm sorry, Donnelly.* I'msorryI'msorryI'msorry. I want to tell him a million-and-one times over.

Eliot and Tom are staring at Beckett more than me. In their eyes, Beckett has the most history with Donnelly, I guess.

Beckett upturns one of the antique chairs. "You can stop looking at me."

"Just making sure you're okay," Tom says. "Seeing as how your favorite bodyguard might not be around for much longer."

Beckett's frown deepens. "I'll talk to Uncle Loren. The article might be bullshit anyway."

"What if it is true?" Tom wonders. "I've seen Uncle Loren glare at Donnelly from across an entire ballroom. Pretty sure he's not Paul Donnelly's biggest fan." He splays a hand out to me, so I'll voice similar sentiments.

Before the whole team-up, I would've said the same thing. My dad *despises* Donnelly. Now, all I know is he's promised to protect him.

I just shrug, a little nervous. I'm walking this super secretive line that I kinda want to hop off now.

"Who do we think is the *inside source*?" Eliot asks.

I can lie.

I *should* lie this time. But I'm really starting to hate that my best friends think this fabrication about Donnelly is true. The only issue— Beckett is here too. And I never pictured myself confessing my feelings for Donnelly in front of *Beckett*.

Is there a way to leave myself out of the equation and tell a half-truth? Is it bad that I don't want to?

"Maybe it's one of Uncle Loren's employees," Tom theorizes. "Someone who overheard water cooler gossip."

"It's not a gossipy employee," I say without thinking.

Their heads whip to me.

"You know who it is?" Eliot arches a brow. "Do tell."

"It's…" I struggle to release the truth. "My dad."

Beckett's face drops. "What?"

"My dad is the inside source, or maybe your dad is. I think Uncle Connor is helping. It's a whole publicity stunt thing…" I mutter, going quiet under their intense stares.

The murmuring bodyguards behind me are causing my cheeks to heat. I peek over my shoulder at the Wreath brothers, expecting to see *confusion*. I search their faces, and they seem irritated.

They know.

Security has to be aware of what's happening today with Donnelly's coffee meet-up with his dad and the media, and maybe these guys are a little peeved that I'm in on a supposed "security" plan. To them, Donnelly is just another bodyguard. He's nothing to me.

"Your dad, our dad," Eliot muses. "Why would they do this?"

"Spill, Luna," Tom says.

"Where's Charlie?" I ask Beckett, trying to avoid. Maybe Beckett can leave naturally? Maybe he has somewhere to be. Maybe I won't have to say these words in front of him.

"Paris," Beckett says casually. "He left after seeing Maeve at the hospital. Why would your dad plant that story on Donnelly?"

My throat becomes suddenly hoarse. "Like I said, it's a whole publicity thing…" The air feels warmer. "Um…he has a plan to make it safe for Donnelly to…"

Date me.

"To…?" Tom has a quizzical look. "What? He's making it seem like Donnelly will be *fired* by Christmas so…it'll appear like he won't be a *buddy*guard anymore?" It's a good guess. An educated guess, actually.

"Yeah," I say into a nod. Why am I such a fucking liar? I blink back that thought before it truly punctures me.

"Beckett," Ian calls out, not too far away that he'd need to shout. "The tailor is done for the day. You three are going to have to reschedule."

Beckett seems unphased. To his brothers, he says, "I'm rescheduling to come in with Charlie. I'm not doing this again with you two. I took my lunch break to be here, and I don't have three hours to waste."

"Fine by me," Eliot says.

"Whatever," Tom mutters, his eyes pinned to me. "There has to be more, right?"

Eliot skims me up and down. "There is definitely more."

I rock on the balls of my feet and tug at my hoodie strings, doing a not so good job at looking innocent. Mostly because I *do* want to gush the truth to them. I glance at Beckett, intimating that maybe I don't want to spill in front of him.

Beckett barely blinks. "They tried to swing a bat at his *skull*. O'Malley's lucky they only broke his ribs and wrist. He barely made it out without permanent head trauma because of Donnelly's family. And I know you're Donnelly's friend, but I think I know him a little better than you, so whatever's going on, I want to know."

My stomach twists. Am I...jealous? Because why do I want to tell Beckett that I slept with Donnelly like I'm one-upping him? Why do I want to claim Donnelly? But really, I wish Donnelly were here to claim me.

Neither can happen right now.

A pit is sinking in my stomach, and I open my mouth to reply— just as the door begins to open. My heart skips several beats.

Like I conjured him from my greatest desires, in walks Paul Donnelly.

13

Paul Donnelly

HER LIP IS BUSTED. Split and bloody. It's all I see when I enter the fitting room, so when Ian speaks, I'm not registering that he's talking to me until he gets in my face.

"Why the fuck does she not have a bodyguard?" Ian hisses.

"She does now," I retort. "Why do you think I'm here?" I sidestep, about to push beyond him, but Ian catches my bicep.

I instinctively rip out of his hold. Fuck him. Fuck them. "You alright, Luna?" I call out to where she stands.

She nods quickly, but I see her twisting the hoodie's string around her finger. Her eyes sort of drift towards Beckett. He's whispering to Eliot.

Luna's cheeks look flushed. Her gaze flits back to me, then away. Something is...off. My chest constricts. All I want is to close the distance and go check on her. See if she's okay, if we're okay.

I'm not losing her to this stupid "waiting" period. I won't.

"She could've been cornered on the street by paparazzi," Ian says lowly to me. "She could've been mobbed by hecklers. She could've been *kidnapped*. But that doesn't concern Omega, right?"

I glower. Of course it fucking does.

"Would I be here if it didn't?" I shoot back in a whisper.

I heard the call over comms. Triple Shield and Kitsuwon Securities have been using the same radio frequency more often ever since these so-called "ops" with my dad keep shaking up everyone's details. Ten minutes ago, Vance Wreath alerted both firms that Luna was at Calloway Couture headquarters without a bodyguard.

He wasn't snarky about it, probably because our bosses threatened suspension if we tore into each other on comms. Frog apparently got shifted to another client already. I'd been in the area and free, so I took the call with no hesitation.

Drove here as fast as I could. But I didn't think I'd find Luna hurt or the fitting room partially wrecked.

I did expect Epsilon to be pricks though.

"You didn't even know she snuck out without security," Vance chimes in. "We had to tell you."

Ian makes a prickish face. "Sounds like you care so much."

"Think what you want," I say, trying to leave them, but Ian grips my elbow.

Again, I tear out of his hold, and my blood begins to boil.

I know I'm enemy number one to Epsilon since my family hurt O'Malley, but they've been trying to take steaming piles of shit on me for much longer than one week. And it's one thing to shit on me, but when I'm trying to reach someone I care about, I'm not gonna be the easy pushover they think I am.

I whisper with heat, "I don't work *for* you. Don't touch me—and you can get out of my fucking way."

"Last I checked, you're a *bodyguard*," Ian hisses under his breath. "You stand here. With us."

"I'm also her friend," I say loudly enough that Luna can hear. "And my friend is bleeding, so move—"

He blocks me again.

I grind my teeth, my nose flaring. It feels like *every time* I try to get close to her, someone else is in my way. Heat brews in my chest, and I'm on a rare edge that I usually meet when someone disses Philly or the Birds, or the occasion O'Malley insults me and my family. This edge, though, feels more fatal. More like I could push everyone off the cliff just to hold her hand.

I bow my head to growl in his ear, "Take your grievances or whatever up with your boss, and get outta my way."

Ian stares me down like I'm a piece of shit.

I glare right back.

He whispers, "I don't know what's happening at your father-son get-togethers, but I hope you're a better nark than you are a bodyguard."

It actually relieves me knowing the three of them haven't been listening in on my conversations with my dad. Since they're on-duty while I'm out with my dad, I bet they're just on regular comms.

"You all can't even keep up with her," Vance says and jerks his head towards Luna.

Luna.

A territorial feeling scalds my muscles. "I can keep up with her better than alright, trust me. Her lip wouldn't be busted right now."

"Keep your voice down," Ian whispers. He was hired only a year and a half before me, and he's acting like he has decades of seniority here.

But yeah, Luna is looking.

The Cobalt brothers are watching.

I couldn't care less about protecting Epsilon's reputation and image right now. Security's dirty laundry rarely gets aired among clients, but they're making me want to dump the entire soiled hamper on their heads.

"It was a family fight," Novak retorts.

I whisper, "You let one of the boys hit her?" I frown though, knowing that's not right. No way would Tom, Eliot, or Beckett lay hands on Luna. I glance back at her best friends.

Eliot sees my confusion and calls out, "Her lip was an accident!" He pauses before adding, "My rage wasn't."

Ian whispers to me, "Her bodyguard would know that if she were here. Where is Frog, by the way?" I open my mouth, but he keeps going. "*Eighteen.* Barely trained. Who's Akara going to hire next—his wife?"

Vance chuckles.

"Like you had any training before you were hired," I tell Vance. "You got the job purely because of your brother." I turn to Novak. "You got the job 'cause of your *dad.*" Silvio Novak is his father, the bodyguard who protected Xander for a while and retired. "Don't act like you're better than us, 'cause you're not."

"We're not fucking our clients," Ian whispers with bite, and truth: it feels like a mic-drop.

I want to sling something pithy back like, *sucks for you* or *sucks to suck,* but I'm not suggesting that he should fuck Luna (makes my skin crawl). And I can't allude that I've also had sex with a client. He has no clue I'm in the same boat.

"Cool," I say tightly and shoulder-check him.

Ian is pummeled to the left, and I make my move to Luna.

Beckett studies me as I approach his cousin, but it's hard to meet his gaze. Still don't know what he thinks of me after the assault, and right now, first, I just want to ensure Luna really is okay.

"You alright?" I ask again.

She nods, but her hand shields her mouth. Even so, she's so fucking pretty. Her light-brown hair hangs in cute scraggily strands and frames her round face. She stuck green star stickers in the corner of her eye, and her lashes are shaded with a cool purple mascara.

"Can I see?" I reach into my back pocket where I stuffed a half-empty bottle of water. The plastic crinkles as I pull it out.

"It was an elbow to the mouth." She lowers her hand, her bottom lip swollen and bloodied. "I just got in the way…I was trying to help."

"Consequences of being a ride-or-die, I know it well."

She smiles a little.

"Can I touch…?" I motion to her lip.

She nods, and I gently peel her bottom lip down, seeing a tiny gash in her gums, made by her teeth—which are all intact. "Doesn't look like you need stitches, but I'm not a doctor." Blood still stains her teeth, so I pass her the water to swish. "If you don't want to swallow, you can spit in the plant over there."

Her flush inches higher with her smile, and it makes me grin back, especially as she says, "You never know what powers you might get by swallowing."

I smirk. "You seem pretty powerful to me already."

She grins into a gulp of water. "I am a swallower."

I make a *rock on* gesture.

"Donnelly," Ian reprimands, still in earshot. He acts like I'm crossing an invisible line. One I've seen him hurdle plenty of times. He's taken whiskey shots on-duty before with the manager of Tom's band, and I said nothing.

As long as he wasn't slurring or stumbling, I figured he could still do his job. Now Epsilon is becoming a buncha Thatcher Moretti clones, and there should only be *one* of him.

"Dude, he's fine," Tom tells his bodyguard. "They're friends." He gestures between Luna and me.

That's all we are.

Reality grates at me, and Luna's smile is gone. She slowly caps the water bottle. I run my fingers through my hair, looking her over—wishing I could draw her into my chest. Still wishing for more.

How greedy do I need to be? It feels like I've already been granted a hundred second chances, but I know those were of my own making. I ran after them.

Fought for them.

I don't even know if I believe in miracles as much as I believe in persistence.

Ian bristles and looks between Luna and Beckett like he's thinking no one should be friends with me.

"Can you wait outside?" Beckett asks SFE as a collective whole. "I know there's some tension between both firms, but I want to talk to Donnelly in private. You can give me that, can't you?"

Ian scowls. Vance and Novak narrow devil eyes on to me. I've seen spoiled ham hoagies that are scarier. They do comply and start to exit, but on their way out, I hear someone mutter, "Fucking Donnelly."

As soon as the door clicks shut, Luna fills me in quickly. "Eliot, Tom, and Beckett know about the fake headline. I told them it's not real, but they were wondering about the *why*."

The why.

Why are Connor and Lo trying to make the world believe I'm halfway out the door? That I'm close to being canned? Too easily, I could just say it's because of the assault—brush it off as if it's only to protect the families, but it's so much more than just that.

14

Luna Hale

EVADING THE WHOLE truth, nothing but the truth, is a skill that Donnelly and I seem to share, and for once, it'd be wiser if we remain *vague*. Even if my heart wants to explode a million honesties.

"What's going on?" Beckett asks Donnelly directly. There isn't malice in my cousin's eyes for everything that's gone down, just confusion. Like Donnelly has trapped him in defenseless fog, and by the knitting of Donnelly's brows, I can tell he hates that. I doubt it's something he'd ever purposefully do to a friend.

"It's a lot," Donnelly says vaguely.

Smart.

Wise.

He is a Ravenclaw after all.

My pulse goes haywire, catapulting up and down, but this is good. *It's good.* It's practical. It's the right thing, and I do want to do the right thing for everyone. The best thing. I don't want to be selfish, but the selfish pieces of me are crying.

"Great, I love excess," Eliot says, still hunting for answers. "I love complicated, *messy*. Where's the fun in safety?"

"No fun at all," Tom agrees and waves Donnelly on. "As you were."

My best friends can be relentless.

Donnelly scratches the side of his jaw, and I try not to imagine running my palms over his stubble. The way he exists is sexy. It's the confidence in himself, in who he is. His biceps look cut and sculpted in his tight black AC/DC shirt, and I have trouble not picturing those arms snug around me.

Sometimes, in quiet moments, I pretend we're a rare species that needs physical touch from a soul mate to survive. Connecting and reconnecting forever. And recently, I've been dying, starved, and longing for Donnelly to run his hands all over me.

To stop my speeding pulse, I chime in, "Donnelly is right. It's a lot. Maybe we should just talk about this another time." *Without Beckett here.*

Beckett frowns. "I'd like to know now." He's staring straight at Donnelly. "Why do you keep looking over at Luna like that?"

"Like what?" I whip my head between them, but they're in a staring contest, neither one blinking.

"What's going on?" Beckett asks again, his voice strained. "Does this have to do with her?" He's pointing at me. Eliot and Tom seem perplexed and a tinge concerned.

"No," I lie.

Why do I keep lying?! Someone save me from my lying, liar self. And yet, I can't expel the truth here, now, with Beckett.

"Donnelly tell them," I say. "It's just security stuff."

He's still locked on to Beckett as he says, "It's always been about her. At least for me, it has been."

My heart suddenly swells, his honesty singing inside of me. Is this really happening?

Beckett looks equally stunned. "Luna?"

I wonder why it's so hard for him to believe.

"Luna," Donnelly confirms, and now my heart pitter-patters like he's hugging me. "I asked her dad if I could date her. He said not until it's safe with my family, so that's what I'm doing. I'm trying to make it safe to be with her."

"Holy shit," Tom mutters.

"'O me, the gods,'" Eliot recites a phrase from Shakespeare, one he usually says when he's shocked. But like me, he's trained on Beckett's reaction.

Their older brother is expressionless. His emotions are caged down, unreadable. His yellow-green eyes shift from me to Donnelly, back to me. The air thickens.

"Beckett," Donnelly says.

"What do you want me to say?" Beckett winces, hurt starting to cross his angelic features. "That I *thought*, in a momentary lapse of judgment or weakness, that you were doing this for me? That you would concoct some dumb, wild fake press story with my father and uncle to keep *me* safe from your family? Because I did. Because I thought you still cared about me and our friendship the way I care about...you know what, never mind." He shuts down again and goes over to a chair, grabbing his T-shirt and jacket splayed over it.

Just like that, the knife returns to my heart. It seems like too many people in my life are vying to be Donnelly's number one thought, his number one concern, and I understand the yearning.

He has this rare ability to make you feel like the greatest, most powerful version of yourself. Being around him amplifies all the pieces I love: the weird, unashamed, daring, *happiest* side of me.

Being without him is just lonely.

"Beckett," I call out.

His stride is quick to the door, and Donnelly looks conflicted on what to say. Tom and Eliot also hesitate to run after their brother or remain beside me.

"Beckett!" I shout.

Not again. I have flashbacks of Xander storming out of my room.

He says nothing, almost in a trance.

"Shit, you broke Beckett," Tom whispers.

"Beckett," Eliot says in concern. "*Brother.*"

Beckett opens the door. "See you guys in New York." And he leaves.

I thought I wanted to one-up Beckett, but now that my jealousy is satiated, I just feel awful seeing him hurt.

"I broke him?" I ask Tom. I didn't know Beckett could break. I pace and bite my thumbnail.

"Donnelly broke him," Tom corrects.

Donnelly opens a pack of cigarettes.

"I broke Xander," I say, haunted.

"Xander knows?" Eliot says with a slow-growing smile, feasting on the chaos. "You've been holding out on us."

Yes, I have. "Is it making you feel better?" He's no longer raging over his theatre troupe. I hope some good can come out of the messiness of my life.

"Somewhat, but I never forget a slight." He steps into his slacks.

"Hey, stop, Luna with No Middle Name." Tom sees me pacing. He grabs my arm with his non-injured wrist, halting me so I don't tunnel into anxiety. "Beckett will be fine. Let's just focus on you."

Donnelly comes closer. Slowly, nearly affectionately, he slips a cigarette behind my ear, his fingers lingering against the strands of my hair, tucking them back. My breath hitches, and the moment is a millisecond. But I grip on to it as he plucks another cigarette for himself.

Eliot is observing. "Seeing you do that to Luna now with this new context changes everything." His lips rise. "You know what the most shocking part is?"

"That you didn't see it sooner?" I guess.

"No, deception is strong with you. It's that *you* asked for permission first." His gaze veers over to Donnelly. "From her father. Why?"

"Shits and giggles," Donnelly says, fitting the cigarette between his lips.

"I'd only be shitting myself confronting Uncle Loren with *that*," Tom notes.

"I'd just be giggling," Eliot says.

"No, he's *so* protective over Luna," Tom argues. "Dude, I'm surprised he didn't immediately nuke your career in security and everything else you love. Wait—are we sure that tabloid is actually fake?"

"Yeah, I'm sure," Donnelly says, deciding not to light his cigarette. He slips it behind his ear. Every time he glances over at me, my heart somersaults. "Lo knows I can't have my family thinking I'm in love with her."

"Love?" Eliot's grin has exploded. He buttons his slacks with an amused, delighted laugh.

Tom is grinning now too.

He told my best friends he's trying to date me. That he loves me. It's sinking in, and I feel my smile mushroom.

Donnelly shares the grin. "You think I would do all of this just for a girl I sort of like?"

"This is beautiful," Eliot says, "and tragic all at the same time."

FANATICON FORUM

We Are Calloway

Posted by @lorensfavtaco616 #wac-mod

Loren/Donnelly Feud Megathread
Discuss the most recent news about Loren possibly hating an SFO bodyguard. (Yes, it's Donnelly. Confirmed via the article linked.) Please be respectful of each other and the families, or you will be banned from the WAC forum.

@fairyduzting: if Loren Hale is that pissed at him, how is he still breathing??

@LionsTigers_andHales: Welp, dude lost GOAT status in less than 48 hrs.

@PoppyRedemptionArc: we should've seen this coming. Aren't there photos of Loren glaring at SFO during charity events? I bet he was looking at Donnelly this whole time. #proof

@TALEasOLDasT1ME: Not shocking that Donnelly is a bad influence. Loren is just trying to protect his son, and if you like Xander, you should want the same thing too. #TeamLoren

@WAC77Lover: can no longer stan.

@Oslie4Ever: I bet he didn't even deliver Jane's baby. Could've been a publicity stunt to try to make him look better, but the truth always comes out.

@rise-of-the-seasons: His days are numbered. No way is he staying a bodyguard after this. Prob for the best tbh

@moomoopants242: Banks & Akara should be fired for ruining Sulli long before Donnelly is considered getting axed, come on. Stupid af

@Iluvcharliecobalt: Just happy it's not Thatcher feuding with Connor. My heart couldn't take that.

@MarrowIsLife: u think Farrow is the reason Donnelly is still around? Aren't they friends? I hope Loren doesn't hate Farrow by proxy too.

@AvengeMe17: Good riddance! Can't wait to see someone Loren LIKES be Xander's bodyguard. Fuck Paul Donnelly.

15

Luna Hale

"SHITSHIT," I SAY quickly as my phone slips out of my hands like a wet fish. It drops in the dark crevice of the security vehicle—the space between the passenger's seat and the middle console, which is typically a graveyard of fast-food crumbs and old receipts.

At least, my car is crumby. Omega's SUV is pristine with vacuumed floor mats and a strong scent of men's cologne.

I unbuckle to try to dig into the crevice.

Donnelly is behind the wheel. He's not reprimanding me like most bodyguards would—and it's been kinda clear he's driving me as a bodyguard, not just as a friend, since we left the Calloway Couture headquarters.

It's rare that he's ever assigned to my detail.

So Donnelly as my bodyguard feels odd. I don't like questioning whether he's here for a job or because he's my natural, tried and true friend who still has feelings for me.

While I try to stick my hand in the narrow crevice and reach down, his eyes dart over to me more than a few times, seeing my struggle.

"I've gotta get gas," he says. "We can fish out your phone at the Sunoco."

Sounds smarter. I wedge my hand out and fall back into my seat. "This is what I get for looking at Fanaticon." I mutter, "Like I didn't regret checking the reactions to the article enough. My phone has abandoned me too."

"Maybe you just have slippery hands. Lemme see." He reaches for my palm, and I start to smile as I let him hold my hand while he drives.

Really, we press fingertips to fingertips, and slowly, his fingertips glide down my palm with featherlight affectionate touch. It's electric, tingling my veins, and my breath catches in the quiet.

"Verdict?" I ask.

"More soft than slippery. Your phone definitely fucked you."

"Knew it." Neither of us pulls away too fast, but I do the good thing, the right thing, and retract my hand. "You really think it's possible to outrun curses and bad luck?" On Halloween, after he confessed he coined the *Hale curse* phrase, he told me that it was.

"Yeah," he nods. "I'm not gonna let it catch us."

I breathe in his hope.

He adds, "And so you know, I don't care what they say about me online. People like to speculate and shit. It's what they do." He picks up his Lightning Bolt! energy drink from the cup holder. "Sometimes I do it too." He takes a swig.

Dark circles shadow his blue eyes, like he's slept poorly, and despite fatigue and the outings with his dad and the article, he's still so…light. Not necessarily weightless, but more so *luminous*.

It reminds me of *Star Wars*, but I don't mention it as we roll into the gas station. Donnelly parks at a vacant pump, and once the car is off, I hop out of the passenger side. He's already swiveling off the gas cap and sticking the nozzle in the hole.

We left Tom and Eliot sort of abruptly at their mom's fashion headquarters since the seamstress needed the room. I said a quick goodbye to them and promised I'd catch them up on the details of how I fell for Donnelly. The start of it all.

They texted soon afterwards.

Since you're just friends at the moment with Donnelly, I propose that the friendship trio become a quartet. — Eliot

I second this motion. — Tom

I'm not sure if I'm ready to give Donnelly a friendship application. It feels more like a major regression in our relationship, and what if he prefers to only be my friend at the end of this? I told them that I'd consider it. I think they're just excited to get to know Donnelly better. A lot of their knowledge comes from observations during family and charity events and things like the triple date.

With the car door open, I stand on the pavement and bend forward, reaching beneath the seat. "Come to me, little cellular device." I stretch my fingers. "*Accio.*"

Nope, still don't have magical abilities. But it doesn't hurt to try.

"Back off." I hear Donnelly's threatening tone behind me.

I peek over my shoulder. Two middle-aged men hoist cameras, and their lenses would be pointed at my ass if it weren't for Donnelly physically blocking them. *Paparazzi.* One has thin wire glasses, a lanky build, and pens are stuck in his blazer pocket, as though he's a respected journalist. The other man is bulkier with thick shoulders and a scruffy beard.

"Do you think you'll be fired soon?" the Thin One nearly shouts.

A college-aged girl hears from the neighboring pump and takes out her phone. Great. She starts snapping pics of us too.

I bend back down and hurry, trying to retrieve my phone. *Accio. Accio!* Mental spells aren't working either, but my fingers brush the case. *Almost there.*

Donnelly pushes their lenses away with a firm hand. "I'm not doing this with you two today. Get the fuck outta here."

"Why aren't you with Xander?" the Thin One persists. "He isn't here, is he?"

I catch the seediness of his voice, the pleasure he's taking from each discomforting question, and a chill snakes down my neck.

Donnelly stands his ground, not letting them pass.

"Why are you with Luna instead?" the Thin One asks. "Is Loren Hale's daughter involved in the friction between you and him?"

My pulse starts racing.

"She has nothing to do with this," Donnelly retorts.

"Why so defensive?" It sounds like the Thin One is smiling. "Is her lip split? Who hurt her? I know you have these answers. You might as well tell your truth now. Never know what'll be printed tomorrow."

Thankfully Donnelly isn't taking the bait.

"Luna!" the Thin One calls out. "What's your reaction to your porn stories leaking online? Do you use them to get off? Are you addicted to porn like your mom?"

"Hey," Donnelly snaps.

My face burns. I finally clasp my phone, right as the Bulky One tries to charge towards me for a close-up or maybe to provoke a frightened newsworthy reaction out of me, and my eyes widen—but Donnelly grips the camera by the lens, about to tear the equipment out of his hands.

The Bulky One tries to wrestle his camera back.

Instead of climbing into the SUV, I instinctively grab my mini backpack, shut the door, and race towards the convenience store several feet from the pumps.

We still need to get gas, and it might be safer if I'm inside. Paparazzi usually won't breach the doors.

Donnelly separates from the Bulky One, locks the SUV, and jogs after me.

The bell *dings* as I slip inside, and I curve around shelves, aimed for the back near the slushie machines. The cashier stares right at me, but I ignore the double-takes and questioning looks as they try to place my face—wondering if I'm *that girl* from the tabloids at the checkout.

I open a fridge door, stocked with single cans of beer and energy drinks.

The *ding* sounds again, and I know it's him, even as he appears beside me and breathes, "You alright?"

"Uh-huh." I pick out a new cranberry flavor of Lightning Bolt!

He glances over his shoulder, looking out the store windows. "You wanna hang out here for a sec?"

Coldness creeps under my skin. "With or without you?"

"With." His eyes lower onto mine again, and warmth spreads.

"What about Xander?" I ask since we were on our way to see my brother. We're going to try and talk to him together. Donnelly heard my brother planned to venture to Arcadia Galactica, and he's supposed to go on-duty to protect him. I imagine Xander will run straight for the X-Men version of *Streets of Rage*. We all loved playing the cooperative battle arcade game when Uncle Garrison and Aunt Willow took us to the mall.

"We'll still make it to your brother. Just taking a pit stop." He watches me tuck the chilled energy drink under my armpit. I grab a wider can off the shelf. A Four Loko. It contains alcohol, but he says nothing about it or how I'm not twenty-one just yet.

His presence is starting to feel less bodyguard-ish and more friend-ish.

"Have you seen those paparazzi before?" I wonder, shutting the fridge. "It kinda seemed like you knew them."

"They've been around." He scans a nearby shelf and pulls packaged jerky sticks off the hook. "They mostly follow Xander. I've been calling 'em Boom Box. One is always louder, more annoying. The other is heavier set and more aggressive."

I like his nickname better than Thin One and Bulky One. "Boom Box haven't left, have they?" I grab a big bag of Fritos.

"Nah, they're gonna hang around until we leave." He returns to the fridge behind me, taking a can of the original flavor of Lightning Bolt! "You don't need to worry about them though."

"I'm not that worried," I say softly as we head into another aisle, empty of people. He's peeling the plastic off the jerky stick while I crouch to the box of Fruit Roll-Ups. I imagine we have nowhere to be, me and him, and we're really dating.

Even if being someone's girlfriend is terrifying, I'm more scared of never having the opportunity. Anxieties around me start to shrink in my make-believe world, and I sing a song under my breath off-key and shimmy my shoulders to the beat. I shift my knees too, still squatting.

I grab two tropical tie-dye Fruit Roll-Ups, and I look over and up at Donnelly. His chestnut hair is pushed out of his face, a silver hoop in his pierced ear today, and as his gaze slips down me, his lips rise like I'm the prettiest, weirdest sight he's ever seen.

He bites his jerky stick and hums a few bars with me. It's a song he knows. One we danced to in Scotland: The Who's "Baba O'Riley."

When I rise, my arms are full of snacks and drinks, but Donnelly walks two of his fingers up my neck and cheek, until he's touching my head. Our eyes only detach as he spins me in a slow circle—really, I turn myself with the movement of his fingers on my head, as though I'm a music box he's winding.

My smile expands, and his grin brightens the dimmest pieces of me. Dizziness whirls my brain, my breath short, and when I come to a heady stop in front of him, our gazes are entrenched inside one another. Desire is a beast we've let crawl inside our hearts, writhing and screaming and needing to be uncaged.

I want him to kiss me.

If it's wrong, then I want to do the worst, wrong things with Donnelly.

He looks just as dizzy, just as overwhelmed, and then the moment breaks with the *ding* of the door. His head whips to the entrance, but he relaxes at the sight of an old man. Not Boom Box.

Juggling my snacks, I use the moment to open my Fritos bag. Sure, we haven't paid yet, but we plan to and the cashier hasn't said anything.

Donnelly takes another bite of jerky. "How come you ditched Frog?" He's not accusatory like Ian. He just sounds curious.

I crunch on a corn chip. "Because the purple people eaters told me to."

"Hate those purple-people-eating bastards."

I nod. "They're nosy too. Snuck into my bedroom in the middle of the night and mentally transferred their histories to me."

"Yeah, no one sneaks into your bedroom but me," he says, hushed.

I begin to smile, but reality hurts knowing he can't really sneak into my room anymore—not as anything more than a friend.

Tension stretches. He tries to break it with another question. "What do they have against frogs anyway?"

"*Everything.* After all the purple people were eaten, their world was cratered with darkness. Legend says, Jar Til, leader of the purple people eaters, was poisoned by amphibians. Frogs are the heroes of the story." I hold out my Fritos.

I'd usually lose most people at this point.

They'd uncomfortably laugh and think the story I made up on the spot is bizarre. Life doesn't have to be that serious all the time, and sometimes it's fun to pretend other species exist. Like you.

Donnelly takes a couple corn chips and tosses them back in his mouth. "Frogs sound dope."

"They are," I sing-song.

"Then how come you don't trust the Kannika Kitsuwon kind?"

"It's not that I don't trust her." I watch him silently observe the few people left in the store. They're stuck in the neighboring aisle, and when our eyes meet again, I say, "Sometimes it's just easier to go unseen if I'm by myself."

"But Frog isn't famous like the rest of SFO. She's not well-known on the internet and the fandom."

"It's not so much specifically Frog. With any bodyguard, it's harder. I would've ditched a temp guard or Quinn or even—"

"Me?"

My pulse spikes, hurt clenching my insides.

His gaze bores into me with an intimacy I've never really felt until him. Maybe because what I feel for Donnelly goes so far beyond sex.

"No. I don't know." I look away. "This isn't the first time I've snuck out without a bodyguard, Donnelly."

"I know." There isn't disappointment in his voice. No judgment. "Are there times when no one has known before though? Not security or your family?"

I walk slowly towards the cashier. He follows as I say, "Would you be upset if I said yes?"

"Upset? No. Worried about you, yeah."

I pause at the end of the aisle. Careful to keep my voice quiet. "I've been able to wander the city alone and without anyone knowing. Mostly in Philly. Center City."

"How old were you?" he wonders.

I shrug. "It was after I was eighteen and moved out of my parents' house. I used to go to some local bars like Thirsty Goose, Tipping Place, Doobies."

"Doobies," he smirks.

It makes me smile, especially knowing he's not condemning me for breaking a ginormous security rule. *Do not leave without a bodyguard.* "No one ever really knew I was there," I tell him. "I'd sit in a dark corner and just people-watch. I guess I could've gone to a library, but most of the time, I snuck out at night."

He looks me over. "Why'd you want to?"

"I don't know," I say quietly. "Sometimes I thought it's because I was trying to feel normal. Other times, I think it just felt freeing. But at the end, it was just kinda lonely."

He bobs his head. "Yeah, best nights out for me have been with friends." We wait to approach the checkout, hanging near shelved bags of M&Ms and Twizzlers.

A long second passes before Donnelly finally asks, "You talk to any guys at the bars?"

I shrug again. "Sometimes."

His face noticeably tightens, and his brows lift while he glances at the entrance again. His six-foot-three build has tensed, and I shift my weight uncertainly.

"Your worry looks angry," I say.

His blue eyes rest gently on mine. "'Cause you're looking at jealousy."

Flush ascends my neck. *Oh.* I give him a once-over, realizing jealousy is hot on Donnelly, the attractive type of *hot.* I realize how badly I just want him to want me, but the yearning is even deeper than that. I want him to consume me, grab me, take me, make me *his* forever.

A little breathless, I ask, "You wish you could've been at the bar?"

"Right there, right beside you, space babe." He searches my eyes for something. "Next time, you planning to throw me an invite?"

"Will you come as a friend or a bodyguard?"

"Friend. I'm joining your secret rendezvous in the great state of PA."

I smile. "We'll dance in the corner."

"To Def Leppard."

"And drink all the green shots."

"*Only* the green ones," he emphasizes.

"Right off my belly button."

He lets out a wanting breath. "Girl, hit me up already."

We're both grinning, but my heart pangs. "Why does that sound like fan fiction?"

"Because we'd both write it." *Isn't that the truth.* "Yours would be better written though," he adds. "I'd read the fuck out of it too."

"You think we'll ever get to live it?"

He canvasses me, up-down. "You losing hope?"

It's been one of the longest weeks of my life. I don't know how we're supposed to do this for months on end. "Maybe just a morsel."

He nods, understanding.

"But I'm trying to stay hopeful," I add now, wanting him to know that I'm not giving up that easily. I won't.

His chest lifts, and we go to the register together.

"You can put your stuff up there with mine," he says, digging out his wallet. His eyes signal for me to please let him, and I've started realizing buying me food means something to Donnelly, so I go ahead and combine my snacks with his. He adds a couple packs of cigarettes to the pile.

The cashier eagle-eyes me, and I catch sight of the nearest *Celebrity Crush* tabloid. The headline: *Who's the Baby Daddy?!*

It's a picture of Sullivan coming out of Lucky's Diner with Banks and Akara. They've circled her barely noticeable baby bump and drawn an arrow with the word, *Preggers!*

Sulli hasn't announced her pregnancy or marriage yet, but the tabloids are rampant with speculations, especially since the three of them wear braided strings on their ring fingers.

"Hun," the cashier says, smacking gum. Nametag reads, *Ash*. "Is this yours?" Ash lifts the Four Loko.

"Nah, it's mine," Donnelly tells them before I can answer. He hands over his ID, saving me from the possibility of being declined.

"Thanks." The cashier returns the ID, then scans the alcoholic drink. "Keep your heads up." I follow Ash's gaze to Boom Box loitering outside. "Some people feel important when they're harassing others, but a lot of us can see who they really are."

It's nice to be reminded that Philly isn't full of haters and bad paparazzi. There are people who genuinely wish us well, seeing that we're human too.

After I thank Ash, I hook one plastic bag on my elbow and Donnelly carries the other. He pushes open the door.

Boom Box swarms us, but I tune out their questions.

The *click, click* of the camera burns my cheeks. It's obvious they're capturing pics of me and Donnelly together. Two minutes pass, and I'm safely inside the car. Donnelly is putting away the pump and screwing the gas cap, still on an *ignore* setting with Boom Box. I release a bigger exhale once we're on the road.

"You think tabloids will post about me and you?" I wonder.

"They might." His voice sounds tight. "Your dad is gonna fucking kill me."

"No, he won't," I assure. "I'll tell him it won't happen again." I don't say why, but the answer is clear: we won't go out in public together anymore. My stomach is in knots at this idea, but I can't let Donnelly's fake feud with my dad become real again.

His eyes flicker over to me while he drives, tension escalating like the ascension of magma in a volcano. He's about to speak, but his hand flies to his mic at his collar. "What was that?" He pauses and mumbles, "Ard." He lets go of the mic, and as soon as he can, he does a U-turn.

"Where are we going?"

"Penthouse."

I frown. "But what about Xander?"

"He's not going to the arcade anymore. He's at home, and Akara said he's not ready to see me."

I sink in the seat. "I didn't think he'd take it this badly."

"Hopefully he just needs time."

Hopefully. But I can see it's also eating at Donnelly.

DONNELLY SHUTS OFF THE IGNITION IN THE parking deck of the apartment complex. Our section of the deck is gated with floor-to-ceiling metal chain-link fencing and a passcode. Jane's baby blue Land Rover is parked beside Sulli's forest-green Jeep, so I know they're home.

Still, Donnelly and I don't hurry to exit the security vehicle. It's dark and quiet, and I pretend it's nighttime. Alone with him.

"Was it hard seeing him this week?" I ask, glancing over as Donnelly places a hand on the back of my headrest. "Your dad?" I finally muster the courage to ask him about his family.

Maybe because I'm less afraid of the discomfort. I'm more afraid of never knowing the depth of what's happening with Donnelly, and I can't really be there for him if I'm in the dark.

Now, alone and in the sanctuary of the car, it just feels like the right time.

"Yeah, it's been hard," he breathes. "It's weird too." His brows pinch, staring off. "Almost like stepping back in time. I was never close, *close* with him. He was too high for that, but he kept bringing up memories." Donnelly shakes his head, his chest falling with a heavy breath. "I have to catch myself not making excuses for him, for my mom."

"What do you mean?"

He cradles my gaze for a fragile beat. "They were *babies* having a baby when they had me. Just fourteen."

It knocks air out of my lungs. "They were *fourteen?*"

He nods.

Slow realizations wash over me. "That's why your dad looked so young when you were a little kid…in the picture you showed me."

"Yeah. It's easy to say, *oh they were too young to be parents. I wouldn't be here if it weren't for them. They were too poor. They didn't have good role models.* Then I start opening my heart to them, and it always ends the same. They disappoint. They never change. So I try not to make those same excuses."

My parents are addicts too, but Donnelly hasn't experienced sober parents. And I've never experienced parents off the path of recovery.

I've never had to make big excuses for my mom and dad. For one, they always take full responsibility for the mistakes they've made and the people they've hurt in the past. For the other, I never grew up with them in the worst of their addictions.

"I think we're all backwards," I tell him softly. "With everything you've gone through, you should be the real-life cynic. I should be the one infecting you with hope."

"I'd still be in South Philly, in the same apartment, never meeting Farrow, never meeting you if I were the real-life cynic," Donnelly says. "And I don't believe you've been hopeless, sad alien." His voice lifts my morose gaze, and there it is—*light* glimmering inside him. "You've just been beat down one too many times. Everyone has a breaking point."

"Even you?" I whisper.

He searches my gaze again. "The way you look at me, Luna…" He seems overwhelmed.

"How am I looking at you?" I'm trapped in his orbit, not wanting to be set loose.

"I'm the hero of your story." His voice drops to the same hushed sound as mine. "I don't know if anyone has ever placed me there, but one of the things I'm most scared of is disappointing you."

I shake my head slowly, then more hurriedly. My eyes burn. "You won't."

He's unblinking too as his gaze reaches into me. "I wanna be your hero—in every story you'll ever write about me and you. I want that, but the honest truth is that...I'm not built to withstand it all. And I don't know my exact breaking point yet, 'cause I don't really know how much I can take. I just know it's a lot."

I choose my words carefully, so I grapple with the seconds, and tension amasses in the car. "You're right...when I look at you, I do see a hero. Not because I think you're indestructible, but because you've chosen the light side despite growing up in the dark." I let out a breath. "It's just *Star Wars* stuff."

His smile is everything to me. The way it effortlessly inches up his lips. "Let's hear it."

I'm caught in how he's looking at me now. If he's my hero, then I'm his queen.

Affection tumbles through my body like a pinball machine, hitting all the pockets that flash neon lights and make high-pitched *pings.*

I swallow hard to control the butterflies swarming my stomach. "Anger, hate, pain—it disturbs the balance of all natural things," I tell him. "In *Star Wars,* it disturbs the Force, and the Sith learned to focus solely on these negative emotions. They empower themselves through the dark side. It's tumorous. Like a disease on the world." I speak softer. "I know people have all different sorts of theories and feelings about the balance of the Force, but I believe light and dark always coexist in nature. And it's Jedi who realize choosing light is what maintains the balance, the peace and harmony. So when I look at you, I see someone who embodies the light side, and maybe I admire you more because you found balance even living among the dark."

His eyes are glassy, but I'm unsure which part struck a chord with Donnelly. His lips part but close, unable to speak.

My heart races wildly, but I dig into my mini-backpack, searching more urgently for something. Donnelly watches in silence while I sift through the contents.

I find a plastic blue crystal. "I bought this a long, long time ago." I hand it to him and rummage around for a second thing.

"What is it?" He inspects the blue tint that fades to clear.

"It's a kyber crystal."

"It powers a lightsaber," he realizes. "Thank you, Illyana_Dallas222 and her *Star Wars* recs for my wisdom." He names me.

"You're most welcome, SB." I name him. *StaleBread89*. I smile over at him, seeing his smile on me, and finally, my fingers brush the long silver chain at the bottom of my backpack. It's tangled around metal bindings of a notepad. I pull both out and unknot the chain. "Do you still have to keep seeing your dad?"

"Yeah." He pinches the kyber crystal between two fingers, but really, he's staring far away. "I've been wearing a wire." He explains the whole security aspect regarding his family. By the end, my stomach is knotted more than the chain I'm untangling.

"Maybe you can wear this next time too." I pool the freed chain in his palm and motion to the kyber crystal in his other hand. "To remind you of the balance of the Force."

He sees the hole chiseled at the top of the plastic crystal and immediately fishes the chain through it. His soulful gaze returns to mine while he loops the long chain around his neck. The crystal reaches his sternum, and he tucks it protectively underneath his shirt.

And then he suddenly unclips his black wristwatch. "I don't have much, but I wanna give you something too." He leans further over the middle console, to reach me, and as his fingers close over my wrist, adrenaline seeps through my veins.

I feel dizzy. Transported to another dimension.

"It's engraved and everything," he says. "Fancy shit." He grins as he shows me the back casing of the watch. A crudely scratched "D" is legible in the silver. He must've used a knife.

It's perfect. The words are stuck in my throat, swelling with emotion as Donnelly clasps the black band around my wrist.

"To remind you of our future together," Donnelly says. "Time is irrelevant when I'm always right here." He hoists my wrist, the watch secured perfectly.

I smile, choked up. "Thank you." He shakes his head like it's unneeded, but before he says it, I tell him, "You can't disappointment me, you know."

"If I fail—"

"Heroes fail all the time. It won't change how I see you, Donnelly."

He looks uncertain.

"It won't." A quiet strain overtakes the car, and I end up asking, "Did you ever read about Ulic Qel-Droma? In the comics?"

"I haven't gotten too far in the reading list you sent. Where does he fall in the timeline?"

"*Tales of the Jedi,* written by Tom Veitch. He appears long before all the movies. I think around 4000 BBY."

"Is he Sith?"

I shake my head. "A Jedi Knight. His Jedi Master died, and Ulic was convinced the only way to defeat his murderers was to infiltrate the Krath. They were these aristocrats who learned dark side Sith magic. He was going to pretend to be one of them, get close to them, and take them down from the inside."

The correlation of what Donnelly is doing with his family is obvious, so neither of us mention it.

"Did he go through with it?" he asks.

"You want me to spoil it for you?"

"Hit me with the spoilers, space babe."

"He does infiltrate the Krath. He pretends to be a fallen Jedi." I frown and stare at the ticking watch on my wrist. "You won't ever disappointment me," I say again. "I think it was brave what Ulic did."

Donnelly sinks back against his seat. "He succumbed to the dark side, didn't he?"

He did.

I look over at him, my heart hurting. "You're not Ulic. That's his story, and this...this isn't just *my* story, like you said. I hope it can be our story."

He comes forward, and his hand encases the edge of my jaw, the softness of my neck. "It is our story, Luna," he breathes.

I fall into his gaze, his touch, my lungs alight. "In the *Star Wars* mythos, you'd be a Jedi Knight, but in our universe, you're something else."

"What am I?" His lips are so close to mine. "Some noble hero of another galaxy? An alien warrior? Or well-traveled bounty hunter?"

"You're human," I whisper. "You're my human hero. And there is no one stronger than you."

We're breathing one another in, and the distance is so painful. I just want him to—and then he does, holy…shit.

He kisses me.

I crash against the passionate wave of his kiss, riding into the storm as our tongues meld, as his hand clasps my cheek tighter and rounds to the back of my head, lost in my hair. *Ohhh wow.* I bask in every millisecond of his possessive touch.

My body throbs, the yearning pieces finally being satiated again. I cling to his bicep, a second from climbing on top of him and bouncing on his lap. I want him so, *so* badly, I can't think straight, but Donnelly pushes me back against my seat, not to end the embrace.

He careens over, still kissing me like he's removing all the hurt, all the pain. Like each kiss is made to cure me, and I melt against the power of his passion and the heat of his skin.

"Donnelly," I moan.

"*Fuck.*" His groan is deeply masculine and sexy. Among our endless, emotion-fueled kisses, his other hand voyages up my shirt. *Yesyesyes.* His thumb flicks my nipple, and I squirm and writhe in the seat.

Yes, fuuuck.

I feel for his zipper. He's rock hard against his jeans. I keep imagining the sensation I first felt when he was inside me. *Again.* I want it again.

Now.

Nothing else matters except being closer than close. Melded and welded and fastened like two bodies and souls becoming one.

Right as he sits up like he's about to crawl over to the passenger side, to me, his lips suddenly break completely off mine.

"Wait, wait, fuck." He rakes a hand through his hair and falls back into the driver's seat, both of us winded, panting.

I blink a lot and wake up. "Sorry, I—"

"I kissed you first," he says and grips the steering wheel. The SUV is still parked and shut off. He presses his forehead to his knuckles.

I bite the corner of my tingling lip, still feeling him on me.

"I don't regret it," Donnelly says, sitting straighter. "I don't regret it, but…" He must be worried about my dad, how he'd perceive him for breaking another promise.

"It'll be the last kiss." I hate these words as soon as I release them.

Pain cinches his face and gaze.

"The last kiss until everything is safe," I explain.

Donnelly skims my features, maybe knowing I'm about as excited to have a "last kiss" with him as I'd be to learn extraterrestrials like you don't exist.

He runs another hand through his hair. "Our last kiss was fire." He tries to grin, but really, he just sounds sad.

It's the last time we talk about that particular kiss, but selfishly and secretly, I leave hoping there'll be another.

FANATICON FORUM

We Are Calloway

Posted by @LorenIsKing1990

THEORY: Okay, so I know we haven't seen pics of Luna in about a week or so since the gas station photos/video. BUT what if she's the real reason Loren hates Donnelly???

The article said Donnelly tattooed MULTIPLE of the Hale children. We know one is Maximoff. She has to be the other. Is there confirmation he inked her tats? Also, where is Luna? Do you think she's hiding since that last outing where she was seen with Donnelly? Something definitely feels off.

@polaris_havoc_domination: Pretty sure she's still embarrassed about her fics leaking and that's why she hasn't been seen. Feel bad for her. Some ppl have said really shitty things.

@connorcobaltseyebrows: There's been no verbal confirmation from the families about Donnelly inking her tats, but we've already confirmed that the lyrics on her forearm is 100% Farrow's handwriting. @ Roses1stDaughter compared a pic of a note Farrow wrote Maximoff at Lucky's Diner to Luna's tattoo.

@hehecallowayxx: Idk about this theory, but Luna should go for Quinn. He's so hot.

@StaleBread89: Seems far-fetched imo. Think Loren just hates Donnelly's good looks.

@lilysandroses4evers: This might be a stretch. Donnelly has been on Oscar and Farrow's socials way more than Luna's. Just seems like Luna-Donnelly have been okay friends. Why would Loren all of a sudden be upset about them now?

@BurnBabyBurn323: We should keep Luna out of this. The beef is between Donnelly and Loren. She's been through enough lately.

@lalaland_11: ~~Has anyone actually read her leaked fics? There's literally tentacle penetration. It's fucking gross. Stop making excuses for her.~~ *Deleted by mod-bot for breaking forum rules.*

@PuffClaws12345: LunaQuinn is such a perfect match. I've been saying this from DAY ONE.

DONNELLY'S DAILY PLANNER
Friday, Nov 23rd

Today's Focus: stop thinking about fucking your friend Luna. (I'm deadass now.)

To Do:

- Ice cold shower. Need it asap.

- See which detail I'm assigned to today.

- wallow. Jk. wallowing is for weeping willows. I'm a mf-ing oak tree. sturdy af.

- Dinner with Xander's dad at his Halway comics office. Just him. Feels sus.

Notes: Another day I'm hoping Xander decides not to hole away. His teachers keep sending all his school assignments over email, so he has no reason to return to Dalton. Don't even know how he's been faring post-homecoming with Delilah. worse: I think I'm the reason he's hiding at home. If he doesn't leave the Hale House, he won't need a bodyguard, and he hasn't requested one to be at home like he sometimes does. Don't know what'd hurt worse. This. Or him requesting Gabe to replace me.

Been in contact with my dad. Saw him for brekky one morning and then a walk (smoke break) another evening. He's 100% bought the fake article. Believes I'm on the brink of being fired. He said Loren is a prick anyway and he tried comforting me, I think. He even bought me a bagel. Not sure how I feel. Still haven't gotten any helpful info for security. He's said I look good tho. Healthy. Fit and all that. was he always this nice? Can't remember.

worried about Luna. She's rippin' a page from her brother's hermit handbook and hasn't left the penthouse since I drove her home last week.

Good news: haven't sleepwalked in weeks. Not since I made cereal in the bathroom sink I share with Luna.

Meals: Might pick up breakfast/lunch at wawa. Dinner with Xander's dad. Probably gonna eat my tongue.

Water: Stop thirsting after Luna. Get a fuckin' grip of your dick. ALSO! Drink actual water.

Question of the Day: ~~Is Loren Hale a human lie detector by proxy of Connor Cobalt?~~ ~~How many broken promises are too many?~~ why is thinking about Qunnie's belly button lint the best boner killer?

16

Paul Donnelly

MY NIPPLES COULD cut glass. Fuck cold showers. I last a second, then switch the handle to a scorching hot setting. Steam gathers around me, and I let the warm water pelt my head and taut shoulders. It's not that I've got zero willpower. I'm just not putting myself through that torture when I'd rather rub one out.

Eighties rock blasts out of my phone, which I left on the bathroom counter. Music bleeds through my hot veins, and while water slips down my build, I push wet hair out of my face.

Before I draw visuals in my head of fucking Luna against the wall, I catch a new sound.

The door is opening.

"Luna?" I crack the shower stall door and peek out.

Yeah, she's here.

I try to cup a hand over my cock, but as soon as she sees me, her gaze falls to my dick. I flex my muscles to avoid a raging hard-on, but my blood is pumping straight to my head.

"Howdy," she mumbles, a tie-dye Fruit Roll-Up dangling out of her mouth like a long tongue. She throws up a nervous Vulcan salute and shifts the Roll-Up in her mouth to speak. "Uh, I just was going to grab some nail polish. I didn't think you'd care."

"I don't care." I skim the length of her. She's in black baggy sweatpants and a green cropped top, my watch still on her wrist. Tiny strands of her long hair are tied with glittery ribbon. "You going to Penn?" I can't tell if it's an outfit she'd wear on campus. Maybe, but maybe not.

"Uh-uh. Not today." She squats to the cupboard and searches for nail polish.

Not today.

Not yesterday or the day before either. Not since her fics leaked, really. What Charlie told her—to drop out—races back to me. I hesitate to influence her too much, but I'm praying she doesn't give up this fast.

I close the shower door and rinse off some soap. "You quitting school?" I ask over the water and music.

I can't hear her response, and it's killing me. So I cut off the water and reach over the stall to swipe my towel. Holding the fabric at my waist, I kick open the shower door.

She's already standing.

I watch her amber eyes trace my abs and my tattoos. Her desire amplifies mine a million times over. Vapor fogs the mirror behind her and thickens the tense air around us. Burning up, I grab the silver chain off the towel hook, and I loop the necklace over my head. The kyber crystal hangs against my wet chest.

"What'd you say about college? I couldn't hear," I say.

Luna glances at the carton of nail polish on the counter but doesn't return to it. "I'm taking a hiatus."

"The internet's still got you down?" I ask. "Or is it about not wanting to see Frog get hurt on your detail?"

"Maybe both." Luna shrugs. "It's also good that I'm not going to campus and being seen outside anywhere. It'll help cool off the article. A perk." She sing-songs that word.

The photos Boom Box took of us outside the gas station were printed in *Celebrity Crush*, but rumors about me and her are fizzling out quickly. The pics were innocent.

Her dad wasn't exactly happy though. Think he tried to imprint his glare in my cerebral cortex.

"It's probably safe now," I tell her, coming closer.

"I'd rather just stay here, for all the reasons above." She watches me near her. "Would you rather I leave?"

No. Not completely.

I shake my head and reach around Luna to my drawer, grabbing the deodorant. Her breath shallows, and her gaze dances all over my face, my body. *I want to fuck her.* The sharp jolt of arousal is a ball in my throat that I'm trying to swallow down.

While I keep the towel gripped at my waist, I use my other hand to roll on deodorant underneath my pits, and I toss the stick back in the drawer. She leans a little against the counter.

I don't want to be the sole reason she's hiding, but I believe Luna when she says it's more than just me keeping her inside this penthouse. And I'm not about to nag her about it.

"You want me to walk Orion again?" I ask.

"If it's not that much trouble?"

"It's not." I can't take my eyes off her.

She slurps an inch of her Fruit Roll-Up in her mouth. With the sway of her head, she dangles the Roll-Up just below her chin. "Want some of my tongue?" She mumbles the words.

I grin. "Whatever you wanna give me, I'll take." I edge closer, our knees knocking.

I bite the other end of the Fruit Roll-Up, not hard enough to sever Luna's end. It's still attached, and I use my tongue to pull it further in my mouth. She does the same on her side, our eyes latched, and as the Roll-Up shortens, our lips are inching closer.

Closer.

I cup the back of her head with one hand, her hair and ribbon soft between my fingers. As the inches disappear, neither of us jerks away from the crash—and our lips meet.

Fuck. Me. The sudden, aching kiss crushes me up against her shorter, thinner frame. I drop my towel to hold her face with two hands. The sweetness of the fruit snack melds with the softness of her lips, and she shudders in pleasure. Her reaction is fisting my cock.

It's been one week since our last kiss, and this one is wrought with as much tension. I'm fighting against the voice that says *end it*.

End it.

Stop it, Donnelly.

One more second.

I tuck her more firmly to me, and quickly, I bite off the fruit snack. While we chew and swallow our ends, her hands scrape down my chest towards my bare ass, scorching trails along my skin. Arousal is thicker than fog, and I tug her shirt up.

She's not wearing a bra.

My chest falls in a shallow breath. Her nipples are perked, and I knead her breast and pull the shirt off her head. She lets out a *wanting* whimper, dousing gasoline in my veins. Swiftly, I hoist her on the counter by the hips.

At a better height to kiss her, I run my tongue along the ball piercing of hers, lips swelled against her lips. Her floral scent is shredding through my barriers, drawing an animalistic hunger out of me. I rasp against her neck, "I want to do seriously bad things to you." I suck on the base of her neck.

Another aching sound escapes Luna. Her ravenous hands glide up my jaw and scratch the back of my head, her eyes consuming me as she says, "Eat me alive."

Fuck. My forehead is nearly pressed to hers. "Careful what you wish for. I could so easily devour every last inch of you." I clasp her cheek. "Then what'll be left?"

"Us," she murmurs. "You with me. For longer than a minute. Longer than a moment."

Forever, I hear, and the pain of this faraway desire translates in how I kiss her. Deeply, slammed together with surging emotion. I nip at her lip, and I push closer while she's on the bathroom counter, her fingers scraping down my biceps.

Luna's legs are spread around my waist. Her cotton sweatpants and panties separate what would be the easiest entry into her pussy. I tighten my hand in her hair, arching into her with each fevered kiss, and the friction of my cock against her pussy is heating us both.

"*Donnelly.*" It's a pleading, *don't stop* Donnelly. She's scared I'm gonna hit the brakes.

Arousal is swirling around us, and I tuck her even closer to my body. I could say I'm drunk on her, but I'm not out of my mind. There is hot, sex-fueled intent in everything I'm doing. I grind into her. She claws against me. My pulse is thudding all the way to my hardened cock.

Be patient.

Don't break another promise to her dad (again).

Wait for her.

These phrases are lost in the steam. Devoured whole by me, and it's not desire consuming all logic, all thought. It's all of me—Paul Donnelly—realizing those phrases aren't rightly made for someone like me, for the cockroaches who aren't gonna count on tomorrow when you know you already have this moment. And it might be the only one.

I'm not wasting anything.

I've never been good at that.

If I were, I would've never gone down on Luna two years ago. And some people might say they're mistakes I keep making over and over again, but if they're mistakes, then why don't I regret them more?

I kiss her stronger, her cries of pleasure driving me to an edge, and I wrestle down her sweats with her panties.

"Donnelly." I hear the *wait* in my name this time.

I pause, both of us breathing hard. Her lips are reddened, her hair ruffled. She's trying to read my gaze. "Are you...are you sure?"

"Not if you aren't."

"I would..." Luna glances down at my hands holding her thighs, her black panties half torn down and in my grasp. "I want to more than anything, but not if you're going to be upset you broke your promise."

"I won't be. And I doubt it'll come up in conversation anyway." It's not like her dad has to know. He doesn't even know I've fucked his daughter once already. Or eaten her out before that. There's a part of me that believes if I wanted, I could get away with murder.

It's the part that I'm sure annoys the shit outta him.

It's the part that I should learn to shut off, but I'm selling my soul every second I'm back in South Philly with my dad, so the least I could do is return to my soul by being with Luna.

Give myself that.

And I do.

She nods me on, and I tear her pants and underwear off. I kiss her more urgently, and she grips my shaft and tugs. Breath heavies in my chest.

I hold her round face with both hands again. "I'm about to fuck you so deep and slow, you'll be on a high for days. You want that?"

"I *need* that. I can't survive without you." A moan is strangled in her throat while I rock forward a little. "*Pleaseplease.*"

My muscles are searing, and I plant a hand on the foggy mirror behind her head. My other palm is against the small of her back, my pierced cock edging up against her smooth folds. I nip her earlobe with my teeth, and her whimper grips me tighter as I whisper, "Your pussy is mine. No one else is allowed inside."

No one.

"Yesyes." She trembles. "*Please.* I need you..." She claws at my back. "Donnelly. I'll die if you don't fuck me." She's squirming in my hold, and I pin her more to the counter.

"I'm never letting you die," I whisper against her lips. "If I have to fuck you all night long, I will."

Her needy arousal hitches her breath. "Fuck me. *Fuckme.*"

My muscles flex into hotter bands. I want this to last so fucking long, but my cock is dying to be buried in her wetness. I slide my hand along her soft inner thigh, the one I tattooed, and then between them. She's already so swollen and soaked. I circle her clit, and her back arches with a gasp.

"*I need...*" she pants, and veins swell in my shaft. Thrusting inside Luna is a primal urge that's gripping me, but I prolong the seconds. "...you have to fuck me twice a day...and I need." She struggles to catch her breath. "*I need you.*"

I whisper against her ear, "I'm gonna *fuck* you alive."

"Please," she whimpers. "*Donnelly.*"

While we look into one another, I position my tip in Luna and I flex into her—inch by deep inch. I slip inside her pussy. A groan is knotted in my lungs. Her mouth parts with sharp breath, and I eat up her overcome expression.

"You better hold on and take me," I rasp, my muscles searing, and she responds with a moan and a nod. Sweat already glistens along my skin, her skin. I clutch her hip and pump deeper, pull out slower. *Deep and slow. In and out.* "You feel how I'm fucking you?" I thrust again, again, then grip her face while her head tries to loll. "Stay with me, space babe. You wanna survive, you've got to take all of me."

"Fuckfuck," she moans and tries to rock back but gives up, drowning in the ascent I'm bringing her on. "*Donnelly.*" It's a high-pitched, I'm-on-the-verge-of-coming *Donnelly.*

So I pull out, then enter even slower to prolong her climax.

She shudders.

I whisper in the pit of her ear, telling her how deep I'm taking her. "You know how tight you are?" I murmur, feeling her pussy pulsate around me. "I'm not stopping." The intensity tries to send me over, but we're both not coming yet. I pump harder into Luna, and I watch her eyes flutter.

Being inside her pussy nearly disorients me: the warmth, the tightness, the way her thighs quake around me. I breathe in her heady, floral scent, and the friction of my hypnotic pace is mind-numbing. I narrate what I'm doing to her, but the words are merged with my grunts and her sharp cries.

"It's too…" She moans.

"Too much?" I pant, thrusting into her, and by now, she's less on the sink counter. I have her ass in my hands, hoisting her against me and controlling the movement. "I'm not slowing. You have to take my cock this hard, this deep to survive."

Another tremor ripples through her body. "Fuck." Her *fuck* is so cute, and I lean over and kiss her lips that part with another hitched breath. "*Donnelly.* I'm…"

I slow into a longer stroke inside her warmth, and when I pull further back, I see blood on my shaft.

Shit.

Fuck.

Immediately, I stop and go rigid, my pulse spiking. I rest her ass back on the counter. Cupping her cheek, I ask, "Are you hurting?" I wasn't that rough, but I'm not gentle either, and blood could mean one of two things.

"Huh?" She's in a sex haze.

I murmur, "You're bleeding, Luna." I start to pull all the way out, but she catches my wrist.

"Wait, I…" She looks down, flush ascending her neck. "I think I must've just started a period."

"It doesn't hurt?" I ask again to be sure.

"Uh-uh." She shies away from my gaze.

I try to catch her eyes. Is she lying? Or is she embarrassed? I can't see why this would embarrass her. Maybe it's because she's only twenty? I dunno.

I haven't been with anyone as young as Luna, except when I was that young. So it's been a while, but when I was a teenager, fumbling through new moments in sex could be more awkward. Though, of what she's told me, she's more confident about sex than she is relationships, so I could be way off.

"You tell me if it hurts at all," I say.

Her gaze snaps to me in surprise. "You…don't want to stop?"

"Nah," I begin to smile. "I'm just getting started."

Her smile reignites and feeds my soul.

I'm realizing now that she thought I'd want to end it here, just because she's on a period. "You'll tell me if you're in pain?" I ask again since she never answered.

She nods vigorously. "I will." She hasn't let go of my wrist, and I kiss her, drawing her body against my chest. She sinks back into our embrace, and I ease deeper inside her.

Fuck. She's still so swollen around me. Breath jettisons from my lips, and I hold her cheek while I thrust. I speak against her ear for a solid minute or two, and I feel her contract. "You're not dying anymore, Luna," I promise, my voice hoarse with need. "You're gonna survive with me."

Her eyes stay fixed to mine, more than just pleasure pooled in them. She manages to breathe out, "I really….really love you."

It plunges into my core. Steals oxygen. I kiss her and whisper, "I love you more." I feel so connected to this girl. It's unreal.

Her lips break open into another cry.

My heart clenches with an angst and passion and love for Luna, and I build us back towards a peak with strong, deep pumps.

I press my forehead to hers again, consumed with her scent—the animalistic instinct to take her is wrapped forcefully around me. "I'm fucking you because you're mine," I rasp into a grunt. "I'm fucking you because I'm the *only* one who'll keep you alive, and no one else will ever fuck you like this again."

Luna Hale belongs to me.

I've never wanted to claim her as badly as I do now. Because she's in threat to be someone else's. Because I'm facing a fear where I could lose her to time.

"Even…when I'm bleeding?" she pants, her body torched with heat.

"*Especially* when you're bleeding," I murmur against her ear. Being inside her while she's on a period is sending her over—which is sending *me* to a new plane of existence. Can't lie, it's hot as hell.

A moan is trapped in her throat. "*Donnelly*. I'm gonna…" Her limbs shake, and she pulses around my length.

I groan and tuck her against my chest, pounding her harder, faster, and her entire body bucks into me. Her eyes roll, and seeing her lose herself to the climax does me in. I release inside Luna, my cock twitching as I unload in her pulsating heat.

Once my ears stop ringing, I hear our panting breaths and my 80s playlist, and slowly, I begin to slip out. I smile over at her, and her lips instantly rise.

I reach for a hand towel. "You sound pretty alive to me." I clean off and throw the towel towards the dirty hamper in the corner.

She hops off the counter, her small boobs bouncing. "For now." She kneels at my feet. Jesus. I look down at Luna while she grips my shaft.

As soon as she licks the side, I harden. Fuck me...again. I rest my elbows back on the counter. "What'd you say you need, two times a day?" I ask.

"Yep, but foreplay doesn't count."

I smirk. "I knew I loved your species."

Her smile morphs into a needy look. "Now?" She licks around my head.

I flex my abs, a breath clenched in my chest. "Yeah, right now." I reach down and clasp her forearm, pulling her to her feet, and Luna is practically beaming as I grab a bath towel and guide her to her bedroom. "Your door shut?"

"Yeah. I locked it already."

Sure enough, when we enter her room, her bedroom door is already closed. She pulls me now in the direction of her closet. I follow and throw the bath towel on the white comforter of her bed. I pass Moondragon, the goldfish floating happily in the crystal clear bowl.

Luna's blinds are shaded with blackout curtains, and I'd think it were night if it weren't for the early a.m. time on her neon clock.

She kneels and digs through the messy bottom of her closet, tossing out a few masks and pieces of costumes. Spider-Man, a unicorn head, a zombie wolf.

I pick up a blue and gray full face superhero mask. It's cheaper, the back just a string attaching one side to the other. I pull the mask on, and Luna glances over her shoulder, seeing.

Her smile reaches her eyes. "That one looks good on you." Quickly, she stands, both of us still naked, and she wears a full head mask from *Scream*.

Alright.

I'm down.

"You're the cutest bad girl," I tease.

"Don't joke. I could murder you in my sleep." Her voice is muffled, and she's by far the least scary Ghostface impersonator I've ever seen.

"I like my chances," I say, then I lift my mask and hers to the top of our heads. Just so I can kiss the hell out of Luna.

I walk her back towards the bed. She still tastes sweet like the Fruit Roll-Ups. Pulse thrumming, my hands glide along her soft cheeks.

She bites my lip, and I nip hers back and breathe, "My little fucking weirdo." I tug her mask back over her face and scoop her up around the waist.

She laughs, and I throw her on the bed.

Pulling my mask back down too, I'm grinning. After I climb on the mattress, I hoist Luna higher up the bed, until she's on top of the bath towel.

Unable to see her face, I watch her breathing pattern shallow, and I flip her on her stomach. She turns her head, and I realize she's looking at the floor length mirror. We're a little out of the frame of the mirror. I draw her an inch or so down, so she can see me knelt behind her ass.

"You good?" I ask, ensuring she's alright.

She nods repeatedly and gives me a thumbs-up.

I skate a hand down her spine to her ass, and with this view, I have some ideas for new tattoos. I wonder if she'd be interested in any. Unlike me, she's mostly bare of ink in this position, whereas I have them scattered nearly everywhere.

After rolling a pillow under her hips, I lean forward and grip the comforter above her head. Her legs are mostly pressed together, and my knees dig into the bed on either side of her frame. This is gonna be a snug fit, and the mere thought of this being *even* tighter is annihilating my patience. Which I got a lot of.

Very carefully, I push into Luna's pussy. Her breath shortens. This is a new, deeper position than the other two times we've fucked. Thank God she's this fucking wet. Still, I take her slow at first.

She's even more swollen—this might not last long for her.

"Have you ever been fucked this good?" I rasp.

She shakes her head and writhes beneath me. The pleasured noises she's making is a playlist I want on repeat. Please and thank yous. Her legs vibrate, and a deeper groan scratches my esophagus. *Fuuucking hell.*

"You've gotta take me again," I remind her into a thrust. "Stay with me, Luna."

She nods into a moan. "Donnelly*Donnelly.*"

"Last with me."

Forever. I wish I could make that a real thing.

The mask is hot against my face, but I watch how she's looking at us in the mirror. Our bodies bare, our faces shielded. My inked biceps are cut as I keep most of my weight off her back and I dig forward. My ass flexes with each thrust, my length lost inside Luna.

Goddamn. This feeling. Being this close to her. This deep.

I don't want it to ever end.

She mumbles and cries out into the mask, and as I pick up speed, I worry about her overheating, so I tear the Ghostface mask off her head. Her face is beet-red, and she pants into another high-pitched pleasured sound as I keep the hot tempo.

"I need…" Her eyes struggle to maintain focus on me.

Veins protrude in my hands as I fist the comforter. The depth of this position is trying to catapult me over. I grit down on my teeth, and I lift my superhero mask to the top of my head. I let her see my aroused expression while we watch one another in the mirror.

One, two—she loses it at the third thrust, and her pussy pulsates around my cock again. Black spots shoot in my vision, and I grunt out, "*Fuck.* Fuck."

Luna is a shuddering, beautiful mess beneath me. I hold her more against my chest and milk my climax inside her. She's spent when I come down right after her, her body limp.

Then she pants out, "Again."

I touch her clit. She jerks like it's too sensitive, too much. "Nah, let's take a breather."

"Five minutes?" She rolls over on her elbows and reaches up to me, just to slip the mask completely off my head.

"You think you can go again?" I collect the towel out from under her, the fabric bloodied, and I chuck the thing towards the bathroom.

"Yeah, I can," she says softly, watching me step off the bed. "I want to go all day."

Naked, I walk to her end table and find her vape. "We have tomorrow."

She says nothing.

A strain wrenches the air. She's worried this might not happen tomorrow?

"I'll be right back," I tell her.

17

Paul Donnelly

I LEAVE FOR ONLY a second, returning with my phone, sketchbook, and I tuck a pen behind my ear. I toss her the vape.

She's already sitting against the headboard, and I join her, neither of us reaching for our clothes. It's warm in her room, and the sheets tangle around our legs.

While I open the sketchbook and she takes a drag of the vape, I'm about to start the conversation where we left off, but she rotates more to me and asks, "Was that the first time you've had sex with masks?"

I shake my head and search her eyes. "Your first?"

"I've tried, but no one ever really wanted to."

"Their loss, my gain," I say and catch sight of her smile. "I have nine years on you though. I'm sure someone else would've said *yes* the older you got."

"I don't want anyone else to say *yes*," she admits, and it drives an arrow through my heart. Cupid did a number on me with this girl.

I skim her. "Have you had sex on your period before?"

She stares at the vape in her hand. "I wanted to."

I stiffen. I'm not gonna like this story, I can already tell. "What happened?"

"Andrew said it was unhygienic."

My brows shoot up. "That fucking—"

"I shouldn't have believed him. It was dumb—"

"No, he's a fucking *dick*."

"Everyone likes all different things." She shrugs. "I think he was just turned off by it."

"So what if he was?" Heat flames my chest. "His go-to was to make you feel like shit instead of just saying that." I motion to her lamp. "Lava lamp, ceiling, Moondragon—new life update: I now severely *hate* her asshole of an ex."

Luna tries not to smile. "Donnelly."

"What a fucking loser." I'm stewing. "I wanna kick him outta Philly." *He's not even from here.*

"Wishes."

"Will come true someday," I finish for her and try to go back to the sketch, but that has me hot. The only thing cooling me down is Luna's smile.

I think about how she wanted to fuck in five minutes. How she might be worried this won't repeat after today.

"We'll have tomorrow," I tell her. "I'm not changing my mind."

She thinks for a second. "I wouldn't fault you if you decided tomorrow that this was *our last sex.* I'd get it." She shrugs again and passes me the vape. "I'm just being realistic."

"I'm just being honest," I say. "I don't want to reestablish a boundary that we've already broken."

Luna frowns. "It's not like we haven't done that before."

I know. God, I fucking know. I rake a hand through my hair and then find a blank page in my sketchbook. I blow smoke off to the side, away from her, and pass the vape back. "It's different this time. I want it to be different."

She nestles against my side, her cheek on my shoulder. "Why?"

"'Cause you don't deserve to be in pain while I deal with my family, and that's what being physically away from each other is starting to be."

Painful.

"You don't deserve it either," she says so quietly; I strain my ears to hear. We don't say much for the next few minutes. She smokes. I draw. Until Luna whispers, "Donnelly?"

"Yeah?" I lift my pen off the paper.

"There's a plastic tub in my closet. Will you take it sometime today? It's yours."

I frown. "What is it?" My chest tightens, already having an idea.

"My fics. The printed ones."

"The only ones you have left," I say the unspoken thing.

"Yeah." She sits up off me. "I want you to have them." Her eyes are earnest but a little scared.

I start to shake my head. "Luna—"

"You've read more of my stories than anyone else. Maybe even more than Charlie. He doesn't reread them like you do, I don't think. I just thought…you'd want them, since I have no use for them anymore."

"I do want them," I say strongly. "But you might change your mind. You might even want to republish them one day."

She seems doubtful. Her face keeps falling.

"I'm borrowing them then," I say. "I'm giving them back when you're ready."

"What if I'm never ready for anyone to read them again?" she asks quietly.

"Then I'll be your only reader, and that's alright." I want to say more, but my phone buzzes. She looks away from me quickly. My chest contracts while I reach for my phone.

I scan the message.

"Shit, I gotta go." I hop off the bed. "Boss just texted. I'm on your brother's detail."

"Xander?"

"Older brother," I correct. "Maximoff has to go into Hale Co. offices for some charity thing, and Farrow is tied up with the med team." She looks a little sad, but before I go, I lean over the bed and kiss her. "Call me if you end up leaving the penthouse. I'll walk Orion before I head out."

She nods. "Thanks, Donnelly."

This is the part I'm starting to really hate. It's where I linger in the doorway, where she smiles back but an excruciating yearning burrows beneath her expression, and my heart concaves.

"There'll be tomorrow," I say.

Hope tries to fill her eyes, and the only regret I have is not making that a promise. The kind of promise on her planet. Tongue to tongue.

It's all I think about as I truly leave.

18

Luna Hale

SEX WITH DONNELLY this morning is a ginormous mental distraction for the rest of the day. I catch myself lost in the blissful memory of him and me, hot and sweaty together. I'm clinging to the minutes and seconds I spent with him, replaying the event so it'll be carved permanently in my head.

Fantasizing this deeply isn't such a problem, not when I'm alone. However, I am now among other humans.

I tune back into my cousins.

"Okay, fucking here me out, *camping* but themed. We could do emo, pirates, fucking space aliens—whatever you want, Luna," Sulli says to the group, which is just me and Jane and teeny tiny Baby Maeve.

Jane and Thatcher renovated their spacious closet into a woodland fairytale nursery, complete with framed paintings of classics like *Rapunzel* and *Little Red Riding Hood*. Behind the bassinet is a bright mural of a castle hidden in a mushroom thicket. It's cozy and perfect for Jane's new little princess.

While Jane is on the plush rocking chair, nursing Maeve, Sulli and I are on a Tiffany blue loveseat, busy entertaining the cats. Thatcher has a rule about not allowing the cats in the nursery, but Jane has amended it to add, "Without supervision."

I'm unsure if he knows this or not, but at the moment, Sulli and I have dubbed ourselves the World's Mightiest Cat-Sitters. I ensure

Ophelia doesn't bother Jane with pets, and Sulli keeps rattling a BB8 cat toy to distract Carpenter from inspecting Baby Maeve.

"Should Jane be camping?" I ask since she hasn't been home from the hospital for long.

She's only a week or so post-partum, and even though she has a glow to her freckled cheeks and maintains her natural upbeat energy, she still just birthed a human being. Sleepless nights with a newborn haven't just been on the horizon. She said, *they exist.*

I wouldn't be able to tell by looking at her.

Donnelly and I think she's powered by Cobalt fuel. It's inexhaustible stuff. But strangely enough, Thatcher is wired the same way. He acts *fine* with only a few hours of sleep.

I'd be an exhausted roly-poly wanting to curl into myself. I'm powered by Hale fumes. Running on empty. But maybe it's potent stuff too. Just in a different way.

"I can camp," Jane says brightly, eyes widening and alight. "We can play charades around the campfire. Or truth or dare. Never have I ever." Jane loves group activities, and I guess that wouldn't change with a baby.

"Oh fuck charades." Sulli loves the actual wilderness. "Last time we played was fucking *awful.*"

Jane smiles with the tip of her head, glancing briefly at Maeve in a blue sling against her chest. "You were the one who decided to announce your relationship via charades. It's not ruined."

"It is tainted."

"I refuse to believe so. Charades are a staple."

They'll both be amazing moms. It's all I can really think while I stroke Ophelia on my lap.

I can feel them staring at me, then exchanging a cagey look, maybe realizing I'm too quiet.

My hermit habits this past week haven't gone unnoticed by my roommates like I thought they would. After Donnelly and I had sex while wearing masks this morning, I spent most of the day reading comics and rewatching episodes of *Beneath a Strong Sentiment.* By nighttime, Jane and Sulli whisked me out of my bedroom.

Sulli wanted to go out.

Jane even offered to go to a *brewery*. "Anything you want," they keep saying.

Sulli's threat level is so high being pregnant, and Jane's has only grown now that the media are salivating over pics of Maeve. When Jane finally left the hospital, it'd been a zoo of paparazzi and press to a dangerous point.

Maximoff and Farrow are now rethinking strategies for Millie Kay Miller, their surrogate, when she gives birth. Everyone is worried about traffic and reaching the hospital in time.

In Maeve's nursery, I look between Sulli and Jane, realizing they're ready to brace the world more than I am. I like sneaking out, so I never thought I'd hide away. But it feels safe. *Easy.* This is also an opportunity for me to be more helpful. If I stay out of sight for longer, then there can't be any "Luna likes Donnelly" theories in the mainstream media. I'm making Donnelly's task of infiltrating his family much easier.

Anyway, I told them I'd rather just stay home, so we've been hanging out in the nursery. Besides the catnip-stuffed mice I brought in for the energetic calico cats, everything is put away and orderly thanks to her husband.

"Hey, Luna," Sulli nudges my side on the loveseat. "Camping was just an idea. We can do literally anything for your birthday."

"Yeah, I know." I slide a brush through Ophelia's white fur. "Out of everything we've brainstormed, it's my favorite."

"Really?" Sulli grins and bumps my arm.

I bump hers back, grinning too. The remnants of our days rooming together in the townhouse are like fairy dust, making me soar higher. I've never been closer to Sulli than back then, but times like this remind me that our bond hasn't totally disappeared or been broken.

"Really, really," I nod. "No media, just all the people I love in the woods, and we can pretend we're all on another planet together."

"So it's settled." Jane steeples her fingers like a giddy mastermind. "Camping with an otherworldly space theme for your 21st."

My excitement gives way to concern. "Are you bringing Maeve or letting your parents babysit?"

"I'll likely bring her with us since she's so little," Jane notes, her hand on Maeve's head. "I wouldn't miss your birthday."

Maeve was too early to be born exactly on my birthday, no cosmic timing after all, but now that she's here, I thought Jane would pass on birthday festivities.

I think she's so used to being present for *everyone*, kind of like Moffy but in a much different way since she has so many siblings. Maybe she's not ready for this aspect to change. She's one of the most reliable, dependable people in the family, and I wonder if she's scared a newborn will make her flaky.

It's okay if it does.

I start, "If you have to miss it, I understa—"

"No, I'll be there."

"Even if you have to change diapers in the woods?"

"Oui," Jane nods, "even then."

It makes me feel good and bad. "We could always do it here. Just have a space-themed party in the kitchen."

Jane looks crestfallen. "It shouldn't be some ordinary, mundane party. It's your *21st*. It's going to be as spectacular as you are."

I try to smile. With the ridicule online, I don't feel all that spectacular these days, but I do my best to absorb Jane's encouragements.

Sulli chimes in, "As long as you and Jane are down, I'm fucking down." She rattles the BB8 toy. "Carpenter! Come here, right fucking now." The cat has leapt onto the armrest of Jane's rocking chair, but he springs off to stalk Sulli instead.

Jane wouldn't want me to alter my birthday plans just for her, I know that.

"Okay, let's do it," I smile.

Sulli pumps her fists in the air. "Fuck yeah."

Jane claps her hands, her bright smile making mine grow. "I'll make a list of everything we need."

"My mom probably has enough camping gear for half of us,"

Sulli says, then glances to me. "Depending on how many people you invite."

Jane is already busy typing notes in her phone.

Invites. "I want all of my roommates there," I tell Sulli, "including Donnelly." Neither of them look overly suspicious when I name him, and I don't really feel like stirring drama tonight by sharing my feelings for Donnelly.

Maybe tomorrow.

"And I want to invite Tom, Eliot," I continue. "...maybe Charlie? If he'll come and if Farrow is okay with it." They haven't exactly mended things, I've heard, and if I need to choose between the two, I'd always pick Farrow.

"Charlie." Sulli makes a soured face. "I can't believe you like *Charlie* more than Beckett. It's like preferring raisins over chocolate chips."

I don't think I'm Beckett's favorite person right now, but I don't mention that. Especially since Beckett is usually nice to me, but besides Charlie helping me with my fics, he has an interesting viewpoint of people. I like talking to him about the world.

"Charlie is like a rogue space explorer," I say. "The times where he's not provoking Moffy, I think he's kinda cool."

"He's a space dick," Sulli says, then tells Jane, "no offense."

"None taken," Jane says breezily. "I'm not taking sides. I love my brothers *equally*, and they both can equally exude dickish behavior."

Sulli tosses a catnip mouse. "Like just yesterday, Charlie said I'm too dumb to help solve the fucking assault on Beckett."

Jane sighs, not at all shocked, "I apologize on his behalf."

"It's so shitty that everyone has to apologize on *Charlie's* fucking behalf," Sulli says. "That's not okay."

Jane sets down her phone and adjusts Maeve against her boob. "I take it Beckett apologized on his behalf."

"He did. He always does."

Jane frowns. "Is there anything left to solve with the assault? We know Donnelly's family is behind it all."

I've been quiet, just petting and brushing Ophelia's fluffy white fur, but my stomach is in knots.

Sulli tucks her long legs to her chest. "The two guys who attacked Beckett's bodyguard are walking free with a flimsy fucking restraining order. I just want to be sure my best friend doesn't get jumped on his way to ballet rehearsal. So I suggested hanging around him more, to and from the theatre, which means my bodyguards would be around him too. Charlie hated the idea. But fuck what he thinks because Beckett *loved* it."

I can see Beckett enjoying being able to spend more time with Sulli. I wonder if Charlie didn't like it because it meant he'd have to share his brotherly time with Sulli too.

Jane is deep in thought. "I do worry that Beckett might not be the only target."

"Why?" I ask now.

"Thatcher seems to believe they tried to attack him because of his association to Donnelly, but why? They didn't mug Beckett or take anything from him to sell."

"I definitely think they fucking tried but his bodyguard got in the way," Sulli says.

I know the truth. Donnelly didn't follow through with stealing Beckett's painting, and it was payback. I'm surprised my dad hasn't spread this throughout security either, or else Thatcher would know. He's protecting Donnelly more than I realized.

Gratitude floods me.

I want to thank him, and I reach for my phone and start typing out a text.

Thanks for keeping Donnelly's story from that night on Halloween safe and thanks for protecting him.

I send it.

Then I add: I love you.

And one more. To Thebula and back again

I tuck my phone in my pocket.

"I just think there might be more to the story," Jane says but shakes off the nagging thought. I really need the Queen of Curiosity to be a little less curious.

I scratch at nail polish I painted on my skin around my forearm tattoo. Neon green is swirled between song lyrics. I even swiped streaks of pink and purple polish beneath my eyes like war paint. The bottle said it was safe on skin, so I thought, why not? Results of being cooped up for so long.

And no, it didn't take my mind off Donnelly. Not one bit.

"Okay, so Charlie's invited," Sulli says, returning to the party planning. "Beckett?"

I hesitate at first, but maybe it'll be an olive branch. "Sure. Beckett…and Xander." Two olive branches.

Jane types on her phone. "Ben?"

"Not if Xander is going," I say. "I think they're still on icy waters with one another, and if there's any hope of my brother attending, then Ben can't come." I remember when Xander visited Penn, he totally avoided Ben the whole time.

Jane looks pained at the idea of leaving Ben out. I don't feel great about it either, but she says, "Let me see if I can get both there. If not, then it'll just be Xander."

I trust her. "Okay. I also want Oscar and Jack to come." Oscar is Donnelly's best friend, and Jack has always been close to all my roommates and even me. I've opened up to him about my persona in the media before—to the point where I had tears running down my cheeks. He's just so genuine and comforting, it's hard to stop the floodgates from opening.

"Good choices," Sulli says, then, "*fuck*," as she knocks a glass of water off an end table. She retrieves a towel from Jane's bathroom and soaks the spill off the carpet.

"Kinney?" Jane asks.

My sister. "I would but…"

"She's only sixteen?" Jane guesses.

"It's not that."

Jane nods in sudden realization. "If you invite Kinney, then you'd have to invite our sisters and also Vada."

Sulli looks up from the ground. "They'll be mega-butthurt if they're left out, but they'll get over it."

"They're just a lot all together," I say.

"Oh hey, I know," Sulli tells me. "Kits would have to be on sister patrol all night, and he wouldn't have any fun."

"Same with most of Omega," Jane says, "and likely, most of Epsilon would have to be there."

"*No*," I say with force.

"Yeah, fuck Epsilon," Sulli adds.

Jane agrees and says more in French. I'm pretending the translation is *fuck them*.

I think this over. "Maybe Tom, Eliot, and Beckett can have temp bodyguards for the party," I tell them, hoping this will be true because three Epsilon bodyguards is three too many. Especially after the run-in with those ones at Calloway Couture headquarters.

"Anyone from college?" Jane wonders.

College. My attendance the last several weeks for Biology 1121: The Molecular Biology of Life is awful. I foresee an F in my future if I don't actually attend the lectures. And then there's the labs. The only friend I've made is barely a friend and more so just my lab partner.

Still, I like her enough that it'd be nice if she came. "Maybe just Harriet."

"What about Frog?" Sulli asks and holds my gaze for an extra beat.

"She'll have to go...she's my bodyguard."

Sulli dabs at the wet spot, staring at the carpet. "You've sort of been avoiding her, and I didn't really want to bring it up. But you know, she's Akara's cousin...and fuck, it's not a big deal anyway. I'm sure it'll work itself out."

Frog has been upset. I can tell just based off Sulli's concern, but Sulli is also my friend and she's trying not to guilt-trip me.

Still, guilt nestles uncomfortably in my stomach. "I'll fix it," I mutter, but I'm not sure if she hears.

"What about Quinn and Gabe?" Jane asks.

Words are thicker in my throat, but I manage to say, "They should come."

And then my phone buzzes.

I check the text.

It's what dads do. And I love you more than chicken tacos — Dad

Spicy chicken tacos — Dad

From the food truck outside S&S — Dad

I smile and text: those are the best in all galaxies. It is known.

Known by me. Taco expert. — Dad

"Who is that?" Jane asks curiously, and I lift my head, realizing she sees me typing on my phone and my smile.

"Just my dad." Then my phone rings. "My mom's calling." I put it on speaker. "Hi, Mom. You're on speakerphone. Jane, Sulli, and Baby Maeve are with me."

"Hi, Aunt Lily," they say together.

"Hey, girls and baby." My mom sounds a little out of breath. "Why is this box so heavy?" She makes a grunting noise. "Sorry, I'm at Superheroes & Scones. New merch came in. But I'm actually calling to see if you wanted to go out, Luna."

Someone told her I'm hermiting.

"Go out?" I mutter.

Dread is a funny feeling. Funny in that it drops your whole stomach like you're on a theme park ride. I usually love the free-fall ones, but not so much this time.

"It's just me and Xander," she says. "I called that new indoor putt-putt place—"

"Putt Palace?"

"You've heard of it." Her excitement is palpable. "Doesn't it look awesome? Eight holes are supposed to be heroes, the other villains. *Golf* holes," she clarifies quickly. "The decorations are hero-villain-esque."

We all smile, and the sinking dread starts to disappear.

"I did want to go there," I say.

"What about tonight?"

"Now?"

"Yeah, I can come pick you up. Jane, Sulli, you both should come too if you can."

"That's okay, Aunt Lily," Jane says, studying me in a quick sweep. "I think it sounds like a perfect Hale outing."

"Yeah, you two go," Sulli chimes in, and they're both mouthing *go, go* to me, and Sulli gives me a thumbs up. Maybe they know the media will be more frenzied and chaotic if they go, and that would be a good excuse for me to bail.

"Xander's coming?" I ask my mom.

"He said he wanted to go. Putt Palace is letting us play an hour after closing time, so we have the whole place to ourselves. Isn't that nice?"

No strangers allowed.

"Yeah, it is," I tell her.

What could go wrong at indoor putt putt? Frog should be fine. I won't be with Donnelly, so no sneaky paparazzi can snap photos of us. And maybe I can patch things up with my younger brother.

It's *very* tempting.

"I'm stopping at the house and getting Xander first," Mom says. "I'll pick you up in a half hour. Does that work?"

Jane is miming swinging a golf club, and Sulli is giving me two thumbs up now.

It's hard not to smile, and it looks like I'm venturing into the earthly world tonight. "Yeah. See you then."

IN THE ELEVATOR, I TEXT DONNELLY THAT I'M

going out with my mom and brother. He responds before I reach the ground floor.

🤘 – Donnelly

Tell him I say hi. We'll catch up later tonight? – Donnelly

For sure. I text back.

He might already be at Halway Comics to meet my dad for dinner. It seems like a cataclysmic event, and so I definitely want the full report on how it all went down.

Slipping my phone in my pocket, the elevator *dings*. I step out and see her.

Frog is waiting in the apartment's lobby. No one would suspect she's a bodyguard—not just because she's thin and unimposing in stature—but because she's wearing a slim emerald-green dress, a trendy velvet coat, and black heels. The only giveaway is the mic cord in her ear.

I've always loved that she blends in so well, but seeing her eyes dart left and right with nervous anticipation stabs my heart.

Here I go.

I slip my backpack-purse straps on my shoulders and trek forward. My sneakers squeak on the marble floor, and anxious heat gathers beneath my black hoodie. I'm thankful for Past Luna (really, Ten-Minutes Ago Luna) who decided to wear jean shorts and fishnets even though it'll be cold outside.

Frog catches sight of me, and her spine straightens.

"Hi, howdy, ho," I greet with a wave.

"Hey." She peeks over to the revolving entrance doors. "Your mom isn't here yet."

"I know. I came down early." I notice about four beefy dudes loitering near the lobby's reception desk, pretending to be interested in the sage paisley wallpaper and gold lighting fixtures. But their eyes noticeably veer to me, and they're wearing identical black suits.

"My backup," Frog says, glancing to them, then to me. "At least that's what they should be called. Frog's Backup Security. Extra reinforcements. Not that I really need them, but those SFE d-bags threw a stupid stink over comms about my 'size'."

It probably didn't help that I ditched her. "I'm sorry for not telling you I was leaving," I say. "I didn't mean to get you in trouble."

"Yeah, well…" Her voice sounds strained. "It hasn't been awesome, but their anti-Frog campaign has been going on since O'Malley got hurt. I can deal with the boys' club and being on the bottom rung. It's not like I was coveted by anyone in Buffalo. Sometimes it felt like the whole state of New York rejected me."

That hurts more. "I'm not rejecting you."

She scopes out my surroundings before looking at me. "It feels like you did. Donnelly told me you're just scared of what happened to O'Malley happening to me, but you don't believe I can escape a situation like that?" I'm sure she hears the doubt enough from Epsilon, and she might be small but she's fast and nimble. I do believe we could outmaneuver crowds together better than any big burly man.

Still…

"O'Malley couldn't escape it," I say. "I'd be scared every bodyguard I *really* love couldn't too."

Frog looks conflicted. She shifts her weight, peeks at her backup security, then tells me, "Maybe it's better if you love me a lot less."

Ouch.

She cringes in pain too. "You're not supposed to worry about me, Luna. That's written somewhere in my cousin's twenty-pound rulebook. *Clients can't worry about their bodyguard's safety.*"

"I know. You're just my favorite bodyguard I've ever had."

Frog makes a face close to the doe-eyed emoji. "You seriously can't tell me that." She sighs into a wounded noise. "I need to like you way less too, but I don't want to."

"I don't want to either." I hold my backpack strap. "I know we're on two polar opposite sides." *I'm famous. She's security.* "But I never want to lose your friendship…and sometimes I'm not so good at keeping friends in the loop, but I know you're different."

She's my bodyguard too. I need to try to respect that more.

Her stiff posture loosens, more open and warmer. "Then can you just like…pretend I'm Wonder Woman or something? No one can defeat me unless they have eight titanium abs and hail from some planet where all the hot guys exist."

My lips rise. "And you can only be taken down by the hottest male specimen."

Her smile appears. "Who also happens to be the sweetest, and the hottest, sweetest guy doesn't exist, so I'll be safe forever."

I laugh, then nod. "I can pretend." It's what I'm good at.

She skims my cheeks that I streaked with nail polish. "I'm liking the new look. It's giving Lost Boy from *Hook*." Her gaze falls to the black analog watch on my wrist. "That is not yours."

I tuck my wrist protectively to my chest. "Has anyone ever told you you're really perceptive?"

"Just my Auntie Mint." *Akara's mom.* Her smile fades since her aunt passed away recently, but before I can reply, she speaks. "I don't know *exactly* what's going on between you and Donnelly, aka Wonder Bread"—I heard she found out about our Fanaticon usernames—"but he better know I am *still* your Number One Protector."

I smile. "Always."

19

Luna Hale

"IT'S NOT BECAUSE of you," my mom assures, her hands tight on the wheel. She's sitting up straighter than usual in the driver's seat.

"Then why else would Xander ditch putt-putt? You said he wanted to go."

"He did, *he did*." Her brows bunch, the Philly streets a little congested tonight. She's focused on driving, but Xander's absence could swallow our car like some freakish aquatic villain. I feel like we're in the belly of a beast and not just headed towards Putt Palace.

Two black security SUVs are also trailing us. Monroe, my mom's 24/7 bodyguard, and Frog drive one vehicle, and Frog's backup squad drive the other. The fact that my mom requested no security to be in our car just means she wants more private family time.

Maybe she knew I'd be upset.

"He hates that I like Donnelly," I say. The urge to sink in my seat is powerful within me.

Mom tries to look at me and the road. "Hate is a strong word, and I think he dislikes that Donnelly loves you." My entire body floats at her use of the word *love*. "And he feels not great about his own feelings."

"So he's mad at Donnelly?"

"I wouldn't say...*mad*." She uses her blinker and switches lanes. She had to take her car into the shop, and this rental has the pungent "new car" smell. It's also missing an X-Men Cyclops bobblehead on the dash and a middle console full of Sour Patch Kids.

The sterileness of the rental car adds some discomfort. I try not to slouch so much, but my back feels stiff. Mother-daughter time is less frequent since I moved out and I'm getting older, and I shouldn't take this outing with her for granted. But again, Xander was *supposed* to be here.

I imagine my brother wishes Donnelly chose him over me. The same way Beckett does. "It's not a competition," I mutter, tendons of my heart twisting.

My mom reaches out and puts a consoling hand on mine. She retracts quickly, just to have two hands on the wheel. "What's with this traffic tonight?" She carefully maneuvers around what resembles a paparazzi vehicle.

Their window rolls. I see the lens right before the blinding flash.

Yep, definitely paparazzi.

We squint, but Mom avoids them really well.

"Xander's just holing up then?" I ask her.

"He'll come out eventually," she nods resolutely. "Like you." Her green eyes dart to my amber. "I don't like seeing you locked away."

Me either. "It was just a week of total seclusion, really."

"For you, that might as well be a millennium. You're my child who's either traveling by imagination or by foot." She honks the horn at the paparazzi, then switches into another lane. "Have you been writing at all?"

I shake my head.

"Did you nod?" she asks. "I can't look away from the street to see."

"I shook my head."

Her frown deepens.

"It's just been hard," I say quietly. "There's too many negative voices in my head, I guess, telling me I'm gross for writing…" I trail off, unsure if I should even bring this up with my mom. It might lead to topics of shame and sex addiction, and it hurts thinking I might hurt her.

She waits for me to say more, but I never do.

"You're not gross," Mom reminds me again. "You're creative and talented. *So* talented."

I look at my hands, fingernails painted a sparkly purple. I want to believe her, but she's my mom—a kind, *amazing* mom who will always try to lift me up, especially when others are kicking me down.

My phone suddenly pings.

I click into the Fanaticon notification and let out a gasp, springing upward in my seat. "*Beneath a Strong Sentiment* just got renewed!"

Her mouth drops. "Whaa...no, it didn't." She starts smiling with me.

I grin at the article. *Renewed.* It's really coming back next year for season two. "They already have plans to start filming. Now you have to finish the whole first season, Mom."

"Oh, I will. Lo and I will binge it this weekend." She hasn't seen beyond episode one because she feared it'd get cancelled, and she didn't want to fall too hard for something that wouldn't last.

Maybe I'm more destructive that way. Falling for things that might have short expiration dates.

I'm about to text Donnelly to tell him the good news, but the car jerks.

"Sorry." Her voice is caught in slight panic. Rain begins to pelt the windshield, and I see several windows rolled down in the cars surrounding us.

I sit more upright and peer out the rear window. "What happened to security?"

"They're stuck behind two cars. It's okay. This happens all the time." She's white-knuckling the wheel.

My phone buzzes several times in a row. I check the new texts.

You're going to Putt Palace without us? — Tom

How dare you. — Eliot

We'll be there in thirty or you'll be turned into a square
– Tom

We can't let that happen. – Eliot

I know they'll understand that I just want to hang out with my mom. Before I can reply, they send an article link.

HALE OUTING ALERT! Lily Calloway is taking her children to Putt Palace tonight!

That's how they know where we're headed? I thought their bodyguards might've told them…

I lower my phone to my lap. "How would *Celebrity Crush* know we're going to Putt Palace?"

"What?" Her eyes dart quickly to my phone, then the road. "They wouldn't."

I read fast. "The article names me, Xander, Kinney, and they speculate that Moffy might even be there."

Her jaw unhinges slowly. "No, they didn't."

"Who?"

"That lying liar of an owner!" She lets out a tiny growl. "He asked who was in my party, and I just said my kids and told him if he could keep that to himself before we arrive, that would be great. He said not to worry. Maybe he told his employees, and they tweeted it. *Uh*, I'm *so* sorry, Luna."

"It's not your fault. Maybe it's good Xander didn't come after all." He would've been more anxious than I am, and Donnelly might've been the one to accompany him. I don't mind that it's turned into a more public affair if it means no "Donnelly-Luna" sightings.

Mom sighs. "Now we know why there's a bajillion paparazzi out tonight." She shakes her head repeatedly, eyes never deserting the streets. Windshield wipers squeak against the glass. "*Call Monroe.*" She speaks to the car's Bluetooth hookup.

"Calling Mom," the automated voice replies.

"Nononono!" Mom freaks as the phone rings over the car's speakers. "Hang up!"

I push the red button on the screen. It clicks off before Grandmother Calloway could answer. "I'll call Frog." I'm already dialing Frog's number on my phone. It's not connected to the car, but I put it on speakerphone.

"You're okay?" Frog asks, sounding worried.

"We're fine right now," Mom says first. "How far back are you two?"

"Three cars behind."

"Temp guards are gone," Monroe says in his Texas twang. All bodyguards are born and raised in Philly, but I heard that Monroe grew up half in Texas. Divorced parents. Spent summers with his mom and the twang stuck. "Flat tire." According to Mom, he's a man of few words, which reminds her of her first beloved bodyguard Garth.

"I think we should take a detour," Mom tells them. After they work through directions, we hang up, and I watch my mom wiggle out of a gridlock and take the next exit.

Most paparazzi can't follow in enough time. They're stuck on the freeway.

And so is our security.

"We'll meet at Putt Palace, ma'am," Monroe says in another call.

"Good plan," Mom says, then hangs up again.

City streets have more stop-and-go red lights, and silence fills the car as she concentrates. Her eyes flit to the rearview mirror more than once.

I crane my neck to see a gray sedan. "They're still tailing us?"

"Just this one car. We can handle it." She nods again, pumping herself up, but she purposefully goes around the block to lose them.

They ride our bumper. Rain blurs their windshield, so I can't distinguish faces inside their car, but I have an uneasy feeling.

Boom Box.

Donnelly said they always chase Xander, and they think he's in the car.

"They just ran a red light," I say, my pulse accelerating.

"Just face forward. It'll be fine." She hasn't loosened her grip on the steering wheel. "I've dealt with worse paparazzi."

I fall back in my seat, facing the windshield.

"Your seatbelt is on?" she asks.

"Yeah." My heart is racing out of my ribcage. "How much long—" We jolt forward. My heart catapults to my throat. Shitshit. They just rammed our *bumper*. Not hard enough to cause an accident but enough to scare us.

Mom presses on the gas. She tries to speed up to lose the tail, but the sedan chases us down the road. "*Call Lo,*" Mom tells the car.

"Calling Mom," the automated voice replies.

"No!" Mom yells. "CALL LO!"

It's already ringing for Grandmother Calloway again, and I hit the red button on the car's dash. The call drops. Once I find her phone in the cup holder, I manually call my dad.

"Hey, Lil." He answers on the first ring.

"Lo, we have a problem."

"Mom!" I shout, just as the sedan tries to cut us off. We almost slam into a brick wall of an old laundromat. *Ohmygod.* I can't blink. I hear my rattled breath.

She speeds out of the close encounter, and I still haven't moved an inch.

"Lily!" Dad shouts, panic shooting in his voice.

"Luna?" Donnelly calls out, his concern palpable. He's with my dad. *Eating dinner together at the office,* I picture them huddled around a box of pizza or to-go cartons of burgers.

"We'reokaywe'reokay," Mom slurs together, trying to catch her breath.

I exhale too. "Mom is awesome," I say in a swallow, trying to calm down. *Calm. Down.*

"Where are you two?" Dad asks. "Shouldn't you be at the putt-putt place already?"

"Paparazzi are chasing us," I say first.

"Where's security?" Donnelly asks.

Mom takes a left turn. "They're meeting us—" The sedan rear-ends us again. Fuuuck.

"What the hell was that?" Dad sounds furious and more alarmed than I think I've ever heard him. "Lily?!"

"They're bumping into us, Lo—"

"Pull over."

"No," I cut in, scared to be in a parking lot with Boom Box. The Bulky One tried to physically come at me, and we have no bodyguards.

"Find the safest place and *pull over*," Dad forces. "They'll run you both off the fucking road."

"I'm going to pull over," Mom says, even though I'm shaking my head a hundred miles a minute.

"No, please," I say "It's Boom Box."

"Stay in the car," Donnelly tells us.

"Boom Box?" Dad questions.

"These two paps—"

"Mom, wait"—I wide-eye the street—"is this…?"

She's turned on to a slim road that resembles a darkened alleyway, a normal shortcut, but road work signs and orange barrels block off the exit. We're in a dead-end.

"Lily?" Dad calls out.

"I'm trying to get out of here." Mom attempts to reverse, but headlights glare in our rear windshield. She hits the brakes. Boom Box is right behind us.

We're trapped.

"Where's here?" Donnelly asks.

I scramble with my cellphone to drop a pin of our location. "I sent you a pin. We can just stay parked, right?" I ask Mom.

She nods, already putting the car in park. Our wipers squeak in the quiet, and exhaust billows out the butt of our car, further obscuring the paparazzi who've confined us here. "We'll be fine," she tells me.

"Lock the doors," Dad says urgently. "Just wait in the car. We're coming to you."

"Security's on their way too," Donnelly tells us. "You alright, Luna?"

"Yeah." I try to control my racing heartbeat with a few breaths. I try to picture their dinner together, only happiness on the menu. I try to imagine we're safe in a forcefield more durable than adamantium and vibranium combined. I try to envision a perfect tomorrow.

I hope.

And believe.

I'm okay. We'll be okay.

Mom stretches over to my side and fumbles in the glove compartment. She hands me the only bottle of pepper spray.

"Mom—"

"Take it." She's already dropped the bottle in my lap, and we keep eyeing the idle gray sedan behind us.

Fear tenses my bones, and I grip the pepper spray like a lightsaber. *We'll be okay.*

And then all four of their car doors swing open. *Four doors?*

"Wait…" *Wait.* My pulse is in my throat. Is Boom Box riding with more cameramen? The two of them couldn't have opened all four doors.

"What?" Donnelly asks. "Luna? You alright?"

Dread wraps around my windpipe like a vice, and I can barely breathe.

"What's going on?" Dad questions. "Lil? Is she okay?"

"They're getting out of their car," Mom tells them.

"Jesus Christ," Dad curses with a string of threats that echo distantly in my pounding eardrums.

"The car is locked, Luna," Mom reminds me, trying to level the shakiness of her voice. "They'll just take some photos and be gone. Poof."

I'm really scared.

My ribcage constricts painfully around my lungs, and I hardly blink as these tall figures emerge on either side of our doors. It's dark, rainy, but as I twist to my window, I catch sight of his hands.

There is no camera.

"That's not Boom Box," I say. "Donnelly!"

"STAY IN THE CAR!" he yells.

They smash our side windows. "Mom!" I scream as we're showered with glass.

"Get out of the fucking car!" someone shouts.

"LILY!" Dad screams.

Everything happens so fast. Mom tries to reverse and run them over, but an arm swoops through her broken window, caging her by the collarbones and pulling her against her door. He's wearing a black ski-mask.

I unbuckle, reach over, and spray his eyes.

"Fucking bitch!" he swears, not letting go of Mom, not even as she fights harder against his iron-like hold.

"We're almost there." I hear Donnelly distantly, but the glimmer of hope is too far away to catch, and my mom's eyes suddenly widen at something behind me.

"NO!" Mom shrieks. "Don't touch her!!"

I glance back, just as another man tries to snatch me around the waist. His face is also hidden in a ski-mask. And my door is already unlocked. Open.

I spin around and kick at him with all my might.

He seizes my foot, only to tear off my sneaker. And then he comes halfway into the car and picks me up like I weigh absolutely nothing. Terror envelopes me, and I reach for my phone. It slips from my fingers as he pulls me out into the rain.

"MOM!" I scream.

"LUNA!" Mom wails. "DON'T HURT HER, PLEASE! PLEASE!"

"MOM!" Tears burn my eyes, and I'm thrown onto the rough cement. Glass shards dig into my hands and knees. A boot slams up into my chest, and I cough. Rain droplets blur my vision, and I try to crawl to my feet.

Another boot to the chest.

I want to curl up. To become a real roly-poly in a soft shell and never emerge. Not until it's safe.

Another boot.

"Donnelly," I cry out.

"Which one of us is she asking for?" A chill rakes my entire body, and my head whirls like I've sucked on too much helium.

"Fuckin' shut up," someone else snaps.

I hear mutterings behind me. "Where's Xander?"

"Not here. Just these two."

"Luna!" Mom yells. I can sense her trying to run after me. Trying to reach me. "Leave her alone!! LEAVE HER ALONE!!!"

I look up. The cratered dead-end road is lit from our headlights. Some masked guy so easily restrains my mom. Lifts her with one arm around her stomach, like we're made of the weakest *nothings*.

"Take anything you want! Just let her go!!" Her gangly limbs flail.

"Mom!" I croak into a scream, my face wet with tears and rain. Adrenaline and fear surge through me—I try to sprint after her, tripping over my feet to stand and move.

It's a stupid idea, maybe, to not run away and save myself.

But it's instinct to want to be with the ones you love, the ones who make you feel safe.

I know I can't overpower these men. Neither can she. But I'd rather be in my mom's loving arms, suffering, than take the futile chance of escaping and being on the cement alone.

Cruel hands suddenly wrap around my hips, stopping me, and I watch as another man throws a fist in my mom's cheek.

"NOOOO!" I scream like a knife is plunging into me. "MOM!" *Mom.*

Their fist flies at her again. I shut my eyes.

I can barely hear anything but my own pulse, my own terror. I can't watch. I can't look. I turn my head even more and squirm in this guy's hateful clutch. "Why are you doing this?!" I shriek. I don't get what they hope to gain by hurting us.

"Find their phones!"

I realize my dad and Donnelly are still on a call, but they've been left in the car.

"DAD!" I scream.

I swear I hear my name. Distantly. And then nothing. My gut drops in pure horror. What do I do? What can I do? "What do you want?!" I yell.

No one answers me.

"Hurry up. Their security is coming."

"Leave her there," someone says. "Let's take the other one."

"You sure?"

"Yeah. She said his name."

Donnelly.

And then they zip-tie my thrashing hands behind my back. They put me on my feet.

I'm shoved forward in the dark. So forcefully, I skip and trip and barrel downwards into the cement. My wrists snag against the restraints, and my head makes violent impact with the cratered road.

Whoa.

Breath ejects. Pain flares. Black spots blur my vision. Dizzy, I barely realize I'm moving. I'm being hoisted in another pair of arms.

I go limp, trying to blink away the throbbing in my temple. My skull is pounding, and I imagine these are his arms. *They're his arms.* My pulse slows. He has me.

I'm okay.

He's right here.

He's always with me.

Donnelly.

TEN MINUTES EARLIER

20

Paul Donnelly

"SO LET ME GET this straight," Lo says, peeling the foil off a chicken burrito, "your dad was lying when he said he took you to the zoo?"

He's referring to the evening smoke break I had with my dad this past week. Sean dredged through ancient history, my childhood, while I wore a wire. So Xander's dad heard everything.

I swallow a bite of steak burrito. "It's not that he was lying."

He scrunches his face. "You just said he'd never taken you there."

"He believes he did. He doesn't remember the part where he forgot to bring me." I have trouble making direct eye contact now. It hasn't been that way. When I arrived at Lo's office, I shook his hand, sat down across from him at the desk, made a couple jokes, felt confident as shit, but I'm starting to wish for an easy exit.

"Sorry," he says tightly.

I look over at him in surprise.

"If I sounded accusatory, I *apologize,*" he says with a hand to his heart and rolls forward on the leather chair. His office is private and warmer than he is. Framed *The Fourth Degree* comics hang along black-painted walls, and colorful collectibles fill a tall glass cabinet. Right next door is Superheroes & Scones, and we coulda eaten in the store's breakroom.

Instead, he invited me to the Halway Comics offices. Been thinking it's so he can kick his feet up on the desk and stare me down on the other side.

But his feet are on the floor. And he keeps rolling closer. Towards me. "Honestly," Lo says with more sting than softness, "there's a part of me that thinks you're withholding details out of spite, and it's putting me on the offensive."

"If I knew something, I'd tell you."

"Would you?" Lo questions, his burrito in two hands, like he's about to take a bite. But he just holds my gaze, not with anger. Not with malice. With something he's rarely directed towards me. *Understanding.* "I've been on PaleyFest panels and been asked about my alcoholic father—with auditoriums *full* of people waiting for the answers. I've sat across my oldest son and been asked about that same dad, and you want to know which was harder?" He takes a beat, alluding to the obvious answer: *his son.*

"PaleyFest," I say jokingly.

The humor falls flat. Mostly because he stays serious.

"It's never easy digging through a shitty past that you'd rather forget," Lo says. "And sometimes it gets easier. Other days, it feels like you're back there. You're playing roulette, hoping not to hit that bad number with that bad memory, and truth be told, I hate that I'm the goddamn dealer, hoping you land on it. But that's where we're at."

I slowly nod, my chest constricted, even if I'm slouched in the chair, looking relaxed. "I'm not some broken toy." I don't know why I say it, but I do.

"Great." His voice is sharp. "Because I'm not trying to fix you."

I nod again.

Same Goal: *Make Loren Hale Like Me...Then Make Him My Best Friend*—it's going alright. Room for improvement. Seeing as how I had sex with his daughter this morning, broke another promise to him, I should be carrying a guilt-sized baby on my shoulder.

But I'm not burdening myself with remorse. Because I wouldn't take it back for anything. Not even to appease him.

We eat our takeout burritos for a few minutes. After I wash down the tender steak with a swig of water, I sit more upright and say, "He was high. My dad."

"Meth?" Lo peels more foil, listening closely.

"Yeah." I wipe my mouth with my bicep. "That's why he forgot to take me to the zoo. That's why he forgot a lot about me, most of the time. It's not like we had the money to even go, anyway. I doubt we would've ended up there."

"Did you see him high a lot?" Lo wonders.

"Enough," I answer vaguely.

Lo swallows a bite, then sips some water, his brows furrowing before he asks, "Was he different when he used?"

I glance at the wall, the memories foggy. Not where I question their existence or anything. I know what they are. I just choose not to go into that haze. What for?

These days, the answer is so vibrant, so clear: *For everything.*

For her.

Lo arches forward again, elbows on his desk. He wipes his hands on a napkin and stacks some drafts of comics in a pile. "My dad was an asshole when he was drunk," he suddenly tells me. "Which was all the time. He was also a shit father, and when he stopped drinking, he tried to be a better dad—but he was still an asshole. Depending on who you ask, he never became a better man."

"You think he did?" I wonder.

Lo looks far away now. "Yeah, I do." He forces a half-smile. "But I'm also the bastard who makes excuses for him, so you're asking the wrong Jonathan Hale offspring."

"Nah." I wad up a napkin, leaning back in my chair. "You're the only one I would've asked."

"Because I lived with him the longest," Lo guesses.

"Because you're Luna's dad." I stare up at the black-painted ceiling. "You wanna know what my dad was like on meth?" I pause. I'm ten, trying to do homework on the floor. There's yelling in the kitchen over their stash being depleted and someone named Lionel.

He's out to get us.

He snuck in here this morning.

Get Paul outta here. He'll kill him.

Lionel didn't exist.

He was my mom's delusion that became my dad's.

I'm eleven, and they're starting to accuse me of stealing their shit, selling the drugs and pocketing the money for myself. My mom is raiding my closet and turning my pockets inside-out.

"Paranoid," I tell Lo. I'm twelve, and my dad hasn't slept in days. He's gripping my shoulders, shaking me and warning me of shadow people. They're in the apartment. Be careful. "Erratic."

I'm fourteen and we're out of cash. They're going through withdrawals, and my dad is screaming at the top of his lungs. Like I'm pestilence and the fucking plague. Not doing enough to help. Not pulling my weight.

"Violent," I say.

"Violent?"

"I dunno." I rake a hand through my hair. *I do know.* She slaps him for screaming at me. She decks him in the jaw, the eye, the mouth. He takes it. I try to come between them. He shoves me in the wall. Says if I don't give them my paycheck from stocking shelves at the supermarket, he'll throw me out.

I blink a few times.

"Where was your mom?" Lo asks, his voice more hushed. Concern sharpens his face, knits his brows.

I turn to my mom for help. She tells me to listen to my dad. "The violence wasn't always at me. It was confusing. One second, she's…" I swallow a rock. "She's beating the shit outta him, then the next, they're having sex loud enough that I can hear."

Lo looks disturbed.

Welcome to the life I left behind.

"You wanted to know," I retort, a little pissed off. "You shouldn't have asked." I'm about to stand, wanting to leave, but he shoots to his feet first. I'm up on mine right after.

"What do you think I'd be like?" His face contorts. "That I'd be *excited* you were in a violent household? That I'd be glad for you." He starts clapping.

I tilt my head and watch, smiling. "Appreciate the applause. You can send me a fruit basket next."

"I'll do that," he says dryly. "Right to 2149 You're Not Funny Lane."

"Sending the basket to yourself?" I nearly laugh.

His eyes are knives. "Oh that's right. Your address is 460 You're *Never* Dating My Daughter Avenue."

Straight to my soul.

Still, I lower back to my seat. "Been trying to move off that street."

"I'm sure you want to." He sinks back into his chair. He could've said, *I'll make sure you never do.* I pocket that positive end note. Keep 'em coming.

We're skimming one another up and down, and I just go ahead and say it, "The more you're getting to know me, I know I'm not someone you'd want for her." I've always known that.

I'm not parents' first choices. Detailing my rocky childhood was never going to help my case, even if he could empathize.

"No, you're not," he agrees. "What you came from is…" His nose flares. "It's not *anything* I'd ever want her to experience."

"She won't," I assure with everything inside me. We want the *exact* same things for Luna.

He nods tensely, his gaze tightening. "I'm sorry you had to go through that."

"So sorry you keep sending the fruit basket to the wrong place."

He rolls his eyes, but we're both starting to smile. His fades first. He clenches his jaw and picks up his burrito. "What you saw between your mom and dad—I hope you know that's not love."

"I do know," I tell him. "I've wanted nothing like what my parents have with each other." I mop up spilt rice out of my burrito with a napkin. "She was happier on drugs. When we couldn't afford 'em, it was like looking in the eyes of a loveless animal."

He grimaces. "That bad, huh?"

"I think she would've sold every organ in my body for another hit." I drag my gaze across the ceiling again. "There were days I wished they could've been high. They were easier to deal with. The desperation, the rage—that wasn't something I tried to stick around for."

He swallows another bite. "Where'd you go?"

"I'd run around South Philly. Go to the library, into Wawa, check out any store I could until it was dark. Then I just snuck back home." I rest my forearms on the desk and hold my water bottle. "I didn't like pulling long shifts at the Acme. Money was alright, but it always created more problems. Cousins would show up. I got fired and rehired about five times in one year alone."

"I get why you didn't want to go back and see Sean."

I nod once, muscles stiff. "He is a bit different, though. My dad. Being out of prison and supposedly not using. He's just..." Calm? Nice? Caring? I shake my head, not sure if there is a perfect word.

Lo narrows his eyes, concern in them. "He's the enemy, Paul."

"Nah, I just thought he was the Hamburgler. Been planning on getting him to steal a Quarter Pounder for you."

He pops a tortilla chip in his mouth. "And suddenly, I'm vegetarian."

"More for me," I say lightly and lean back.

He dunks another chip in salsa. "I also hate Van Halen." He stares at the old, ripped Van Halen tee I'm wearing like it's radioactive. He's throwing darts at my favorites when I thought he'd mention how I need a new wardrobe. Gotta get a new fit to impress his daughter and all.

"That's alright, Xander's dad. Not everyone has good taste."

He reaches for his water on the desk. "That's exactly what I was thinking about you." He flashes a dry smile.

"Like minds." I give him a *rock on* gesture.

"Yeah, no—" He's cut off by his phone's loud Skrillex ringtone. He answers fast. "Hey, Lil."

"Lo, we have a problem." The office is so quiet that her side is audible without speakerphone.

"Mom!" Luna yells in pure fear.

Adrenaline shoots in my veins.

Lo fists the phone. "Lily!" he shouts, panic crashing him forward in the chair. I'm on my feet and unclipping my radio. The cord is wrapped around the device, unplugged. Turned off. I'm not in contact with the security team.

Where the fuck is their security? Where's Frog? Monroe?

"Luna?" I call out, and once Lo puts the phone on speaker, I hear her heavy breaths.

"We'reokaywe'reokay," Lily slurs, panting for breath too.

Lo has a tense hand on his forehead.

"Mom is awesome," Luna says in a steadier voice. *Is she alright?*

I plug in the mic cord. Are they on the road?

"Where are you two?" Lo asks with urgency while I fit in my earpiece. "Shouldn't you be at the putt-putt place already?"

"Paparazzi are chasing us," Luna says.

Fuck. "Where's security?" I ask her.

Lily answers, "They're meeting us—" A loud *crunching* noise, like a collision, blares over the line. Luna intakes the sharpest, gasping breath.

It jars every instinct in me. To go. To find her.

"What the hell was that?" Lo shoots to his feet, looking volatile but terrified for his wife and daughter. No one answers. "Lily?!"

"They're bumping into us, Lo—"

"Pull over." He speaks sharply into the receiver and comes around the desk. He motions for me to hurry with security.

I'm about there. I click my mic and whisper, asking about Frog's location.

"No," Luna cuts in. Fear is still clung to her voice. Something's not right.

"Find the safest place and *pull over*," Lo forces out. "They'll run you both off the fucking road."

"I'm going to pull over," Lily says shakily.

"No, please," Luna nearly cries. "It's Boom Box."

Shit. Fuck. "Stay in the car," I tell them.

Lo is glaring at me. "Boom Box?"

"These two paps—"

"Mom, wait," Luna interjects again, her breath hitched. "Is this…?"

What is it?

I don't wanna be here. I don't wanna be stuck in this office. I need to find her. Now. Lo has the same idea, and we're already deserting his office with lengthy, scorched strides. Bypassing the small lounge of couches and chairs, we exit through the front door, and the Philly sidewalk is strangely empty of cameramen, of fans. Dark clouds rumble in the sky, and the world feels on a tilt.

Off-centered.

Rain begins to pelt the asphalt and us. No jackets, but Lo parallel parked his Bugatti close. Quickly, he's behind the wheel, and I'm in the passenger, shutting out the rain. His light brown hair is damp, droplets soaking his long-sleeved black shirt, and I run my fingers through the strands of my hair.

Lily and Luna haven't responded in at least a minute.

Lo starts the car and glances at the phone. "Lily?"

"I'm trying to get out of here."

Where the fuck are they? "Where's here?" I ask.

One second.

Two seconds.

Three.

"I sent you a pin," Luna says, her voice abnormally pitched. "We can just stay parked, right?" It sounds like she's asking her mom.

My phone buzzes.

I put the location in my GPS, and Lo takes off. Reading the address, I know where they're stuck: a cut-through skinny road that must be blocked by something. If paparazzi are behind them, they're not getting out.

I ask for Frog again on comms, and this time, she hears me.

"Frog to Donnelly, we're meeting our clients at Putt Palace."

"Reroute," I say quietly into my mic and text her the pin. "Luna and Lily are in trouble. Paparazzi. I sent you their location."

"Got it." Her voice is tight.

"Tell the temps to follow," I remind her.

"I'm on it."

"We'll be fine," Lily says with shallow breath. She's consoling her daughter, and I want to be there to do the same. I grip my knee as we speed in the direction of this small cut-through road. We're fifteen minutes away from them without traffic.

"Lock the doors," Lo says, a death-grip on the wheel. "Just wait in the car. We're coming to you."

"Security's on their way too," I tell them. "You alright, Luna?"

"Yeah." She audibly exhales. Inhales.

I just want to hold her.

I rub a hand over my mouth. *She's okay.* She'll be alright. We'll make it to them. Maybe not before their bodyguards, but we'll be there. Fucking *Boom Box* might just try to terrorize them through their windows for a money-shot.

The thought flames my insides, a gathering inferno. Blood boiling, I just stay alert, watching the road, listening to the call.

"Mom—" Luna starts

"Take it."

Take what?

Lo isn't speaking. I bet, like me, he doesn't want to cause more panic. He's weaving through the city streets and cars, beating the red lights. His amber gaze is venomous, and he's hardly breathing.

"Wait…" Luna chokes out, and her voice tapers off.

I go cold. "What?" I ask. "Luna? You alright?" Something's changed.

The call is eerily silent. I can't even hear their breathing anymore. Then we hit grid-locked traffic. Our car rolls to a full fucking stop behind a Volvo.

"What's going on?" Lo asks, putting our car in park and picking up the phone. "Lil? Is she okay?"

"They're getting out of their car," Lily whispers.

"Jesus Christ," Lo grimaces. "These sick fucks are dead. They are so goddamn *dead* after this. They're going to be slapped with a thousand lawsuits until they're buried beneath hell."

"The car is locked, Luna," Lily says to her daughter, a tremor in her voice. "They'll just take some photos and be gone. Poof."

Lo is shaking his head repeatedly. His cheekbones and jaw are blades as he grits down on his teeth. We're not acknowledging one another while they're in danger. Tension is suffocating. I watch the unmoving traffic. Wish these motherfuckers would stop honking.

I glance back at the phone in Lo's hand.

Lily and Luna are quiet again. I hear the ping of rain on our end and theirs. They said the paparazzi are walking towards them. Out of their vehicle. Moving closer.

Something still feels so off-kilter, and my gut is nose-diving to an abyss. But it couldn't be…?

"That's not Boom Box," Luna says and screams, "Donnelly!"

Horror slams into me. "STAY IN THE CAR!" I yell, but I already know what's gonna happen a second before it does. The sound of shattering, crunching glass *booms* over the line and slices into me.

"Mom!" Luna shrieks.

"Get out of the fucking car!" That's a man. South Philly accent. Don't know who.

"LILY!" Lo screams into the phone, his gaze bloodshot and rattled. Traffic is starting to clear a bit, and he steps on the gas. He's gripping that phone like it's the sole lifeline to his wife and daughter.

I click my mic, sick to my stomach, but I'm speaking. "Someone call 9-1-1. Frog has the location. Lily and Luna are being attacked. Can't talk. I'm with Lo." Bodyguards flood the comms channel, but I tune them out and shout, "Lo, watch it!"

He hits the brakes as traffic slows.

I ask, "Can you driv—?"

"I'm fine!" he shouts, clearly not fine. Neither of us are, but someone needs to drive—and he's already behind the wheel.

He impatiently waits for a lane to clear, and he speeds over to the fastest one. We listen to Luna and Lily's grunts and breaths, and my eyes burn alive.

A man groans in pain. "Fucking bitch!"

Lily screeches like she's fighting him.

Lo puts a fist to his mouth, his face ashen.

"Get off the exit," I tell him.

He cuts the wheel. We're still ten minutes away.

"NO!" Lily shrieks. "Don't touch her!!"

Blood rushes to my brain, dizzying the shit outta me. *Someone's touching Luna.* Lo nearly careens back into his seat, his eyes red and looking as tortured as I feel.

Luna screams and wails, and I scrape a hand down my face, bile rising in my searing throat. *I'm coming. I'm almost there.*

If they fucking hurt her…

They are hurting her, and rage and anguish are pulverizing me. It's taking everything not to scream, and to just call out directions to Lo. I'm not even sure if he can see the road through his filmy, pained gaze.

"MOM!" The sheer terror in Luna's voice is killing me bit by bit.

My eyes blur, but I blink and flick the wipers to a higher speed.

"LUNA!" Lily wails. "DON'T HURT HER, PLEASE! PLEASE!" I'm being stabbed repeatedly, and if a knife is plunging into me, then a bulldozer is running over Lo's whole being. He's sheet-white, and when we reach a red light, he opens the car door. And vomits onto the cement.

Shutting the door, he wipes his mouth, and the light turns green. He hits the gas.

"Your phone," he chokes out. "Pull it out."

I dig out my phone.

"Mom!" Luna's voice is fading. She's likely out of the car, away from the phone.

They pulled her out of the car. Pain is nailing my eardrums. I pinch my eyes, but then force my hand off my face. I keep blinking to stay focused. To see what's in front of me.

"Text my brother," Lo tells me in a single breath.

I assume I'm supposed to tell Ryke Meadows to meet us. So I briefly shoot him a message about the situation. I keep it short but urgent.

Lo has a hand rooted over his mouth, the other on the wheel.

"LUNA!" Lily yells in despair. "Luna!" Until her voice drifts into an echo too.

He rubs at his wet eyes. "Fuck!" He slams a hand on the wheel, accidentally hitting the horn. It causes other cars to honk back.

"Leave her alone!" Lily screams in the distance.

"I can't..." Lo is choked. He presses the heel of his palm to his forehead.

"We're almost there." I breathe through my nose. A wreck is up ahead, causing more stop-and-go traffic, so I tell him to weave over and take the closest right turn. After another right, we're clear, and he steps on the gas.

"Noooo! *Mom!*" Luna screams bloody murder. My chest collapses.

"What the fuck is happening?" Lo's voice breaks in raw agony.

I can't look at him.

"DAD!" Luna yells desperately for him.

"LUNA!" he shouts back at the phone. "WE'RE ALMOST THERE—" He cuts himself off. Because the call just dropped.

"No," he nearly cries into a scream. "*No. Goddammit.*" He tries to call back, but it doesn't ring through. A tortured, angered, wounded noise wrestles out of Lo in all his pained fury.

A ball is lodged in my throat, my muscles just strict bands of anguish and determination and sheer utter pain. It's taking every... fucking...thing inside me not to break down. I'm clinging to my nerve with my fingernails, and I so badly just want to let go and scream for her.

But I can't...I can't. I'm security first. Her friend second. Her boyfriend not at all.

Five minutes out, Lo volleys between rage and grief, like he could slaughter the world and then fall to his knees. Then his bloodshot eyes nail on to me.

"Why would they go after them?" he rasps. "Why would they touch Luna?"

I shake my head. The chances my family is behind this is too high. I know that. Unbearable weight has been bearing on my chest, and I try not to picture what Lo said. Their hands. On her. I can't without losing my shit, and I can't...

"What are they doing to her?" Lo chokes out.

"I dunno."

"They're your family!"

"I DON'T KNOW!" I yell with every breath inside me. "You think this woulda happened if I were closer to them?! You think I woulda let it happen?! They tell me *nothing*."

We're too late.

I'd barely even started to get in my dad's good graces, and then they jump on this opportunity—to what? What are they even doing?!

I grind down on my molars. "Take the next right—the next right!" He almost misses it, but he swerves and we're still on course to reach them. Lo drives. I'm silent.

Until Xander's dad says, "I swear to Christ if they rape her, I'm going to burn every one of them alive until nothing's left."

Nausea roils in my stomach, and I want to do worse to them. I'm clenching my knee with one hand, and my other is on my mic piece attached to my collar. I click it. "What's that?"

I misheard something while Lo spoke, and Monroe repeats, "We're pulling up. Only Lily's rental car is on the road."

The guys who jumped them must've left already.

I relay this to Lo, and he's waiting for more info. We're less than a minute behind Frog and Monroe, but several security SUVs beat us to the scene.

Lo parks and jumps out of the car. I bolt ahead, but he catches up. His legs pump urgently beneath him, face full of panic. We run past security SUVs. Bodyguards spill out and sprint with us toward the rental car. Ambulance and police sirens pitch into the dark sky. *They're on their way.*

"Lily!" Lo shouts in the light rainfall.

I shadow Lo, not stopping. *Where's Luna?*

"Luna!" I call out, my heart pounding. "LUNA!"

The rental car is still running. Smoke billows out of the exhaust pipes into the night, and our boots crunch over broken glass. The windows are smashed, and I peek quickly inside. No Luna.

"LILY!" Lo sees his wife on the concrete several feet beyond the rental car. Monroe and Frog are crouched around her unmoving body.

The wind is knocked out of me, and I stagger back and slow to a deadened stop.

This isn't happening.

This isn't fucking happening. I whirl around, my world spinning three-sixty degrees.

"The Keenes are coming," Monroe tells Lo, right as he drops down to his wife.

"*Lily.*" His voice is punctured, fractured…obliterated. "*Lily, Lily.*"

"She's still breathing," Frog says shakily, but she staggers to a stance, her hands to her mouth while she sees Lo shatter completely.

"*Lily.* No, no, *no,*" he cries into a scream, his face twisting and his fingers featherlight across her battered skin. The anguished, guttural noises he's making could freeze rain and time. I almost puke. I pinch my eyes tightly and wince at the wall, the concrete, the sky.

Pain is relentless in my body.

Luna.

Luna.

She's not here.

The road is small. Construction barrels obstruct the exit and form a dead-end, and Luna. Isn't. Here. I rest a hand on my wet hair. My chest rises and falls heavily.

"I can't lose you," Lo sobs. "You're okay. Come on, love. You're okay. Wake up. *Please, wake up.* Lily…*Lily.*"

Bodyguards speak around me. "Someone get Ryke on the phone."

"He's already on his way."

I can't watch Lo being split into a million pieces. Can't listen to his gutted voice. It's unbearable, and no one pulls him away from her. I wouldn't even try. It'd be like separating two halves of one soul.

Luna. Lo is being torn apart, and I don't think he's fully here anymore and realized his daughter is missing.

I whirl around again, looking left and right.

She's not lost among the stars. She didn't rocket off to another planet like I know she wanted to after her fics leaked. She's not invisible. 'Cause she wasn't supposed to disappear without me.

With a single breath, I dig out my phone and call him.

My dad.

Phone pressed hard against my ear, I hear the ring and ring and ring. He doesn't answer. I hang up on his automated voicemail and shoot him a text.

Can we meet up and talk?

And another. Where are you?

He's not responding fast, so I pocket my phone. My muscles won't unwind. I brush back my wet hair, pressure not unmounting.

Frog teeters backwards away from Lo and Lily, and she turns and sees me in the dark. As she takes a few steps over to me, pain constricts her face. "Donnelly..." Her voice cracks, and I know she's searching for solace in a friend.

I know she thinks that friend is me.

And it sounds easy—to just hug Frog. But my eyes sear as emotions barrel into me at caustic speed. I just want to be holding Luna, and I can't be anything for anyone else right now.

I don't know how to be.

"I'm sorry," I say quietly to Frog and walk away, both hands on my head.

Breath is caught in my burning lungs.

I squat down and grip the brick wall out in front of me, the other hand shielding my face. They took her.

I need to find her. It's a desperation now. *I need to find her.* Except, my dad isn't answering and I'm stuck here for more than a second, trapped in a tornado of people. Police. More private security.

"Donnelly!" Price shouts and catches me by the shoulder.

I'm being whisked off to the side, near a black security SUV and the brick wall. Alpha bodyguards huddle around me.

Ryke Meadows is rushing past us, his motorcycle helmet beneath his armpit.

"LO!" he calls out to his brother.

The Keenes (the med team)—Edward, Tripp, and Farrow—are already surrounding Lily and shouting to the paramedics as ambulance doors swing open. My head rotates in each new direction.

Police say *crime scene* and push most bodyguards outside the rental car's perimeter.

"Where'd they go?" Price asks for the fourth time, drawing my gaze back to him. "Who was involved?"

I shake my head. "I didn't—"

"How many were here?" Bruno asks me.

"Who did this?" someone else questions.

"We need answers."

I don't fucking have them! I wouldn't still be here if I did!

"Hey, back off!" Akara shoves into the huddle.

"He's our only *in* to finding her quickly, Akara," Price retorts. "I don't care about his feelings right now. *We need answers.*"

"He doesn't know anything." That's not Akara.

Oscar Highland-Oliveira has pushed into the cluster of bodyguards. Severity edges his assertive posture.

"You can't be sure of that," Price shoots back.

"I legitimately can," Oscar retorts, rain droplets slipping down his golden-brown skin and stubbled jaw. Curly pieces of his brown hair are wet against his forehead, and he's squinting through the storm. "Because if Donnelly knew where Luna was, he wouldn't be standing here listening to you. He'd already be gone."

"I'll find her," I suddenly say, knowing what I need to do.

"Where?" Price questions.

"I gotta go." I turn out of the huddle, but multiple hands jut out and grab me. For fuck's sake.

"You do this *with* us," Price retorts and looks to my boss. "Akara."

Akara stares into me. "He's right. We do this together."

"I can't wear a wire, and there's no time. Just let me go."

Let me go.

"Give us three minutes," Akara says, almost pleading. "That's all. Just three minutes to form a plan."

What if that's three minutes too long?

Oscar squeezes my shoulder, and I end up nodding. "Alright. Three minutes."

It takes four, and as the huddle breaks and a plan is set, we split off. I move towards the middle of this narrow road. Farrow's father, Dr. Edward Keene, is climbing into the back of the ambulance with the stretcher, Lily strapped on—her face bloodied, beaten.

Sickness burns my throat again. Lo is the next to board the ambulance, but as he twists around, his destroyed gaze catches mine.

"Donnelly?" he calls out as wind whips through this dead-end. I approach, just as he says, "Luna—"

"I'm gonna get her. I promise you."

Lo has no clue I've broken every promise I've ever made to him, but this one, I can't break. Because this is the promise that will break me if I do.

A shred of hope is in his amber eyes—hope that I've ignited, hope I can't let extinguish—and the paramedics close the doors on him. The last thing of Loren Hale I see is his hope in me.

Sirens ring in the air. Red strobe-lights flash against the brick walls, and I watch the ambulance speed off on to Philly streets.

Someone sidles next to me. I already know who. His calm, readied demeanor resets mine, a trauma bag slung on his shoulder. There is no wait. No yesterday. No tomorrow if she's not here.

There is only now.

Farrow watches the ambulance disappear. "We'll be with you."

We.

Oscar comes up to my other side, dangling the keys. "I'm driving."

21

Paul Donnelly

MINIATURE PINK BOXING gloves dangle on the rearview mirror of an old Ford. I'm in the backseat of Joana Olivera's car, and I'm hunched forward, hands cupped and knees jostling beneath me.

Oscar is driving towards South Philly. I check my wrist for the time, but I have no watch on me. *Luna has it.*

The blue kyber crystal necklace lies heavier against my sternum. Did I kiss it before tucking it in my Van Halen tee? Better believe I did.

"Why the fuck does my baby sis have her steering wheel positioned so low?" Oscar is trying to adjust the wheel while he's driving.

Could say a lot about that, but I don't speak.

Farrow's annoyance is visible. "Man, stop fucking with it. Just pick a position."

Oscar locks the wheel in place and tries to peek back at me. "No comment back there?" He's concerned since I'm not ribbing him about sex positions. I see the joke alright. Just don't wanna make one right now.

My legs won't stop jostling. "Your adult sister has probably been hooking up with someone in the driver's seat."

Oscar short-circuits. "First off, *no.* Secondly, I'm sorry I asked."

"Me too," I mutter. "You sure Jo's okay with us taking her car?" We needed a non-security vehicle and nothing related to the famous ones. Something more inconspicuous. Oscar called his husband and his sister, but Joana was closer to the crime scene than Jack. Literally only a minute away. Been the only good fortune I've had all night.

"She's not just okay with it, she's motherfucking thrilled," Oscar says to me. "The more favors I ask of Jo, the more she can cash in IOUs."

"Think she just likes when you treat her less like a kid," I tell him, scraping a hand against the back of my tensed neck.

He frowns. "She's twelve years younger than me. I can't change that."

Yeah.

Silence thickens.

We haven't been talking about the attack on Lily. Drowning in the dark parts of a night isn't something any of us like doing. It's a reason I've always loved hanging around Farrow and Oscar, and I'm guessing it's why they like my company too.

But right now, they're taking me towards a certain darkness.

It's in the landscape. Looming over us. At some point, they're gonna have to leave me. Together, it's easier to stay calm in the light.

The light side.

I think of Luna. My eyes burn again, and Farrow pops a bubblegum bubble and fiddles with the stereo. "You pick, Donnelly."

"You choose the music." My choked voice sounds unnatural to my ears.

Farrow casts a glance back at me. He's wearing Maximoff's blue *Superman* baseball hat, a birthday gift from SFO to his husband. It conceals his ash brown hair, and the brim shadows his gaze. Can't tell his level of concern, but he just faces forward and connects his phone to the car's sound system.

Back at Yale, we'd all bar hop and end most nights in Farrow's apartment playing music videos, drinking whatever cheap liquor he had in his pantry, and laughing about Oscar's pop-genre obsession. Good times. Those still exist. I haven't lost 'em yet.

What do they matter if I've lost her?

I blow out a strained breath.

Farrow picks a song.

The second the beat starts playing, I recognize "Tried and True" by Ween. My legs go still. Slowly, I lean back against the seat, and the soothing music washes over me.

God, this song reminds me of Luna. But maybe it made Farrow think of me.

I stare out the window, the rain letting up. Brick row houses fly past us as we enter South Philly. *I'm gonna find her.* I'm convinced I will. Because I won't stop until I do.

The power of this certainty holds me upright, ready for whatever needs to happen. Confidence is a weapon I've had to wield most of my life, but usually that went hand-in-hand with self-preservation. Now, not so much.

What I'm doing is self-destructive.

Damning.

Pretty sure I'm either gonna walk away with her, or I'm not walking away at all.

"Where is he?" I ask after the song switches to Third Eye Blind. I'm without my radio. Don't even have a gun on me. So I can't locate anyone I care about.

Oscar glances back at me. "Where's *who*?"

"Xander?" Farrow asks, lowering the music.

That's not who I was wondering about, but now he rushes to the front of my mind. "Him too," I say. "All the Hales."

That family is being pulverized tonight, and though I had nothing to do with this, any harm done to them feels like my fault at this point. This wasn't supposed to happen. I was supposed to take down my family before they got in arm's length of anyone I love.

"Last I heard," Oscar says, "Xander and Kinney should be headed to the hospital."

"Their aunts are taking them," Farrow confirms, since he has the direct line into the Hales. Being a Hale himself by marriage and whatnot. "And Kinney is blowing up my fucking phone." He's texting with one hand. "She's asking for 'vivid' details. Like fuck I'm giving them to her."

"Do they know what's going on?" I ask.

"No," Oscar says tensely. "There's been orders on comms not to say anything about Luna or Lily to the teenagers. Parents want to do it themselves."

"They need to hurry," Farrow says, more quietly. "If police are involved, this is hitting the internet tonight." He rests his forearm on the middle console. "Maximoff is on his way to the hospital."

My initial question still hasn't been answered. I ask outright this time. "Where's your son?" *Ripley*.

He's the baby. He's biologically a *Donnelly*, and I want to make sure he's nowhere near South Philly tonight.

"He's with Maximoff—" Ringing cuts off Farrow, the phone call coming through the car's speakers.

"Speaking of the Husband," Oscar says, then asks Farrow, "Have you talked to him yet?"

"Just texted. It's all I've had time for. He knows I'm not with his mom." He motions to Oscar to answer it, and Oscar presses the *accept call* button on the wheel, connecting the car speakers to the eldest son of all the famous ones.

Resilient, steadfast, headstrong—that's how the world sees Maximoff Hale. Right now, I just see him as Luna's protective older brother. She's missing, and maybe he'll think I'm to blame.

"Hey, Thatcher and Akara aren't telling me a goddamn thing. My dad isn't picking up his phone. My uncles are being cagey, so what the fuck is going on, Farrow?"

"Does he always come in this hot?" Oscar asks Farrow, and I imagine Farrow is either rolling his eyes or glaring at him.

"Oscar and Donnelly can hear you," Farrow warns his husband. "I'm in the car with them."

"I've been told to go to the hospital to see my mom—I'm not about to come in fucking cool," Maximoff retorts.

"Good," Oscar says, more seriously. "Neither would we."

"Farrow—"

"I can't tell you what happened, wolf scout," he says, his voice abnormally constricted. "Not while you're driving."

Long dead silence tries to eat away at me.

"I can drive," Maximoff finally replies. "I'll be fine. You know I can handle it. Just tell me what the fuck is going on. *Please.*"

"I know you can drive. I know you won't wreck."

"Then why are you doing this to me?" His hurt is crushing.

"Man, don't say it like that," Farrow breathes, tortured too.

"You always let me in on everything. If you're worried about our son, he's okay. He's asleep in his car seat."

"It's not about Ripley." Farrow lowers the brim of his baseball cap. "Promise me something and I'll tell you."

"Anything."

"Don't follow me."

"What?" Maximoff says. "Where are the three of you going? Why aren't you with my mom?"

"Promise me, wolf scout."

"...it's my sister?"

"Promise me."

Another long pause, only with this one, I can see Maximoff wrestling with the tough choices in front of him. He's felt a responsibility to protect his sister, but he's gonna need to hand that off to someone else.

To me.

I want to tell him to trust me.

I want to tell him that I'll die a hundred times over trying to save her.

I want to tell him that there is no stop in me. There never really has been. I'll do more for her than he ever could. He's got a husband. He's got a son. He's got another baby on the way.

She's all I have.

She's all I want.

But I don't interrupt their conversation. Not as Maximoff says, "I promise. I'll go straight to the hospital, Farrow. Just tell me."

"Luna is missing," Farrow starts, then disconnects his phone from the car speakers. He puts his cell to his ear. "We're on our way to find her."

Oscar parallel parks outside an old run-down biker bar. Black paint is peeled off the brick siding, but I still make out the name. *The Rhino.*

Time to see my dad.

22

Paul Donnelly

THE RHINO IS AN OLD relic of 80s hedonism. Think some famous hair metal bands used to frequent this spot in its heyday. Dollar bills are stapled to the ceiling rafters, and regulars graffitied the walls with pen and Sharpie.

I see him.

He's behind the bar, absentmindedly wiping a beer glass and glancing at the only TV screen. Hockey is airing. I walk past a couple brawny guys playing pool, the only other people here. Billiard balls clink together in the quiet, but I hear my heartbeat hammering.

He sees me and stops wiping. "Paul." His lips rise, then fall. "What's wrong?"

"I texted. You didn't answer." I rest my elbows on the bar, stiff as can be. "I need to talk to you fast. It's important."

He's digging in his pocket, unearthing his phone. "Shit, I had it on silent." He frowns at the phone screen, then calls out to the other men. "You boys need a refill, help yourself. I've gotta take care of something for a sec."

They nod. "Thanks, Sean."

"This way," he tells me.

I follow my dad into the one-stall, one-urinal bathroom. Smells like piss, and the mirror is fully covered with band stickers.

"Don't bullshit me," I start off, my chest rising and falling. "Who took her? Where is she?"

"Whoa, *whoa*." He raises his hands. "You need to rewind, son. I don't have a fucking clue what's going on here." Concern flares in his blue eyes. "Who took who?"

"You really know nothing?" I can't believe that. "You're not on the periphery."

"Periphery? When did you start using words like...*periphery*?" He acts like it's gross. Being book smart and all, and I don't have time to play dumb with him. Or point out how he still hardly knows me.

I shift my weight. "You've gotta be in touch with someone who's involved."

"Involved with *what*?" He looks me up and down. "I can't help you unless you're honest with me."

"Lily Calloway was jumped tonight, and someone took her daughter."

His face plummets. "They didn't...Jesus." He takes out his phone again.

"You know something?"

He has trouble looking me in the eye. "I know Flynn and Hugh's kids have been talking to some shady ass journalist at some media firm."

"Why?"

"For the money. They're two degrees from those families through you, and they couldn't give a shit about burning your career alive." Flynn and Hugh are Uncle Raff's sons. That side of the family isn't warm towards anyone related to Uncle Bobby (my grandpop), which includes me, my dad, Scottie.

"Why would they hurt Lily though?" I ask him.

He doesn't answer. Just puts his phone to his ear. "Ollie—" Long pause. "Are they fucking insane?"

I strain my ears to hear Ollie's reply. "...I can't control my brother any more than you can yours. Roark is all over the damn place. Now he's got his stupid son roped into this mess with Raff's grandsons. They're not gonna come out of it this time, Sean. Just stay away."

My dad stares right at me, tensing.

He has to help me. He can't hang up. I mouth, *where is she?*

He hesitates.

"Where is she?" I almost yell.

"Who's that?" Ollie asks on the line, and my dad switches the phone to *speaker* so I can hear clearer.

"My kid."

"*Sean—*"

"I trust him."

"Is he alone?"

My dad nods to me. "You alone?"

"Yeah," I lie, knowing Oscar and Farrow will be close by wherever I go. They're my tail.

"You don't want to be a part of this, Sean," Ollie cautions. "This isn't gonna be good for either of you."

"He's right," my dad tells me. "They'll set you up and take you down with them. The damage is already done—"

"No," I cut in. "They have Luna."

"The daughter of the rich prick who hates you?" He frowns. "So?" Then he sees my torn expression. He takes an agonizing beat before speaking to his cousin. "Tell me where they are, Ollie."

He sighs. "This is a mistake."

"Where are they?"

"The place where you and I first got high."

No address I can plug in or text to the team. A place I know nothing about.

"Thanks," my dad says.

"Bye, Sean." It sounds like a solemn, forever goodbye.

After they hang up, I tell him, "You don't have to come with me. Just give me the address."

He shakes his head. "I just got you back. If you go in there alone, I don't know what they'd do to you. They don't all like you. So you want to see her; you need me."

Can I trust him? Before this, I'd say *barely* and *not at all*. Now, I'd say, *I do*. Unrelentingly and almost undoubtedly, I do. Don't know why exactly. It's more feeling than logic, but feelings can betray you.

I wonder if it's because he's my only shot at finding her. I have to trust him. There is no other path. No other way to Luna.

There's no time to argue. "Alright. Take me to her."

He leads the way, and as soon as we exit the bathroom, my head snaps to the TV screen. A breaking news story has replaced hockey.

"...again, we have limited information," the news anchor says over helicopter footage of the smashed rental car and dead-end road. "But it's confirmed that Lily Calloway has been hospitalized after an assault in Center City. It's unclear whether this was a mugging or a targeted attack. We also don't know which of her children were present with Lily at the time of the assault...but okay, we have more breaking news to report. We've just received *graphic* photos of the scene with Lily Calloway. Please remember, these are *graphic* and should be viewed with caution."

Don't air them.

"Don't air them," I mutter out loud. "Why are they gonna fuckin' air them?"

My dad watches me twist away from the TV as soon as the first brutal image hits the screen. He tells me, "There's how they got paid."

The money. They took photos of Lily and sold them to their journalist connection. Did the journalist also know they were the ones who beat her up? Were they okay with that?

"Why would they take Luna?" I ask him.

His gaze darkens. "I dunno. Honestly, I don't."

I can't waste time. "Let's go." I hurry, and on our way outside, he tells the bouncer to man the bar for a few hours. Then we're on the curb. A motorcycle peels down the slick road. Rain has stopped.

"You bring a car?" he asks.

"No."

"We'll walk then. It's not too far."

I stay at his side, the chill biting my arms. "You have an easy out," I say to him. "You don't need to help me more than you already have." I've never known him to be selfless.

He stuffs his hands in his jacket and glances over at me, our strides quick and lengthy. "Despite whatever I've done, whatever you think of me, I didn't set out to be a dad who abandons his son. Maybe given the choice now, it's not something I wanna do."

I nod a few times, but I can barely wrap my head around that. Luna is taking over four-fifths of my brain.

He lights a cigarette. "When we go in there, you can't act like you're a cop or private security, you understand?"

My muscles burn.

He blows a line of smoke out through his nose. "They won't let you inside if they think you're gonna turn them in."

"Will they even believe I'm on their side?"

"They will 'cause I'm with you, and we're gonna pretend we're there to help clean up their mess." He passes me the lit cigarette while we cut a corner. We walk briskly past more brick row houses and a deli. He hugs closer to me since cars are double-parked and sit half on the curb. "I don't think it's a good idea if they know how much you like this girl—"

"I don't—"

"Now you don't bullshit me," he interjects, his breath smoking the cold air. "I saw it when you said her name. I'm betting her dad hates you because you fell in love with her—and you're attached to scum of the fuckin' earth." He motions to himself, then out towards the row houses. "And they can't know how much you love that girl. You can be concerned about her, but remember we're here to protect them. Otherwise, they won't give us what we want."

"I just want her," I admit.

He eyes me for another extended beat. "We'll get her."

Don't fuck me over. Please don't fuck me over.

I thought Loren Hale would be the one at my side, and in the end, all of my trust is in a dad who hardly knows me and who I hardly know too. Truth be told, I'd take Xander's dad over mine—any day, any night.

But this is the only dad I've got at the moment.

Putting the cigarette to my lips, I take a long drag and focus on the road ahead. *I'm not leaving without her.* It's the only certainty I'm carrying.

23

Paul Donnelly

FIRST TIME OLLIE and my dad got high was at Uncle Marty's row house. He's been dead since I was a little kid. House then belonged to his only living son, but he went to prison. I can't be sure which cousin owns it now, but even in the dark, the shabby outside looks forgotten and unloved.

Grime coats the tan stone siding, and the yellow overhang is faded and dirtied. It shades a black door that my dad raps his fist against.

Door cracks open, and a chain snaps taut so we can't bulldoze through. Colin peeks out at my dad, then me. "It's Sean and Paul," he calls out to someone behind him.

I'm not shocked to see Colin, considering he's Roark's son and Ollie named him on the phone. Plus, he was the one who blackmailed me during Halloween. Figured he might be involved in this too.

"Let us in," my dad sneers under his breath. "You dumb fucking idiots left a trail. We're here to make sure you're not sent back to prison."

Colin hesitates. "Just you. Paul can stay outside."

"Ah, *no*. He's the only reason you're not all being booked as we fucking speak."

I hear muttering behind Colin. People arguing. I barely move.

"Roark," my dad calls out in a hot whisper. "What is this, an investigation? I'm trying to help *you* out here. Let me fucking inside."

The chain suddenly drops, and the door widens.

"Thank you." My dad enters first, and I'm a step behind.

The smoky living room is dated from the nineties with torn floral wallpaper. I try not to rapidly scan the place, but I let my eyes flit around. *Where is she?* Cousins are everywhere. I spot dark-haired and chin-dimpled Ryan and Patrick. Most are standing around and watching the old TV play on low volume. A news channel.

Some are crammed on the lumpy couch. They pass around a glass pipe.

I look away.

"Your phones," some guy with a green Eagles beanie demands. Don't know who he is. He seems a lot younger than me, but by the darker hair brushing against his ears and his broad shoulders, I'd guess he's one of Raff's grandsons, like Ryan and Patrick.

My dad glowers. "We're not handing over our phones."

"Liam," someone calls out. "They're fine. It's Sean."

"*Paul* works for the Hales," Liam retorts. "He could be recording us."

"I'm not," I snap. My pulse tries to accelerate. "I'm barely even employed at this point."

"Only *his* phone, Sean," Roark says, coming forward. He's scrawnier than the others. Pock marks scar his cheeks, and he's missing some bottom teeth. "It is what it is. Call it insurance."

My dad motions to me with his head.

Where is she? I swallow the words I want to scream, and I give Liam my phone. I'm banking on the idea that Oscar and Farrow never lost sight of me on my walk here.

They could have.

I didn't see Joana's car.

Liam unlocks the phone by hoisting the screen at my face. He checks my recent texts. I'm not an idiot. I deleted most threads before we arrived.

Then he throws my phone on the scratched floorboards. Screen shatters, and he stomps his boot on the device. Cousins laugh in the background, and others come over to kick it into the wall like a soccer ball. Pieces break off.

I control my breathing and speeding heart rate. I'm only moving my eyes. *Where is she?*

"That's good enough," my dad declares.

Liam locks gazes with me. "Strip."

My dad glares. "Come on."

"Most of us haven't seen your kid in over a decade, *Sean*," another man sneers, descending the staircase. Is Luna up there? Can't see beyond the darkness of the stairs, and I'm rocketed back to a memory. The townhouse in the Rittenhouse-Fitler district.

The fire.

I ran into the burning house. I ran to the staircase and looked up.

I was looking for Luna.

Back then, I was ordered in another direction and I couldn't go find her. I couldn't make sure she was okay.

Staring at this darkened staircase now, the urge to race up the steps throttles me. *Find her.* I gotta find her, but I can't alarm them. Can't make it seem like I'm against them.

"Paul," the man snarls, forcing my attention on him. He's reached the bottom few stairs and assesses me from head to toe. I can't place this guy at all, but he's around my dad's age. Looks more like Uncle Raff with the chocolate brown hair. His scruff hasn't grayed yet, and his surly expression is souring on me.

"Hugh," my dad greets with bite. "I just thought your kids were up to this shit. You really got in this mess too?"

"You want me to talk? He needs to strip down."

I'm not wasting more time. Quickly, I shed my old Van Halen shirt, each boot, each sock, and I step out of my jeans. They're gonna want me buck-naked, so I take off my boxer-briefs and cup my dick and balls.

"Turn around," Hugh orders.

I do a three-sixty. *Hurry.*

Colin comes at me with a laugh. "What's this shit?" He tries to rip off my kyber crystal necklace, and I expose my cock to shove him.

"Don't touch me," I warn.

"Jeezus." He glares like I bitch-slapped him again. "You've got serious problems, you know that?"

"You kidnapped a *Hale*," I sneer. "You're the one with the serious fucking problem." The living room tenses. Cousins exchange panicked glances.

"It wasn't kidnapping," someone says.

"Yeah, she came willingly," another guy says. "That's what you'll convince her to tell everyone. Won't you, Paul?"

I grind my teeth, tasting acid in my mouth. "No one in her family is gonna believe that."

Voices jumble, everyone throwing in their two cents at once.

"Time is of the fucking essence here," my dad cuts in harshly.

"Let's go to the kitchen," Hugh says and motions to Liam. "Pick up his clothes. Someone get Paul some underwear."

Just like that, we're in the cramped kitchen. Linoleum floors are peeling, and pizza boxes are stacked on a cheap plastic table. It stinks like spoiled milk, and sugar ants march up broken cabinets.

I'm putting on someone's boxer-briefs. Smells clean, otherwise I'd rather stay naked. They throw my clothes in the sink. Instead of running the faucet, they squirt lighter fluid on my oldest shirt. I watch them torch the Van Halen tee, and I feel nothing.

Absolutely nothing.

She's all that matters to me.

"Where's Luna Hale?" I ask them.

"Hold on." Hugh extends a hand. "Why do you think this is going south?" He's talking to my dad. "No one tracked us here."

"We heard they did. Through one of his security buddies." He turns to me to confirm.

"They know you're in the vicinity," I tell everyone. "We came here to warn you."

"We *never* shoulda taken her, Hugh," Roark chastises. "That wasn't the plan."

"You think I don't know that?" Hugh retorts angrily.

"Plans change," someone defends. Don't know him.

"What was the plan?" my dad asks. "Because this one was dumb as fuck. What'd you think would happen? They'd come looking for her. They'd find you. You'd all get slapped harder than you've *ever* been."

"I wasn't there," Hugh glares at Liam, at Ryan, at two others I can't name.

And then I hear a *thud* above us. My eyes shoot to the ceiling. "Is she up there?" I ask, and when no one answers, I can't help myself—I can't stay stationary—I run.

I bolt out of the kitchen and back towards the staircase.

"Paul!" they yell and chase after my breakneck speed. I've run away from that name most of my life, and I don't turn back.

I never turn back.

As I reach the banister, a cousin at the stairs tries to grab me, but I jerk out of his hold and thrust him against the wallpaper. He's skinny and coughs like I gut-punched him. Letting him go, I race up the stairs. No one else catches me.

"SEAN!" they yell at my dad.

"He's fine! *He's fine.* He's with us! Let him be! He's just worried about the fucking girl." Their arguing becomes background noise. Blood pumps in my head. My ears ring.

"Luna!" I yell and open a door in the short hallway. Bathroom. Empty. "Luna?!"

"Donnelly," she calls out, sounding near the end of the hall. *She's here.* It propels me to the last wooden door. I fling it open and step inside. Alarm barrels into my chest.

She's disoriented on a lopsided bed, her right wrist handcuffed to the wooden headboard. Her damp hair is tangled with ribbons, her eyes swollen from crying.

I latch the lock on the door and rush over. "Luna?" I press a knee to the mattress, and I touch her splotchy, tear-streaked cheeks. *Luna.* What'd they fucking do?!

"Donnelly." Her voice shatters, overwhelmed tears slipping out.

She's intaking the sight of me like I'm just fiction inside her head. "*Donnelly.*"

"I'm here. I'm here. *I'm here.*" Her tears roll over my hands, and her surge of relief rattles her body. I kiss her forehead, pain wrapping around my heart. She tries to embrace me but her handcuffed wrist tugs against the restraint.

An anguished noise claws up her throat.

"I'm getting you out," I say. Hurrying, I unclip my makeshift earring, a safety pin, from the cartilage of my ear.

She tries to steady her breathing. "My mom...where's my mom?" She blinks hard.

"She's safe with your dad." I sweep Luna quickly again. She's still wearing fishnets and shorts, but her hoodie is gone. "Did they touch you?" Sickness and wrath sear my throat, but there's no time to drown in feelings. I'm only rushing with the safety pin. I see a lamp lying sideways on the floor. I'm guessing that's the *thud* I heard from the kitchen.

"They just...picked me up," she croaks.

"They didn't try anything with you?" I ask, unable to even paint the fucking picture.

"No." She rubs her eyes with her free hand. "They...said something about...selling my hoodie, I think." Her voice sounds so small. "Donnelly."

"I'm right here." I clutch her cheek again, pink and purple streaks swiped on them. "I'm not going anywhere."

She tries to hold my gaze, but her eyes are flooded with tears. "I'm really scared," she cries. My heart breaks into a million serrated pieces.

She was never supposed to be in this house.

She was never supposed to meet my family.

She was never supposed to be swept into the darkness of my childhood. I'd left it all behind me, and to think that the *one* girl, the *only* girl, I've ever loved is hurtled to *this* place is fucking sickening. I hate it more than I've ever hated anything.

"I'm getting you outta here." I wiggle the safety pin into the lock of the handcuff. *Come on. Unlock, you motherfucker.*

She squeezes her eyes shut in pain.

"What hurts?" I ask.

"My head." She gulps air.

"Did they hit you with something?" I shift the safety pin to the left and hear a click. The handcuff comes undone, but Luna is slow to move. I help lower her weak arm to her chest.

"No. I think...I think I fell on the concrete."

I inspect the top of her head. No gashes. No blood. Just a small bump near her hairline. I think she'll be alright, but she needs a real doctor. She might have a concussion.

When she sits up more, she winces and her hand hovers near her abdomen. I lift her white T-shirt. Red welts blemish her ribcage like bad watercolor art. One rib looks sunken in, probably fractured. My blood boils. *I'm gonna kill them.* Whoever did this to her—I want to strangle against the wall.

I've never felt this furious, this *destructive*. Not in my lifetime.

"PAUL!" Someone knocks. "Come out!"

Luna clings to my biceps with panicked breaths. "Donnelly." Her fear is killing me all over again.

I gently touch the back of her head and whisper, "I'm not leaving you. *I'm not leaving you.*"

She blinks a few times, woozy, but she's trying to root herself to my assured gaze. Her eyes start falling to the blue kyber necklace.

While I'm bending to her, the crystal hangs between us like the force between me and her, and a swell of emotion pools underneath me, through me, through Luna. Love and light are the powers that've guided me. Been racing towards them my whole life. I just never realized all this time I've been racing towards her.

She wraps her weakened arms around me. "Where...where are we going?" she asks.

"To your planet, space babe." I scoop Luna into my arms, cradling her carefully against my chest, and she closes her eyes, seemingly breathing in my words like morphine. I whisper, "You're safe now. We're gonna fly there together."

She curls herself closer to my body. Her breaths slow.

"Don't fall asleep, alright?" I worry about her going unconscious. "Stay awake with me."

She barely nods.

"PAUL!"

"I'm coming!" I shout back. With Luna in my arms, I exit into the short hallway. Someone half my age, a *teenager*, is blocking my path to the stairs. He puffs out his chest like he's a threat, but a bad mixture of anger and pity rise inside me. "Get outta here, man." I walk past him.

He doesn't fight me. All bark.

Descending the staircase hurriedly, I hit the bottom stair. Everyone in the crowded living room zeroes in on me and Luna. My dad has his arms outstretched like he's been keeping the peace.

"What the fuck are you doing?!" someone shouts at me.

"What is he doing, Sean?!"

"Put the girl down!"

Luna is trembling in my arms. I hold her tighter to my firm chest. "You all go!" I shout at them. "Leave me here with her. I'll take the fall."

Mutterings, dismissals, refusals.

"How do we know the cops are even coming?" Ryan snaps. "They could be lying!"

My dad scowls. "Why the fuck would we be lying? Are you really that dumb?"

I glance at the door. Could I just bolt outside? *No.* Liam and someone larger are guarding the exit and eyeing me skeptically. If I charged at them, I couldn't fight 'em off. Not while carrying Luna, and they'd pry her out of my arms.

"They'll probably be here soon," I warn. "You could let me take her. I won't say anything to anyone."

"No fucking way," Colin spits. "We should at least take some pictures of her before—"

"Nah, there's no time," I cut in. *And fuck you.* Venom bleeds through me, and I shift my gaze so nobody can see that I'm pretending to care about them.

"No one has the names of who's involved tonight," my dad announces. "Either give Paul the girl or leave him with her. It's the smart thing to do."

They start talking over one another. Discussing more seriously. No one has left the row house yet, and suddenly, Luna goes limp in my arms. Her body slackens, and my pulse shoots to the moon.

"Luna," I murmur.

Luna. Luna. Luna.

She's dead weight. Unconscious, and I round the banister. "Get up. All of you. Get the fuck up," I tell the four guys on the couch, a boulder in my lungs.

They stand with their pipe and drugs, and I place Luna on the lumpy plaid cushions. Crouching down to her face, I touch her cheek tenderly. "Luna?"

She looks asleep. I press my fingers to her neck, feeling the slow *thump, thump, thump* of her pulse.

"Is she dead?" someone asks.

"Fuuuck," another guy curses. "I'm not going down for *murder*."

"Let him take the fall. He offered. We should let him."

More agreements.

"Nah, she's just playing," someone says.

"Just kick her. That woke her up the last time I did it." He laughs, and my head whips in the direction of that voice.

Patrick. He's a foot from me, and rage flames like lit gasoline in my veins. I stand and whirl around on him, my fist slamming into his face with the strength of my entire fucking body—physical, brute strength that I never had as a kid, not to this degree. The *crack* of his nose causes a few "ooohs" and winces from cousins, but no one assists him.

And no one stops me.

Not even as I throw a second, a third, a fourth *furious* punch into his face, and he's on the floor. My knuckles sting. My muscles and lungs sear, and I inhale the fire of my wrath like toxic fuel. Anger isn't a darkened boiling pool I ever blister this deeply inside, but I can't crawl out. A fifth, a sixth, a seventh fist to his face. I'm beating the shit outta him—he should be writhing or moaning, but he's trying to block my hand. He spits out a tooth. And he's laughing.

I hate meth.

He's numb to this pain. Now at least, and it staggers me back and on to my feet. Panting, I twist towards Luna, safe on the couch. I hover over her thin frame, about to lift her in my arms. She needs a doctor now.

"Shhhh!" my dad yells. "Do you hear that?"

Everyone goes quiet. I freeze, only hearing my heavy breaths.

And then...sirens.

"Cops," Colin says, sprinting to the backdoor, but it's too late. Every entrance whips open, and police swarm the row house.

"Hands up! Everyone!" Cops chase after my cousins who try to hurdle furniture and flee out kitchen windows. "Stay where you are! Don't move!"

"Shitshit," cousins curse.

"*Fuck.*"

I raise my hands, my pulse jackhammering. I haven't taken my eyes off Luna, so I don't sense a cop at my back.

I'm shoved hard to the floor. Chest meet Ground. His knee digs into my spine, and I turn my head so I can see Luna. "She needs—"

"Shut up," he sneers, yanking my wrists painfully behind my back. Cold metal clips around my wrists.

I can't leave her. I promised I wouldn't fucking leave her. I'm unblinking, knowing not to struggle, but I can't leave her. I can't leave Luna.

"On the floor!"

"Against the wall!"

"Hands behind your fucking back!"

The commands are jumbled with grunts, curses, and bodies thumping around the house. Police are saying something about the drugs and collecting evidence. I'm a second from shouting how she needs a fucking doctor, and then in sprints my best friend.

Farrow is running straight for Luna, his trauma bag already half-unzipped, and for a brief second, his eyes flash down to me. I'm handcuffed. On the ground. His focused gaze is suddenly stabbed with pain.

My chest collapses. Then the cop pries me off the floor by the wrists, pulling me to my feet. I stand and shout to Farrow, "She said she hit her head."

"On what?" He drops the trauma bag and assesses Luna.

"Concrete. The ground. She fell." The cop is pushing me towards the door. "Check her ribs!" It's all I can release before the cop carts me outside.

Holy fucking *shit.* Flashbulbs of cameras glare in the night. Police aren't the only ones on this skinny South Philly residential street. Paparazzi have arrived, and as soon as they see me, they go nuts in my face.

"Paul Donnelly!"

"Why are you being arrested?!"

"Are you behind the attack of Lily Calloway?!"

No.

No.

I stare hauntedly ahead, almost numb. Cold barely bites at my flesh, still only wearing a stranger's boxer-briefs.

"Where are your clothes?!"

"Get a shot of his tattoos! The one of Satan on his back!"

"What'd you do to Lily Calloway?!"

It wasn't me.

Defenses ring in my ears, but I know not to say anything.

Squinting against more camera flashes, I spot Joana's car on the curb. Nearby, Oscar is talking heatedly in his phone, and once he sees me, his lips stop moving.

The world stills.

Bet this wasn't on his Bingo card. *Watch Donnelly get arrested for his family.* If there was a time my friends thought I'd go to jail, it'd be for pissing outside after a night at the bars. It'd be for streaking on a college campus. It'd be for defending one of them at a club and getting in a fucking brawl.

It'd never be for my family.

It'd never be for this.

Truth is, I've never been arrested. My rap sheet is squeaky clean, thanks to my cockroach tendencies and a whole lotta luck.

Guess that's changing.

Oscar steps forward, then halts, looking tormented. He can't help me. *It's alright*, I wish I could tell him. *I was always going to survive.* I'm not the one he should be worrying about.

Luna is still inside, and the only thing keeping me calm is the fact that Farrow is with her.

"Get in." The cop pushes my head down while I duck into the police car.

"DONNELLY!" paparazzi shout over and over.

He slams the door, drowning out the mayhem.

Arms imprisoned behind my back, I cast short glances at the window, hoping to see Luna come out with Farrow. Every time I look outside, flashes ignite and I can't see shit. I can't even contemplate what kind of photos they're capturing of me or what'll hit the internet.

I don't even care.

An older cop with a grayed mustache slides into the driver's seat. He shuts out the chaos, and the car is hushed again. He taps on the screen near the steering wheel. "Sorry about the cuffs. We have to treat you like the others." His brown eyes meet mine through the rearview mirror. "We can't let anyone know you're the informant. You understand?"

I nod once. "Yeah."

"We'll have to book you."

I blow forward. "I need to be with her at the hospital. I can't be stuck in a holding cell—"

"It's important that no one in your family knows you drew us here. It'd put you at risk, and that'd put the Hales at risk again. And frankly, your involvement is an asset we can't lose right now, so just hang tight."

I go quiet. I barely blink in the passing minutes. My eyes feel dryer and dryer.

I only awaken when he gets off the phone and tells me, "We're putting someone else in the car with you."

I edge over to one side and make room for them. God, I hope it's not Colin. Or Patrick. The car door opens, and mixed emotions course through my body as my dad slides next to me, hands bound behind his back.

He's silent at first. His face is set in harsher lines while he looks ahead. "What's the saying?" He speaks as we're driven to the station. "Like father, like son."

I lean back into the seat. Unable to glance at him. All I can think is, *fuck me.*

"HEY, *HEY*," I CALL OUT IN THE JAIL CELL, MY ankles and wrists chained and a thin metal bench under my ass. Blood is caked and dried on my busted knuckles. The cop on duty ignores me completely. "I need a phone call. Just one call! Please!"

Nothing. *Goddammit.* Frustration and fear are eating at my patience, and I just need to know she's alright. I've heard from no one in probably five hours. Time is agonizing here.

"They're not gonna let you call anyone." My dad is chained beside me. He's the only other person in this holding cell. Must be purposeful since private security and the police have been working together for a while now. Police have been informed that I'm the rat for a lot longer than just tonight.

My dad, though—he has no clue I'm the reason the cops *actually* showed up. He didn't know Farrow and Oscar were tailing me from the Rhino. He has no idea what I've been doing, and even if he stuck his neck out for me, I couldn't tell him the truth and take that risk.

Still can't tell him.

Guilt shouldn't gnaw at me like a monster at my heels, but it's arrived somehow. Probably because I couldn't have convinced my family I'm on their side without him. They would've never let me inside that house.

"You still on parole?" I ask quietly.

"Yep." He stares ahead like this is same old, same old.

He'll be thrown back in prison for breaking parole. They one hundred percent found large quantities of meth there. Kidnapping and assault—he might have a good alibi from bartending at the Rhino, but it won't matter too much. He was around drugs tonight, and that's enough to send him back.

He's gonna go back to prison because of me. It's never happened like this before. I've never been a cause or a reason my dad has hit this bad square on the Monopoly board.

"This is your first time?" he asks me.

"Yeah." Feels like bees stung my throat.

"They might let you out."

I say nothing.

He shifts his ass, the seat uncomfortable, and the chains jingle at his ankles. "Someone will come post bail for you."

"Why are you so sure?" I ask him.

"'Cause you're not like the rest of us, Donnelly." It takes me aback, hearing him call me that. His blue eyes finally meet mine. "You never really were. And according to your mom, that's always been a good thing."

"And according to you?" I wonder.

"I've never wanted you to follow us to prison, if that's what you're asking, but I do wish you stuck around." He lifts his shoulders in a tight shrug. "You're my kid. I do love you, you know."

Nah, I don't know. The love he had for me was buried underneath his love for drugs, and I didn't spend time trying to dig it out. Now, it feels different. It's like he's been unearthing that love himself, without asking me to do any heavy-lifting, and it's making *this* hard—sitting handcuffed in jail beside him, knowing he's taking the fall for me.

He looks me over as though mourning time soon-to-be lost. "Ey, it was a good run." He smiles off in the distance. "Can't ask for more, can I?"

I can pull strings. Could I?

Maybe that's not the right question.

Should I?

"Donnelly," a cop calls out.

Our eyes shoot forward.

She glances up from an electronic tablet. "Paul Donnelly. You've posted bail." In a matter of minutes, she's unlocked the cell and me from the bench and chains. Rubbing my sore wrists, I step out while the hefty metal slings shut.

"What about him?" I ask her under my breath.

She leads me down a hallway and whispers, "With major felony charges, the court has suspended the right to post bail for the rest of your family. He'll likely be held until his hearing or until the court changes its decision. There's a vehicle waiting for you out back. Press can't see you've been released this quickly, or else it'll blow your cover."

I'm shocked they decided to release me at all then.

She sees my surprise. "Your security firm has ensured us you'll enter the hospital undetected."

The hospital. I don't ask her about Luna. I'm brought to the rear lot of the police station, where paparazzi are forbidden to go, and I climb into the back of an SUV, windows tinted pitch-black.

The driver throws a red baseball cap and a pair of gray sweatpants at me. "That's all I had in the car."

"Thanks, boss." I sound a little choked, but I put the Studio 9 baseball cap on, brim low over my eyes.

"You okay?" Akara turns to me.

"Is Luna?" I ask him.

He can't hide his wince. "She hasn't woken up, Donnelly."

My nose flares. My heart is being shredded alive. "And Lily?" I wonder now.

He just shakes his head, unable to speak. It takes him a second. "We're headed there. You did a really good job tonight."

"No," I tell him, my insides crushing with this cold reality. "I was too late."

PART·TWO

"While you slept, the world changed."

- Xavier, House of X #6

24

Luna Hale

STERILE LIGHTS BEAM down on me in hot waves, and I imagine this is it. *I'm on a spaceship.* Taken away by an intergalactic species to be experimented on or be crowned queen. A hammer swings against my head, *thumping* and *thumping*. My bones feel like seven-tons of bricks. Are there bricks on this planet?

Have I turned to stone?

Am I still even on Earth? I'm sinking…or I'm too drained to move.

I squint harder and try to distinguish shapes, but everything is just *fuzzy*.

Maybe I'm dreaming. One of those half-awake kind of dreams that's sleepy and fogged. They're not my favorite. I like the vivid tapestries of my imagination to overtake my subconscious. Not this cloudy, murky distorted confusion.

In a concerted effort, I fight to wake from this blurry no-good dream. I blink more and concentrate on the harsh lights. My surroundings gradually sharpen into a clearer picture, but the throbbing in my skull doesn't recede.

My stomach lurches as I take in the beige drapes and ugly matching chair pushed under the window. A TV on the wall plays a rerun of *Gilmore Girls* on mute. Closest to me, a heart monitor beeps, and cords are attached to me, plugged into hefty machines and IV bags.

What…

Beeping quickens on the machine, and my heart tries to jettison from my body.

This is a hospital room.

I'm in a hospital room.

I'm stuck on the one thought, mentally stepping into superglue. My mouth is so dry, tongue thick and strange. I lick my chapped lips.

"Hey…" Someone speaks gently.

I follow the sound of the soft, soothing voice to the darkened corner of the room. Sitting on a cushioned chair, the man slowly stands and approaches the hospital bed. I squint harder, piecing together his features.

A hoop piercing in his lip, barbells in his brow, a black dangly earring—I think I know him. The tattooed skull and crossbones on the tops of his hands seem familiar, as do the inked swords on his throat and wings on his neck.

Why is his hair brown? "You…dyed your hair," I croak, my throat raw. Words come out coarse. *Is that his natural hair color?* Have I seen it before? I swallow, and I skim his black V-neck, black pants. He often wears the same thing, and this familiarity tries to ease me.

I do recognize him.

Farrow. *Farrow.*

The name washes over me with not enough tranquility. I'm too confused to relax, and I feel like I've been in a head-on collision with the Millennium Falcon. My whole body *hurts.*

He's filling a plastic cup of water and studying the machines and me. "How are you feeling?"

I can't even wrap my brain around how to answer. I blink a few more times, hoping to clear more fog. "What…happened?" I rasp and look around for my mom and dad. My brothers and sister. If something bad happened to me, they'd be here, right? Unless…unless…

Dread heavies my stomach.

If they're not here, it means something bad happened to them. I'm too afraid to pose the question. Beeping goes haywire on the machine, and the sound intensifies the gavel swinging in my head.

"Just take a deep breath," Farrow says in a comforting voice. It coaxes me out of my jumbled thoughts, but the beeping is escalating my headache.

"Stop," I plead into a wince.

"It's your heartbeat," Farrow tells me, still calm. "Just take a breath."

I do as he says, and I silently remind myself that all is okay. *Farrow is here.*

Farrow is here. Why is he here? I intake a sharper breath. Where's his dad? Dr. Keene? The questions blip in and out of my brain.

I try to lift myself up, but my bones shriek in protest. I wince and cringe, pain blossoming throughout my body.

"Stay still. I'll sit you up," Farrow tells me, coming to my rescue with the bedside remote. "What's your pain level? From zero being no pain to ten being the worst you've ever felt?" Slowly, the bed elevates on its own, and I'm propped in a sitting position.

"Seven, maybe," I whisper. "It just hurts."

"What does?"

My whole body. I think I answer him out loud. Maybe I didn't. I can't be sure.

He snaps on new gloves, fiddles with the IV. I dizzy watching him move around the room, so I stop tracking his steps.

"Just relax," he says casually, his voice helping me breathe.

Once he pulls a stool closer to the bed and sits beside me, I fixate on him again. He offers me water from the plastic cup, and I take small sips to soothe my raw throat.

"Can you describe how you're feeling?" Farrow asks.

"Confused," I mutter. "My head hurts a lot."

Farrow nods like that's understandable. I don't see how. "You had a traumatic brain injury. You fell and hit your head on the street, on concrete."

Oh.

I frown. "I don't remember that," I say quietly. "I feel fine except for the headache. Can I go home?" I don't want to be here. I want to see my mom. My dad. Moffy. Xander. Kinney.

My heartbeat accelerates again. *Beepbeepbeepbeep.* The frantic noise is a violent jackhammer in my brain. I let out a soft groan.

"It's okay." Farrow stands up to lower the volume on the machine. My breathing steadies, and I zone in on the mirrored blood-red sparrows on his collarbones. They fly through masts of identical pirate ships. Between them is a half-skull on his sternum.

Beautiful in all its symmetry. I've always loved his tattoos. *But is that one…new?* Next to a red sparrow is a name. Inked clearly. Visibly. *Maximoff.*

My brother's name.

I must be dreaming now. Or hallucinating.

"Why is Moffy's name tattooed on you?" The words are tight in my aching ribs.

Farrow steps away from the machine and glances at his collarbone peeking from the V-neck. Then he looks at me. He frowns for a second before gently taking a seat again. "Do you know your name?" he asks.

"Luna Hale," I say, confident about this. "Luna with No Middle Name Hale. That's what Tom likes to call me." My voice sounds frail.

I gulp more water and taste my strange tongue. How long have I been asleep? Is that why my mouth feels so odd? The questions flash in and out again.

Farrow nods like I'm on the right path with my name. I try to relax, and I rub at my tired eyes.

"Do you know what day it is?" he asks.

The calendar feels fuzzy. *How long have I been here?* I search the room again, eyeing the TV. *Gilmore Girls* is playing. I notice the beeping monitors. The IV bags. I recognize Farrow on the stool, bent forward with a serious face.

Why isn't his hair bleach-blond?

"What happened?" I ask quietly. I barely hear my own voice. "Why am I in the hospital?"

He's calm as he answers, "You fell and hit your head on concrete."

Oh.

I don't remember that.

He takes a deep breath and adds, "You had a CT scan done, and there's no hemorrhaging or clots in your brain. But you might experience some post-traumatic amnesia. That means storing memories and information right now might be difficult. It might also be hard to access past memories from before the injury."

My stomach somersaults. "How long does that last?"

"It varies," Farrow says.

I frown harder, not liking the vagueness of that answer.

Farrow runs a hand over his mouth and lip piercing, contemplating something. After a second, he tells me, "For mild brain injuries, less than twenty-four hours. For moderate brain injuries, that could be anywhere from one to seven days. Anything more is severe."

Mild. Moderate. Severe.

I'm afraid of where I fall, but I'm more afraid to ask how long I've been in the hospital. Farrow—the more I inspect him, the more he's the same but different in a way. I can't pinpoint why other than I'm still half-asleep.

"So this isn't a dream?" I ask while he refills my water. "Because it feels an awful lot like a dream." The fuzziness, especially. Like my brain hasn't fully *awakened* yet. Fear clings to me like too tight plastic wrap around my head. What if I can never wake up? What if I'm stuck floating through a haze forever?

"It's not a dream," Farrow assures. He stands, grabs an electronic tablet from the wall, then returns to the stool. "I'm going to ask you some questions. You up for that?"

My eyes sting, too dry. I blink a few more times. "I guess." I scan the room. "What about my mom and dad? Can I see them?" *Are they okay? Why aren't they here?*

"You can see them after you're evaluated," Farrow says. I suppose that if I can't see my family right now, Farrow is the next best option. He's a person I'd choose to be with me.

"You're the one evaluating me?" I ask hopefully, but also a little puzzled. "Nobody else?"

He nods. "Right now, it's just me." He reaches out and takes my hand.

I inhale, exhale. His tattoos are so beautiful. I look around the room again. The drapes are too beige, but I recognize the Stars Hollow gazebo on the TV screen. Some network must be airing *Gilmore Girls* reruns. Soft beeps emit from the heart monitor, and I focus on Farrow, about to ask him why I'm at the hospital.

But bits and pieces of information float around my brain.

Head injury. Something like that?

I fell, I think.

I don't ask.

I try and think hard about the injury. But nothing pops in my head.

Except for the mental image of a room. Not one in the hospital. This looks more like a home. Drab with scuffed floorboards and old floral wallpaper. It's a weird image, barely even a memory. Feels more like a movie I once saw and not somewhere I've been.

In all the fics I've ever written, I don't think I've ever penned a story with amnesia. Then again, would I even remember if I did?

"WHAT'S YOUR NAME?" FARROW ASKS THE FIRST question.

"Luna Hale." I use the remote to prop myself even higher. He's already asked about my pain levels again, and I feel a little less run over. Likely, I'm being pumped full of meds, and I'm not complaining. The baby blue hospital gown swallows my frame, and I stay underneath the white blankets. The tubes and wires on my body aren't annoying me as much as my foggy mind.

I touch strands of my light brown hair. Green…ribbon? When did I tie ribbon in my hair?

Farrow types on the skinny keyboard of the tablet. I wish I had X-ray vision to see if I'm on the right track. At least I know who I am.

Right?

Riiiight?

Okay, what if I'm *not* Luna Hale? What if she's a famous pop singer, and I woke up believing I'm her. Uhhhh, that sounds like a total nightmare.

I grimace and slouch a little.

I'm starting to hate my imagination.

"When were you born?" he asks question number two.

"November thirtieth." I include the year after Farrow asks for it, and again…he scribbles. *Please do not fail this, Luna.* I pick at my thumbnail and watch him type. He could just be checking off correct answers too.

"Where do you live?" he asks.

"Philly," I answer and try lifting myself a bit more. Strength, come to me! I've never been great with upper-body activities, but this shouldn't be so tough. My arms are jelly.

"You want to sit up higher?" He reaches for the remote.

"No, I'm fine," I say quietly. *I wanted to do it myself.* I whack-a-mole my disappointment pretty poorly, but maybe I should just concentrate on his questions and not my body. To show I'm cognitively aware, I add more details, "I live with my parents in a gated neighborhood."

His fingers hover over the keyboard for a split-second before he types again.

I frown. "Not Villanova. That's where my grandparents live."

He nods.

Okay, that was good…right? I sweat a little, but pushing aside the blankets seems too strenuous right now. I tug at the collar of my hospital gown.

"You want the heavier blanket off you?" Farrow asks. So perceptive, he's studying each of my tiny movements.

"I'm okay." I don't want anyone to worry. I want to ace this test. Return to my regular abnormal life.

"You're not hot?" he questions.

"No," I lie.

Farrow looks straight through me. It's unnerving, but I don't look away.

"I'm fine," I whisper.

"Wanting to be okay and needing the help to get there are two different things, and you shouldn't be scared to need help. See, I won't judge you. I won't treat you like you're fragile glass, if that's not your thing. I'm just here to help you."

I want to trust him. He's Farrow, but he's…different. I still can't place how or why. I'm struggling to even trust my own thoughts right now.

"I'm a little hot," I say more honestly. "But the blankets can stay."

"You change your mind, I can help." He raises his brows, and I nod. His gaze softens in a comforting way. He asks, "Where are you now?"

I look around. "The hospital?" I don't know why I phrase it like a question.

"Do you know the name of the hospital?"

Drapes are closed, shutting out the light or the dark. I'm guessing I'm still in Philadelphia, which would mean… "I think Philly General." I try to sound confident.

Farrow types. This time, he takes a bit longer. I sip more water.

"When were you admitted to this hospital?" he asks.

I set the cup down slowly, my stomach dropping. "I don't know." Has it been days? Weeks? Months? *Years?*

"How did you get here?"

"I don't know." Panic shoots through me. "Should I know this? Was I even conscious?"

Farrow takes a steady breath. "I can't give you information until I see how much you remember on your own." I wonder if he already broke a rule by telling me I hit my head.

Then again, I still can't remember the exact details of *how* I hit my head. Did he mention it and I just forgot?

Farrow focuses on me. "What's the first event you can remember after your injury?"

I think about that room. Floral wallpaper. Scuffed floorboards. Was that before or after my injury? And…and is that even real at all?

It might be from an *actual* movie. Like *Matilda*? No…that's not it.

My temples throb. "I remember you. Here in this room."

"Can you give me more details?"

"We've been talking…or I've been asking questions, I think? Now you're asking questions. There's a lot of questions." I let out a nervous laugh.

Farrow gives me a warm smile that instantly eases me inside this awful situation. Like my life isn't imploding before my eyes.

"Can you describe the last event you can recall *before* the accident?" he asks.

"There was an accident?" I say. "Like a car accident?"

His face tenses. He pauses, assesses, then says, "Before your injury."

I wrack my brain. *Before* my injury? What was I even doing yesterday? Or was it this morning? How long have I been in this hospital?

Shit.

Um…oh I know! I have it!!

I inch up the bed. Barely budging, but in my excitement, I gain some super strength. "We had family dinner last night," I say into a confident nod, the words surging out of me. "Mom cooked meatloaf, and Moffy told everyone that Declan is retiring. He's getting a new bodyguard soon, and he's completely freaked out about it because Declan has been with him forever."

Farrow isn't looking at me. He's busy typing. I think I aced this. I blow out a breath. It's okay. I'm going to be okay.

"What time is it now?" he asks.

The draped windows aren't offering any answers. I search for a clock. Is this cheating? Maybe, but I can't find a good resource anyway. "Early morning maybe? Seven a.m.?" It's a wild guess.

"What day of the week is it?"

I bite the edge of my lip. "Saturday."

"The month? All I need is the date."

I puff out my cheeks in another breath. Let's see. I remember Moffy's 22nd birthday. It was a few days ago. He was born on July 13th. So it has to be… "The sixteenth."

Farrow presses the delete button. I swear he does! I blink a ton and press my head back to the fluffy pillow. *Calm down.* If I freak out, no one will think I'm healthy enough for answers.

I want answers.

"What's the month?" he asks.

"July." I imagine opening the drapes and seeing the sunshine and blue skies of summer.

"The year?"

I do mental math and give Farrow the correct year. The best part of this year will be my eighteenth birthday, which can't come soon enough.

He's trying to type faster, maybe seeing it's jolting my nerves. My stomach twists as my confidence begins to wane.

I stare at the ceiling panels. "How hard did I fail this thing?" Maybe I should be asking how hard I *fell*.

"This test isn't a pass or fail," Farrow says casually. "I'm just trying to determine if you still have post-traumatic amnesia. It's important we keep track of that because once your PTA ends, we can determine how severe your brain injury is and what kind of care and treatment you need."

I really like that Farrow is providing info like I'm an adult. Like I can handle this even with a head injury.

He adds, "Your orientation to your own person and to place is accurate. However, your orientation to time tells me that you still have post-traumatic amnesia."

Time.

How much time am I off by?

He tells me PTA can be retrograde or anterograde. Basically, I can experience memory loss of past events from before the injury or memory loss of future events.

I don't know what's worse.

He doesn't tell me which I have yet, and I don't ask. I don't even remember if he's told me how long PTA is supposed to last. Maybe he has.

I don't want to ask again and seem worse than I am.

"So what now?" I wonder.

"We're going to keep you here overnight for observation," Farrow says. "Tomorrow, we'll see how you're feeling, and I'm going to call a neuropsychologist to come and talk to you and your family."

Awesome.

"Can I see them?" I wonder.

He nods. "Yeah, but I'm going to talk to them first, so it'll be a few minutes at least." He trashes his medical gloves.

I take a breath, my gaze falling to the red sparrows along his collarbones. His tattoos are so, so beautiful.

Wait…is that…? My brother's name! My eyes widen. I'm about to inquire more about it when I notice a *wedding* band. It has to be one. It's on his ring finger!

What.

The.

Fuck?

Does that mean…?

The ring. The new tattoo…?

Is he married to my brother??? When did this happen?! How *could* this happen?!

"Wait, Farrow!" I call out. He spins around to face me, and my pounding heart tries to eject from my body again. He eyes the monitor as I ask in a whisper, "You're married?"

He swallows hard, then combs a hand across his hair. He just nods.

"To whom? When?" I press my fingers to my forehead, and in doing so, I catch sight of black ink on my arm. *I have a tattoo?!* My pulse spikes. "Is-is this your handwriting?" I stare at music lyrics in Farrow's familiar scrawl. I instantly recognize his handwriting from all the birthday cards he's given me throughout the years.

"Luna—"

I touch my tongue with my fingers now. "Oh my God," I mumble. No wonder my mouth felt strange—I have a tongue piercing! Anxious tears begin to build, and in a panic, I kick down blankets so I can see my legs. What if they're missing too?

Farrow rushes back to me. "You're okay, Luna."

"Nonono." Uncontrollable tears squeeze out of my eyes, and Farrow helps roll down the hefty blankets. Both of my legs are intact. I'm not a bionic woman, but is that…? I lift the hem of my hospital gown. Intricate lines swirl around my thigh in a gorgeous galaxy— another tattoo. I trace inked planets and stars. How many more do I have? Why don't I remember getting any of them?

"Take a big breath," he says.

I'm taking short, sharp breaths. "Who did you marry?" I rub at my wet eyes. "Did…did I miss your wedding while I was asleep? How much have I missed?" It terrifies me, and only when Farrow sits on the edge of the bed and hugs me do I stop gasping for breath.

He whispers consoling phrases, "You're okay. Just breathe with me." His heartbeat is powerful and reassuring, the thuds comforting me in silent seconds.

I hang on to him like he's a buoy in a turbulent ocean. "I need to know," I say shakily. "I need to know, Farrow."

He pulls back a little, his hands on my shoulders. He holds my gaze, and I search his eyes for the past. I can't see anything beyond the present.

Then he says, "I married your brother." He pauses. "But he'd tell you that he married me."

Happiness is submerged beneath a swell of despair. "I wasn't there." *I missed it.*

"No, you were there," Farrow says, getting choked up. He clears his throat, looks to the left, then back at me. "You were in my grooms' party. You were in the procession walking ahead of me."

I'm crying. "I don't remember."

He snatches a tissue box off the nearby tray table. "You've been through a lot—"

"That's just it," I cut him off. "I don't even know what I've gone through. I don't even know how much time I've actually lost." I blow my runny nose in a tissue that he hands me. My eyes feel more tender and swollen. "I mean, you married my *brother*?" It seems unbelievable.

How could this amazing thing happen? How could I have forgotten?

"And-and," I stammer, "you're acting like my doctor, but you're just a bodyguard. Your dad is my doctor."

He shakes his head. "I'm your doctor, and I'm also Maximoff's bodyguard."

My jaw hits the floor. "*You* replaced Declan? Moffy would've hated that…" I trail off, not just because Farrow is starting to smile but because I remember my brother married him in the end.

"This all might come back to you soon," Farrow reassures me. "Don't get too hung up on it." He can tell I'm overwhelmed.

I've just discovered I have multiple tattoos, a tongue piercing, and a brother-in-law. It's the tip of a humongous iceberg, and to dive even deeper is a brain freeze I might not be ready for. But I don't want to panic more and overly concern him and my family.

I wet my dry lips. "Can you just tell me how long I've been here? In the hospital?" *How long have I been asleep?* "Have I missed years?"

"No," he says with certainty.

I inhale a stronger breath. "Months?"

"It's barely been six hours," Farrow says.

The accident happened recently then. Was it an accident? Did he say it was a car crash? I can't remember…

"When can I see my mom and dad?" I ask him. "Where's Moffy?"

He tells me he's going to talk to them first. They'll come in soon. *Okay.* I breathe fuller breaths. "Can…can I see my phone?" I mutter as he heads to the door.

He nods. "I'll have a nurse bring in your personal items." He takes a beat, sucking in a wince. "But I'd advise *not* looking at the internet. Can you do that?"

"Yeah," I say, but I don't even know if I'm lying to him or to myself.

He nods again, sweeps me from afar. I spot his concern, but I'm unsure if it's normal doctorly concern or something more personal. I'm missing time, and in that time, did my relationship with Farrow change at all? Did we grow apart or closer?

It tries to unsettle me, so I focus more on the familiarity of him. "Thank you," I whisper, resting back against the bed with a deep exhale.

"You need me, I'm one call button away." He motions to the buttons on the bedframe, and I nod. Farrow gives me a warm consoling smile before leaving, but I wonder if he's stepping out into the hallway with certain dread.

I wonder if he thinks I'm a lost cause.

I bite the edge of my fingernail. "Memories, don't fail me," I whisper to myself. I try so very hard to remember what happened to me.

Another flash.

Another picture frame.

Another glimpse.

Anything.

But it's like grabbing air in a darkened room. There's nothing to hold on to. Nothing to touch. Nothing to see.

It's all just...

Gone.

25

Paul Donnelly

OSCAR TOWERS ABOVE me and tries to hand me a flimsy paper cup of water.

With my head in my hands, I'm sitting against the hard hallway wall outside the visitors' room in Philly General. Glass doors to the ICU remain locked right now. No visitors allowed, and so everyone's relegated to a morbid, stuffy room with blue chairs, a coffee bar, and a few tables. Haven't been in there though.

For one, it seems like a morgue.

For another, it's mostly full of Hales—plus, Lily's sisters and their husbands. Everyone else is back at the Cobalt Estate with Jane and Thatcher, I've heard.

Don't know where I should be, so I've just waited in the hall for better news. I shake my head at Oscar and rest my forearms on my knees. "I just want her to wake up," I mutter. *What if she never does?* I'd lift the collar of my shirt to my burning eyes, but I'm not wearing one.

Still shirtless.

Still in Akara's sweatpants.

Still reeling from tonight.

Oscar downs the water in one gulp. "We all do, bro." He crushes the paper cup and free-throws it into a nearby trashcan. "For both of them."

I shut my eyes, pushing back horrific images of Lily on the news.

She'd been in so much pain that doctors put her in a medically-induced coma. I can't stand knowing I'm a piece that caused this shit to happen. I can't stand seeing the families this broken up.

"I shouldn't be here," I choke out and rise to my feet. I don't know where to go. I can't leave the hospital and risk paparazzi seeing me.

"Hey." Oscar catches my shoulder before I turn. "*You* found her. You just got arrested and sat in jail to protect the Hales. You are a shirtless motherfucker right now, but you're not a villain."

Jokes wither in my head. I stare at one of my best friends like he's watching a different movie where I'm the star. "I'm cleaning up a mess I made. Does that seem very heroic to you?"

"*Their* mess isn't yours." He points down the hall. "Your family is here. You've never been a dumb motherfucker, so I know you get this. Your family is *here*."

It digs deeper into me.

His phone starts ringing. "Charlie," he reads the screen and sighs. It's been a long night, and I'm still playing catch-up with all I missed while in jail.

I nod for him to take it.

He props the phone to his ear. "Yeah?" While Oscar disappears down the hall, I stare ahead at the visitors' room. *The Hales.* They're in there.

I wish I had something to give them. Tomato pie. Some Wawa coffees. I have no wallet to even buy vending machine candy bars. All I've got is me.

Normally, I'd say that's more than enough.

As I stride forward, I've still gotta believe it is.

I want to brave the sight of Luna's family, and I open the door and slip inside the eerily quiet visitors' room. Been here before. When I was much younger, I tried to find Farrow during his rounds or rotations. I don't remember the correct terminology, but he'd been out of med school.

It was empty then.

Now it's half-full. The room deadens even more on my arrival.

Last time I saw Lo, he'd been destroyed and just barely holding it together in the ambulance. I know what I expected now. I thought he'd be smothered with worry by his brother Ryke, but he's not.

Ryke is offering Lo a wide berth of space. So is Connor.

The two of them are standing with Maximoff near the coffee bar, the only three on their feet. Ryke is also holding a sleeping Baby Ripley.

I can't look at the baby for too long.

Seeing me, Lo goes from a slouch to a pin-straight position. He's next to Xander. My little elf wears bulky red headphones, likely listening to music in the corner. The seventeen-year-old looks the most shattered of anyone—when I thought that'd be Lo. It's his son.

It sinks my gut.

I take off my baseball hat. Seems like the polite thing to do.

"I..." What do I even say? I just tore through my past to pry out and protect what I thought would be my future. *Luna.* Every time I picture Luna in that house, handcuffed on that bed, pain and rage rip inside my heart, and oxygen is acid. Burning me alive, inside-out.

I blink away the image. Suffocated by it, I turn around to leave.

"Stay," Lo says, his voice sandpapered but sharp.

He wants me to stay? By the time it processes, he's walking over to me. Everyone is watching, but I can't tear my gaze off Xander's dad. What'd I think he'd be? Angry, judgmental, pissed off that I'm the malevolent thing attached to his family, ready to kick my ass to Montana, wishing he'd already done it weeks ago?

But he's none of those things.

His reddened eyes are windows into my heartbroken soul, and I blink back the surge of emotion. Flashes of the row house, stripping down, clothes on fire, Luna in my arms, knuckles searing, leaving without her, then the bright cameras, cop car, behind bars, waiting—it all courses through me.

I just want her to wake up.

"I tried..." I hear my voice shake.

Lo puts a hand on my shoulder. And he pulls me into a hug. It almost breaks me. Then he whispers, "I know."

I start to shake my head.

"You did enough," he breathes.

My hand flies to my pained face. Been thinking I could never do enough in his eyes, so I can hardly believe it. "I didn't." *She might never wake up.*

I don't want to survive without her. I've never felt this crushing feeling in my life. It's worse than drowning. Worse than being lit on fire. Worse than Luna's biggest fear—floating endlessly in space.

I'd rather do all of those things than feel this.

He pulls back. I pinch my wet eyes and face him as he says sharply, "You didn't put her there. You got her out." He sounds as choked as I feel. "And I know…" He trails off, his throat thick with emotion. His brows are cinched. He runs his tongue over his molars, collecting himself. "I know what that took." He's trying to be grateful, but it's buried beneath a lot of anguish. "They'll make it out. Luna. Lily. They look small, but they're tough."

The shred of hope I'd given him earlier tonight, he's returning to me. Can't lie about how much I need it. I'm carrying this hope like a lit match. One wrong breath and it'll extinguish.

"Yeah. They will," I say quietly.

He pats my bicep, and when we split apart, he goes to talk to his brother. Across the room, Kinney is avoiding my gaze. Her fingers are paused on a page of a comic book. She's at a table with the Calloway sisters and her Aunt Willow. A *Superheroes & Scones* tote bag of comics is spilled out in front of the sixteen-year-old Hale.

I see Xander all alone.

He's studying me, so I approach my client—one who's been holed up at home since he learned I love his sister. So I haven't been on his detail in weeks.

"This seat free?" I ask, nodding to the one beside him.

"Yeah." He lifts himself out of a slump and watches me sit. "It's morbid over here, just to warn you."

"That's alright," I say softly. "It's morbid everywhere. Hospitals aren't usually cheery."

"No kidding," he mutters, then sniffs hard. He yanks the head-phones to his neck, his amber eyes glassy from tears.

"Watcha listening to?"

"Uh…" He sniffs again. "Bob Dylan. Loretta Lynn…" He shrugs. "Banks got me into it a while back. I like it, but…honestly, it's all kind of depressing right now." Quickly, angrily, he wipes an escaped tear off his cheek. "I was supposed to be in that car, Donnelly. My mom—she asked me to go to the fucking Putt Palace, and I said *no*." His voice cracks. "I said no, and I should've been there. Then you might've been in the car with us. *Everything* would've been different. Better."

"We don't know that," I breathe.

"Yes, *I do*," Xander professes quietly to me. "It's like my choices in life have these catastrophic repercussions. I made a shitty selfish choice that hurt my sister, my mom, and now they're both in the ICU. For what? Because I was scared to confront you?" Face twisting, he slumps back in his chair. "I'm such a fucking—"

"Elf," I interject.

"What?"

"Didn't you say elves were sorta selfish? I dunno, they've always seemed dope to me." I know he loves them the most in fantasy worlds too. I catch him staring at my busted knuckles. "You wanna know something?"

He nods once, listening.

"I've made a bunch of shitty selfish choices in my twenty-nine years, and I can't say that I regret a single one."

Xander frowns. "How?"

"'Cause it's okay to put yourself first and chase after the things you want or run away from the things you don't. Life's too short to try to be perfect for everyone else."

He's quiet for a beat. "What if I'm not happy with myself?" He's staring at the floor.

I look him over, my lungs tightening. "You bailed on putt-putt, man. You didn't bail on your sister or your mom."

He rubs his runny nose with the back of his arm. "I'm sorry." It comes out constricted.

"Don't be."

"I am, though," he says more clearly. "When I heard you had feelings for Luna, my whole...fucking world crashed. It feels so stupid now." He tilts his head to meet my gaze. "I used to want the Moretti brothers to marry into my family, you know? I thought it'd be cool to always have them around."

I frown. "They did end up doing that."

"Yeah, and it's not the same as how I thought it'd be...so when you came along, I liked knowing I have *all* of your attention." His shaggy hair touches his wet eyelashes. "And I thought you'd stick around forever. Not for her, but for me. And now—*now*, I'd give *anything* for my sister to be okay. I'd change places with her in a heartbeat. I'd rather be dead."

It stabs me. "She wouldn't want that," I tell him quietly.

His chest caves. He stares at my bloodied fists again. "I'm selfish enough to hate when I am selfish, but not selfish enough to thrive on my own. I'm doomed; Luna's not. Her future is *better*."

She might not have one.

It all hurts. I say, "I wanna see yours too." His tears surface as he looks back at me, but I just tell him the truth, "I hope I can be there, whatever happens. I wanna be there."

"You're not going anywhere?" he asks.

I'm still gripping on to the lit match of hope. It's burning near my fingers. *She's alive. She'll wake up.* But in a future where she doesn't— could I even stomach being around her family without her? For Xander, maybe I could.

"I'm not going anywhere," I say.

He inhales a full breath, then sniffs again. "You have any music recs, wise one?" He wipes at his wet eyes again, then scrolls through songs on his phone.

"Yeah, I've got one." I type in the song and press *start*. Ween's "Tried and True" plays around his neck until he lifts the headphones to his ears.

Xander eases back, breathing in and out, and I stand up, thinking about joining Maximoff, Ryke, and Connor at the coffee bar. I worry they'll ask about tonight. Pry for more details I don't have. Like full motives.

My family said taking Luna wasn't the original plan, but I don't know what was yet.

Before I can decide where to go, an older woman enters, toting an expensive handbag and clutching pearls at her neck.

No one looks thrilled to see Grandmother Calloway, who's more accurately referred to as the Crow. Mostly by me.

"Where is she?" the Crow barks at her daughters, not even acknowledging the Hales. As though Maximoff doesn't exist. Like Xander and Kinney aren't teenagers coping with their sister and mom in the ICU right now.

"*Mother*," Rose snaps, marching forward. "We told you to wait at home—"

"No, Lily called *me*."

"Jesus Christ," Lo grimaces, looking fed up with this conversation. "Not this again."

Yeah, I missed some family fights while in jail.

"She called me twice! Right before—right before the *accident*." The Crow is spouting crocodile tears, if I do say so. "And I need to see her. She called *me*."

"This isn't about you," Rose sneers.

"Oh, be quiet, Rose," the Crow retorts. "For once, in your life, just shut up."

"Excuse me?" Rose's eyes flame.

"Samantha." Connor walks over quickly. He touches the small of Rose's back. His other hand dives into Rose's hand. "Now's not the time. You need to leave."

"I—" she starts.

"Mom." Daisy tries to corral her out the door. "Visitors' hours aren't for another *four* hours. You don't want to be here for that long. We'll call you—"

"Will you?" she snaps.

"No, we fucking won't," Ryke declares.

Lo comes forward. "Unless your name is Garrison Abbey and you're bringing breakfast bagels in ten minutes, you're not allowed in here. I don't care if you have goddamn *proof* that Lily called you. I know Lil better than anyone. She won't want you here, and over my dead body will you be the first face she fucking sees when she wakes up, you understand?"

Her cheeks are bright red. "I can't even care about my own daughter?"

"You can. At home."

Her lip curls. "I'll remember this."

"I *sincerely* hope you do." He can't even flash a half-smile. He's too broken up for that. Once she's gone, air returns to the room.

"Why is she always so intense?" Kinney mutters.

"Don't worry too much about her," her Aunt Willow says. "Have you read *Powers of X* yet?"

The door swings open again.

"Garrison—" Lo stops himself short.

"Not Garrison," Farrow says in a tensed breath, a tablet under his armpit. Everyone seems to spring to a stance, and Farrow extends a hand, as though saying, *wait*. "I need to speak to two people. Lo and Donnelly."

Me?

The Core Six as they're called in WAC forums—really, the Core Five without Lily—all shift and look back at me. Never in my wildest imagination would I picture this movie moment, and I wanna send the script back to Luna. Ask her for a rewrite. Replace the setting to a tropical beach and turn their frowns upside-down, thank you *very* much.

"Why Donnelly?" Rose questions, turning to Farrow, hands on her hips.

"He was the last person who spoke to Luna before she became unresponsive. He has information we need."

"We? As in doctors or security?" Connor asks.

"Doctors."

I go to the door with Lo, not arguing or complaining.

Lo asks Farrow under his breath, "You can't talk in front of everyone? It's that bad?" He already seems gutted.

"It's complicated. Bring Maximoff if you'd like." He motions for us to exit, and Lo waves his oldest son out the door with us.

Security has crammed the hallway, more than before. Most of SFO are here, especially the rookies. Quinn, Gabe, and Frog try to catch my attention. I divert my gaze and take interest in the ceiling tiles.

Not sure what those three want, but I'm struggling to make most chitchat light and easy. Partly, too, I'm still their cool bodyguard camp counselor, but I felt more like a role model when I flashed my pierced nipples and deep-throated a hot dog at two a.m. than I do today.

Being arrested, even for show, isn't something I wanna be known for.

I look fully away as a few Epsilon and Alpha bodyguards scrutinize me head-to-toe. Probably wondering where my shirt went.

"What's with security?" I whisper to Farrow.

He casts a quick glance at Omega. "They're here because the cops are being pricks." Off my confusion, he whispers, "They want to throw you back in so you can get more information off your dad."

Wow. Alright. I want to smoke, but I can't in a hospital. "Could this night get anymore fucked up?"

Farrow stares right at me in a way that decimates my insides.

It can.

26

Paul Donnelly

FARROW BRINGS THE three of us to a smaller waiting room. Sad in here. Just a magazine rack and five lonely chairs. None of us fill them.

Maximoff hasn't uncrossed his flexed arms. "You look pissed," he says. He's talking to his husband. Farrow does have an angry furrowed brow.

"I want to choke out my colleague right now, so *yes*, I'm extremely fucking pissed." He's scrolling hotly through the electronic tablet. "But first, I need to ask"—he looks up at me—"when you talked to Luna at the row house was she coherent?"

I nod slowly. "Yeah." I'm frowning. "Why?"

"Did she understand where she was?"

"Yeah, I think so."

Lo and Maximoff are drilling daggers into me, but I'm trying not to take it personally. That's her dad. That's her older brother. Being overly protective is in their DNA, and if I had a daughter or sister, it'd likely be in mine too.

"I need you to be sure," Farrow says.

I run my fingers through my hair, thinking back in clearer detail. "She could tell me how she fell and hit her head. When I asked her questions, she could answer. She never seemed too confused, just...scared."

Farrow is typing at rapid speed. "Okay, so she woke up—"

"She woke up?" I jolt, paddles to my heart.

"Jesus, why wouldn't you start with that?" Lo retorts, about to charge for the door.

"Wait, wait!" Farrow shouts, extending his arm to keep Lo here. "You can't see her yet."

Lo goes pale.

"She's not okay?" Maximoff asks.

"She's *confused* about time, and unfortunately…" His glare punctures the door, then the tablet. "My colleague decided to ask Luna if she'd like a rape kit. I wanted to wait until she was in a state where she could consent or at least process this request, but they asked when I wasn't there. And Luna said *yes*."

My head whirls three-sixty degrees. Why would she ask for a rape kit? She knows they didn't touch her. She told me they didn't.

"The results came back two minutes ago," Farrow says.

Oh fuck me.

I scrape my hands over my head, breathing harder.

"She gave me permission to disclose the results with family." Farrow glances over at Maximoff. "Don't break anything, wolf scout."

Maximoff is already up in flames. He squats down to cool off.

Her dad looks even more homicidal.

"There was semen…" The medical jargon goes in one ear and out the other in a snap-second daze. All I hear: semen, no abrasions, no signs of force.

Of course there wouldn't be. *I* had sex with Luna. *Me.* That morning. Twice. Consensual, loving, smoldering, extraordinary sex.

"She wasn't raped," I cut in—or maybe Farrow just finished talking. I can't be sure. "She told me when I found her. I asked if they touched her like that. She said they just picked her up and took off her hoodie. To sell her hoodie. She wasn't raped."

Farrow's brows pinch at me in confusion. "There was semen…"

I stare harder at him.

Sudden realization sobers his face, but like a good friend, he doesn't speak the answer; his eyes flit cagily to Lo.

Lo is already glaring at me. "Whose semen?"

I scratch the back of my head. I never thought he'd find out I broke this promise. Never imagined a scenario where he could or would need to know. My luck has completely run dry.

Fuck.

Me.

Fuck this situation.

He adds, "Because I could've sworn you promised me that you'd wait for her."

My nose flares, stifling emotion. "I didn't wait. We didn't...I slept with her this morning. Or..." *What's the time?* "The morning before Lily picked her up. It probably hasn't been twenty-four hours yet."

Lo grinds his teeth, his gaze lethal on me. "I don't know if I want to hug you or strangle you."

I can barely breathe. "I've got that effect on people." I nod to him. "I'm not really into strangling though. I vote hug."

"I vote *you better get out of my face.*" He's pissed but relieved, and that's all I can hope for at this point, honestly. He's glad his daughter wasn't sexually assaulted. She had sex with me. Her...well, I'm not her boyfriend. Not yet, anyway.

Maximoff is upright again, cracking his stiff knuckles. "Do they need DNA proof it was Donnelly?" He's asking Farrow.

"If Luna lets the police admit the kit into evidence, then they'll need it. It's a good idea to get it anyway."

"Whatever I need to do," I tell them.

Blood test, apparently. I just keep nodding as Farrow describes the medical process. He'll take me to get my blood drawn. Then he tells Lo and Maximoff, "Wait here. I'll be back to talk about Luna."

Lo turns to me. "Take a good look, *Paul.* Maybe you'll understand what it means to *wait.*"

Oof, right to the nuts. Not exactly the jugular, but it definitely hurt something.

Thought I earned a *Donnelly* and not a *Paul* from Xander's dad, but I fucked that up in less than a half-hour. "I'm looking," I say seriously, but he still seems peeved.

Even on my way to the ICU with Farrow, the heat of Lo's scolding still stings. I dig in my pocket for cigarettes that aren't there. "I probably deserved that."

"You had sex. No one knew about that until now, and the threat of your family was the whole point of waiting. Most of your family is already in jail." He swipes his medical ID at the glass ICU entrance. "He's only upset about you lying to him."

The doors slide open. "Feels like I keep putting myself in positions where I have to."

"Don't make promises you can't keep," Farrow says like it's so easy.

"You read that life lesson over a toilet?" I quip. "Was it framed or what?" It's my first joke in a while. I'm happy she's awake, but the tensed side-eye from Farrow starts to strain my muscles and puncture the humor.

"This way." He leads me through the ICU. Most doors are shut, curtains drawn over glass walls, but his head careens to a door labeled B2.

"Is that Luna's room?"

Farrow slips me a warning glance. "Don't think about it."

I am thinking about visiting Luna and not during visiting hours. I've breached the locked ICU doors where only medical personnel have ventured through in a long while. Her room is in sight. She's awake.

She's right there.

Once he flags down a nurse, I'm seated in a desk-chair in the ICU's hall, and she's tapping at the veins on my forearm.

"*Donnelly*." Farrow catches me eyeing Luna's room again.

I frown. "You don't think she'd want to see me?"

"Man, it's not that—"

"Dr. Hale!" a white coat calls from down the hall. I also spot Dr. Keene, Farrow's dad, peeking out of the same room, waving his son over to them. Must be where Lily is.

Farrow is quick to leave and disappear into Lily's room.

Patience maybe isn't my strong suit anymore. Waiting might just eat away at my heart. Now with Farrow gone, the young brunette nurse scrutinizes me with apparent disdain.

I stiffen. "Something wrong?"

She flicks my vein. "No. You should be used to this."

I know what she's insinuating. Needles. Syringes. Shooting up. "I don't get my blood drawn on the regular," I say lightly, eyeing the B2 door. *Luna.* Racing after her is the only thing that makes sense to me.

"I meant the needle," she states, wielding a needle.

I'm taken aback by how forward she is. "Not used to those either, Nurse Becky—*fuck*," I curse as she stabs me outside the vein.

"Sorry, and it's *Macy*." Apologies aren't on her face.

"You sure it's not Ratched?" Bad joke, considering she's the one poking at my vein. I grit through another missed attempt to draw blood.

"Oops," she states. "You have really small veins. Sorry. That might bruise tomorrow." She thinks I'm evil, but maybe she should look in the mirror.

"You want a go at the other arm too?" I ask. "I have plenty more veins for you to stab."

She bristles. "Maybe you should see Lily Calloway later. See what you've done—"

"That wasn't me." *Whatever you read in the news, it's not true.* I have no phone. Can't even check the internet to see what's been posted.

Macy humphs, skeptical, and after finally drawing a test tube of blood, she smacks a bandage aggressively on my forearm.

"I got it." I stand up, ripping out of her hold.

"Take care." Her words are brittle. I watch her vanish behind the nurses' station, and with a quick sweep up and down the ICU hall, I realize no one is in the vicinity. Coast is clear, and in four steps, I reach the door labeled B2.

I knock first, then hear, "Come in."

Her soft voice almost sends me straight to the moon.

It does send me right to her.

27

Luna Hale

I'VE OPENED A LARGE plastic baggie with my belongings—what I guess I carried or wore tonight. Farrow attached a sticky note on my phone.

Don't look at the internet.
(You said you wouldn't.)
× Farrow

I trust that Farrow is telling the truth, and I do remember fragments of our conversation. Him advising me not to check the internet. Me saying...*yeah?* Or maybe I said, *I won't*.

It's a little hazy, but I set my phone on the hospital bed and sift through clothes: jean shorts, sneakers, fishnets. It all seems familiar, except for a plain black watch.

A knock raps the door.

"Come in," I call out and pull the watch from the baggie. Does it even work? I tap the watch-face, the hands stuck on three a.m. Why would I wear an old broken watch? Maybe I bought it with Tom and Eliot at a thrift store.

"Luna?"

The new voice draws my gaze upward. *Who...?*

Slowly, at my own leisurely pace, I canvass this bare-chested, tattooed guy. Gray sweatpants ride low on his toned waist. An inked scorpion, tail on fire, peeks out of the elastic band near his...*his dick*, really, and it's hot.

Flush is ascending my neck, crawling to my cheeks. His chestnut hair is swooped back, a silver hoop in one ear and nipples pierced. I dive into the blueness of his eyes for a moment.

I'd categorize him as out-of-this-world sexy, and maybe it's not just because of the tattoos scattering his carved arms and ridged abs. It's not even his height or his handsome face. It's how he's coming towards me like a bright comet soaring through a darkened galaxy... headed for a favored planet.

Headed for me...

And then I see the chain around his neck.

I freeze.

"Hey..." He slows to a stop, a few inches away. "You alright?" His South Philly accent is thick, and I want so badly to place his voice. I squint, and I think...I think I remember his features more. But from where?

I don't know. It's more frustrating than panic-inducing now.

I nod in reply, wanting to believe I'm alright more than I probably am. The watch is warm in my palm, but I'm mostly eyeing the stranger.

He sees the contents of the baggie strewn on the bed and fixates on my phone. "I didn't think the cops would hand that over."

The police had my phone? I try to remember if someone already told me about collecting evidence. Maybe I'm too quiet for too long or blinking too much because concern pinches his eyes.

He casts a quick glance to the closed door, then to me. "Farrow said you might be confused...?"

I know him. I have to know him. Why else would he be here?! I bite too hard on my lip. "It's coming back to me, I think," I lie.

It's a quiet, awful lie that makes me feel terrible. Pushing aside the frustrations and guilt, I lift myself a smidge higher on the bed, my arms shaking a little.

"You need help?" He's at my side, touching the bedframe buttons.

A weird sensation tingles my skin at his closeness. A good weird. I love weird. *I do know that.* While I'm rising, my face inadvertently moves closer to him, and my breath hitches in a strange pattern. I have to ask… "Who gave you that kyber crystal?"

Because it looks an awfully lot like mine.

The bed is propped better, but now that I'm motionless and sitting up, I realize how much *he's* frozen.

"You gave it to me," he murmurs. "You don't remember?"

I could lie again, but the instinct to trust him with the truth is a powerful force inside me. "I'm trying to remember."

He runs his fingers through his hair, his Adam's apple bobbing. Another glance to the door and he mutters, "Now I know why Farrow told me to wait."

"You know Farrow?" Right as I say it, I gasp. "I know who you are!"

Relief rocks him. "Thank God."

"Donnelly," I say with total confidence. "You're Beckett's bodyguard."

He goes still again.

No, *no*, I know I'm right! My brows bunch together in aggravation. "You're my cousin Beckett's 24/7 bodyguard. And you're a tattooist! You tattooed him…" I trail off, a pit in my sore ribs. *I have tattoos.* Oh… *Ohhhh.*

Does that mean…? Did he tattoo me?

"Are we friends?" I whisper.

He looks to the door again. "I should go wait with everyone—"

"Nonono," I slur together in haste. "Please, stay. *Please.*"

Donnelly hesitates, seriously conflicted.

The kyber crystal—I spent my thirteenth birthday money on that necklace at Philly Comic-Con. It took me *two hours* to pick out the collectible, and it's not something I would part with—but I did.

I gave it to him.

I must trust him.

He must mean *something* strong to me. After another soft "please" he rolls the doctor's stool closer and takes a seat at my bedside.

"You are Donnelly, right?" I ask, just to be sure. It surprises me how I'm not as worried about appearing too lost in front of him.

"That's me." He cups his hands, seeming a little tentative. Not like he's scared of me, more like he's cautious of not wanting to hurt me. "How much don't you remember?"

"I don't know," I admit. "What's today?"

Donnelly scans the room like he's unsure too. It relaxes me for some reason, knowing I'm not the only one playing catch-up. "I think maybe the 24th."

"Of July?"

"July?" His brows jump.

"It's not...July," I say, and I risk staring at the harsh fluorescent lights for too long. Thinking, thinking, grasping for something. "It's like I can *almost* see my eighteenth birthday. Like I know I had it."

His hand shields his eyes, then he rubs them in a type of angst I can't make sense of.

If I can't place Donnelly beyond being Beckett's bodyguard, then he must be part of the timespan I lost. He's totally gone. Vanished from my mind.

"Sorry." He clears his throat and drops his hand. "I know this has gotta be harder for you. You, um..." He looks right at me and takes a breath. "You're turning twenty-one this month."

Twenty. One.

"Holy shit," I mutter, alarm coursing through me. "I'm missing three whole years." What happened in those three years?

His neck twists towards the door. "I'm sure if we brought Farrow in here, he'd say something about getting your memories back. It might not take that long."

Mild. Moderate. Severe. "Yeah, I think he already told me something like that." I calm down, but I blush a little at how he's looking me over, as though he wants to scoop me up and carry me off to a place that'll never harm me. Has anyone ever looked at me like that? Someone who's not related to me?

In the past few years, maybe they did. Maybe he's not the only one. I wouldn't know, would I?

The more my face heats, the more I realize this is real *attraction* roasting me. For another beat as his eyes sweep me, I study him like he's a new specimen on my homeworld.

Protective.

He's protective of me.

"Are you my bodyguard?" I ask quietly. There must've been security transfers in the last three years. Maybe J.P. retired from my detail.

"No." He shakes his head slowly and sees me examine the old defective watch. I flip the thing over and trace the scratched silver casing.

The letter *D* is etched crudely.

Donnelly. "Is this yours?" I ask, my heart skipping.

"Yeah." His eyes redden. He sits a little straighter. "I gave it to you."

I tap the face. "Was it always broken?"

"Nah. Gimme."

Passing him the watch, our fingers brush in slo-mo, and hairs rise on my arms, an electric feeling zipping through me again. How many times have I discovered this sensation?

Was it only with him?

While he fiddles with the tiny gears, I click into my phone. Only four percent battery. Whaaat is…this? My lips part, and I go cold at the unfamiliar lock screen picture.

In the photo, I must be dressed for a costume party. Likely as Polaris from X-Men. The sprayed green hair, green lip gloss, and sparkly matching dress are giveaways, and I think I look a little older in the pic—but that's not what's shortening my breath.

The baby.

I'm holding a little baby dressed as a purple dragon. Lockheed. Only this baby…his eyes are so, *so* blue. I glance up at Donnelly.

He looks over at me. "You alright?" *His eyes.*

I glance down. *The baby's eyes.*

"Luna?"

I eat air, until I manage to blurt out, "Do we have a baby?"

"What?" He's frozen-faced, only his eyes growing. *Those blue eyes.*

"Do we have a baby together?" I ask again, trying not to freak out. I wonder if this seems as unbelievable to him as it does to me, and I'd one-hundred percent jot this down for a future fic. It's a *great* sci-fi plot, but I don't exactly want to live it!

He reaches for my phone, but I spin around the screen first and point to the lock screen photo. "That's me. And that's a baby that looks a whole lot like you."

It dawns on him.

I wish it would dawn on me. Before anxiety fully kicks in, he's telling me, "That's not your baby." I wait for the release of oxygen, the breath, the relief, but my stomach sours, thinking the baby still might be his. Why do I even care?

"This is your baby?" I whisper.

"No, he's not."

"He...he has your eyes." *Am I wrong?*

"Yeah, he looks a bit like me...but he's not biologically mine. That's Ripley Hale."

Hale. It's unlikely he's my parents' kid, so only one thing really makes sense.

"As in...?" I can't even finish. Tears well. Overwhelmed tears. Happy but also sad that I've *forgotten* this monumental moment in my brother's life. The brother I'm the closest to. "Moffy has a son." I wipe at my wet cheeks. "He has a husband *and* a son...when he said he'd never have either." He sacrifices so much for others, I never thought he'd choose a family of his own. I'm so happy for my brother, but the mourning of this memory tries to swallow me whole.

Donnelly passes me tissues, but he seems like he'd rather do more. Struggling to stay seated, he's rooting his hands on his kneecaps. I zero in on the dried blood and broken skin along his knuckles.

"Were you there tonight?" I ask after blowing my nose. "Or... maybe it wasn't tonight. Last night? Whenever I hit my head."

"Time's a little fucked up for me too," he admits. "I wasn't there for the whole thing." I see how he's looking *into* me. I crave to reach that expression, to understand and know and feel, but it's like my fingers are pressed to frosted glass and he's stranded on the other side.

Or maybe I'm the one isolated and marooned.

"What are we?" I whisper.

It blows him back. He looks to the ceiling, then the wall, trying to hide his face in every direction.

Maybe I didn't ask that right. I blink a ton. "Are you...my boyfriend?"

Donnelly runs a hand against his neck. "Not exactly." He returns to my gaze. "We were hoping...but we didn't get there yet."

Oh. I search my brain, but nothing is there to unscramble. I keep thinking this new info will crop up a puzzle piece, a memory, but I can't fill the missing picture if my mind is empty.

"You said...you said you were partly there tonight," I say softly. "Does that mean you know about...?"

"About?"

I shouldn't ask him. I could ask anyone else, but if Original Luna hoped to be with Donnelly, then maybe confiding in him is what she would do, most of all. And isn't she still me?

"I can't remember anything about what happened, and I had a rape kit done. And they said it came back...I just want to know if you saw anything or—"

"You weren't raped," he cuts in and then reaches out a hand. *He's holding my hand.* I like how he encases my palm. It slows my racing pulse.

But I blink, emotions barreling towards me at full speed. "Uh-uh, that doesn't make sense. I'm a virgin. And they said the test came back..." My voice tapers off at the way he's staring at me. He's offering the answers in his eyeballs.

I want to scoop them out. Eat them up. Metaphorically. He'd probably think I was a total freak if I mentioned that out loud.

"I…." I grapple for words.

"You aren't a virgin, Luna," he says, helping me out.

When did I lose my virginity? I gasp for breath a little. How is this possible? *Three years.* I'm missing three years!

He adds, "We had sex."

"We had sex?" Shock widens my eyes.

I had sex. With Donnelly?

Whoa. *Whoaaa.* I give him a short once-over. I can hardly believe that happened. He's so much older, probably twenty-six…or twenty-eight? I'm older too, I know, and maybe he's more experienced. It wouldn't stop me or bother me. But no way would my dad be understanding of that age-gap. Maybe he doesn't know.

Donnelly clarifies, "The morning before all of this"—his eyes flit around the hospital room, then back to me— "we had consensual sex. So whatever bodily fluids they found in that exam, they were from me."

I touch my eyes, real relief hitting me. "So I wasn't…?"

"You weren't," he says strongly.

A tidal wave crashes against me, lurching me back into the pillows. My hands fly to my face, and I sink down to hide this breakdown beneath the blankets. Cocooned underneath them, I choke out, "I thought…I thought the worst."

"It didn't happen," he reassures and pats the blanket lump that is me. "That's your forehead?"

"My nose," I sniff, and my lips rise a little just thinking about him patting me. His presence feels needed, necessary, as if he's the sole light among space and time. I calm myself in two breaths, peeling the blanket off my splotchy face, I ask, "Can you…can you come closer?"

He rises off the stool but stops short. Distraught, he clamps a hand on his head. "Look, I'd already be on that bed, *holding* you—"

"Then why aren't you?"

His face nearly cracks. "You don't remember me."

"I want to." I hate that I can't *see* what I've already lived through.

"I know," he says. "I know." He's looking around the room. *Don't leave.*

I prop myself on my weak elbows, fighting to stay more upright. Donnelly is a stranger to me. I have no idea who he really is—no memories, no past conversations floating in my brain. He's nothing to me now, but he was something.

Original Luna had three years' worth of failures and mistakes to learn from. She has knowledge, and I trust her.

"Can we pretend for a second?" I ask him. "Please."

"Pretend that you know me?"

I nod rapidly, and I already prepare my heart for him to say, *that's a bad idea.* Or worse, *that's dumb.*

Instead, Donnelly is game.

He climbs on the hospital bed without falter, and I scoot to make room. Carefully, gently, his muscled arm curves around my bony shoulders, and I find myself resting my weight against him. My cheek to his heart.

True to his word, he's holding me.

It feels really good to be held, but the newness of this embrace is tingling my skin, speeding my heart. Do I remember this with him? Is that why this feeling is hyper-sensitive?

I wish I knew. One of his hands is on my hip, and I trace his veins running from his knuckles to his wrist. Maybe being in the arms of a stranger should be more nerve-wracking, but I've never been the cautious type. I think it worries my parents more than anyone.

"You in any pain?" he asks.

I shake my head a little. "It's dull."

His heart *thumps, thumps, thumps* against my ear. I can't believe I had sex with him. In what position? Where did he fuck me? How many times? A billion questions attack me all at once, but I startle at a realization.

"What's wrong?" He feels me jerk.

"You came inside me."

"Yeah?" He's confused.

"I'm not on birth control." Off his expression, I see that Original Luna had that covered. "Or am I?"

"You are, but we should probably make sure your doctor knows you might've missed taking the pill while you've been here." He glances back at the door, and when chatter sounds outside, worry spreads across his face.

I realize, "You're not allowed to be here. Farrow told you to…to wait?" It's becoming easier recalling the talks I've had in the hospital.

"Yeah, and there's a No Fun Nurse out there who thinks I'm a piece of garbage that's going to stink up your room. Joke's on her because I smell great."

I sniff his bare chest, a bit tentative knowing it's a strange thing to do. Yet, I want to sniff Donnelly all over like a bloodhound.

He watches with a rising smile. "Smell away, space babe."

My heart pitter-patters. He calls me *space babe*? "My nose is powerful," I warn.

"Good. I'll triple-down. I smell amazing."

I smile. "Gutsy."

"Been taking risks all my life. Think I can handle this one." He raises his arm off my shoulders, opening himself up to me and letting me go free. I inhale around his collar, up towards his neck. It's difficult to pry my gaze off his while I smell him. His eyes…they remind me of blue spinel gems. How many times have I drowned in those blue pools?

More questions infiltrate. How did we become friends? Are we technically dating even though he's not my boyfriend? Are we just friends-with-benefits?

Why do you look like you want to kiss me?

I inhale deeply at the nape of his neck. "Mint," I whisper against his skin. "And sweat." I love his scent. His strong hand is suddenly on my other hip, and feeling the force of him pulses a need in me. Only, Donnelly is lifting me *off* his body. I had somewhat crawled up him and straddled his waist, and now he sets me delicately on the mattress.

"Shit," he curses, tangled in some wires and tubes connected to my arms. He's careful about unwinding them.

I notice the bulge in his sweatpants. Heat burns my cheeks. "Were you my first?"

He flinches. "Your first what?"

I'm more afraid of this answer, and I hesitate to ask again. "...did you take my virginity?"

It takes him a second before he says, "No."

Then who did? My eyes grow. "Do you know who it was?"

"You really wanna know?" he questions, stifling a cringe. "You could just wait. These memories might come back tomorrow for all we know, and you'll have the answers then."

I nod, wanting to believe that.

After untangling the wires, I tell him, "I like your scent."

Donnelly looks me over. "Doesn't seem like you like it if it turns your smile upside-down."

"I just wish it triggered a memory." I glance nervously at the door, like an invisible hourglass has flipped. All the sand is nearly collected at the bottom. "If my family thinks I don't remember the past three years, they're going to be so concerned. I just don't want that kind of worry or pressure. It's already hard enough not remembering."

He nods. "I get it."

"You do?"

"Sure," he breathes. "You and I are the same. We keep our issues to ourselves because letting other people see 'em makes them bigger than they have to be. Gives power to them. Makes them feel more unbeatable than they are. It's easier to just keep that stuff *here*." He touches his hand to his heart.

I nod strongly, and a knock sounds before the door opens.

"Miss Hale..." The brunette nurse skids to a halt. "*You*. Get off her bed, right *now*." Her scathing glare at Donnelly sends a chill down my spine. "Now!"

"I'm going," Donnelly says. He's being careful not to yank any cords attached to me.

I grasp at the wrinkled sheet where he sat. Too slow to catch him. "Wait," I say, panic reigniting. "Let him stay. He can stay."

"No, he can't," the nurse forces out coldly. "Visitors aren't allowed right now. Especially not *him*. Get. Out."

What? My perception of reality is fogged, but I hang on to one belief: *I can trust Donnelly.* He has my crystal.

I have his watch.

Donnelly is walking towards the door.

"No!" I shout abruptly, worry pelting me like rain on glass.

The nurse frowns. "Luna—"

I'm jumping off the bed, wires tangling and ripping painfully at my wrists. "Nonono, dontgodontgo."

Donnelly reroutes. He's suddenly at my side, grabbing on to my hand, stopping me from pulling out my IV. "It's alright," he whispers. "Luna, it's alright. I can go—"

"You can't go!" My heart rate is spiking. "Please don't go," I beg. I don't even like this nurse. Why is she acting like he murdered my whole family?!

I go very still.

Did he…?

No.

No.

I can trust him.

Can't I?

"Luna," he says, a knot in his throat. "I…"

I shake my head on instinct. "No. *Please.*" I death-grip his hand. He's not peeling me off him. If he were a murderer, he'd have handcuffs. He'd be in jail. And when I look at him, I know—I know he's good. Why would I give my kyber crystal to someone bad?

He is light.

He is harmony.

He is *love.*

The Force is within him. I saw it. I knew it.

I've just forgotten it somehow.

"You can't be here," the nurse sneers.

"He can't leave!" I scream, uncommon rage storming me. *Anger.* I just want to cling to someone I know I can trust. And she's trying to take that away. In the last three years, I have no clue what my relationships with my family and friends are like, but I *know* this.

The crystal. The watch. The sex this morning. He's here. He fought to see me when everyone else told him not to.

I trust Donnelly.

"He. Can't. *Leave*," I repeat, almost out of breath. I'm working myself up, and her hatred of him volleys into concern for me.

"Ditto," he says to the nurse. "Can't leave. Stuck here like glue." His hand still tightly clings to mine.

"I'm getting your doctor."

"Do that," Donnelly tells her. "Go get my best friend, Becky."

She glares but beelines out of the room.

Best friend? I frown up at Donnelly. "You're friends with Farrow?" *Since when?*

While helping me back onto the bed, he tells me it's not something they advertise all that much. "It's mainly Farrow though," he says. "Always acting like he's a take-me-or-leave-me *meh* friend." Donnelly smiles a little at this, like it's an inside joke. "But the guy has never wanted me to leave. He's made it easy for me to stay."

"Farrow is a caring bean," I say, letting out the last anxious breath.

"Nah, he's a kidney bean. Full of piss..." He trails off at my laughter, and his smile matches mine until the noise dies down.

Time is ticking. Someone will come in any minute now. Donnelly surprisingly risks another round of the nurse's wrath by sitting on the edge of the bed.

I pick at my thumbnail. "I'm a really shitty intergalactic detective. I thought I had a baby." I speak so softly; I doubt he hears. "I would've never guessed he was Moffy's. He would've been last on my list."

"You're not a shitty intergalactic detective," he tells me, which jars me in surprise. "I'd hire you."

"For all your interstellar troubles?"

"I've got plenty of those."

"Same. A lot can go wrong in space," I say and relax into the casualness of this conversation. I like how it's broken into the intensity of the others. "Everything can really be solved by discovering a perfectly mined mineral on an otherworldly planet. Then you've created super space medicine. Super space condoms. Super space lube."

"You sharing your super space products?"

"Maybe." I shrug. "For a fee."

He sucks in a breath. "Girl, take…" He doesn't finish, his voice dropping off.

"What?" I look over at him.

He skims my features. "Take my money," he mutters, sounding sad.

I struggle to speak because it hurts how he's seeing me. His face is fracturing. Pain lances his blue eyes as if he's realizing that he's lost something too.

Lost me.

He's stopped pretending that I remember him.

I blink back tears, but I swallow the lump. "I could use a partner in this detective case," I say. "The Case of Luna's Missing Memories."

He smiles, even if it's a sorrowful one. "Sign me up."

Chatter escalates outside until I hear a forceful knock. "Don't leave," I remind him, a little more whiney than I meant.

"If I can help it, I won't."

28

Paul Donnelly

"DONNELLY," FARROW says with a sigh and an eye-roll like I'm in deep shit this time. *Don't I know it.* Luna thinks I'm just some run-of-the-mill bodyguard. Background. Wallpaper.

She thinks I'm no one.

The girl I've given my heart and soul to doesn't know she even has my heart and soul.

But she's alive. She's awake. Can I really ask for more?

The fact that she's demanding I stay is another checkmark in the *plus* column. Gotta hang on to those good things. They've been hard to come by, and this whole night, morning, whatever has crushed me enough.

"He needs to *leave*, Dr. Hale," Nurse Macy says with heat while she's latched to Farrow's side. "He can't be in here." Her glare slices to me. "And get off *her* bed."

My ass is barely on her bed. "Sure, Becky." I stand, trying to brush her off, but Luna panics, her chest rising and falling in uneven patterns. *I'm not going anywhere.* I reach out and hold her hand, showing her I'm staying.

She has a tight grip, but I can tell she's weakened from either the pain meds or just everything tonight.

"Like I told you before, it's *Macy*," the nurse retorts, then spins to Farrow. "It's not right for him to be here while she's—"

"We can talk about this outside," Farrow says hushed. "Not in front of the patient."

"You're *seriously* letting him stay alone with her for even longer?"

"He's not leaving!" Luna shouts in distress. "I want him to stay, Farrow. Please! Get *her* out!"

Farrow is as jarred by the uncharacteristic yelling from Luna as I am. This is a girl who speaks so quiet at times, I strain my ear hairs to catch the noises. Worry stampedes inside me.

"Sweetie," the nurse tries to console. "I'm here *for you.*"

"If you were here for me, you'd listen to me." Luna gasps for breath.

I lower to her side. "Luna, it's alright. Look at me." I cup her hand with more force. "I'm here. You see me?"

She rubs at her eyes, almost hiccupping for breath. Is she having a panic attack? I glance back at Farrow, but he's in a heated conversation with the nurse.

"Absolutely *not*," Farrow says, louder.

Back to Luna, I set my ass on the edge of the bed again. "I know you don't know anything about me," I tell her, watching her gulp more air. Talking seems to help, so I continue, "But I've traveled to your planet and back again countless times."

She inhales slowly, exhales slowly.

"Go ahead and try to bring in Dr. Tack. She's *my* patient," Farrow says to the nurse. "Again, you need to leave. Now."

Luna is only fixated on me. I dunno why. She could hang on to the familiarity of Farrow, who she knew growing up, but she's more absorbed with the mystery of who I am. I'm not complaining about it.

"I promise I'm not leaving you if I can help it," I tell her more strongly this time. "And I know how promises are made on your planet."

She catches her staggered breath. "How...how are they made on yours?"

"Promises on my planet?"

"Uh-huh."

I think for a second. Our hands are still clasped, but I hook our pinkies. Leaning closer to her, I say, "Kiss your thumb the same time as me. Yeah?"

Her lips twitch into a tiny smile, and together, with locked pinkies, we kiss our own thumbs. When I let go, she whispers, "That's a very earthly promise."

I start to grin. "That's 'cause I'm from Earth, space babe."

She takes a bigger breath, smiling back, but the slam of the door flinches her and swings my head. The nurse is gone, and Farrow is beyond aggravated, especially as the door flings back open and a bearded doctor in a white coat strolls stiffly into the room.

"He can't leave," Farrow tells Dr. Tack, his name embroidered on the coat, then my friend is motioning for me to join them near the draped window.

"I'll be here," I assure Luna.

Her heart rate spikes on the machine as I leave her bedside, and Dr. Tack studies her while I meet them across the room.

"She wants him to stay. She's attached to him," Farrow whispers to his colleague. "I don't give a flying shit who thinks it's a conflict of interest. I'm not pulling strings because of security or because he's my friend. All I care about is that girl while I'm her doctor—"

"You don't need to convince me. I'm not Dr. Lewis," Dr. Tack interjects. "I heard her yelling from the hall. I think it's necessary for him to stay too, at least until we have a better sense of her PTA."

PTA?

"Thank you," Farrow says, easing. They mention something about the staff taking sides and to have a new nurse assigned to Luna.

Once Dr. Tack has left, Farrow sees the needle marks along the crease of my elbow and forearm. The bandage only hides the main puncture. Pure rage flashes across his face, and he catches my elbow for a better look, but I jerk out of his grip.

"You've already got one patient. I'm fine." I ask fast, "What's PTA?"

He works his jaw but ends up answering, "Post-traumatic amnesia." *Shoulda known.* Context clues and all. He shifts his focus to her. "Luna, the neuropsychologist is talking to your family right now. They're coming to see you after."

She nods. "Donnelly's staying?"

"Yeah. He'll be over in that chair when your family comes in." He motions to a beige chair in the corner.

"My name's on it already," I say lightly.

She smiles, her cheeks a little flushed. Someone cleaned off the painted streaks beneath her eyes, but they left the ribbons in her light brown hair. She looks like Luna.

She *is* Luna. *She just doesn't know me.* Plus, I didn't even start getting to know her until the FanCon tour. We had such few interactions at the beginning, and so many other events eventually shaped her throughout the years—and those are gone in her head.

While Luna relaxes against the pillows, Farrow pulls me to the side to talk privately, and the first thing I say is, "She doesn't remember anything about me."

"She's missing about three years?"

"You know?"

He keeps his voice low. "Man, she thought *Declan* just retired." He combs a hand through his hair. "I can't say too much without breaking HIPAA." *Patient-doctor confidentiality*, I know that. "Once she's able to give consent about discussing her health—and *if* she does consent— I'll talk to you more."

"I get that also means I can't know about Lily...but how's she doing?" Last I saw, he rushed into her room.

"She's okay. Lo is with her now."

"She's out of the coma?"

He just slides me a look that means, *yes.* "Did you tell Luna about her mom?"

"No way. I couldn't."

"Anything about what happened?"

I do a quick run-down of the bits and pieces I shared with Luna. Nothing major. "How long will the amnesia last?" I ask him just as quietly.

"We won't know yet," he admits. "You want a shirt?"

"Nah." I try to breathe in something lighter. "I like the chill on my nipples. Keeps them perked."

He rolls his eyes into a slight smile. "She's watching you."

She is studying me from afar like I'm the most interesting patient and she's the most inquisitive doctor. When I catch her, her cheeks go rosy. It's cute. Gotta say that I'm glad I still have some positive effect on her. If she completely feared me, I don't know what I'd even do. Go sob on a deserted island for a solid millennium. Befriend a volleyball.

That's not too accurate, really. In my heart of hearts, I know I'd use every ounce of self-given, self-accumulated resilience to show her I'm not someone to fear.

I wouldn't give up.

Farrow's brows rise. "She's *really* watching you."

Yeah, she's not being shy about it. "Don't know why," I whisper to Farrow. "She doesn't know me."

"She knows you meant something to her. Clearly, that's enough."

"She's also had exes," I remind him. "Firsts with other guys. Once she figures that out, she could want to go explore those too." If her memories never resurface, the chances of Luna moving on from me could skyrocket. She might want to stay single. She might want to date around.

She might want everything but me.

"She fell in love with you for you," Farrow says with the tilt of his head. "You don't believe she could fall for you again?"

It might seem far-fetched, but I have to believe it's possible. Perseverance is what I'm good at. That never-giving-up attitude has saved my ass more than once, and I won't give up on us now.

MAXIMOFF IS THE ONLY FAMILY HERE AT FIRST.

They're easing Luna into seeing everyone, but after she asks about their parents, he's the one who drops the news: their mom was admitted to the ICU; their dad is at her bedside right now. Luna's been crying for the past three minutes, but she's hugging her brother and it's making this horrific situation more bearable.

Farrow keeps checking his buzzing phone.

I'm sitting in my chair in the corner. "Security, I'm guessing?" He's not wearing a radio, so he's probably stuck in group chats. Unlike my phoneless self, I *still* have no communication with anyone, and it's not fun. But it beats sitting in jail.

"Yeah." His voice is tight.

"Police still wanna send me back to jail," I guess again.

His jaw muscles tic.

I think about information I could pry from my family if they lock me in their holding cells. Maybe I could learn about the original plan, but some of them aren't that stupid. They're not gonna talk in jail.

Still, there are loose ends, and if I'm the best shot to tie 'em up... "I could go back."

Farrow stares down at me like I'm the one who's lost my mind. "Your family could be locked up for *months*. The hearing has no date yet. We don't know when it'll take place, so if you go back, the police will try to keep you there."

"Am I supposed to hide for months? They're gonna know I snitched on them if my dad is in there while I'm out. He has as much to do with this as I do."

"Of what I've heard, they don't want to release him."

"Well maybe they should."

Farrow side-eyes the wall, glaring. "I hate your dad, and being honest here, it's a little disturbing you want him out—"

"I don't like him either," I remind him. "But I couldn't have found Luna without him. You know that, and if letting him out means I can be seen freely in public without blowing my cover, then maybe that's what should happen. Or else, throw me back in and let me get more information—"

"You're *not* going back in," Farrow forces out. "And this isn't even me trying to shake you. *She* needs you." He motions with his head towards Luna. "She's more important than whatever you'll find sitting in jail. Which could be nothing."

I'd never disagree with that.

29

Luna Hale

EVERYTHING HAS CHANGED. It's impossible to feel like it hasn't. And I don't know whether to crumple into myself and cry or scream in rage. But I do neither while I'm around Moffy. He's already looking at me like I might dissolve into the carpet, and I really don't need his worry to mount.

Speaking of carpet—it's ugly. An ugly shade of *blah* gray runs down a deserted, maze-inducing hallway. After being at the hospital for two days, I've finally left. Now I've just entered a back entrance to the apartment complex from a parking deck, and I'm utterly lost.

At least we're out of the clutches of the media. Fiendish paparazzi (as Eliot would call them) were camping outside the hospital, and leaving undetected was a challenge that the security team aced. A horde of bodyguards flanked me and obscured me while I exited Philly General, and I was skillfully dipped into an SUV. After being dropped off in a parking deck I've never seen before—and entering a building completely foreign to me—I just keep waiting for something to *click* in my brain.

Nothing has yet.

"This is where we live?" My brows scrunch.

Moffy looks to me with the same toughened green eyes, as if he's ready to football-tackle the monster who stole my memories. Right now, I like to think of my oldest brother as my memory guide into my missing years, and it's probably good he's a protective one.

"This is just the hall," he answers with a gesture around the undecorated area. "Not that we usually take this back entrance."

"We don't?" I peek back at the locked rear door, a sign above saying *emergency exit*. The horde of bodyguards didn't join us. Farrow wasn't among them since he's needed at the hospital. Nor was J.P., but I'm not sure why my bodyguard was MIA.

While we'd been safely in the backseat of the security SUV, I told Moffy, "You could've brought your son." I kinda wanted to meet him. Soft baby cuddles would've maybe lifted my spirits.

Moffy seemed uptight with someone else driving. *Normal. What I remember.* "You'll see him soon." He pried his eyes off the driver to focus on me. "I just want to make sure you get home okay first. There's a ton of paparazzi."

He wasn't wrong about that. I couldn't remember a time so many ever tried to follow me. "Who's your baby with if Farrow's working?" I wanted to call the baby my nephew, but it felt too bizarre.

"Ryke and Dad are watching him."

"Not our aunts?" I would've thought they'd be the first in line after our mom.

"Ripley likes when Ryke and Dad hold him more," he explained, still trying his best to train his gaze on me and not the driver. Screens blocked our windows, so he couldn't peer outside that easily. "When he was really small, he used to cry a lot, except when he was in my arms. So I think they remind him of me."

I wanted to ask if Original Luna already knew this, but I just assumed she did.

Walking through this ugly carpeted hallway now, Moffy clues me in more, "We usually go in the front entrance. The lobby."

"So we're still not that afraid of any lurking cameramen?"

"Yeah," he smiles. "You and I still brave them like they're total background to our *awesome* abnormal lives." He slips me another brotherly smile, and it feels the same.

Not so different.

The escalating pitter-patter of my heartbeat slows a little. He is a very good memory guide. Chosen wisely.

"We're going up." He points ahead after we've weaved between halls and worked our way towards the lobby. "It's a private elevator. No one else has access to it without our keycard. No strangers allowed."

I want to ask if I seem like a stranger to him.

But I'm limiting my questions. My family and Farrow agreed not to overwhelm me by filling in every single blank in my memory. Instead, they're letting *me* ask the questions. And I'm trying my best to filter out the stupid ones.

"Private elevator," I muse under my breath while he scans his card, and we wait for the elevator to drop to us. From here, I spy a snapshot of the lobby. Seems glitzy. Marbled floors. Gold light fixtures. I like the green paisley wallpaper.

Still, is this apartment snazzy or something? I glance back at my brother.

He's *older*. Three entire years *older*, and I see the changes. His jawline is stronger with age. He's more built, but he still stands poised for a meteor shower. He's never been Atlas, crouched down while bracing the world.

My brother is upright, the entire globe perched on his strong swimmer's shoulders like it weighs as much as an inflatable beach ball. *The same.* That's the same. Or is he pretending for me? To not frighten me?

But his hair—his hair isn't dyed light brown like the last I remember. The natural dark shade makes him look more like our Uncle Ryke, which was why I thought he'd been dyeing it in the first place. To look less like him. So he could show love and loyalty to our dad and give a middle finger to the "Ryke is Moffy's real father" rumors.

I look back to the elevator, then the snapshot of the lobby. I can't imagine my brother living in anything extravagant or pricey. He's not flashy *at all.* I'd be more freaked if he were wearing shiny loafers and a button-down. He's just in Timberland boots and a plain white tee.

The elevator dings.

When we're inside and begin rising, anxiety presses hard on my chest, not knowing what I'll be walking into. So I think *good thoughts*. Like how I saw my dad at the hospital.

He sat on the edge of my bed after he hugged me. His relief at seeing me alive and awake flooded the room. "You feel okay?" he asked and his sharp gaze snapped to Farrow like, *pain meds stat!*

But after a decent night's sleep at the hospital, my body didn't ache as badly this morning. Just tender ribs. I learned I fractured two.

I wasn't totally sure how. I was told there was an assault. The details surrounding that night were still fogged, and they were careful not to paint the whole picture for me. I gathered that it could do more harm than good.

"I feel better," I told my dad. "How's Mom?" It hurt even asking. His eyes were bloodshot, face unnaturally torn.

My parents—their souls were intertwined. In my life, their love had always been one-of-a-kind. Stuff of legend and fanfiction, and the fact that it was *my* reality, that I got to be raised by two soul mates, was a treasure I wouldn't trade for anything. Not even dirt from Mars or the *guarantee* I'd write the best sci-fi novel in the world. It was that precious to me.

"She's doing better," my dad said tensely. His brows never uncinched in their *fuck the world and everyone in it* wrinkled position. "But uh…" He had to clear his throat. "She wants to wait a bit until everyone sees her." He forced a pained smile.

Had he broken his sobriety? Will he break it?

It wasn't the first time the thoughts invaded, but they seemed the most warranted in that moment and even now.

I frowned. "Why doesn't she want to see me?" I was hoping to say *hi*. Hug her. I just wanted to be with my mom.

My question eviscerated him.

I hated that. I hated how I was making things worse, not better. I guessed in that instance, it was proof I was still the same failure and fuck-up.

"It's not you," he said with his whole heart. "She'd love to see you, Luna. Trust me." *Trust him*. He was my dad, of course I did.

Of course I do.

But I just didn't understand. "Then why doesn't she want to?" My temples thumped.

"She's...not ready yet." He peered up at the mounted TV, hiding more suffering from me, but I could see. I stopped asking him about her. My throat swelled too much anyway. He cringed at the Rory and Jess drama on the screen. "That reminds me *way* too much of your Aunt Willow and Uncle Garrison. Gross." He acted repulsed like an older brother would be about his younger sister's love life, which made me smile. (Willow is his sister, after all.) "We'll get *Guardians of the Galaxy* up there."

Stellar distraction techniques from my dad.

I no longer questioned why my mom didn't want visitors, and my dad stayed to chitchat about Star-Lord and Gamora for a while. He did put my favorite movie on the TV too. It comforted me. Once he left, Xander and Kinney replaced him.

They didn't say much.

Kinney kept sucking down tears. "They told us not to overwhelm you or whatever." She shrugged like it was nothing.

"Does it hurt?" Xander asked. "Your head?"

You both look so much older. It stunned me and raced my pulse.

Kinney is *sixteen.* My brother is so close to turning eighteen. A senior in high school. What I thought I was! He's even had a growth spurt. The more I studied him, his jaw seemed sharper (if that's possible), amber eyes more intense.

And just yesterday, Kinney had been in middle school. Little. Twig-like. Yeah, she was still gangly like our mom and me, but she wasn't as soft-cheeked anymore. I couldn't tell if the makeup was to blame, since our dad never let her wear *that* much eyeliner or black lipstick.

When did that change?

It all changed. They've changed.

Pain radiated inside me. It was too much.

I kept looking over at Donnelly in the corner. He'd give me a thumbs up. There was no Past Donnelly to gauge Present Donnelly.

I just had this one Donnelly before me, and unlike with my family, it made things easier.

"What was the question?" I had to ask, a ball in my throat.

"Does your head hurt?" Xander asked again.

"Not as much anymore," I muttered. "I just can't...remember everything." I searched them for answers, but discomfort lied in his face and hers.

"Maybe that's a good thing," Kinney said.

Xander shot her a look.

"What?" she snapped, her cheeks reddening.

I'd never been that close to Kinney, but in three years, I figured our relationship might've changed into something better. Time heals all, right? Not that we were broken, but we'd never had a super strong bond like Sulli and Winona or even Jane and Audrey.

At the hospital, I couldn't tell what we currently were to one another. Xander seemed to be harboring more under the surface than I could comprehend too.

"I'm just glad you're..." Xander couldn't finish, too choked up. I knew he meant, *alive*. He glanced back at Donnelly and took a deeper breath. *Strange*.

"That's a given," Kinney stated, wiping away her tears before they even fell. "And you can't die that close to your birthday. It's bad luck."

I almost died? Or was she exaggerating?

Xander pushed hair out of his face. God, he looked *so much* older. It kept slamming against me.

So I just asked about our mom. "Do you know why I can't see her?"

"We can't either," Xander said.

"She's only letting Dad, plus aunts and uncles," Kinney explained. "We overheard them talking. I think she doesn't want to scare us."

"Why would she...?" I trailed off, seeing Xander's tortured expression and downturned gaze.

"She got beat up," Kinney snapped, incensed, and she glared back at Donnelly like *do something*.

"Kinney," Farrow warned from Donnelly's corner. To which, he had to clarify to me, "Donnelly wasn't involved with Lily's assault."

Kinney was about to retort, but Xander cut in, "We can't, Kin. Don't overwhelm Luna."

Our mom got beat up.

Assault.

I imagined her face puffed. Eyes black-and-blue and swollen shut. Legs and arms in casts. My stomach lurched, and I sincerely hoped my overactive imagination painted a worse picture than reality.

She'll be okay.

It's not as bad as you think.

Farrow gave me those reassurances when I asked him after my siblings left. Still, it made total sense why she wouldn't want many visitors. I feared having the real picture superglued to my brain, and she was saving us from that image.

As the elevator ascends towards the unknown, my good thoughts are more of a mixed bag, and anxiety still bears on me.

Moffy sees. "You okay?"

Great, now my memory guide is overly concerned. I like it more when he's pissed about the Time Thief in my head. Plus, I'm angry too.

"Fine." I chew on the corner of my lip. "Just thinking about Mom." I was released from the hospital this morning, but they wanted her to stay longer.

"She'll be okay." He sounds certain. "I think she's more worried about you."

My memories. Everyone must be freaked. Honestly, every time I say the wrong thing or do the wrong thing, *I* worry Moffy is gonna think I've been body-snatched and a Variant Luna has entered his universe.

Or maybe that's my fear talking. Because I'm fucking terrified that everyone will look at me and think I'm not *me*. And they'll mourn the Original Luna that was put to rest when she hit her head. They'll wish for her. Long for her.

Instead they get this subpar, mediocre copy.

My hands sweat, and I rub my palms on my jean shorts. Someone brought me clothes from home.

Home.

I don't even know where that is. Not yet.

NUMBERS CLIMB ON THE ELEVATOR PANEL. 28, 29, 30…

Each floor higher is another dollar sign. My eyes grow as the elevator slides gently to a stop at 33. "Is this the very top floor?" I ask.

"Yeah." He leads me into a short foyer, a door staring back at us. "There's no creative name for this place. We just call it what it is." He already grimaces. "It's a penthouse. And I know, I know, you're going to think, *what the fuck, Moffy? How could you ever?*"

I'm already thinking it.

"But the townhouse burned down—"

"It burned down?" I gape, shocked, then sad. I fantasized about living there with my brother and Jane so much. "How?"

"Electrical problems." He unlocks the door, then meets my gaze. "But we needed more space. I had Ripley, and you were my roommate."

"We lived together? In the townhouse?"

"Yeah," he begins smiling off my rising smile. I'm ignoring the grief that tries to tank my stomach—grief over the memories I've lost at the townhouse. *I'll find them. I have to.* They haven't been gone for that long.

Living with Moffy is something I *really* wanted to happen, but I also knew that I could've chosen Tom and Eliot. I also figured the townhouse was small. Would Moffy have even wanted me there?

"I lived with you right after high school?" I ask.

"Right after," he says, still smiling. "Pretty much immediately."

"And we still live together," I say, looking at the door that hasn't opened yet.

"We do. Only we have a ton more roommates."

I've been told that already. The penthouse upgrade seems logical, and Moffy wouldn't only consider himself in that decision. He'd put it up to a vote, and I must've voted for this too.

As the door opens, I walk behind my brother and round the wide hall into a spacious living room. Warm earth tones, brick walls, and industrial lighting—I can feel remnants of the townhouse here. But Jane's explosion of grannie furniture is gone. Instead, I see a mod pastel blue couch and masculine leather chairs. The floor-length window showcases a beautiful view of Philadelphia.

"Wow," I breathe, just as furry felines bound over to us. Squatting, I pet Jane's black beauty at my side, remembering her well. "Hi there, Lady Macbeth." She brushes up against me and purrs.

Good news, I haven't become cat repellent.

"None of the roomies are around?" I ask Moffy.

He's checking the mail on the coffee table. "They'll be here tomorrow. They wanted to give you a chance to acclimate."

My dad asked if I wanted to go back home with him. Stay at my childhood house since it's where I remember living, but I want to jog my memories. The best bet I have is going about my life where it is today and not where it was three years ago.

So I have roommates now.

Moffy and Farrow, plus their son.

Jane and Thatcher. *Weird.* Plus their newborn daughter. *Still weird but cute.*

Sulli and Akara and Banks. *Weirder.* And I say *weird* with the utmost love. I adore weird things, but it's also really hard to grasp. Like trying to piece together a puzzle made of clay.

Farrow suggested I let Jane and Sulli answer my questions about their lives, so I keep those to myself.

Oh, I do have one more roomie.

Donnelly.

He shares a bathroom with me apparently, which makes living here easier. At least, I know he'll be nearby.

Suddenly, a giant dog ambushes me. The excited ball of fluff nearly knocks me out of my squat and onto my butt.

"Oh shit," I curse as the dog licks my face. "Nice to see you too…" I pause. What's its name? I laugh when the fluffy black dog nuzzles into my cheek, tail wagging haphazardly. I pet under its scruff. "Did Sulli get a dog?" I ask Moffy.

He's watching me from the middle of the room, mail tucked under his armpit. His face stays a little unreadable, but his eyes glass in a sadness.

"He's yours," Moffy says.

My stomach knots. *I have a dog.* When? How? There are too many questions. Too much time to fill. I try to figure things out on my own and reach for his collar, looking for a name.

Panic trembles my hands, and I squeeze them tight, trying to catch my breath.

"His name is Orion," Moffy says, helping me out.

"Orion," I nod and gulp air. Okay.

I named a dog after a constellation. That makes sense at least. So does his breed. "He's a Newfie," I say. "Like Nana from *Peter Pan.*"

Moffy nods, then eats his next words, rethinking. He cracks a few knuckles.

There's more? I could ask. He's clearly trying to filter out what's unnecessary info, so I'm not hit over the head with details and history all at once.

"You remember me, Orion?" I ask, scratching his fluffy head with two hands. He licks my cheek again. *I wish I could remember you.*

I rise to my feet, and Orion circles my body frenziedly. "He has mega puppy energy."

"He is still a puppy," Maximoff says.

"Really? He's huge."

"Newfies stop growing when they're two. Which he won't be until April." Moffy smiles down at a drooling Orion.

He'll be bigger? His torso reaches my waist, and he'd hog most of the couch if he jumped on the cushions. The more he races around me like a cumbersome adorable oaf, the more I gather that Orion loves me. I share my brother's smile and give Orion one more pat and scratch.

Just then, a *second* fluffy Newfie suddenly trots up to his side. Moffy pets him under the chin. The puppy is almost identical to mine. Except for the brown fur.

My lips slowly part.

"You can ask," Moffy encourages.

"I don't need to ask." I lean my weight on one foot, trying to be casual. "He's Orion's brother." It's an educated guess, but it's enough to light up my brother's eyes.

"You remember Arkham?" He's tentative, but the hope attached to his voice sends a wave of wasps through my stomach. Stinging my insides.

"Yeah, a little," I lie.

His brows pinch. "It's okay if you don't know something. I'm not going to judg—"

"I *know* you won't judge me," I interrupt him with unfamiliar bite.

He nods slowly, not even put off by my tone. My brother is still a good, moral bean, I think. "Just making sure you know."

"I know," I mutter. Silence stretches more tension.

Moffy clears it. "Ready to see your room?"

My biggest gateway back to Original Luna.

Anxiety flits away, replaced by more eagerness. "Yeah, let's do it." I hope my confidence vanquishes my brother's worries.

"Think of the penthouse like a square box," Maximoff tells me while we walk down the wide hall. "Emergency staircase is in the middle, along with the elevator lobby or foyer, whatever you want to call it, and the elevator. Then this hall pretty much connects everything. You can do an entire loop of the house just following it."

That's not so hard to figure out.

He points to a door. "Game room." Then another door. "Your room." He opens the door for me but lets me be the first to enter. Well, technically, I'm the first human.

Orion barrels ahead. Plopping down on a fuzzy dog bed, he pants and drools.

One step inside, I take it all in.

Plastic glow-in-the-dark stars are stuck to the ceiling. Same ones I had in my bedroom growing up. A lava lamp projects violet colors on dark-painted walls. I recognize the beanbags and tapestries. My pillowy comforter is new, but it looks as cozy as the purple nebula quilt I once had. A multi-colored woolen blanket I knitted in high school rests at the foot of the bed.

For the most part, everything is somewhat familiar.

It relaxes me. Maybe I haven't personally changed so much in the last three years that I'd be perceived as a stranger. Maybe I am still me.

Then I see the desk.

A goldfish is swimming in a glass tank—or I guess it's more of a bowl, complete with purple coral and a treasure chest. "I have a fish," I say, confused. "I'd *never* get a fish. Mom couldn't keep a goldfish alive. Why do I think I can?"

"Wait, what?" Moffy is at my side in a flash, confused. "You have a fish…?"

Whaaaaat?

"You didn't know?" I frown deeply.

He's my memory guide. He should know, right? Only, I understand I'm not in a cool sci-fi thriller. My older brother isn't all-knowing about my daily life, even if we're super close. And he has no mind-reading superpowers (that I know of).

Still, he should know I have a fish.

He shakes his head once. "I had no clue."

"You've been in my room before, right?" I bend down to the bowl.

"Yeah, a bunch of times."

"Maybe I just got the fish?"

"Yeah," he nods, but his brotherly worry hardens his face.

I make eye contact with the goldfish. *What's your name?* Sadness grips every part of me, thinking I've erased this fish from existence. If I don't remember it and I didn't tell anyone about it, then it might as well be gone.

I turn to Moffy. "So I'm guessing you don't know its name?

"Sorry," he says, shoulders squared. "I wish I did."

Maybe Tom or Eliot know. Still, I can't get over how I kept this from my brother. Why? Why did I not tell him about my pet fish?

I just don't fucking understand. "Did we grow apart?" I ask suddenly.

Moffy is taken aback. I give him a second to collect his thoughts. He gestures to his head. "I think about everything *all* the damn time. Me. You. Xander. Kinney. The four of us and our lives from childhood to now, and I could spell out exactly where I thought our relationship was and where I think it is—but I doubt that'd even help, Luna."

I still don't understand. "Why not?"

"Because I know how *I* saw you, but I couldn't tell you how you saw me. Do I think we grew apart? *No.* Even after my marriage and a baby, I believe we're close. But I also have no damn idea why you would've hidden a goldfish from me." He makes a face at the bowl. "I should've seen it. It was probably here this *whole time*, and I just didn't see."

"It feels like a *me* thing," I say quietly. "I could've just been cagey with everyone." If Original Luna hid a lot from those around her— which I've been known to somewhat do—then I'm in serious trouble. "I haven't told you that I had my first kiss yet."

Creases line his forehead, and he swings his arms, maybe to shake out the strain. "You did end up telling me."

"I did?" Pride for myself swathes me like a comfy blanket. I wanted to confide in Moffy about my life while I was in high school, even at the risk of flipping the *Big Brother Protect Little Sister* switch.

"Yeah, but I couldn't tell if you were joking or not. Which was a hundred-and-twenty percent a *me* thing that time."

I smile a little, but my lips droop fast. I can almost see that moment. *Almost.* "When did I tell you?"

"Sometime before Halloween, around the start of your memory loss, I think."

I sigh, frustrated. "I can almost picture the leaves in October and hearing about Camp Calloway for some reason."

Moffy goes rigid. "Some of us did go to Camp Calloway that year. You weren't there, but I hosted a Camp-Away for H.M.C. Philanthropies."

"Did I go to the lake house around that time?"

He nods strongly, then takes out his phone. "You okay with me telling Farrow you're remembering this?"

"Sure." I shrug. "But when I was in the hospital, I had glimpses of that time period. My eighteenth birthday...I think we had spaghetti family dinner. Did Xander pierce his ears?"

"So did Kinney. Farrow did it."

Right. The Farrow part is a bit hazy. "Then Camp Calloway. But everything is totally dark at the lake house. I can tell it was cold, but I think we were there early..."

"It was before Christmas," he confirms.

"We weren't there for the holidays?"

He shakes his head.

"Why not?"

Now he *really* stiffens. He mentions a Big Event that brought everyone there before the holidays. Nothing he's comfortable retelling for my sake. I *could* do an internet search. But I'm scared to be drowned in a rabbit hole of Big Bad Events.

"What happened back then has more to do with me and Jane," he says. "You weren't really involved in it, but you did join us on the damage control tour."

Huh. I learn all about the FanCon tour. Okay, not *all* about it. He gives me a brief synopsis, and it sounds way too fun to miss. *Do not mourn the tour.*

Too late.

"You remember nothing about the tour?" he asks.

"Uh-uh. I barely remember anything past *arriving* at the lake house." My ribs throb against my aching lungs. "I've still forgotten three years, haven't I?"

"About, yeah." He pockets his phone, his burst of happiness popped. He thought I was getting better. Moffy is good at caging emotions, so I can't tell if he's disturbed by Variant Luna (aka *me*). "You'll remember when you're ready to, sis. You know?"

I try to nod.

Moffy bops my head lovingly, and our childhood tries to lift my spirits. He says, "Don't put too much stress on yourself over it. I'm a knower of things, *and* I have this super annoying husband who practically drilled in my brain: Stress Bad, Relaxing Good."

My brother loves Farrow.

It pummels me again. Two of the most important, influential people in my whole life cosmically collided together—and I can't even reminisce with him.

Because I never saw them fall in love.

I spin around, pretending to examine an old Sagittarius tapestry thumbtacked to the wall. Walking forward, tacked beside the cloth is a black pen drawing of the Leo constellation. My heart leaps.

"Do you know Donnelly's birthdate?" I ask my brother.

"August…13ᵗʰ, I'm pretty sure, but I can double-check—"

"No, that's okay." *August 13ᵗʰ.* Donnelly would be a Leo. I run my finger over the stars. Another sheet is stuck beneath this one. I lift the paper and a hidden sketch steals my breath. Stars and planets swirl around two figures: a girl, a guy. *Is that us?*

Why did I hide it?

Then again, would I even be that forthcoming if I got a boyfriend? I could see myself not sharing with so many people. Less voices mean less opinions, and sometimes it's easier to just keep things to myself. Seeing a romantic sketch concealed beneath another just saddens me though.

"You have any other questions?" Moffy asks.

"Why can't I remember anything about him?" I turn to face my brother.

He tries to exhale a breath. "No one really knows."

"You have theories?" Does Maximoff Hale still have a philosopher's heart? He's had to have thought about this! I perk up, but he's making a cringey face. "Please, *Moffy.*"

Scraping a hand along his tight neck, he says, "I think your brain is probably protecting you from…trauma, or it's safeguarding memories with him that you don't want corrupted. Maybe both."

Trauma. "He was with me part of the night," I remember what Donnelly said. "When it happened…" *What happened?*

"Yeah," Maximoff says, just as Arkham barks and scratches at the door. "I have to take that one out for a walk. You need anything?"

Orion springs off his doggie bed, whining at my feet. "Does he…?" I trail off with insecurities.

"I'll take Orion too." Moffy whistles, and Orion follows him to the door. Guilt heavies my lungs for not taking care of my dog. Am I a bad pet owner? Orion looked happy to see me, so I can't be too neglectful, right?

Moffy stops at the door, hesitating. Glancing back, he says, "I'm not bothered at all if you need anything. I'm seriously one phone call and Bat signal away." He's earnest. "I'm still your big brother who'd fuck up anyone if they fucked with you."

I want to believe that's true.

Still, I say, "This kinda feels like Bizzaro World where everything is backwards and the sun is square." He'd know the DC comics. He was the one who lent them to me to read when I was nine.

"I'm the same." He touches his chest. "I still *love* my face plastered to *Celebrity Crush.* I'm a headline whore, and I tear up *far* too easily. I'm practically a waterfall." His brand of sarcasm is 100% the Moffy I know, and I try to smile. "Ask Farrow, I've drowned him a billion times." Quickly, he adds, "Metaphorically."

I try to ease. "Still speed on freeways?"

"All the damn time." He's rigid though.

"Besties with Charlie?"

"Hell would freeze over first." He licks his lips, looking away. Is he actually close to Charlie again?

It's okay if you've changed. I can't say it. Because I'm more frightened that he has. "You are close to Charlie?" I actually ask.

He tries to shrug. "A bit. Yeah. We're not trying to kill each other." He motions to me. "You're in contact with him a lot more too."

"I am?" I've always liked Charlie from a distance, but I haven't made large strides to close the gap. Charlie is someone who can create multiple Grand Canyons of his choosing, and it's a calculated risk to exert the effort to even reach him.

"He's been editing your fics."

Makes a little sense.

Moffy grips the doorframe, about to leave. "I am the same enough," he reiterates, and I realize he's afraid I'll think he's too different to trust or love this time around.

It's a rational fear.

Because I'm thinking, *can I trust him?* He's right—he only knows what *he's* seen. Maybe I need to enlist Detective Donnelly to help me.

I throw up a Vulcan salute, not wanting him to worry much. "Thanks, memory guide," I tell him.

Moffy tries to smile back, but he knows I'm placating him. I know he's trying to convince me he's worthy of trust.

It's all screwed up. Warped.

After he leaves with the puppies, I crouch back to the fishbowl. "Polaris?" I ask. Nope, no response. Well, that sucks. Miracles *don't* happen. But if a miracle were to fall into my lap, I can think of a thousand better ones than my fish magically responding to its name. *Like getting my memories back.*

I walk over to another door in my room and enter...a bathroom. Two sinks, a glass shower stall—everything is tidy. No toiletries spread on the counters. No water stains on the faucet. I'm guessing sharing a bathroom made me neater than usual...I don't know.

Letting out a frustrated breath, I eye another door. "Donnelly's room," I think out loud.

To snoop or not to snoop, that is the question. Biting my thumbnail, I wonder if something in that room will jog a memory. If my brain is protecting memories that surround Donnelly, then wouldn't he be the key to unlocking them? Or...if I was close to Donnelly, then those memories could be the strongest to burst through.

More educated guesses.

Not that I'm good with education. I'm failing out of high school... or no...I'm not in high school anymore. Did I even graduate?

I let out a long groan. There's just *too much* that's missing. It pushes me forward. I grab the knob and turn.

30

Luna Hale

THIS IS OH SO WRONG. I'm likely booking passage to hell. Yet, I can't stop scoping out Donnelly's room—which I've come to realize is a *guest room*. How else do you explain the frilly grannie shams and floral comforter? It screams Jane Cobalt. Plus, *The Commencement of the Empire* painting is hung on the wall. *Jane's* painting. Donnelly must've not cared about redecorating.

Maybe he didn't think he'd be here for long. That freaks me out—because wouldn't Original Luna want him to stay?

I tug open a dresser drawer. Empty.

Second drawer. A couple shorts. Bathing suit trunks. Boxer-briefs. So few items that they all fit together.

Crouching, I slide out the third drawer. Among socks is a ripped open box of condoms. I wonder if we ever used these or not. *Maybe he used them on another girl.* I crinkle my brows, not sure how to feel about that idea. He never said we were *exclusive.* I could've been sleeping around.

He could've too.

Shoving the condoms aside, I find an old cigar box: a place where people usually store mementos. I only hesitate for half-a-second before I flip the lid.

Passport.

I unfurl a sheet of paper. *His birth certificate.* The answers are handwritten and not super legible.

Full Name of Child: *Paul Donnelly*

County of Birth: *Philadelphia*

Born on: *August 13th* (Moffy was right)

Weight: *6 pounds 1 ounce*

Father's Full Name: *Sean ~~Ketty~~ Donnelly*

Mother's Maiden Name: *Bridget...*

I squint hard, unable to really decipher his mom's maiden name. I refold the birth certificate. He hasn't kept any old IDs. The only things left in the cigar box are...wedding programs.

Jane Cobalt & Thatcher Moretti

They were married last year. Jane...and a bodyguard. Jane... and Thatcher—who just so happens to be my little brother's 24/7 bodyguard. Quiet, a bit broody, an identical twin, that's what I remember. It's not like I know him too well. He barely talks at all. Jane could talk for *hours*. Evidence that opposites do attract.

I read the other program.

Maximoff Hale & Farrow Redford Keene. I skim the list of the grooms' party and freeze at the sight of Donnelly's name.

Oh wow, he was Farrow's *best man*. They are closer than close then.

I place the cigar box in its original spot and check the end table drawer.

Phone charger.

Bullets? *Probably since he's a bodyguard.* He has a gun somewhere. Then I unearth a notebook. Milky Way swirls and basic stick figure aliens...I used to draw these in my school binders all the time. I recognize my crappy artwork. These are *my* doodles.

Why would he have my notebook?

Is this a diary?

I exhale a burst of fear. *Okay*, he could've thieved this from my room. But am I much better? I'm digging through his belongings like a thief in the night (or morning, it's morning).

I've never kept a diary though. In the situation I'm in, it'd be way too helpful if I did. Heart accelerating, I open the notebook and see my handwriting on the inside cover.

Donnelly,

I don't know if you use this sort of thing, but I figured you might like writing down your daily thoughts in pen. Sometimes it feels good to seep out all the gooey stuff in your brain and put it somewhere else. So this is for your gooey brain matter.

Merry Christmas,

Luna

Not my diary. It's *his*.

My stomach twists with this information. I gave Donnelly a Christmas present, which definitely means I trust him. He's good. A good guy. Knew it!

More eagerly, I flip through a few pages and see the words *Daily Planner* and different typed sections: *today's focus, notes, meals, water, question of the day*. In each one, Donnelly has added his handwritten thoughts.

Today's Focus: Be chill (you are the freeze)

Question of the Day: Has Rose Calloway ever farted in front of Connor?

I laugh hard, smile spreading, and I flip another page and another. Not reading everything, I'm just seeing how much Donnelly has used this notebook. So, *so* many pages are filled. My heart swells.

I tuck the notebook under my armpit and turn my sights to the closet.

Once there, I whip open the door. T-shirts, a suit in the very back, some hung slacks—your regular variety closet occupants. No skeletons. No monsters. *Yet.* (I really hope those don't exist.) Bending down, I pull out a plastic tub and pop the lid.

Manuscripts? I pluck one out.

The Bluest Night by Luna Hale. My manuscripts...I thumb through the stapled pages. Red pen strikes through some lines, and little notes in the margin read, *check consistency* and *this word doesn't make sense in this context. I think you mean "dissipate."*

Charlie's notes.

Quickly, I snatch the next manuscript. *Born to Roam* by Luna Hale. The next. *The Chasm of Elsewhere* by Luna Hale. And the next. *See You in the Stars* by Luna Hale. I've never read any of these! I can't even remember writing them.

My ribs tighten painfully, and I swallow a rising knot. Slower, I reach in for the thickest bound manuscript.

Human Him, Cosmic Her by Luna Hale. Subtitle: *The Thebulan Saga.*

Of course I've been continuing my longest-run series, and I've had plans for how the next stories would pan out, not just for me but for the handful of readers on Fictitious who keep up with the story. The slight *positive* to losing my memories, I can read my stories for the first time like I'm just a reader and not the writer. I put the printed story back in the tub, I can access them online. Original Luna must've had a ton of guts to lend these to Donnelly.

He's read my stories. The startling thought comes crashing down.

My cheeks burn, feeling a teeny bit exposed. Did I know he'd like them? Or did I just risk it? What if he read the smuttier ones? Maybe he hasn't had the chance to flip through any of them. They could just be collecting dust in his closet.

It lessens my nerves, and I return to the closet-hunt. Next to the tub, I find his tattoo machine, ink, and other supplies, some carefully packaged for sterilization. Sketchbooks are stacked neatly nearby, and I examine the top one.

Each page is full of tattoo sketches. His style of art is bold and colorful. Pirate skulls, lions, roses, a ship in a bottle, horseshoe with a *good luck* banner…an alien head. I smile at the alien with a crown, a banner reading, *galaxy queen.* I flip a page. A ringed planet with a new banner says, *chart your own galaxy.* My lungs fill, and as soon as I turn the next page, I solidify.

This is…not a tattoo sketch.

Or maybe it is, but the style has changed from thick black lines to a thinner pen. He's drawn a girl. Inside her eyes are twinkling stars, and I'm lost in the expressiveness of those lively orbs, as though she's seen universes of light.

And her hair—oh wow, her *hair* floats around her soft face, the tendrils whirling into flying saucers and comets and crescent moons and hearts. I've never seen anything this stunning or this beautiful, and I wonder if she might be…could this girl be me? Involuntary tears leak and one drips on the page.

"No, no," I panic, the wet droplet bleeding the pen around her eye. "Shit." Gently, I dab at the paper, but her eye is already smudged. She looks horrible now. Pain is an unwelcome companion in my life, something I find myself bumping into, and now it's sitting on my chest.

I keep patting at the wet blotch, but another tear soaks the paper. *Shit.* I rub my watery eyes with a harsh hand. Then I hear the patter of footsteps outside the room—I'm in *Donnelly's* room.

I not only have his sketchbook in my clutch, but I never put back his daily planner. Frantic, I tuck the notebook under my butt like contraband.

The door swings open.

Donnelly goes still, hand on the knob. He peers backwards, and I catch a glimpse of the towering Moretti brothers passing through the hall behind him. Right as Thatcher and Banks nearly lock eyes with me, Donnelly steps further inside and shuts the door.

"They're just grabbing some things," he says, scanning me and my suspicious self. "They aren't spending the night yet."

I nod, unable to move off his notebook. "Cool."

"You going through my stuff?" He doesn't sound upset at all.

He should be.

Then again, he's a little difficult to read at first glance. Maybe inside he's soul-crushed thinking about how Variant Luna is a shitty version of his perfect Original Luna. Jealousy is growing like thorny vines in my body, and how can I be jealous of myself? This is so, so screwy.

"I messed up your drawing." I cop to the mistake because it's the right thing to do, and I hold up the sketchbook, opened to the smudged girl.

Donnelly comes forward, his stride so unencumbered, and his nearness skips my pulse. He takes the sketchbook and looks. Disappointment isn't on his face, but he hasn't pulled away from the drawing either.

"With my tears," I murmur. "I ruined her."

"Nah," he breathes, studying the page. "You made her better." He flashes the sketch to me.

She seems worse off. "Her eyelashes are blobs now."

"'Cause she'd been crying," he says like it makes perfect sense, and he does make perfect sense to me. He spins the sketch back to himself. "Sad tears?"

"Overwhelmed," I tell him softly. "I thought the drawing was very beautiful." I hesitate to ask, so I say, "Whoever the girl is, you made her look out-of-this-world extraordinary."

His lips begin to rise. "You are, Luna."

Brightness explodes in my body, an inward radiance that I haven't ever felt before, not to this degree. He's making me feel *overpowered.* An

OP character in the novel of my life. And despite all of that, it's hard to agree with him. "The Luna you know was extra spectacular, and I'm not sure she would've gone through your things."

At this, I unearth the daily planner from beneath my butt.

I hold it out in confession. "I didn't read too much of it."

Donnelly squats down to me, still wearing the kyber crystal necklace. Like me, he was brought a new set of clothes at the hospital (tattered jeans and a black long-sleeve tee), and he showered there too. As he reaches for the notebook, eucalyptus soap permeates off him, but I also smell his natural musk. It's a heady, dizzying scent, and I find myself inhaling deeper.

He eyes the doodled cover. "You gifted this to me a while back."

"*She* gifted it to you."

His face pinches in pain. "You are her."

Am I? "I don't even know who I become in the three years I missed." It's *frustrating*, and the pestering, annoying emotion won't go away.

He sets aside the sketchbook and planner. "You don't think you'll remember?" He doesn't seem shocked.

"Was your Luna a cynic too?"

"Cynical, yeah. Pessimistic, sometimes. But you wanted so fucking badly to *believe*. Mostly in aliens."

I smile a little.

"And yourself," he adds, "and in us." He tips his head, catching my gaze. "You were still adamant that the world was shit and people sucked."

Sounds like me. I ease. "You don't think the world is shit?"

"The world can be shit." He sits with me, his arms hanging on his knees. "But living in it can also be amazing. Like ate the best ham hoagie of your life *amazing*, danced your heart out at 3 a.m. *amazing*, kissed an alien and shot to the moon *amazing*."

I glance at his lips, butterflies swarming me. "You've communed with the extraterrestrial?"

"Just one." He's looking at me. "And she's the prettiest alien I've ever seen."

"*Wannabe* alien," I correct.

"Sad alien," he amends, his tone flirty. I bite the corner of my lip, smiling more, especially as he sweeps my features. He nods to me. "I think you've crashed on my planet this time."

He crashed on my planet the first time then. I picture Donnelly orbiting my universe and landing at my feet. It excites me as much as this inversed reality where I've fallen at his. "Uh-huh," I say, breathless.

"Welcome to Earth, space babe."

"It's peculiar here," I sing-song. "But I already like one of its inhabitants." I'm looking right at him. "I just wish…" *I could remember you.*

The pressure to remember has amassed since seeing my family. I've wanted to remember to comfort them and ease their worries, but now, more than ever, I crave to uncork these memories of Donnelly. Not just for him, but for *me*.

I pick at my bitten thumbnail, and more cowardly, I stand up and avoid his gaze.

Donnelly rises to his feet. He makes no effort to put away his things. He just rests against the wall, giving me some space. "You scared?" he asks.

Yep. "I want to remember, and I don't know how your Luna fared, but I'm not always that successful at things I put my brain power to. I just seem to always fail in the end." I shrug. "I could be considered Luna the Failure."

"Failures are those who don't even try. You always try—"

"And face-plant."

"And pick yourself back up. Sounds more like Luna the Fighter to me." He's such an encouraging human, and he's right—he already knows I'm gonna try to remember, even if I'm frightened of the worse outcome.

I give him a once-over. "You're not mad I went through your stuff?"

"Whatever helps you," he says honestly, then motions to the bed. "You check the real hiding spot?"

"Under your mattress?"

He grins. "Not under, no." He lets me wander over to the bed, and only one place really seems likely.

I belly-flop on the mattress to reach his bed pillow, and I roll over on my butt. "Am I getting hotter?" I squeeze the fluff of the pillow.

"Girl, you're roasting."

While he comes closer, I dig inside the pillowcase. "Careful of me," I warn. "I could burn you. I am hotter than hot."

"No lie," he smirks. "I'd burn up from you."

Flush bathes my cheeks. Now he really is scalding me inside-out, but I manage to scoop out the contents tucked in the pillowcase.

A small roll of cash tied with a rubber band.

A pack of cigarettes.

"Why do you keep these here?" I ask.

"Just habit." He watches me scooch to the edge of the bed. My bare knees knock into his legs, and a ripple of sensitivity shoots through me, then goosebumps pimple my skin. Donnelly stays standing above me as he says, "My parents would go through my room and try to sell my things to buy drugs. Most everything I had I bought myself with money I made working."

I frown. "That's awful," I mutter.

He takes a seat beside me. "I got used to it, but the pillowcase was one spot they didn't really look too often."

The last thing I find in the pillow: an old photo. The edges are yellowed and creased, but the picture is clear. A smiling little boy is on the shoulders of a young guy, whose cheeks are a bit sunken but he's smiling up at the boy too. They have the same chestnut brown hair. Same blue spinel gem eyes. Only, the little boy's gaze is a billion watts brighter. Livelier.

"Is this you?" I point to the boy.

"Yeah. And my dad."

I study his father again. He's really young. "He kinda looks like Ethan Hawke."

He smiles, scratching the back of his neck. "That's what you said the first time."

"You've showed me your hiding spot before," I realize and slip the cash, cigarettes, and photo back, wishing this jarred a memory. Alas, I'm memory-less.

He's shaking his head.

I freeze. "You didn't show me?"

"I just showed you the picture. The hiding spot didn't come up."

So perfect Original Luna didn't know every little thing about Donnelly then. I may have a leg up on her in this stupid pseudo competition in my head. I've never been competitive, so I don't know why I've decided to compete against myself. Maybe it's another amnesia symptom: the sudden urge to defeat my alternate version.

I would rather *become* her and seep into her memories of him, but that still seems unrealistic.

I place the pillow behind me. "Why show me now?" I ask.

"Guess I'd rather tell you now than later." He reaches back and reclaims the cigarettes from the pillow. "It's not easy for me to talk about my upbringing and some deeper things, but I wanted to with you. I meant to."

"Did I share a lot about myself with you?"

"I think so. I got the sense you did, anyway." He leaves the bed, digging in his pocket and unearthing a lighter. "But you had limits and *not nows* or *not tonights*."

He must not have been pushy.

Slowly, I stand and glance at his drawer. *The condoms.* Questions spring in my mind again, but he asks if I'm hungry.

"I could eat," I say.

So after a kitchen pit stop and pantry raid, we end up in my bedroom with three cans of Pringles, cinnamon Pop-Tarts (untoasted), and warm glass bottles of Fizz. He's lounging on the fuzzy rug, and I've occupied this white globe chair that'd be perfect in a NASA spacecraft.

Now that he's in *my* room, intrigue tries to overtake my appetite. I only munch on a few Pringles and sip my Fizz. I watch Donnelly lean back on one hand. He seems at home here.

Yet, he asks, "You care if I smoke?"

"Did your Luna care?"

He opens his mouth, words caught for a millisecond. "You didn't."

"So…why get my permission twice?"

"Because you don't remember the first time, and I think it's only right that I ask again."

I hate the idea that I might change my mind on certain things and be too different from Original Luna, but at least I know, in this, we're the same.

"You can smoke." I even switch on the air filter on my nightstand. Back on the chair, I ask, "Where's the best ham hoagie you've ever had?"

"Wawa." He says it so fast, then smacks the cigarette pack on his palm.

"Never been…or maybe I have." I spin in a circle on the chair, rotating back around just in time to catch the shake of his head.

"You haven't been," he tells me.

I wonder why.

"I'm gonna take you there," he adds, putting a cigarette between his lips.

"For a ham hoagie?"

"Whatever hoagie you want, I'll get you." He lights the cigarette, taking a deep drag, then blowing off to the side. "It's a date."

A date. I start to smile. "We have those a lot?"

"Sadly, no." He squints like this past is a harsher light. "We never really dated outside our rooms."

I tap my glass bottle. If we wanted to be together, then *what* stood in our way…or rather, *who*? "Was it my dad? Did he forbid us from seeing each other or something?"

"He didn't make it any easier, not at first," Donnelly says, "but it wasn't him in the end. It was my family."

It takes him several minutes, but he explains how *his* family has been trying to extort *my* family. With the downturn of his gaze and the tightness of his voice, I get the sense they're behind my injury that night. Everything becomes a bit clearer—and not because I remember—but because the nurse's foul attitude towards Donnelly has context. Especially knowing he's been undercover trying to rat out his family.

When he finishes, he has a glazed look in his eyes. He sucks on his cigarette, his tattooed forearm resting on his knee.

I haven't totally considered how hard this must be on him. Partially because I didn't know what actually went down. Now that I have more pieces, I ask softly, "Can I do anything?"

"For what?" He blows smoke over his shoulder, away from me.

"For you." I shrug. "You've been doing a whole lot for me."

"This is enough," he breathes.

I frown. "But I'm not really doing anything."

"You're alive, Luna." He holds my gaze. "And I get to look at you and talk to you and go on dates with you. What more could I want? That's everything to me."

It barrels into me in the brightest, most luminous way possible. I'm choked for a second, but I manage to say, "So we're dating?" *Is that what we are?* "And we've never dated outside our rooms before?"

"You just got out of the hospital." He looks me over, and I wonder if he's thinking, *you don't remember me, Luna.* "We should take this slow. But I can talk to security about going out in public together. I'm hoping we'll be able to now that most of my family is locked up. If you'd want to, that is."

"I want to," I say with a nod, eagerness brewing in my body. The Pringle can is tucked between my thighs, and I eat another chip, not taking my eyes off Donnelly as he picks himself off the floor. He's holding the glass soda bottle and cigarette leisurely with one hand, and he comes towards me.

My heart flutters. "I think earthlings have a strange effect on me."

"All earthlings or just me?" He spins my chair, and I sit cross-legged while I rotate 360.

My room whirls past me. "This is the first real close encounter I've had with your species, so I can't be too sure."

He keeps spinning me, and my heart keeps flying. The lava lamp, fishbowl, and his tall build blur together as he says, "So you know, I'm one-of-a-kind. There aren't a lotta humans like me. Just ask the mirrors, the floor, Moondragon, they'd all agree."

"Moondragon?"

"The little fishy guy over there." He twirls me in another circle, and I catch a glimpse of the goldfish swimming laps in the bowl.

I intake a sharp breath. *I told Donnelly about my fish.* Moondragon. It's not lost forever, which means I confided in *someone.*

I confided in him. And I'm starting to wonder if Original Luna more than just "liked" Donnelly. Did she really love him?

He said he's one-of-a-kind, so if I look elsewhere, I might not *feel* the tingles and electricity that I feel with him—but I wonder if OG Luna had proof.

"Did she date a lot before you?" I ask during another spin.

He halts me in front of him, his face unreadable, but he's tensed. "A bit. Right before me, you were mostly into casual hookups."

That's not so hard to believe since I've been interested in having sex. "She likes sex?"

"You love sex."

It scares me that I might be compulsive in bed, and I don't even *know.* Maybe that's why it's easier to still consider Original Luna a separate entity from me. *Her* and *she.* Not me. It's reassuring, though, hearing Donnelly keep referring to her as me. I like that he's hopeful I'll remember everything again, even if I'm not so sure that's possible. It's making me feel like…it might be. Maybe.

I hope.

"Am I a sex addict?" I ask so quietly, I'm unsure if he hears.

He drops the burning cigarette into the glass bottle. "You haven't been diagnosed or anything, but I know you think about it."

"Do you think I'm one?"

He shakes his head. "But we also haven't had sex that many times. You and me—the two of us—we're fairly new."

Didn't expect that. Something about Donnelly makes me feel like

I've known him my whole life, as if we've been together millenniums already.

I stand on the cushion of the chair, double-fisting Pringles and soda. "So she was into hookups until you. What'd you do to her?"

He grins. "Only you know that, space babe."

I wish that were true. "You rocked her universe somehow."

"With my good looks and wit." Donnelly spins me while I'm standing, and I balance, smiling as I whirl around and around and around. During each turn, I try to pin my sole focus on him, and everything begins to blur except for Paul Donnelly. He is the most vivid thing ahead of me, and I never want to lose sight of him.

"Do you think," I say in another rotation, "that we could trigger memories of you and me?"

"How so?"

I see his blue eyes.

I see his pink lips.

Anticipation and attraction swirl like a toxin around me, but I want to believe it's the opposite of poisonous. Being this close to Donnelly could reawaken me.

"We could kiss," I say. "It'd be like an experiment."

He breaks the chair's momentum again, but this time, I feel like I've flung off. While I stare down at him, his expression makes *zero* sense to me.

31

Paul Donnelly

EXPERIMENT. **THAT WORD** rings in my ears. 'Cause this is *exactly* how we started, and what are the chances this could be happening all over again?

"Bad idea?" she asks quietly, searching my gaze for answers.

Not sure it's one. I never regretted eating her out for the other experiment. I'd do it *all over* again—I've always known that. And given the opportunity a second time around, my instinct is to rush forward, to race right after her desires. Which have become mine.

Kissing Luna? Can't turn that down if you paid me to.

"Doesn't seem like a bad idea to me," I tell her, the air thickening with a hotter tension. She's still standing on the chair, an inch or so taller than me. I set aside our sodas and her Pringles. Then I reach out and cup her soft, flushed cheek, blood pumping like I'm boarding a rocket.

She's grinning.

My lips begin to rise. "I'm at your earthly service, space babe."

Her breath deepens and grows stronger.

I'm on a high. The biggest high I've been on in a while, and I'm not looking to come down. But I know, *this is different than the first experiment.* For me, not for her. She has no memories of me and our first kiss, but I have so many more of Luna—of us together—but I try to imagine this is the first intimate moment of our existence.

I latch on to the eagerness in her gaze. "You ready for takeoff?" I breathe.

"Yes," she whispers, her hands on my shoulders. "Let the experiment commence."

I bring her head down with gentleness, and very slowly, I press my lips to hers. Light bursts in my chest, and I urge her lips apart in a sensual motion. Her tongue slides against mine in exploration, and I want to go on every journey to every fucking place with this girl.

Don't leave me behind, Luna.

Deepening our kisses, my fingers thread through her light brown hair, and I step onto the chair with her. The instant I tower above Luna, her breath hitches. Swiftly, I place a hand on the small of her back, holding her body against mine. Stabilizing her. Then I carefully kick the desk, and we spin.

Rotating 360 on her chair, we haven't stopped making out. My heart is hammering in a hypnotic tempo. We share a lethal attraction, and I've never fully understood Romeo and Juliet till I found a love I'd rather die inside than live without.

Remember me.

She glides her fingers from my forehead down to my cheeks, along my jaw and neck, as though hoping her hands will remember what her mind can't. Heartache tries to grip my insides, but I won't let it ruin the purity of this moment with Luna.

No matter what happens to me, to us, I can't let darkness shade my world. It's the brightest it's ever been with her. That's the happy truth.

As we continue to spin, her arms wind around my waist. I can't get enough of her sweet scent and taste—they start overriding my other senses. Clutching her cheek, I kiss her stronger, and her hips buck against me. A grunt scratches my throat, my lungs, my muscles blazing.

Whenever I skate my hands along Luna's skin, shivers ripple through her, and as she becomes breathless, I break our lips and ask huskily, "You remember how I kissed you?"

"Not yet." She's eyeing my mouth. "Help me remember." She pants, "*More.*"

She wants more.

"I'll give you more." I cup her ass and lift her against my chest. She hooks her legs around my waist, sharing my grin. After I hop off the chair, she catches my lip in her teeth, and I nip her lip back, until we're kissing over and over and over again. She's clinging tighter to my build.

This is her first time with me.

It's a jolting thought.

If she asked for more years ago, after I gave her head, I woulda done it. So why is that thought trying to rattle me now? I shake it off and push her up against the wall, the midnight blue and gold-stitched Sagittarius tapestry at her back.

Muscles flexed, on fire, I hold Luna and suck the nape of her neck, spurring tiny noises out of her. Each breathy sound is fisting my hardened cock. Her feverish hands drift up my shirt, raking hot trails along my abs. *Fuck.*

"More," she moans.

Keeping her hoisted with one hand, I use the other to draw down her loose top and expose her tit. I kiss and lick her perked nipple, and she writhes against me. Heat gathers, blood thrumming in my veins, and I'm in a perfect position to fuck her against the wall—if we weren't clothed.

"*More,*" she pants and pleads, trying to grind and bounce on my dick. When that's not enough, she fumbles for my zipper. Luna unbuttons and unzips me, and my gut drops. I can't go this far—not like this. Quickly, carefully, I set Luna on her feet and lift her shirt back up.

Her face plummets, and I go cold. Ah *shit.* Fuck. I feel way worse, like I jumped in a ditch and shoveled dirt on myself.

"It's alright," I assure, staying close. "It's a me thing." *You didn't do anything wrong.* I'm resting my forearm on the wall beside her head.

She bites the edge of her lip, thinking, before she speaks quietly.

"Does kissing her feel better than kissing me?" It plunges a knife in my chest, but I'm not letting on how much that hurts to hear.

"No," I say strongly. "Feels the same to me."

She still looks worried.

I'm not cheating on Luna with Luna. They're the *exact* same person to me, but with amnesia, Luna is a tad bit more sensitive since she's comparing herself to herself and all. Been learning more here and there.

"I…don't understand then," she murmurs, and frustration bunches her brows and downturns her lips. "Is it because the experiment isn't working?"

She still doesn't remember me.

I shake my head.

My desperation hasn't been as strong as my desire. Because I haven't been banking on being able to trigger her memories through a kiss. I figure she'll remember when she's ready.

"You love role-playing," I tell her. "We both do, and I sorta saw this as that. I'm not upset that it didn't work out."

Her shoulders untense, and I wonder if she was scared that I'd be disappointed the experiment failed.

I ask, "Are you upset about it?" I skim her, unable to tell.

She shrugs. "I kinda believed it was a long shot too. But I thought it'd be fun…to kiss you—I wanted you to kiss me." Her cheeks flame. "I wanted to do more too." She glances at my unzipped pants. "I feel so…" She winces, then tries to palm her reddened face to hide.

"No, no, Luna," I breathe, holding her warm cheeks. She's never hidden like this from me, like I'm her prick of an ex-boyfriend causing her to question herself. My second go-round with Luna—I can't fuck it up this quickly. "You wanna know who I am?"

She nods, clinging to my gaze.

"I'm the guy who's never been ashamed of anything I've ever done. I've stripped down in sweaty nightclubs, humped bronze statues at 2 a.m., skinny-dipped in strangers' pools, pierced my cock, tattooed you." She's barely blinking, and I don't stop. "Went down on you after your dad threatened my job *over* tattooing you, then tattooed you again."

Her eyes well.

"I've been the son of addicts, a high school dropout, a slut, a tattooist, and a bodyguard, and I love everything about myself, despite so many people telling me I should *hate* who I am. That I'm shit. That I'm nothing. Not worth air. Not worth this life. I know I'm worth *everything*. And the girl I've fallen for—she's loved herself tenderly. Wholeheartedly." A tear escapes her eye and slips over my hand against her cheek. "Despite so many people telling her she should be embarrassed of the things she does, of who she is." I cradle her watery gaze. "You don't embarrass me, Luna Hale. You never have, and you never will. It's something you already knew, but I'll tell you a million times if I need to: I'm the guy who's never gonna be ashamed of anything you *ever* do. I'll likely do all those things with you too."

She sniffs hard, then wipes her runny nose.

More urgently, I say, "I've fucked you wearing a superhero mask. I'd fuck you wearing a unicorn head. You going at my zipper isn't a turn-off or anything."

"Then what made you stop?"

Why did I stop?

Slowly, I drop a hand from her cheek, just to scrape my palm against my taut neck. The words are tar in my throat, but somehow, I get 'em out. "I don't wanna be an experiment."

It's one of the hardest things I've ever had to say. Harder than broaching the topic of being exclusive way back when, because at least she could confidently say she wanted a committed relationship with me based off her prior experiences.

She remembers so few now, and years ago, I was her great head baseline when she was looking for more *experiences*. We didn't end up together right away. She got into casual sex. I slept around too.

The first experiment was a steppingstone for her to go figure out what she liked to do with other guys, and I'm not gonna be her gateway lay again. I can't lose her like *that*.

She's processing, so I add more, "You've only known me for a couple days; I'd rather take this slow until you're sure you want to be with me and only me." I'm giving her room to choose to sleep around if that's what she needs to do. It seems unfair to tell her she can't, knowing that's what she pursued the first time.

I just can't be hooking up with her if she's having sex with other guys. I can't handle it. I will break.

"Okay," Luna nods rapidly. "We'll go slower until I'm more certain." She's holding onto my beltloops. "I'm not planning on doing anything physical with anyone else in the meantime though. I think it'd hurt Original Luna...and maybe me, too."

I start smiling. Didn't think she'd say that. Relief breathes more life in my body. What a top tier feeling.

I tell her, "Slow is also good since you're mentally a virgin still. We don't have to rush anything."

She shrugs again. "I never put much stock in my virginity. I don't really care how I lose it."

Seems about right. Considering she lost it to some high schooler and afterwards that fucker spread a rumor about her being a slut at Dalton Academy. I don't have the heart to tell her that.

Her brows crinkle. "I can...*almost* remember my first time, but it's hazy. It happened before the lake house, right?"

"Yeah, I think so." Most of what I knew about Luna before the FanCon tour was from rumors in security. *Security*—I've only gotten confirmation that I'm still on the team. *Thanks, boss.* Don't know much else at this point since the press is taking a dump on me.

She frowns. "I think my first time was disappointing." She peeks up at me for confirmation.

"I wasn't with you in bed, space babe."

"Damn. I wish you were stuck on me."

"The barnacle to your ship." I give her a *rock on* gesture, then I curve an arm around her shoulders, pulling her away from the wall. She's smiling while I say, "Don't worry, I'll get stuck on you." *I already am.*

A fist raps her bedroom door.

I drop my arm off Luna, just as her brother calls out, "Luna, you okay? Can I let Orion in?"

"Yeah, come in!"

Maximoff emerges, unleashing her excitable puppy. The fluffy guy comes bounding for...*me.*

My grin returns. "Who's a good boy?" I squat and scratch behind his ears. "That's you. Yeah, you know it, don't you, Orion? My happy bud." I feel Luna studying me and her dog like she's never seen Man's Best Friend before. I look up at her. "We're best bros."

"Huh."

"I love dogs and dogs love me." I leave out the fact that Kinney's puppy would like to murder me in my sleep. Orion licks my hand, slobbering on me, but I'm more aware of Maximoff's domineering presence.

Her older brother might not approve of me being in her room, considering she doesn't remember *shit* about me. Causing friction between brothers and sisters is never something I wanna do, and she needs Maximoff right now.

"I can go," I say as I stand.

"No," Luna panics. "You don't have anywhere to be today, right? We're hanging out."

Maximoff uncrosses his arms, gesturing to me. "You should stay. This is your home too, Donnelly."

That strikes me, right to the core.

Maximoff could so easily tell Luna to trust him more than me, and she would believe him. He's been her closest sibling. Maybe I shouldn't even be shocked that he'd put faith in me to take care of his sister. He's only wanted Luna to be safe and happy, and he must see that both lie with me.

And *safety* is not something I could guarantee for her, not with my family attached to me, but now that most are in jail—I have a better shot.

I nod to him. The Hales are something else. *The Bad Luck Crew.* Never thought I'd grow to love them as much as I do.

"Alright," I say. *I'm staying.*

"I DIDN'T FLUNK OUT OF HIGH SCHOOL," LUNA

says, still mulling over her past that I dole out in spurts. On her bed, we've been smoking and drinking Four Loko and *trying* to watch *Beneath a Strong Sentiment*. Thought I pitched her current (forgotten) favorite sci-fi show well, if I do say so.

Except we're two minutes through episode one and the freeze-frame of Callie, Luna's ride-or-die character, fills the TV screen. And Luna has no clue how she would've burned at the stake for this girl.

Goal: *Get Luna invested in Bass before the convention in San Francisco.*

It shouldn't be this hard, but I can't blame her for being more interested in pieces of her missing history. It's the more engaging story.

Propped against the headboard, I blow smoke towards the air filter on her nightstand. With barely any sleep, cigarettes are the only thing keeping me awake.

I ask, "Graduating surprises you that much?"

"Yeah." In the darkness of her room, I still catch confusion in her eyes from the blue light of the TV. "I thought there was a chance I would've quit. Jeffra was being...*awful*. She's—"

"I know who she is," I tell her.

Luna nods. "I guess in three years, I did more and less than I thought I would. I graduated high school, which is awesome. I'm taking college classes, but I'm not fully enrolled for some reason." Her brows bunch. "Fear, maybe. It's easier not going all-in. Less chances to disappoint myself and others, and I didn't think I'd be so disappointed in myself right now just knowing I took the *easy* out."

"You were really tired," I mention. "You had to pick yourself up too many times."

So softly, she asks, "She went through a lot, didn't she?"

"Yeah." My throat tries to close. Maybe hers does too because she sips the alcoholic drink. Don't think she's supposed to have too much alcohol right now with her injuries and pain meds, so I've been downing bigger gulps when she passes the can to me.

Just when I'm about to press *play*, her phone buzzes. Reminds me that I need a new phone. Stat.

Luna checks her cell. "I have an appointment with the neuropsychologist tomorrow morning." She types out a text. "Will you come with me?"

"I would, but I gotta check with security." It also might be better if she goes on her own. Her infatuated attachment to me could be a bad thing, and I wouldn't know.

She's on her phone for a hot second longer.

"Watcha looking at?" I ask, concerned.

"I just don't understand." She growls in frustration, practically fisting her phone. She types feverishly again. "It's not working."

"What's not?"

"My Fictitious password." She slams back against the headboard in a huff.

I ease an arm over her shoulders, and she expels a calmer breath. Putting the cigarette between my lips, I nod to her phone. "There's a reason for that."

"You know the password?"

I take a drag, blowing smoke away from Luna. "You deleted your account." Having to retell a heartbreaking history isn't so easy for me, but I'm doing it for her. In as many necessary words, I recount how her fics leaked recently. Spread on the internet. The blowback from media and people online, all of it.

I'm bracing myself for a round two of Luna breaking down. I'm prepared to hold her, comfort her, anything to make this better—except, she's not sobbing.

She's not frozen in shock either.

"The manuscripts in your closet?" she starts to ask.

"You gave them to me to hold on to."

"That's all that's left?"

"Yeah." I pause. "If you wanna read your stories, that's where they exist. You didn't get rid of 'em completely. They're not online or in your computer, only printed."

Her face pinches, as though examining the puzzle of her life. With my arm still around her, she touches my hand that's hanging near her bicep. She traces a vein with her thumb, the soft touch flooding my lungs.

"People were shitty," she says quietly. "*Are* shitty, I'm guessing. They're calling me what…a *freak*?" She frowns. "Luna the Tentacle Smut Lover?"

"That's what I call myself."

She smiles over at me. "You love tentacle smut?"

I suck on my cigarette, nodding. Blowing smoke at the ceiling, I say, "It's a favorite. I love yours."

Flush creeps up her neck, but she's interlacing her fingers with mine and turning more towards me on the bed. "I can't believe she let you read our smut." Her smile widens. "I kinda love her for it."

"Ditto." I'm drawn into her emerging effervescence. Big word, *effervescence*, I know. It'd shock the pants off my dad, but I do read.

Luna rolls onto her knees, sitting more in front of me. I spread my legs open so she's a bit closer, and after she passes the Four Loko to me, I say, "You've been crushed about the leaked fics." I explain her absence at college, holing up in the penthouse, and avoiding the public.

"This is all recent?" she asks again.

"Yeah." I sweep her reaction. "You're not torn up about it?"

"I mean, it sucks, but what doesn't?" She shrugs. "Maybe Original Luna was beat down so much that this was the final straw." She watches me swig the drink, cigarette in the same hand. "And being told a horror story isn't quite the same as living it."

"Yeah, I get that."

"What if I can help her?" Luna says, perking up. "What if some *good* can come out of my memory loss? If she couldn't face the world after what happened, maybe I can." She adds, "This is my chance to get over the internet trolls and go to college *fully* this time."

Pride is a sappy emotion, and I'm bathing in it right now. "I think you would've been proud of yourself, Luna Hale."

Her smile only grows, then she stares at our clasped hands and her lips soften. "I'm scared I'll never be Original Luna again, but I can try to be a Better Luna in the meantime."

I'm keeping hope she'll remember the past. It hasn't been that long that she's forgotten. "I have to talk more to security, but if you do go back to college, no one can know you've lost your memories."

"I've heard," she nods. "They said if my medical records leak and anyone outside of my family, doctors, and security find out I have amnesia, it'll put me at risk."

"No one wants you to get taken advantage of is all, and there are some slimy fuckers out there."

"Who'd try to manipulate me," she mutters, understanding. "It'd be a good villain arc."

"God, I hate villains."

She sits cross-legged now and lets go of my hand to reach for the Four Loko. "Even if they make the story more interesting?"

"I just don't want 'em to surround me—or anyone I care about."

Luna rattles the can. *Empty.* Then she eyes me up and down a little more tentatively. "Can you be my bodyguard?"

The question comes so far out of left field that I do my best to recover with another drag of my cigarette. Reclaiming the can, I snuff the little nub on the aluminum rim. "I don't think I can."

"It was just an idea I had. I'd feel bad taking you from Beckett anyway."

"I'm not on his detail. Haven't been for years."

Her lips part. "Really?"

I see the time on her phone. *It's late.* We've been talking for hours. Exhaustion is trying to maul me into the covers, and my body still aches from being chained on the metal bench in jail. "I'll tell you about it another night."

"Wait, but who…?"

"I've been Xander's bodyguard."

"Oh." She stares far away.

"I've promised your brother I'd stay with him—and I've been shit at keeping promises that matter to your family. I wanna make sure I don't break this one. I'm trying to be a Better Donnelly."

Her lip quirks in a slight smile. "Cheers to being better among our respective species." She lifts a finger toward me, and I press my fingertip to hers like we're in *E.T.*

"Is this where I get powers?" I ask her. "Or are you gonna abduct me?"

"Abduction, obviously."

We're laughing, and I tell her, "I'm ready. Take me to your planet."

More softly, she says, "I forgot the way." It tunnels through me, and we gaze into one another, searching. Quieter, she whispers, "I'm lost with no map."

"You'll find your way back," I reassure. *She will.* I could light another cigarette. I could go pop open an energy drink. Fuck sleep, right? Except she's battling a yawn, and I know it's time to go.

So I climb off the bed, throwing the trash in a bin, and she's reluctant to crawl beneath the covers. "Donnelly," she starts, an emotional tension straining the air this time.

I have to cut in first. "I need to warn you—since I sleep over there." *And I haven't slept in a while.* "I sleepwalk."

She considers this carefully. "What helps?"

I shake my head. "I dunno. Some years it's worse than others." I glance to her bathroom door. "I thought being next to you might help, but you've seen me sleepwalk before."

Luna touches her comforter. "I was gonna ask if you want to sleep in my bed with me. You were with Original Luna, and it's something I think I want…but if you're not into it, that's okay. I don't know if it'll help your sleepwalking or not, but if it can, then…" She shrugs. "I want to help you too."

Lying in bed alone or lying in bed with the comfort of the girl I love?

No brainer. And that's how I find myself stripping down to my boxer-briefs and beneath the comforter with Luna. Naturally, we gravitate toward one another. On our sides, she nuzzles her back against my chest, spooning, and our deep breaths sync up.

I hold her, and as I begin to drift, I hear her murmur one last thing to me.

"I wanna do all the amazing things in this world." The tail-end is too quiet to catch, but I'm hoping she said, *with you.*

Please let it be with me.

32

Paul Donnelly

RAGE ENVELOPS ME like a violent inferno. I'm suffocated in the fumes of anger. My knuckles sear. Breath is smoldering in my lungs. I scream a noiseless scream while my fists fly into Patrick's face. He's still laughing.

It's gasoline to my wrath, and I can't stop.

I can't stop.

I can't see his face anymore. I can't hear him. Blood-red fury overpowers me—scares the shit outta me—and I thrash awake.

Holy shit. I'm in bed. Luna's bed. Panting, I've shot up to a sitting position, and she's startled awake. Sweat soaks the sheets all around me, and I take a second to collect my bearings.

"Donnelly?" I hear her concern.

"I'm alright, I'm alright, I'm alright," I say so fast in one staggered breath, then ask, "I didn't hurt you?" I skim her features with urgency, hoping I didn't throw an arm at her face. God, if I hurt her…

She shakes her head quickly. "No. You just started kicking."

Alright. I brush a hand through my wet hair. Fuuuck. I smear a hand down my damp face, then climb out of the bed. Jabbing a thumb to the door, I say, "I'm gonna get a water. You need anything?"

"No," she says. "You sure—?"

"I'm alright," I say again. "Talk tomorrow?" *Don't wait up for me.* "I might crash in my bed so I don't wake you again."

She nods, then scoots back beneath the covers.

Orion tries to follow me, but I close him in her room and whisper, "Stay with Luna. She needs you." He sits more patiently, then rounds back to her, hopping on her bed. She wraps an arm around his furry body, and it eases me out.

Once I'm in the dark kitchen, I abandon the task of getting a water. I'm gripping the butcher block island and trying to breathe out a strange weight on my chest. The chain around my neck might as well be a choker. I keep tugging at it, the kyber crystal like two-tons against my sternum.

I fucking hate this feeling. Anger has never lived inside of me, not long enough to take root and grow thorns, but every single time I think about that night…in that row house…it simmers beneath my skin. Crawling. Restless.

Weight.

I clench the counter.

"Hey?" Farrow flips on a warm kitchen light. In point-two seconds he scans me and he's looking at me like he's never seen me before.

"Couldn't sleep?" I ask him. He's only in black drawstring pants, his body covered in tattoos I inked on him.

"I was woken up by texts. Hospital paperwork." He's chewing slower on gum. "You look like shit."

I smell like roses, I'd joke. Come see. I'd stuff my pit in his face. He'd shove me and tell me to go stink up Oscar. All of those easy-going things just wither in my head. Asphyxiated beneath this dark fuel.

"I'm alright," I mumble.

Farrow kicks open the trash bin, spits out his gum, then eyes me once again.

"Stop," I sneer, acid burning the word. Burning me.

He frowns. "Man, this isn't like you. What's going on?"

"I'm fine!" I shout. "Just get the fuck away from me."

Farrow shifts his weight uneasily, glancing at my death-grip on the counter—at my hardly healed knuckles—and his hand outstretches calmly, coolly. "Donnelly—"

I push him. Farrow is taken aback. It pisses me off, and I can't say why. So I push him again, harder. His jaw muscles twitch, and we're breathing heavier. Then I snap, and coming at Farrow means meeting the floor. I've known that since I was a teenager—when he brought me to his MMA classes. Signed me up. Paid for me.

Don't worry about it, man, he'd say.

I did get him back, with tattoos.

I always tried to get him back, even when he never asked for an IOU.

"Donnelly," he grits out, putting me in a submission lock on the kitchen floor. "Just stop."

I can't. I struggle against him, and we're not teenagers anymore. He's thirty. I'm twenty-nine. He shifts again, until he's sitting up against the cabinets, his leg like an anchor fastening mine to the floor. My back is against his chest, and his arm goes around my windpipe— but he never chokes me too tight.

"Breathe," he urges.

I can't.

"Talk to me."

I can't.

I wanna scream, but the violent noise is like my nightmare, just soundless inside me. "I...need it to stop."

"What to stop?"

"This...feeling, man." I grind my teeth, eyes burning. I cover my face, and Farrow adjusts, knelt on one knee in front of me, gripping the back of my head. Before he says anything, I choke out, "Just go. You're gonna have another baby." I've said it before, but he doesn't need to deal with me and my shit. I've never wanted to drag him down with me, and I'm doing it now.

"Look at me," Farrow urges, his clutch strong on my skull.

I let my hand fall off my hot face.

And with everything inside him, he tells me, "You are my family." Tears gather in both our eyes, tears I don't think we've ever shared like this. "That's never changing."

It splits me open, and I bawl into my hand, into his chest. Glimpses of that night try to tear through me, and I just cry. It gushes out of me, and I can't stop it any better than I could cut the anger. This time, though, the weight is releasing bit by bit.

Easing off me slowly.

I breathe.

After some time, my tear ducts run dry and throat feels hoarse. Then Farrow snags waters out of the fridge, and we're leaning on the cabinets side-by-side.

I swig, the rush of water cooling my throat, and I spin the cap back and forth on the plastic bottle. "I woke up thrashing."

"You haven't slept," Farrow says, hushed in the quiet of the kitchen. "Being overtired can cause night terrors."

My nose flares, emotion funneling back into me. "It's Ulic Qel-Droma."

"Who?" Farrow makes a face like I'm speaking gobbledygook.

"He's a Jedi Knight."

"Luna," Farrow realizes.

"I read some of the comics in the hospital, while I was waiting for her to wake up, and Ulic—even with his good intentions, he was consumed with rage." I rest my arms on my knees like Farrow and look out at the kitchen island. "I walked into that row house, and I genuinely thought nothin' could hold me back from the light. I've walked through so much shit my whole life, and nothing has latched on to me like this. But seeing her there—I brought it back with me."

He extends a comforting arm over my shoulder. "We'll get through it, and being honest, PTSD is a typical outcome with what happened."

"PTS-who?" I play dumb. "I just told you I'm a Jedi Knight."

"Shut the fuck up." We're both smiling, but with a softer one, he pinches the kyber crystal off my chest.

"Hales," I say.

"Gotta love them," he says.

"Truths." I take another deep gulp of water.

"Technically, I'm not your doctor—"

"You don't say?"

"—but you do need a sleep study, like I've told you for years, and therapy might help."

I tried therapy once and didn't like how every time I joked, the therapist would prod me to be more serious. Which is the point, but I'd rather be in my happy place with people I like than endure a therapy session with someone I hardly know. It works for some, but it's not for me.

"I might just go grab a bagel at Lucky's." The diner is open 24/7. "Incognito and shit." Since no one can know I'm out of jail yet.

Farrow picks himself off the floor. "I'll drive. You text Oscar, see if he's awake."

"No phone."

He tosses me his.

I look up at my best friend.

The closest thing I'll ever have to a brother. And I know I'm gonna be okay, even if it takes some time. Bagel. Friends. Easier nights. Better tomorrows.

He clasps my hand, and I rise.

FANATICON FORUM

We Are Calloway

Posted by @lorensfavtaco616 #wac-mod

HALES' OFFICIAL STATEMENT MEGATHREAD 8
Discuss the most recent official statement released by
the Hales' (i.e. their publicists) regarding Lily Calloway's
assault & Luna Hale's kidnapping. This includes the part
about Paul Donnelly **not** being associated with the attack
and that he has not been fired from their security team,
like some of you speculated. (Official statement linked.)
Please be respectful of each other and the families and do
not repost images of Lily Calloway after the attack, or you
will be banned from the WAC forum.

@charliezbiggestcrush: There are photos of the ass-
wiper coming out of the house where Luna was taken.
Handcuffed. Then put in a cop car. It's not a deep-fake.
He's clearly a part of this. What are they doing???

@WWRCD: Can we not make "ass-wiper" a thing? We
don't know if Donnelly is *bad* or not, and it's just mean.
#StilltheAssKicker

@dragons_breakfast15: he's an ass-wiper.

@CapAndWidowBesties: aren't there grainy pics of Farrow, Oscar, and Donnelly eating at Lucky's Diner in the middle of the night? They're all still friends if that's real.

@XanderOnlyXander: 3 points. 1...we don't know how long he sat in jail for. 2...there are rumors all the charges were dropped with no evidence against him. 3...if he really was involved, there is no way Farrow & Oscar would associate with him.

@MarrowIsLife: agreed. Farrow is #TeamHale. He wouldn't be with someone who kidnapped Luna or hurt Lily.

@not_ur_beauty_queen: I can't believe there are ppl here who actually think Donnelly is innocent. WTF

@kitsulletti134: it's not that simple. We need to trust what the families are telling us.

@moomoopants242: oh look, the one kitsulletti stan. Go suck two dicks. Deleted by mod-bot for breaking forum rules.

@WACorDIE: Dude, he's related to ALL the guys who assaulted Lily. Red flag central.

@ILikeBigMorettis: Maybe he had the address to where Luna was being held?

@Coballoway_Child: BETTER QUESTION! Why wouldn't the families fire him??? Connor is smarter than this. Something's up, ya'll.

@wut_up9: He's WITH Beckett. I'm telling you all. He's protected bc he's NEVER been a real bodyguard. He's in a fucking relationship like the rest of SFO.

@rise-of-the-seasons: Looks like they aren't gonna get rid of him after all. If he survived this w/o getting axed, he's not going anywhere.

@AvengeMe17: Fuck Paul Donnelly.

LUNA HALE'S JOURNAL

<u>Eliot Alice Cobalt</u>

Where does he live now?

~~Are we still friends?~~ Dumb

How's his job going at the theatre? (He signed a 2 yr contract still in high school. Did he still go?)

Is he single??

<u>Tom Carraway Cobalt</u>

Does he live with Eliot?

How's the band doing?

Is he dating anyone??

Does he know about my fish ~~too~~?

33

Luna Hale

FROM THE GUIDANCE of my neuro-doctors, I'm now the owner of a memory journal. It's been four days since I woke up with amnesia, and they said it *might* help temper my frustrations. But with the sloppily written pages set before me, my brows have yet to unfurrow. "This is dumb. I have too many questions, and it's hard to think of any other pertinent question than *what have you been up to for the past three years*," I say in distress.

Donnelly ditches the wiped-down food counter of Superheroes & Scones, just to approach me at a red vinyl booth.

My mom's comic book coffee shop hybrid has been "closed until further notice" since the accident. A move my dad made when reporters and paparazzi started appearing and harassing staff for more info about the famous Lily Calloway.

I've talked to her on the phone. Just short convos so far.

"How are you doing?" I asked.

"Great, really great." She sounded hopeful. "I should be out of here soon. The food's not so bad, and your dad has brought me cinnamon rolls every morning. I have a cinna-belly now."

I wanted to laugh, but the phone calls just made me miss her more. I swallowed the words, *I wish I could see you.*

"How are you holding up, Luna?" she always asked.

"Better than yesterday." It's the main reply, because each day does feel a teensy bit better. More questions are answered; more of the puzzle is filled. "I love you to planet Thebula and back again."

"I love you so, *so* much." She sounded teary at the end of the last call, and I think her prolonged stay at the hospital has been just as hard on her.

The media's need for *details* doesn't help.

She's doing well at Philly General and not critical. She would appreciate if everyone would respect her privacy at this time. That statement was not juicy enough for the press, so they're waiting in the wings for fleshier meat, but while the store is closed, I'm using it as my base camp. The penthouse hasn't jogged any memories, and it's been nice to venture out into a new environment.

Donnelly leans a hip against the booth, and he clutches on to a half-wrapped breakfast bagel. As he careens over my shoulder and peers at my journal on the table, I cage a fluttering breath. Absorbing the fact that Original Luna kinda dated him is like sucking on helium (even if we technically aren't dating), and I feel floaty around him.

So much about Donnelly compels me towards his bright energy field and pushes me to get to know him more. No amount of time spent with him feels like enough. I wonder if Original Luna experienced that too.

I'm still holding in air. Like if I breathe too hard, I'll blow away this new reality into a puff of smoke. And I'm hanging on to this piece of my life with a death-grip.

I need him.

Maybe, too, I've been growing to want him. Crave him. *Desire* him.

"Nah, this isn't dumb," Donnelly says, then takes a giant bite of the bagel sandwich. "You're asking all the right questions."

"I am?" I say unsurely. I hate that bits of my confidence have disappeared along with my memories. Maybe they're a package deal.

He bobs his head strongly. Before he can answer, bodyguards that've been manning an emergency exit have entered the front of the store. Stoic faces, cagey eyes, they join another five quiet bodyguards posted at the main entrance.

Donnelly watches them, then puts a couple fingers to his earpiece, eavesdropping on security talk. Is it considered eavesdropping if it's also his job? He said he's a part of the security team as a whole today, not specifically on my detail. All the bodyguards were really careful to make sure Donnelly wasn't seen in public with me. We didn't even come into the store at the same time.

When he admitted to being Xander's bodyguard, I was actually happy in a selfish way. From the life I remember, I wasn't the closest to Beckett, and there's a better chance I'll see Donnelly if he's protecting my younger brother.

Still no sign of J.P. He's copper-haired, white, and about three-hundred pounds of squishy beef. Hard to miss from his size alone. Lately, I've been flanked by three times as many bodyguards as I'm used to. I'm almost certain he's no longer on the team, which has only spiraled my questions.

Maybe my new 24/7 bodyguard hates me. Is that why no one has told me who they are? Or did something happen to them during the assault? Did they get hurt? *Oh my God*. Why am I just now thinking of this?

"Donnelly," I say quickly, catching his attention. Though he still seems casual, taking another bite of the bagel sandwich. I ask, "Is my full-time bodyguard okay? Because no one has reintroduced me yet, and now I'm thinking maybe they got hurt—"

He's mid-chew of his breakfast bagel when he interrupts me to say, "She's fine."

She.

My gaze widens. One of my favorite bodyguards was a woman. Alana. I grew up with her, and when she retired, I wrote a story about Alana living forever in a queendom on Thebula. I tried to preserve her memory on my home planet, where I wished she'd always be.

I have a new bodyguard. A female bodyguard.

Sliding a little out of the booth, I crane my head to see the entrance where security has gathered in a team huddle. *No women.*

"Where is she?" I ask.

"I dunno, but I think she'll be on your detail later." Donnelly swallows the last of the bagel and crumples up the napkin wrapper in his fist. "You sure you don't wanna eat?"

I already rejected a breakfast bagel, a hashbrown patty, and a scone. My nerves don't pair well with hunger. I shake my head. "Why wouldn't you know where my bodyguard is?" I question, confused. "You're on the security team."

"Yeah, but I don't get looped into all the big boss meetings. I'm not a lead so…" He trails off when the front door chimes. Security breaks apart to let them pass.

I elevate out of my seat, thinking it's Eliot and Tom. It's not them…

A woman struts inside with a graceful power-walk, and I go from nervously excited to just plain curious. *Is this my bodyguard?* She's likely in her mid-thirties, black, and dressed for success in a taupe silky blouse and high-waisted pants. Her curly pony is styled so beautifully.

Something about her is a *wee* bit familiar, but I can't place her in my mind.

"Is she my bodyguard?" I whisper to Donnelly, but just as I ask, I notice how the other bodyguards bristle around her, even more so when two other men slip inside the store.

It registers the same time Donnelly says, "That's Ali Miller. She's production."

Behind her, I recognize the very tall Jack Highland—he's the exec producer on the unit that films my older brother and older cousins. He's Filipino and white, and at his side is a guy who looks like he could be Ali's twin. Just as fashionable and poised.

"Ambrose," Donnelly tells me quietly. "Ali's brother." *So maybe not twins? Or else I think he would've led with that.* "And that's Jack. All production."

There are three production units that film my family, and I'm a part of the third one, so I'm not around Jack's team as much as Maximoff, Jane, and Charlie. But…I think I was supposed to be shifted to Jack's team after I graduated high school, so maybe Original Luna knows him better than I do.

Disappointed, I lower back in my seat. And so, the mystery of my bodyguard prevails.

"Give us some space here," Ambrose tells the bodyguard fleet.

"We could move some of the shelves," Ali says to Jack and acts as if security is invisible. "It'd give the guests more room."

"Do you have to do this now?" a late-twenties bodyguard asks with slight edge. He kinda reminds me of my Uncle Connor's bodyguard—a younger version. Golden-skinned, warm brown hair curled at his ears .

Donnelly sees me squinting. "Cruz Jr. He's Kinney's full-time bodyguard."

Huh. "What happened to his dad?" *Cruz Sr.*

"Retired."

So many bodyguard changes, but I wasn't always that aware of them even when I didn't have memory problems.

"Well, we aren't going to do it later," Ali says, still surveying the store. She points at the espresso machines and whispers to Jack. He's typing on his phone.

"Aren't you guys done with post-production?" a burly white bodyguard asks. "The new season of WAC already premiered."

I usually always watch the premiere with Tom and Eliot. I wonder how many months the new season covers and what big events they filmed. Tuning into the docuseries might help fill in blanks. I sense a binge-watch in my future.

"This is for a *wedding*," Ambrose emphasizes like they're air-headed jocks. "We already explained we're seeing if the store can hold two-hundred people for the welcome party."

"We'll be out of your hair in ten," Jack tells security. "I promise, it'll be quick."

"Who's getting married?" I whisper to Donnelly, careful so they don't hear. Production has no clue I have amnesia. Not yet, at least.

"The story supervisor and boom operator on Jack's unit. Jane's their wedding planner."

Jane is a wedding planner? *That suits her.* I want to smile, but bodyguards start muttering, pissy over production occupying this space when it's supposed to be safe for me, maybe.

"There's always another fucking wedding in production," a bodyguard grumbles. I'm guessing security is full of Single Pringles while production is getting hitched left and right.

Ambrose rotates back to him. "Maybe go out once in a while. Take a day off. Go wash your body with soap and you'll find someone who wants to touch it."

Ali snorts into a laugh.

Jack is trying not to smile. "Ambrose."

"Me?" Ambrose plays innocent.

Ali says pointedly, "My brother is full of relationship tips that nobody wants to hear."

"Jack wants to hear them," Ambrose says.

"I do, but later," Jack smiles.

Bodyguards voice their opinions over one another.

Ambrose turns to the fleet again. "You're all invited to Faye and Hudson's wedding, so I don't know why you're so angry."

The door chimes. Security goes deathly silent. *Eliot and Tom.* I rise again, only to sink back in my seat.

Still not them.

"Oscar," Donnelly whispers to me, just in case I can't remember Charlie's bodyguard.

Another bodyguard snaps, "Oliveira, tell production to scram."

Oscar blinks. "Scram?"

"Yeah, *scram.*"

Oscar's brows crinkle. "Call me nuts but this isn't the *West Side Story*, and I'm *not* participating in a fucking rumble." He extends an arm between production and security. "Play nice."

Bodyguards groan and cough, "*Traitor.*"

Even so, Jack's bright grin hasn't faded. Strange. Oh wait, Jack is approaching Oscar, and they're kissing! Whaaat in the world.

My jaw slowly unhinges.

"They're married," Donnelly says to me, and he's full-on grinning like it's the best news he gets to tell me. Oscar, I've come to realize via *We Are Calloway* Fanaticon Forums is super close to Donnelly. (Yes, I've been snooping online but just recent posts.)

One of the worst things I've seen: an article about my dad feuding with Donnelly. To which, Donnelly confessed it was fake to help him infiltrate his toxic family. He needed to distance himself more from mine.

It was a good reminder that I can't believe everything on the internet. Which is why I haven't combed through too much online.

Production is true to their word at Superheroes & Scones and depart after ten. Oscar goes with them. Only a few minutes later, the door chimes for a third time.

This has to be Eliot and Tom.

My nerves double. Of all my cousins, I thought about confronting Jane first, but Eliot and Tom reached out to me in a group text.

We've been told to wait for you to contact us, but you know what we think about rules. – Eliot

Meant to be broken – Tom

100%, so this is us saying we're still your best friends. Let's hang out when you're ready. – Eliot

So last night I texted back: Superheroes & Scones tomorrow at 11AM?

We'll be there – Tom

Wouldn't miss it – Eliot

It is them walking through the door.

I press my journal against my chest seeing my best friends for the first time. Eliot is…*tall.* That hasn't changed, at least. He carries himself like the world is his stage, a player amongst mortal men, while Tom walks with an earnestness like he has somewhere important he needs to be.

"Luna, No Middle Name, Hale," Tom greets first, nearly jogging to reach me, as if I'm so far away. *I'm right here*, I want to yell, but it'd be a half-truth, a half-lie.

Parts of me are gone.

Coming out of the booth, I step forward like it's the most natural thing to do, and then we collide into a tight hug. I fist the back of his leather jacket, the familiarity overwhelming. He still smells like Tom—like sage and apricot, the fragrance of some expensive cologne Beckett got him into when he was fourteen.

Eliot joins us, his long arms wrapping around me and Tom. He encases our three-person hug, as though protecting what we are. Tears prick the edges of my eyes. It feels like no time has passed—but I know it's all an illusion.

How much has really changed?

A knot in my throat, I back up slowly.

Eliot has a hand clamped on his mouth, like he's forcing himself not to say anything triggering. His gaze carries a million worries for me.

"Let's go this way." I motion for Donnelly to follow. We vacate the café section of the store and slip down an aisle of Halway comics and Marvel merch. We're further out of the security team's sights, sans Donnelly, but he's hanging back a bit too.

"Just to be clear"—I face Tom and Eliot—"I still don't remember the last three years, so I have questions." I hoist my journal. "I've been writing them down."

Eliot smiles. "How very Luna of you."

"The most Luna thing you could do, really," Tom adds, his eyes a little reddened. "On brand."

It makes me feel good, and I catch Donnelly's supportive gaze at the end of the aisle. I take a deep breath. "You already know Donnelly." Do they despise him and me together? Do they think we're a bad match? I just go ahead and ask, "Are we all cool?"

"Cool as a cucumber," Tom says with a big nod. "The four of us are like the Four Musketeers. Unbreakable. Unstoppable."

"Thick as thieves," Eliot chimes in.

Behind them, Donnelly's brows rise in disbelief. "This happen when I was asleep or what?"

My stomach tosses.

Eliot gives him a hard look. "We were on our way to becoming a four-pod, ride-or-die friendship group. Right on the *cusp*," he says dramatically, then waves to his brother. "Tom and I just decided to fast forward the awkward beginning, so we can solidify the inevitable."

Tom nods wholeheartedly. "We're basically all friends."

"Basically?" I ask, confused.

Eliot bops a Groot bobblehead on the shelf. "Like I said, you were just beginning to bring Donnelly into the fold."

"So for clarification, we're not the Four Musketeers?" I squint hard at Donnelly. He's shaking his head.

Eliot sees. "But you're invited. Luna was going to tell you that we all wanted to be friends."

I was?

"You didn't tell Donnelly?" Tom questions.

Original Luna either ran out of time or didn't want Donnelly to join the friendship trio.

"She can't remember," Eliot reminds his brother.

"Sorry," Tom says, looking a little torn up. Their best friend was kidnapped. They might've even feared she wouldn't survive. I'm likely a lousy fill-in for her, but I'm trying.

Since I already brewed coffee, we wind up at the Superheroes & Scones bar. Donnelly posts up on a stool, and Eliot pours a few mugs of dark roast behind the counter. Just as I sit between Donnelly and Tom, my phone buzzes.

"Uh, who's Harriet?" I ask. "Do I need to answer?" I still have to keep up appearances with anyone who's *not* family or security. The outside world needs to think all is well. I have all my memories. Nothing to see here!

The whole pretending thing sounds like I've been planted in a *Parent Trap* movie and instructed to take the place of my long-lost twin. Only, I don't have that twin to help guide me in this charade, which makes it infinitesimally harder.

"Harriet," Tom groans. "Just hang up."

"Luna wouldn't be rude to her," Eliot defends.

I'm befuddled. "So do I like Harriet or not?" The call is about to ring out. "Someone tell me fast."

"You like her," Eliot and Tom say together, and Tom adds, "But I personally have mixed, mostly negative, feelings."

I look to Donnelly.

"She's your lab partner at Penn." He tells me the name of the class super quickly, and I answer on the last ring, putting the call on speaker in case I need help.

"Hey, Hi, Holy Cow," I say and then cringe. I doubt OG Luna would say that.

"Hey, Luna," Harriet says casually, but her tone has a bit of sour bite. "So I know you're dealing with family stuff. But the professor told me to tell you that if you miss another lab, he's going to fail you. He's being more dickish than usual. I can cover the lab work—but you know I can't actually clone you, so you're going to have to show up."

I don't say anything.

"Luna?"

"Yeah, okay. I'll be there." *I must have a schedule somewhere. Maybe on my laptop.*

"Cool. Cool," she deadpans. "Sorry to be the bearer of shitty news."

"It's okay. Thanks for looping me in."

She says a quick goodbye. When I end the call, Eliot applauds. Tom claps, a little less enthused since Harriet is involved, I'm guessing.

"Brilliant," Eliot says and tosses sugar packets my way like rose petals. "A masterclass in acting."

"Ten points to Hufflepuff," Tom says.

I smile, even if residual nerves swim in my stomach. "What's with the Harriet hate?" I ask Tom. "She sounds nice."

"To *you*, yeah." Tom combs a hand through his golden-brown hair. "She auditioned for the Carraways to be the drummer—"

"Daniel is on drums."

"Daniel quit."

"Good riddance," Eliot says, setting down the steaming coffee pot.

Donnelly is half-listening. He's glancing back at security. He must be tuning in more to comms.

"Harriet was *good*," Tom says. "I admit that, but she's seventeen, and the label doesn't want minors in the band. So she sends me an email and asks if the spot is still available when she's eighteen can she be considered. I say, *we're not interested in pursuing you in the future.* It was very professional, was it not?" He's asking Eliot.

"It sounded professional to me," Eliot says, "but a little angry with the way you recited it."

Tom lets out a long groan again. "Then she sends this *ranty* email to Warner about how I'm going to sink the band—*my* band! She's trying to…*usurp* my authority, and I barely know her."

"How'd she get your personal emails?"

"She was sending them to the band's email but addressing Warner personally, so I could see everything she wrote." Warner is the bassist in the Carraways. *Still the same there.*

"But you still have no drummer?" I ask.

Tom buries his face in his hands, groaning for the umpteenth time.

"That's a painful *yes*," Eliot says.

Tom seems over the subject. He even says, "Let's talk about something else."

"So I have to go to school sooner than I thought," I realize. I planned to enroll full-time next semester after Christmas, but now I need to finish what Original Luna started with this biology class.

"You could drop the class," Tom suggests. "No one would blame you."

I want to do *more* than OG Luna, and adding a failure on my long list of failures is not the move. "Then everyone will think it's because I can't hack it, and I want to hack it." I shrug. "I'm going."

Eliot passes me a Hulk-shaped coffee mug. "You need reinforcements, we're there."

I still have them in my corner. I take a deep breath and warm my hands on the mean green mug.

"Donnelly!" a bodyguard waves him to the entrance.

"I'll be back," he whispers, his eyes lingering on me for an intimate second. His fingers even glide over my arm, and the touch zips a shockwave through me. Quickly, I rotate to my friends. "Okay, so when did Original Luna fall in love with him?"

"Original Luna?" Tom asks.

"It's the Luna you knew for the last three years. She's gone. You have me now."

They look semi-freaked—Tom, more so—but if anyone will roll with the oddities of my mind, it's them.

"Who are we speaking to now?" Eliot questions, flipping a lighter open and closed.

"Variant Luna, I guess."

"I love it," Eliot decrees, making me grin.

Tom rubs his eyes harshly. "You know…I'm getting kinda hungry." He hops off the stool, mood changing in a snap of a finger. "Does Aunt Lily keep any peanut butter scones in the back?" He's rounding the bar counter where Eliot has been serving us coffees.

Eliot catches his brother's shoulder, not letting him disappear in the storage closet.

Tom glares at Eliot, then under his breath pleads, "Just let me go." Darkness flashes in Tom's eyes, battling a deeper emotion from surfacing fully.

"It's fine, brother."

I go cold.

Tom shakes his head, his gaze storming. "It's *not* fine, dude. I told you she'd be looking to us for answers, and we're shitty fucking friends—"

"We're not," Eliot refutes. "We're her *best* friends." He turns to me. "We're *your* best friends." His conviction feels genuine, but I also know he was the lead in almost every school play. "We're friends that don't slice each other open like every time we meet it's another therapy session. We let each other talk about things on our own time. That's how it's *always* been."

He's right, but am I the most closed off of the three of us? I hold my breath, tossing his words over and over in my head. "I'm guessing...I didn't tell you about Donnelly."

Tom crosses his arms over his chest. "You didn't tell us anything about how you two got together or what he means to you. And we didn't care that you hadn't yet, Luna. But it matters now because..." He looks away in excruciating regret.

Because they can't help me.

Because they don't know everything about me.

"That's okay," I say in a small voice. "It's okay." I know they still love me. I still have the memories of every single time they stood up for me against my bullies.

"It's okay," Eliot repeats my words *for* Tom because Tom looks about ready to cry. He lets out a long, frustrated growl, then grabs Stormbreaker, Thor's axe, off the wall beside the espresso machine.

He twirls the plastic toy in his hand like he's ready to just swing.

I know the feeling. "I guess we're all on the same footing," I tell them. "You guys don't know some things about me. I don't know many things about you."

"The difference is we can actually tell you about ourselves," Tom says, pointing Stormbreaker at me. "It's not fucking fair."

"Life's not fair," Eliot says. "We accept the hands we're dealt." That is very diplomatic of the Eliot Cobalt that I know. He sees my surprise and flips the lighter open. "I'm trying my best not to burn everything down."

Says the guy with a flame beside his face.

"Yeah, well I'm fucking tired of Luna getting the shittiest hand," Tom decrees and points Stormbreaker at his brother now. "And this isn't a fucking Shakespearean play. Fuck you for spouting Brainy Quotes at me."

Eliot touches his chest in mock hurt. "You wound me, brother."

Tom fights a grimaced smile. "I'd never."

When Eliot sees that Tom is less pent-up, he looks to me, "We might not know *everything* about you, but we do know a lot. And you're looped into our lives. You know some things we haven't even told our brothers and sisters."

"Like what?" I bow forward on the stool, elbows to the counter.

Eliot checks that security is out of earshot. Yup, and he takes a readying breath like this isn't easy to spill. I wonder if it'd been just as difficult the first time, and now he has to say it for a second.

"I…" His voice tapers off, his gaze faraway. "It was…"

I've never really seen Eliot lost for words like this. My heart slowly crumbles. "Wait," I whisper. "You don't have to. Maybe I'll remember soon, and we can avoid this."

His Adam's apple bobs, his eyes reddening. He ends up explaining how he quit his job at the theatre, so he's currently unemployed. It's not what he planned to say, I gather.

A wave of silence lingers for a second, and Eliot speaks again to break it. "Tom has a secret crush."

My eyes widen. "Who?"

"It wouldn't be a secret if I told you two, would it?" Tom retorts, clearly seizing tight to this.

"A secret from us," I sing-song.

"From *everyone*." Tom drums the table to my tune. "The way it should be." His face is beet-red. "And I called Phoenix."

"Phoenix who?" I frown.

"Phoenix St. Pierre," he says with disdain. "The drummer that I refused to hire because he's a *diiiick*, and now he's playing for a band that's blown up called Nothing Personal. He's selling out shows while The Carraways are struggling to finish our album because no drummer is good enough."

"Good enough for you," Eliot rephrases.

"Same difference, dude," Tom breathes out.

"What's not good enough for you is not good enough for me," Eliot decrees.

"Thank you," Tom sighs. "If only *Charlie* agreed. He said I'm being more obstinate than him, and that is just…" He cringes. "*Not* true."

"Unfounded," Eliot agrees.

Tom tears open a sugar packet. "The drummer for the Carraways *has* to be as good or better than Phoenix. That is the bar. Jax wasn't it. Levi isn't it. Harriet isn't going to be it."

"Wait, wait." My brain is overloaded. "So you called Phoenix? Is that good or bad?"

"*Bad*," Tom says. "The guy is a fucking prick, and I nudged him to quit his shit band to come join mine. And he told me to *beg* him, and he'd consider it."

I wince.

"Yeah, exactly," Tom says off my expression. "And I'd rather be buried in a coffin than anyone else find out I stooped so low to call that guy. *Never again*."

"I knew this already?" I wonder.

He nods. "Yeah, I actually told you before I told Eliot."

"Because I offered retribution," Eliot says.

Tom shakes his head. "The only retribution I need is never seeing or hearing Phoenix St. Pierre again, including his music." He grimaces. "Even his name is douchey."

"I kinda like it," I say.

Tom begins to smile. "Yeah, I know."

My brows jump. "I already told you?"

"Yeah, you said it sounded like a comic book hero's name." To which, Tom looks ready to upchuck.

I laugh, and Eliot is grinning. At the sound of my laughter, Tom takes a robust breath too.

I'm still trying to piece apart my history. I stare at the watch on my wrist, the little hands ticking thanks to Donnelly fixing it, and I ask, "Do you know about OG Luna's fish?"

"She has a fish?" Tom frowns.

So only Donnelly might know about Moondragon, I've deduced.

"Did Original Luna date anyone?" I want to reconfirm what Donnelly has told me.

"Sure," Tom nods.

"There was only one real ex-boyfriend," Eliot says. "After him, she'd been into casual flings."

I frown. Donnelly never mentioned anything about an ex. I stiffen a little. "What's his name?"

"Andrew Umbers," Eliot says just as Donnelly returns. The air stretches like a taut rubber band, and I don't fully understand why. Was he a bad guy? Did he hurt me?

Do I even want to know? Maybe this is fate and I should just be happy with *not* knowing. I shelter my questions since Donnelly casts another quick glance at security. His lips are more downturned than usual.

"Everything okay?" I ask.

He nods once. "Yeah." Then he says, "My dad just got out of jail."

34

Paul Donnelly

MY COBALT BRETHREN telling Luna about her dog-shit ex-boyfriend is back-stabby, traitorous behavior. Something no friend or Musketeer would do. But like I've known, they're *her* friends, *her* Musketeers. Not mine. So they're true to Luna, and I can't fault 'em, especially if she asked outright.

As much as I've looked up to the Cobalt Empire—been close to their brother Beckett too—Tom and Eliot don't owe me anything. Not a sock, not a toothbrush, not loyalty.

I've done nothing to earn that sort of devotion from them. On top of that beautifully steep mountain I haven't tried to climb, my dad is gonna be on their hit list. It's a long list though, considering those two eat, sleep, dance, and sing vengeance.

"How'd he get out?" Eliot asks, his eyes flashing hot like the devil himself just got freed from hell.

"Charges didn't stick," I say vaguely and more quietly. "We knew it was coming. He has an alibi." *He was bartending at the Rhino.* I'm not telling them more than I have to. Like how it's suspicious I was the only Donnelly let out of jail that night. My family was gonna start questioning if I sold them out.

Police finally agreed that having my dad on the outside would be better for everyone. It means I have a tie to the rest of my family still out of prison, and I can ensure no one else is plotting anything.

"Was more of your family released?" Tom asks.

"Just him." I'm about to glance at Luna, but comms go off, vibrating my eardrum.

"You should be posted at one of the doors," Ian Wreath tells me, like he's my boss or something.

An Alpha bodyguard pipes in, "The clients don't need a play-by-play of what's happening in security."

Not giving them one, but thanks for caring. They're bugging me, really, and this sorta bullshit doesn't usually get under my skin that easily.

Their echo chamber of "Donnelly Sucks, Let Him Know" has been in my ear since I arrived with Luna. Helping find Luna at a South Philly rowhouse—that wasn't a brownie point to Triple Shield bodyguards.

They're aggravated that I'm friendly with Luna enough to cross a line between *bodyguard* and *client* right now. A line that I know most of Triple Shield reestablished when Beckett almost got attacked on Halloween.

After what happened to Luna and Lily, it's now written in stone for them: *Don't be friends with clients. Stay serious. Stay alert. No buddyguards allowed.*

When they figure out I'm more than friends with her, there might be another civil war between the two security firms, but this one feels like a long-time coming.

"When's the take-down?" Eliot suddenly asks.

My head swerves to him. "The what?"

He closes his lighter. "Sean Donnelly. He can't walk free. After all he's done—"

"Did he do anything bad himself?" Luna asks them, then looks to me for answers.

"He was *involved*," Tom emphasizes. "That's way more than enough."

Eliot nods, "He's a part of it all. He should pay."

My blood is ice, and I can't disagree with them. My dad isn't all that good. He's been a shit parent and a bad person deserving of prison time, which he's paid. That being said, Luna wouldn't be here without him, and for me, that's worth too much in my head.

"I'm taking care of it," is all I tell them.

Eliot pockets the lighter. "You need a helping hand, I'm always available for payback."

"Nah, I got it," I say easily. "Payback's a bitch and my favorite one." Not all true. I haven't been completely revenge-hearted, or else I would've transformed into John Wick and slaughtered my whole family decades ago. But Eliot doesn't catch my humor since he doesn't know me all that well.

"Like minds," he replies.

Comms go off abruptly in my ear.

"You going to be over there all afternoon, Donnelly?" a bodyguard snaps.

"What do you have to talk to them about?" another says.

I click my mic at my collar and whisper, "Maybe you should be worrying about what's happening to your face. It's looking pretty ugly."

A few guys growl out my name, along with *fuck you.*

"I'll fuck myself later, thanks for caring," I mutter over comms.

Luna whispers to me, "Security is glaring really meanly at you."

I refuse to glance back at them. "We're not seeing eye to eye right now about something." Suddenly, my new phone beeps, and I take out my cell.

SFO emergency meeting in 30 mins. Penthouse library.
– Akara

My pulse spikes into my throat. "I've gotta go back to the penthouse," I say quietly to Luna and show her the text. "Enough temps are here that'll protect you while I'm gone—"

"I can come with you." She's hopping off the stool, and even though it might be better to protest and tell her to stay, I don't.

Tom and Eliot make it too easy. They tell Luna they'll catch up later. Apparently, they need to go to Calloway Couture HQ for another suit fitting, and maybe they're being cautious to not overwhelm her with too much information at once.

So I'm headed back to the penthouse with Luna for an SFO emergency meeting.

One that I asked Akara to call.

It's really happening.

35

Paul Donnelly

"WHAT'S WRONG WITH this picture? I'm *early* but all the motherfuckers who live here are late," Oscar says while flipping through a worn hardback. Didn't get a good look at the title.

I'm sitting on the wooden rung of a ladder, old books shelved behind me. The penthouse library isn't that quiet since Gabe, Quinn, and Frog have been arguing in the corner. Been eavesdropping on them until Oscar started talking.

"I live here and I'm early," I tell him.

"Besides you…" His voice tapers off, catching sight of the unfolding rookie drama.

"He didn't *kill* your girlfriend's crybaby Gerber Gerbil," Frog protests, waving her iced coffee toward Quinn. "He's not a psychopath."

"You met him, what? Three days ago?" Quinn says. "I don't expect you to know what he's capable of doing or even his middle name."

"Middle name's probably Fred," I joke to Oscar, but we're both on guard. Who is Frog even bringing into their apartment? Does Akara know? I've been out of the security loop since I was thrown in jail. On the fringe. Trying to race back to the middle.

"Fuck Fred," Oscar says. "He's out here killing my baby bro's gerbil."

His girlfriend's gerbil, but I don't correct Oscar.

"He's *not* a gerbil killer," Frog repeats. "His intentions are good. Stop trying to turn him into some evil archetypal villain when he's been nothing but *there* for me."

"There for you?" Quinn shakes his head roughly. "You've known him for three days!"

"I didn't like him," Gabe Montgomery states, his thick biceps crossed over thicker pecs.

Oscar shuts the book. "When's the last time you've heard Montgomery hate someone?"

Not sure. "Why are we trusting Monty's intuition over Frog's?" I ask Oscar.

Gabe adds, "He smelled like oat milk."

I grin, nearing a laugh, and Oscar mutters, "That big buffoon."

"Team Froggy." I make finger horns.

"He isn't an oat milk smelling gerbil murderer," Frog says, then swings her iced coffee in *my* direction. What the fuck? "Donnelly knows him. *Donnelly.*" The rookies spin towards me. "You know Scooter. He said you go way back."

My brows catapult up my face. "Scooter?"

"Who's Scooter?" Oscar asks me.

Yeah, we go *way* back—before I met Oscar at Yale. Hell, before I even tagged along on Farrow's collegiate adventure and left for the Ivy League.

I tell Oscar, "When I apprenticed in Old City, he worked at the same tattoo shop. I was seventeen." I eye Frog, wondering what she's doing with someone like Scooter. "He's five years older than me."

Quinn chokes on air. "*What?*"

"Yeah, guy's gotta be about thirty-four now." I keep talking, even though Oscar has gone from a relaxed slouch to a Tin Man position. "Don't remember much about him other than he has a full sleeve of an octopus and submarine girl."

"He's *nice,*" Frog insists. "I met him at the tattoo shop. I was thinking about getting something done to represent my aunt, and we got to talking about life and Philly during the sketch session."

I ask her, "You didn't wanna come to me?" I frown. "I would've given you a friend's discount."

Frog wiggles her straw. "You've been busy. I didn't want to take you away from what's going on with…" *Luna.* "She needs you, and you *better* be there for her." The heat in her eyes makes me smile.

"Said like her Number One Protector," I say.

Frog nods, but uncertainty stiffens her posture. Her position on the team as Luna's bodyguard is more up in the air since Luna's threat level has increased, and I haven't heard if she's being transferred yet.

To all of us, Frog decrees, "You might not like Scooter, but *I* do. It feels good being heard, you know? And he listens."

It brings me back to the crime scene. The cratered dead-end road. The rain. How Frog turned to me for comfort and I brushed her off—and she hasn't tried to come to me again. Instead, she's now seeking refuge in a complete stranger.

I'm lost in this thought, not even noticing Quinn approaching me and Oscar. Frog and Gabe are bickering in the corner about Scooter's hygiene and oat milk.

"What's a thirty-four-year-old dude doing with an *eighteen*-year-old girl?" Quinn whispers to us. "Tell me you both think it's weird."

Maybe not weird. I like weird, and I don't like Scooter hanging around Frog after she just witnessed something traumatic.

"Sus for sure," I say casually, then look to Oscar.

He's observing Frog while she gesticulates with her iced coffee at Gabe. He tells us, "We might need an SFO come-together about what happened."

I hear *group therapy.* Not excited, but I try not to show it. "Only if there's muffins."

Quinn sighs, pushing up his sleeves in a heated huff. I spot a bruise on his forearm, and my gut drops. Looks like fingerprint marks.

"What's that?" I ask, but as soon as I catch him, he quickly tugs down the sleeve.

"What's *what?*" Oscar's attention veers over to his little brother.

"A bruise," Quinn says. "I ran into a fucking door. You want me to take a picture and sign it for you?"

"You want some ice to cool the fuck off, bro?" Oscar says, eyeing him skeptically.

"I'm *fine*," Quinn retorts.

I tell him, "No one said you weren't."

"You two have *that* face."

"I've got the face of an angel," I say easily, trying to get him off the defense. "I don't think I look anything like your big bro."

Oscar is still trying to solve this Quinn equation, and it's making him appear too intense and constipated.

"You know what, leave me the fuck alone," Quinn states.

"Whoa, how'd we go from zero to two-hundred?" Oscar questions, hands up in surrender. "No one is coming at you, Quinn—Quinn!" He's already distancing himself from everyone, taking a seat near the fireplace and stewing alone.

"What'd I do?" Oscar asks me, concerned.

Nothing. I have this uneasy feeling Nessa, Quinn's girlfriend, is to blame for the bruise. If her gerbil died, maybe she blamed Quinn and physically took her anger out on him.

But it could just be all in my head. I've been trudging up my childhood, the past with my mom, and that's making me a paranoid fucker. The bruise might not even be a handprint. I saw it for a split second.

Didn't get that good of a look.

I glance to Oscar. "I think he just wants us to stay out of his shit."

"I see that," Oscar mutters, upset because he finally mended the rift with his brother and he hasn't wanted to create another one.

The door opens. In walks Farrow and Thatcher, only Thatch has a sleeping Baby Maeve cradled in his arms. Says something about how it's Jane's turn to nap, so he's clocking in father time.

"Sorry, we're late," Akara tells us, coming in last and pushing back his black hair. "Banks lost his wedding ring."

"Fuckin' found it in the garbage disposal," Banks mutters, shutting the door behind him.

"The string ring?" Oscar questions.

"Yep, it's destroyed," Akara says like *that's the story of our lives.* Banks isn't happy, but Akara assures him they'll figure out a solution.

Oscar tries not to laugh. "Who would've thought braided twine wouldn't last forever? Did you, Donnelly?"

"Thought that shit was like titanium," I banter. "Should've used spit to seal the knot instead of glue."

Banks grumbles something about the "fucking Yale boys" and maybe this is the wrong time, wrong place to crack a joke, but no one is a bigger Kitsulletti supporter than me, myself, and *I*.

Except maybe Beckett.

Trying to figure out a bridge between me and him. Maybe one day we can have a longer conversation about everything. It feels like we've only reached the surface with the one talk about cocaine and me being transferred off his detail. And I dunno if I want to sweep it under the rug and act like him doing drugs never existed.

In the penthouse library, Akara gestures for everyone to congregate. "Let's get down to business." Thankfully everyone pushes in closer to the bookshelves, so I stay seated on the ladder. Farrow is at my left, resting a foot on the bottom rung below me.

My pulse picks up speed, thinking I'm about to make a speech or plea or something of the like.

Then Akara says, "I'll open the floor to Donnelly at the end."

Fuck. I gotta wait until the *end* of the meeting? Yeah, my patience has been sledgehammered. I just nod.

Akara snaps his fingers to his palm. "Okay, so we've all been through a lot recently, and I'm still *trying* to be on an even playing field with Price and Triple Shield. This means, what he does for his firm, we need to do the same, and I want to preface that I agree with *most* of his decisions. Like psych evals."

I try not to react, but my stomach tosses.

"For the whole team?" Oscar asks.

"For everyone," Akara confirms. "Even me. I know it's not fun, but we need to make sure we're all mentally prepared to protect these families, and your health is a priority, not an afterthought."

What if we don't pass the test? I will. I have to, so I'm not even asking about the worst-case scenario.

Quinn is. "What if we fail it?"

Frog shifts her weight, then asks him, "Are you looking at me?"

"I wasn't looking at you," Quinn says more softly.

Akara answers, "Then you'll be suspended until you're cleared to be on-duty. I'll be setting up appointments that work into your schedules. I would also appreciate if everyone completed their daily logs. I've slacked on making you fill those out since I started Kitsuwon Securities—*especially* since you've all had your hands full training temp guards."

"Most of us," Oscar corrects.

My hands have been mainly free of that task. Oscar has taken on the brunt of teaching temporary newbies the ropes.

"Most of you," Akara agrees. "Thanks to Michael Moretti taking over temp training, you all should have time to fill out your daily logs."

Farrow looks unenthused.

I don't mind them as much.

Akara reads off a list on his phone and continues, "Now, mandatory check-ins"—*please no*—"it's something Price is trying with Alpha and Epsilon as a group, and I think it's a decent idea for us to do."

I raise my hand.

"Donnelly," he calls on me.

"Don't we already do that with these meetings? Seems redundant and all."

"Agreed," Farrow says. Best friend coming in with a vote of confidence.

But Akara shakes his head. "They're not the same. In meetings we're usually talking about the future. What events are coming up. What extra security measures need to be taken. These check-ins, we'll be discussing the past together, and I'm not talking about mistakes and things we could've done better, but more like..." He searches for the word.

"Our feelings," Thatcher concludes, more sternly.

Akara nods. "Our feelings on past experiences while on-duty."

"Group therapy?" I call it what it sounds like.

"There won't be a professional therapist in the room. Just us," Akara explains, acting like it's just SFO shooting the shit, but it won't be that if we have to dig through bad nights. Still, I try to be a team player and open to the concept, even if I can't picture how it'll go down.

Oscar eats some Filipino corn chip snack. "Legitimately took my idea right out of my head." He crunches. "I think it's a great one, Kitsuwon."

"Perfect," Akara relaxes, maybe thinking there'd be more pushback.

Can't say the rest of us are jumping for joy. Quinn is scowling, and Frog seems more nervous, maybe about the psych evals.

"Check-ins won't start until after we're all cleared for duty," Akara tells us. "One thing at a time." He scrolls on his phone. "So Luna…"

My bones lock up, and I bow forward in a bit of anticipation.

"Her threat level has increased," he explains what I already know. The public can't find out she's lost her memories, and on top of that, she's a hot button topic in tabloids after the kidnapping, which means a greater paparazzi presence will follow.

When he finishes, Frog asks, "What does this mean for her detail?"

Akara looks sympathetic towards his cousin. "This *isn't* a reflection on anything you've done, Frog, just on the circumstances surrounding Luna now."

"I'm no longer her bodyguard, right?" She speaks softer, more morose.

"No, you're staying on Luna's detail, but she needs a second 24/7 guard. We can't keep rotating temps and have them tag along with you. It's better if we just make a permanent position happen."

I'm moving.

He's making me her bodyguard.

The shitty thing, I don't want it.

I don't want to act like Luna's bodyguard when I just want to be her boyfriend in the future. Sure, I can do both, but I like switching to her detail on my terms and not being there 24/7 because I'm paid to do it every day. Other guys would've *killed* for this—I know Thatcher and Farrow would've when they couldn't be on Jane and Maximoff's details—but they're not me.

And I made a promise to Luna's brother.

Can't believe I'm already one step from breaking it.

"Am I an option?" I ask fast. "'Cause if I am, I'd like to be benched. Thank you."

Everyone looks shocked.

Even Farrow and Oscar.

"Why?" Thatcher asks, rocking Baby Maeve in his arms.

Why?

Bench looks lonely, I almost say. *Thought I'd let it see my ass for once.* But this is my chance to plead my case, and I step on the gas, not the brakes. "Because I made a promise to her brother to be on *his* detail. Not hers. Because everything I've ever done for security regarding my family has been so I can be with *Luna* and not as her bodyguard—and I know I haven't told you all that, but I'm telling you now. It's about her."

It's always been about her.

I love her. I'm in love with her, I almost profess like I'm gripping to the future that misfortune keeps trying to rip out of my hands, but I stop short of saying those fragile, vulnerable words. Not letting anyone touch 'em but me.

Though, I continue hotly, "And I know some of you might say she's not the same—but I know, *I know* she's in there. She's still Luna to me."

They're all quiet for a solid second. Farrow and Oscar seem surprised at how much I shared, but they already know it's about Luna. Frog has had her suspicions, and the rest...I dunno.

"Goddamn," Banks mutters, toothpick between his teeth. He side-eyes Akara. "I do not envy you right now."

Akara winces, his fingers rubbing his temple. "You really want to be with her *right now*? The timing is crap, Donnelly."

I go still, stuck on the fact that none are leading with shock and awe. "You knew we've wanted to be together?" I ask all of SFO. "Did you read her medical records or what?" *They know I've had sex with Luna. Just like her dad knows.*

Shit.

Farrow is glaring at me, though, like I'm being more illogical.

"Why would her medical records matter?" Thatcher asks intensely.

Shit.

So she didn't let security have access to those files? I scrape a hand down my face and mutter, "She had a rape kit done—I thought it went to security, no?" I glance to Farrow, who's shaking his head.

Fuck. I'm so ready to stop being out of the loop with security. Don't need to be a lead or top dog with the most responsibility, but put me back in the middle where I belong.

Quinn looks devastated and murderous all at once. "She had a *rape* kit done? And we're just now hearing about this?"

"It was thrown out," Farrow says plainly, then eyes me. "You going to tell them or do you want me to?"

I'll do it. "I had sex with Luna before the…incident or whatever you're all calling it. Sperm matched me." I make a loose *rock on* gesture with both hands.

Akara has a palm over his face, stressed to the max. "*Donnelly.*"

I open my mouth, but I can't figure out what to say. I knew that trying to be with Luna would be bad for Security Force Omega and Akara's firm as a whole.

Oscar munches on the corn chip. "Are we shocked they've been having sex?"

"It hasn't been a lot," I mention.

"*That* is shocking," Oscar says.

I'm more shocked he didn't place a bet on it with the rookies, but maybe it'd be an unfair one since I tell him more shit than them.

Banks bobs his head. "I thought you've been secretly fucking since you moved in."

"I had my suspicions," Thatcher says.

"Same here," Quinn says and motions to Frog and Gabe too.

I'm frowning, not realizing that all of them thought we were already together. Maybe even longer than we actually were.

"You two just click," Frog says simply. "Everyone who's anyone can see it and believe it." My friends are smiling, which are all of SFO in case that's not clear.

More than friends, actually.

Family. Best I've ever had.

Frog adds, "I'd like to mention that Epsilon *hates* the idea of you two together. Like *despises*."

Figured.

Akara slides his hand down his tensed neck. "You weren't going on Luna's detail, Donnelly."

That...stuns me. "What?"

Akara sighs out, "We're actually concerned about her attachment to you post-trauma and mixing that in a professional setting."

"Especially since it's only been four days since she woke up," Thatcher adds.

Alright. Makes sense.

Thatcher explains further, "We weren't sure if it'd be a good idea to put you in a position where you'll need to protect her 24/7 while she's still processing who you are to her and healing. It's a relatively big change from what you were to Luna, and her therapist advised us against it."

I try to ease. "Who's shifting then?"

"I've already talked to Farrow about his son having no security for a while," Akara starts, and Quinn begins to arch backward, knowing it's him.

He's been Baby Ripley's bodyguard for some time now. A big position, but this one might be just as big, considering Luna's threat level.

"Quinn," Akara says, "you're being transferred. You've already been Luna's bodyguard, and she needs you now."

She needs you.

A pit wedges in my ribs, but I try not to take his words to heart. *She needs me too.* Just in a distinctive, unique, unduplicated way. Just like I've needed Farrow and Oscar and not only her. Still, I want to be the most necessary, vital thing to Luna's life.

Gotta say, this transfer is a good call from Akara. He's reverting Luna to her past with Quinn and keeping her present with Frog. He's not changing to something entirely new. Maybe it'll help her find her memories too.

"I'll be there," Quinn assures our boss, then eyes Frog.

She eyes him back skeptically. They're now working together as a bodyguard duo. Seeing as how they've been bickering, it's not looking so bright, but they're friends at the core.

"Donnelly," Akara begins, waving me forward. It's my time to shine and plead my case.

I step off the ladder, more concerned this won't end well for me and Luna. "I asked for a meeting today 'cause I know the timing seems bad. I know it's important that my family still believes I'm on their side. They can't know I was behind getting them locked up, and the *best* you've done, Akara, is make it so I can still be on the team. I know that."

I'm appreciative of that.

I tell him, "I have to maintain my cover with my family, but I have a way to make it safe if I'm seen out in public with her."

His perplexed eyes are on mine. "What way?"

And I explain my plan. Really, it's not easy to say at all. I end with, "I wanna tell Loren Hale after the meeting, so you don't have to relay it to the parents."

"Okay," he agrees almost instantly.

Thatcher nods in approval too. It truly dawns on me that they all want me to be with Luna. They're not trying to stop me or be a buncha hypocrites about it.

"This could work," Akara says, "but I still need to talk to Price. I might have to work out a deal with him so he doesn't have a heart attack and come for my firm." This isn't the first romantic relationship sparked within Omega. Not even the second or third.

Akara doesn't say what the deal might entail, but a storm is looming over him. I hate knowing I summoned it there.

36

Paul Donnelly

MEETING IS OVER, and I find myself on the phone with Loren. I'm in my shared bathroom, alone, and sitting on the toilet lid.

"Are you shitting?" Lo asks with bite. We're video chatting, so he has a pristine view of the bathroom wall behind me.

"Nah, I'm relaxing. Toilet is where I do my best thinking." My voice sounds a little tighter than usual. "Must be where you do yours."

He's leaning on a blue tiled wall of what resembles a bathroom. Likely the one in Lily's hospital room. "I'm not having a come to Jesus with the toilet, Paul. That's all you." He flashes a half-smile, and regardless of sleeping with his daughter, I have to believe the strides I've made with him count for *something*. I'm not all the way back at the bad start with him.

I nod a couple times. "How's Lily?"

"Better," he says quietly, then his eyes flit around. "I only came in here because she's sleeping. I didn't want to wake her." Xander's dad looks exhausted, honestly. Dark half-moon shadows are under his amber eyes, and his face is sharper, more lethal. Like he's had more reasons for murder and less for loving these days.

I understand the feelings.

His daggered gaze returns to me. "How are you holding up?"

It catches my breath. "Don't you wanna know about Luna first?"

"I talked to her this morning and yesterday and the day before that. I haven't really talked to you since I saw you here." *At the hospital.*

I sense him studying my features, same way I studied him, and I end up staring at the shower stall and the purple Saturn bath rug. "I'm making strides," I say quietly. "Most everyone is worried about you. What you've been going through is a lot..." I trail off. Just as I look back to my phone, he's dropped his gaze.

We're silent for a long beat. Minutes, maybe.

And then he says, "When I was younger, I used to wish everyone would just *stop*." His reddened eyes are off to the side. "Stop goddamn worrying about me. It was...suffocating. Even the days where I wasn't fucking up, they were a reminder that I could. That I have. Then, as I got older, I wondered what it would've been like to never have people looking out for me, and I know I wouldn't be here." He shakes his head once. "It would've been easier to grab a bottle. My brother went to the ends of the earth to stop me from drinking myself into oblivion. But he shouldn't have had to do that. There are people, family, friends, who spend their *lives* fighting for their loved ones. Worrying about them. And I can say that sometimes their worry isn't enough. All it does is make me want to drown it out." He pauses, still staring off. "This disease is won and lost with me, but I can't tell anyone not to worry, and if I do, it's a lie—because I'm just as afraid of the moment they stop."

Lo has never been this frank about his addiction with me. I try not to think about my own father and mother.

Partly, I wonder if Lo has already relapsed. I'm not sure if he'd even tell me if he had, and I don't ask. Instead, I say, "I don't know how you got through that night. With both of them in the hospital..." I remember how he'd still been holding his shit together in the visitors' room. How he'd even stood up to comfort me.

"I kept rereading her texts," Lo says, sniffing hard and tapping his phone.

"Lily text you something?" I ask.

"My daughter. Luna. That night, she texted...*thanks for keeping Donnelly's story from that night on Halloween safe and thanks for protecting him.*" He chokes up, but it's choking me up too. His hand is against his mouth before he reads, "*I love you. To Thebula and back again.*" His voice cracks, and he clears his throat to say, "We joked about tacos." He sniffs, nodding. "That's what kept me together all night." He wipes the corners of his watery eyes fast. "Then I heard you slept with her and strangling you seemed more satisfying than a bottle of Macallan."

Damn. "Glad I could help your sobriety."

He lets out a weak laugh. "As *fun* as this catch-up has been, you never call me to say hi, so what's going on?"

"You worried about me?" I wonder, seeing concern cinch his brows.

"You're attached to my daughter, so by proxy, yeah, sure."

I'll take it. "The worst of my family is locked up," I remind him. "So I figure it's safer to been seen out in public with Luna, and before you say anything, we're taking things *slow.* We're not rushing into anything while she's dealing with amnesia. There's no labels at the moment—"

"Wait, hold on." His brows are scrunched even more. "You're forgetting your family can *never* find out you're the reason they're about to be in fucking hell for *eternity.*"

"I know it's soon—"

"It hasn't even been a full week since they were thrown in jail! Give it a few months—"

"I think it's better if I don't," I try not to shout, but my pulse is speeding. "I have a plan."

Lo looks hesitant and more fretful. "Jesus Christ, another plan."

"SFO already approved it, so it's a good one."

He gestures me to speak, but his face is all tight lines.

This is the hardest part. The part that takes effort and force to pull out from my core. "If I get spotted out in public with Luna, I'm gonna tell my family that I'm just using her." It's a knife in my gut just saying the words, but... "This is the way."

Lo lets out a breath.

"It's the only path forward," I add. "The only path with her, really. And in the future, if I ever date Luna publicly, then my family will just believe I'm faking this relationship to stay close to you all so I can help them, but I won't be able to help 'em. And years later, I dunno, I pull away completely from my family. They realize I fell for her for real, and I'm just gone. Detached from them and attached to all of you. They won't ever think I ratted them out years prior, and they'll have no reason to come for me."

Lo is processing, his hand raking through his light brown hair.

"Everyone will know the truth that I'm really with Luna," I say. "The only ones being duped are my family. And if I stay in their good graces, I might be able to figure out their real intention that night, which wasn't to kidnap Luna."

Lo is wincing.

I frown. "What's wrong with it?"

"You. Your family. Going back there." He points off to the side. "That was *not* the plan. It was supposed to end."

I sit up further on the toilet lid, phone tightened in my fist. "I'm not planning on befriending long-lost cousins, Xander's dad. I'll be talking mainly to one person."

"Your father," he says like that's no better.

I run a hand down my jaw. "You're not gonna like this, but he has to be in on the truth too."

"What?" he snaps.

"He knows…" I swallow a rising lump. "He knows I have feelings for Luna. I don't wanna get into it, but he still helped me that night, even knowing. He'll help me again and vouch for me when it comes to the rest of the family."

"At what cost?" Lo questions. "What's he going to ask from you?"

"Hopefully he'll just want a relationship with me," I mutter, but I can't even say it's a strong enough pull. "He went to jail for me. He was willing to go to *prison* for me. He has more to gain by helping me now than he did before—that's all I know."

Lo groans and cringes, not a fan it seems, then he sighs. "Just keep me informed. Trust." He motions from me to him, since our trust in each other has been like walking a rickety plank off a pirate ship.

Truth is, I trust him more than I do my own dad.

I nod and say, "I like green grapes and Granny Smiths." Off his confusion, I add, "For the fruit basket."

"The one I'm never going to send you," he reminds me. "You still *didn't wait* for her when you told me you would. Don't press your luck, Paul."

I want to laugh. Because all I've done is try my hand at luck, especially with his daughter. Hasn't always turned out in our favor, but I'd rather keep taking my chances. At least then, I'm still racing towards her.

POCKETING MY PHONE, I EXIT THE BATHROOM TO find Luna chilling in the living room with her puppy. She's upside-down on the sofa, flipping channels rapidly, but she mutes the TV as soon as I appear.

Seeing her just makes me smile. "You hungry?" I wonder.

"Yeah, I could eat."

Before she moves, I go to the back of the sofa and reach down, catching her hands. I pull her up and over the furniture, and her body melds against my chest. Luna is in my arms, breathless, and I remind myself, *she just met me*. Slow.

Be slow with her.

Doesn't mean I have to be distant. I carry her against my chest to the kitchen, her legs wrapping around my waist.

She's grinning. "I bet she loved when you did this."

I know she's referring to her past-self. The self she doesn't remember. "Carrying you to the kitchen wasn't something we did on the regular." *Or really at all.* "We were mostly friendly outside our rooms."

"This isn't friendly?"

"Not to me," I breathe.

She's eyeing me with an eagerness that heats my blood. "How'd the meeting go?"

"I'll tell you about it."

So I set her on her feet in the kitchen, and I rehash everything to Luna while we're making turkey sandwiches. I'm spreading mayo on a sourdough slice. She's topping tomato on the deli meat. Saying the plan a third time isn't any easier.

It's harder than the rest. After unleashing the brunt of it, I tell her, "You won't be around my dad or my family at all. You're not dealing with it."

She squirts mustard on her bread, considering this quietly. "I just want you to be safe. I think Original Luna would want that too."

"It's safe," I assure, and I believe it. I have to 'cause this is the only path I want to take. "Most everyone I know is locked up."

"It's a good plan then," she nods, slapping the top bread on her sandwich. "If it allows us to be out in public together, it's something I want." Luna is patting her sandwich. "Love pats add extra flavor."

I grin, licking mayo off my finger. "Is that so?" I rinse the knife off in the sink. "Did the sandwich tell you?"

"I'm not proficient in the sandwich language, unfortunately, but love pats tend to bring joy, not misery."

"You're telling me," I wipe my hands on a dish rag, and I pat my finished sandwich a couple times. She's smiling over at me, and I edge closer while her body shifts toward me. I pat her cheek lightly before cupping her face. "How'd that feel?" I breathe her in.

"Loving."

I watch her eyes roam over me, and so easily we could just take this to the bedroom. Go back there. Stay there. *This has to be different.*

"Wanna watch Bass?" I ask. "We could start over." We barely got through episode one.

She nods repeatedly, and we break away to grab our sandwiches— but pieces of me always feel entwined and bound to Luna, no matter how far apart we truly are.

37

Luna Hale

WE'RE THIRTY MINUTES into episode one. Roommates are elsewhere throughout the space, so the living room is free for my TV-watching marathon with Donnelly.

Turkey sandwiches made with heart, in a fancy penthouse, with a bout of amnesia, while casually seeing a guy who was dating my original self—it's a great setting for a sci-fi fic, if I added time travel. It'd be cool if I could speak to Original Luna. Get more info from myself and not just everyone else.

I wish.

On the blue sofa together and plates on our laps, Donnelly chews methodically, his attention super-glued to the screen. He really loves this show, and I've abandoned half my sandwich in favor of the "evolved" drama on the Peak between Callie, Frost, and Strider.

"That's how episode one ended?" I ask, wide-eyed. "I have so many questions. Is Frost an Anger Dominant but controlled? *Beneath a Strong Sentiment*—his sentiment has to be Anger? He's definitely not Sadness or Lust."

"You'll see. We've got eleven more episodes to go."

Sandwiches eaten and three episodes in, I've made a comfy home on the sofa with Donnelly. Tucked closer to him, his arm has fallen around my shoulders, and I sense him absorbing my reactions.

Was this her favorite show?

It's a *really* addicting one. "Wait, go back to Strider," I say to the TV and huff. "Why are his scenes so short? He's the most interesting character." I lean back into Donnelly's arm but notice he's tensed. "What?" I frown. "Is Strider secretly awful or something?"

Donnelly has a cool, calm expression. "No spoilers in this sacred Bass household." He points the remote at the TV. "Keep watching."

By episode five, we've stretched our legs onto the coffee table and eat gummy bears. Evening has fallen and we consider ordering take-out, but we fall victim to our obsessive binge-watch and forget about a future dinner.

I hear footsteps behind the couch, and Donnelly and I turn our heads as Sulli crosses the living room. Looks like she'd been working out, her brown hair sweaty in a top bun and water bottle in hand.

"Hey, Luna," she says to me.

"Hi." I lift a hand in a wave and return to the show. I doubt she'd want to stick around a TV all night with me.

Two seconds later, I hear her walk away. Donnelly watches Sulli leave, a strange look in his eye that I can't decipher. And I glance back at her shadow, then I frown.

"Should I have invited her?" I ask, glancing back again. "I didn't think she'd want to watch it."

"She likes hanging out with you."

"She does? Are we...friends?"

"Yeah," he says softly.

I nearly sink down. It hurts a ton knowing this friendship makes no sense to me. Sulli and me. Me and Sulli. In our adult years? We're friends with Cobalt boys, not with each other.

I try to let that interaction go. Bass helps.

By episode seven, I stand to stretch my legs. "Are there ship names?" I ask him. He's swigging a water and nods to me. I wonder, "What's Strider and Callie's?"

"Stallie."

"They're my favorite," I profess at the TV, but when I look to Donnelly, he has blown back against the sofa cushion in shock, plastic water bottle crunched in his hand. I say, "You're not a Stallie shipper?"

"*You* like Stallie?" His face contorts in pure confusion. "Why?"

"It's mainly Strider," I shrug, then return to my spot beside Donnelly. "I don't know he's…" I frown, trying to unearth the words. "He's misunderstood. He can't control his anger, and no matter how much Frost tries to reason with him, it's not making sense to Strider. Even though it's *clear* he's trying to be better." The TV screen is paused on a twenty-something guy with an angelic, tortured face.

Donnelly has bent forward, his forearms on his thighs. He's deep in thought.

It's not hard to guess where he's gone.

Sadness heavies the room, and I whisper, "She loves Callie, doesn't she?"

"You are—were a die-hard Callie fan, yeah. A vocal Frostie shipper, but…" He shakes his head. "I dunno, it makes sense why you wouldn't love her as much as you did. You don't remember being called a *slut* in headlines or being called a sex addict after doing close to nothing. You related to Callie and she reminded you of your mom, too."

I'm missing the memories of being eighteen in the public eye. My love life would've been greater clickbait and more of a free-for-all in the tabloids. I have bits of my birthday, but beyond that, it's still gone.

I want it back.

I hate that I'm yearning for something that I might never find again.

Donnelly can see I'm sad. "We don't have to watch the rest now—"

"I want to finish it," I say quietly.

He tucks me more against his side. The embrace tingles my skin, but it's not familiar. It's purely new and warming.

By episode eleven, it's so late that no one in the penthouse stirs, except a few furry felines. Even Orion has fallen asleep on a leather chair. The dark living room is bathed in the glow of the television.

On-screen, the monster of all twists drops. "Callie is *everything?*" I question. "Not just a Lust Dominant?" I slowly digest how she's the most powerful evolved. It puts a weird feeling in my stomach. "Original Luna couldn't have liked this."

"You didn't."

"Good," I nod. It feels like they gave extra reasons to make Callie special and likeable to the audience.

"Ready for the finale?" He's about to press play. "Hold on to your bootstraps."

"I'm holding tight and buckled in."

His arm curves around my ribs, tenderly and carefully since they've been bruised, and at first all I can concentrate on is Donnelly's hold on me. His arm. His touch. My lungs balloon with bright feelings I don't ever remember feeling.

I snuggle against him, my cheek on his collar. He strokes my hair, and I could fall asleep to the motion of his fingers gliding through the strands.

I love this. I'm discovering what I love in being with a guy, but there is a creeping notion in the back of my head telling me, *you've discovered this before.* But with who? And how could this possibly be a feeling I've felt with more than one person?

The finale is gripping enough that I pull out of those bad thoughts. "Ohhh whaaa, no way." I sit up off Donnelly. "No freaking way." I gape at the television screen. "Nowaynowaynoway." My hands fly to my head. "Strider is Callie's *son.* That's his mom…" I was shipping a mother and a son! "What the…shit." I sink backwards, then look over.

Donnelly is grinning.

"It's not funny. I feel like crying." I cringe and shiver, all gross inside.

He wraps an arm around me. "I'm not smiling 'cause I'm happy your ship sunk."

"No, it *burned* to a crisp," I mutter, still not understanding his reaction. "Why do you look happy?"

"'Cause you were spoiled the first time you watched the finale. It's cool seeing you watch it without knowing what's gonna happen."

I smile. "I got a redo."

"Yeah, you did."

"Amnesia perk," I sing-song. "There aren't many."

"We'll make more," he says like it's a real possibility and not fiction. I hang on to the depth of his expression, his sincerity as it burrows into me.

He's attractive. The way he had been gripping a *sandwich* today was hot, and I wonder if I always found his mannerisms and his whole being so sexy.

With the quiet, the TV paused on the credits, and the glowing space, I start diving down a rabbit hole, imagining our first time together. Was it like an explosion of passion? Fast and forceful? Or slow and sensual? How did he take her? He said they wore masks one time…or maybe it was more than once.

Will he even want to have sex with me if I don't have those memories?

"You like the show?" he asks, even though my brain is halfway down his pants. *I want him all the way down mine.*

"Yeah, it was epic." I look to the TV. "I'm definitely going to do a rewatch sometime, see if I can pick up any hints that I missed."

"We were gonna go to a convention next month together in San Francisco, if I can get off work. The actors will be there."

"Really?" I smile. "We're still going?"

"That's what I was gonna ask you."

"I'd go with you."

He smiles. "I'll put it in my calendar. Doodle stars and planets next to it."

"With glitter pen."

"Only glitter pen."

I start to smile too. I wonder if this is an official date, but we don't bring it up. As he collects our snack trash, cleaning up, my stomach tightens. I'm not ready for him to leave.

Stay.

"Did you care a lot about your virginity?" I ask out of left field. It brings him back down to the sofa, and honestly, I could stay up talking to him for hours upon hours, or really, just be with him doing nothing at all. At the way he's looking at me, I wonder if he could too.

"Why do you want to know?" he breathes.

I shrug. "You know I didn't care a lot about mine. I was just thinking about yours."

"Did I care about it?" Donnelly thinks, outstretching his arm on the back of the couch right behind me. "Not really. I lost it in the most unspectacular way possible. Back of a Chevy. Girl told her friend, who then told someone else."

Kinda sounds like a typical first time, I guess. "Would you have changed it, if you could've?"

"Maybe not." He looks up at me. "Everything I've ever been through has led me to better things. If I changed a part, maybe I wouldn't have found you."

It tries to swell inside me, but I can't remember everything that led me to Donnelly. Frustrations attempt to invade, but I try to banish them.

"Do you want to…?" I start to ask softly, but I sense his hesitance. "I was just going to see if you wanted to sleep in my bed with me again—we don't have to do anything."

"I want to," he breathes.

I'm bracing myself for the incoming rejection. "But we can't?"

"But I don't think we should." He scratches the back of his head, trying to wipe pain off his face. For me, I think. *He doesn't want to hurt me.* "We've gotta be slow about this, and plus, I don't wanna kick you in my sleep."

Right. He had a nightmare when we slept in the same bed, and I couldn't do much to help him.

I don't want to make this harder on Donnelly either. "Slow," I nod. "I agreed to slow and I can do slow." I can try, at least. "You're just a very irresistible human."

His lip rises. "Trust me, I feel the same about you, space babe." With this, he presses the most tender, electric kiss to my forehead, and he elevates off the sofa like a figure of my imagination. I'm in a dream state as we say our goodnights, as he's left for his bedroom.

I star-fish the couch, a gooey mess of giddy feelings. I look to my furry Newfie. "Did Original Luna feel like she flew a billion lightyears in his presence too?"

Orion perks up, as though I said, *time for bed.*

"I'll take that as a yes," I smile.

DONNELLY'S DAILY PLANNER
Friday, Nov 30th

Today's Focus: festivities and all that birthday magic for Luna's 21st. Gotta smother her with it (politely).

To Do:

- Tattoo Akara + Banks their forever wedding bands. (Still honored they asked me.)

- Check in on Xander's detail. Happy to be back.

- Maintain texting relationship with Dad?

- Best birthday party!! Only happy things for my space babe.

Notes: Heard from the boss man that Alpha & Epsilon threw a big ole pissy pants party after hearing I want to be with Luna. won't let 'em bring me down. Not sure how Akara's gonna smooth things over with Triple Shield yet. Need to find a penny to throw in a wishing well for him, where are all the pennies? Baby Maeve is a nighttime wailer. She's cute tho. Also! My psych eval is scheduled for Dec 10. Do not forget.

Quinnie is avoiding me. Think I messed that up bad. Maximoff + Farrow headlines are bonkers. Countdown to their second baby is on and it's fucking maaaadness. I'd be hyped too. (I am hyped.) Things with Beckett are meh. Could be better. Haven't had time to meet up or anything. Still feels like we need another face-to-face chitchat at least. Good things, Lily should be released from the hospital soon. Glad she's ok. Really glad.

Meals: Don't care. Eat my heart out, world.

Water: Hydrate all day, every day.

Question of the Day: How often does Luna snoop through my planner? Is she reading this now?

38

Luna Hale

IT'S MY 21ST BIRTHDAY and I can cry if I want to. That's what Tom sang to me this morning since I did not magically wake and merge with Original Luna. Here I am—the memory-less variant. Birthday magic isn't real after all.

I'm not so much in the mood to shed tears. I'm still just a jumbled mess of confusion and frustrations. It's been six days since I woke up, and the more the days pass, the more I've been learning about the years I've missed.

I'm not any closer to my little sister Kinney. Her familiar brush-offs should be comforting. Nothing has changed, right? Except, I was hopeful that maybe we were the kinda sisters who text every day and send memes. We're not even *that*.

I went through our text thread, and she barely messages me anything. I barely respond to her. It's just sad.

I've also discovered that despite being friends with Sulli, I never told her or even Jane about my feelings for Donnelly. *Why?* It puzzles me in an anxious, nervous way. If I am such good friends with Sulli, wouldn't I have confided in her?

Catching up on info about everyone in my family feels like binging ten seasons of a reality show in ten days. Like real life isn't *my* life. I hate this feeling.

I'm hoping my birthday can take my mind off these lost memories.

Focus on the present, not my missing past for a night. Even doing so, a part of me feels like I'm failing myself. Like I'm not trying hard enough to find Original Luna.

And now I'm in a slow-burn (maybe casual?) relationship with *her* guy. Who is technically *my* guy. But it weirdly feels like I'm stealing Donnelly from myself. Is that even possible?!

I stab a slice of Funfetti birthday cake too many times, wearing a Roswell Crashdown waitress costume: bobbing alien antennas, a 50s throwback mint diner dress, and a silver alien apron. It's one of my favorite Cosplay outfits I made for Comic-Cons.

I smash the frosting spaceship.

"Is she okay?" I hear Xander ask our older brother, not quietly enough. "She's mutilating the cake."

Moffy has empathetic, kind eyes on me. When my big brother (aka my memory guide) asked what I wanted to do for my birthday, I said to keep the plans I had already made.

Apparently, I chose camping in the woods with an otherworldly theme. Not so strange. It sounded fun, but *camping* was promptly thrown out the window by security and my parents.

Yes, I am a legal adult.

Yes, I am freshly twenty-one.

Yes, I just experienced a head injury and horrific incident of some sort—which I have no memory of experiencing.

Yes, my parents are overconcerned and overprotective because of said experience.

So I didn't protest when the venue changed from the state park to a bowling alley. It's shut down for the private event. Safe and sound with a tight guest list and heap of security.

Neon lights flash over the alleyways, and silver streamers dangle celestially from the ceiling. Balls smash into pins down the ten lanes, and I've camped out at Lane 8 with my brothers, as most everyone keeps their distance from me.

Don't overwhelm Luna. Don't overcrowd Luna. Don't pressure Luna. I've heard these phrases muttered more than a dozen times since I've woken from the hospital. I wonder if it's a reason why I haven't met my bodyguard yet. Maybe she's here, but bodyguards aren't attached to their clients as much during these types of private events. They mill around and focus on entrances, exits. That sorta thing.

My brothers and I have taken a pause on rolling balls into the gutter (mainly, I am the Gutter Queen) for a dessert break at our lane.

I pick at the lumpy green frosting.

"You know something about the cake that we don't?" Moffy asks me, eyeing the mushy mound on my plate.

"It could be sentient," I mutter.

"Yeah, I don't think it'll grow hooves and attack us," Xander says, lounging on the swivel chair beside me. The retro 80s swivel chairs have always been my favorite part of bowling. As a kid, I would imagine we were on a spacecraft in Star Trek, commanding the USS Enterprise together.

Moffy feigns confusion. "Huh, that's weird. I thought we bought *murder*fetti cake."

I smile.

Xander laughs and shakes his head at Moffy. "Sometimes I can't tell if you had the dad jokes before Ripley or not."

I would know this better than anyone. "He did."

"I did," Moffy says, gesturing to me with his fork. "I'm the same *amazing* interstellar big brother." He motions to his *Pizza Planet* shirt.

"With the corny dad jokes," Xander adds, smiling. His costume is more elaborate than Moffy's simple T-shirt. Xander is cosplaying my favorite character from *Dune,* Paul Atreides, by wearing a black stillsuit made for the harsh desert climate of planet Arrakis.

"The same but different," I sing-song.

I wish I didn't say it.

The air tenses between me and my brothers, and I don't know how to course correct.

He is the same in all the ways that matter and count, but the more I'm around him, the more I know he's not the Maximoff that I knew.

"He's not that different, Luna," Xander consoles. "He's still there for us, and he's still running circles around everyone in *everything* he tries for the first time."

I'm still having a hard time looking at Xander. He's so much older now. So I stare at my cake while I say, "He is different." I look up at Moffy. "You're someone better."

His brows knit together, emotion bobbing his throat.

In such a short time, I've come to realize this. He's not easily triggered to fight anymore. He's not speeding down highways. He's not afraid of the media seeing his public affection or writing stories about his parentage.

He's happier.

Envy burrows inside me, and I don't want to be envious of my brother's ability to find pure happiness within himself and his life. I just want to know that I, too, can be better.

I eat a huge bite of cake, hoping to avoid my feelings more than the conversation. I wish Donnelly were here.

I brave a glance at the shoe closet.

Donnelly has been among the racks of retro bowling shoes for thirty minutes and counting. He's in a serious conversation with my dad and my therapist. I've only caught brief glimpses of him through the crack of the door.

The intensity of my therapist isn't sitting calmly with me. She's holding up a firm hand in front of Donnelly's face, and he's raking a tenser hand through his own hair.

During our last session, Dr. Raven asked me if she could speak to Donnelly, and I gave her permission. Now, I'm regretting it. I mistakenly believed she wanted to help him sort through what happened, but she's *my* therapist.

She's advocating for me, and she's already thrown out words like "trauma bond" and "codependent attachment" to me. As if I *only* like Donnelly because of my fractured mental state, but it's only made me defend him more during those sessions.

I feel strangely protective over him, and I have no clue why.

I'm afraid Moffy and Xander will also conclude that Donnelly is *not good for me and my amnesia recovery* and I'm *too attached*, so I'm doing my best not to anxiously watch the shoe closet.

Moffy stands. "You want another drink?" He collects my empty can of Fizz.

"Yeah, but I'll take a vodka cranberry."

He pauses, just briefly. We're all the children of an alcoholic, but I've always imagined I'd drink on my 21st. It's not like it's my first sip of alcohol. To my knowledge, I've never overindulged before. Though, what I did the last three years, I can't be so sure.

"Unless..." I start, but he interjects fast, "I'll get you a mixed drink. What about you, Summers?"

"I'm good." He swishes his soda.

Once Moffy is gone, I'm left with my seventeen-year-old brother. He casts a glance to the shoe closet, then to me. "Donnelly's been in there with your therapist for a while," he says.

"Has he?" I play it off cool. Solid deflection tactics, I think.

"You've looked over there like twenty times," Xander tells me, but not as a dig or forcefully pointed. He seems concerned.

"I don't know what they're discussing," I admit softly. "But I can guess it has to do with me."

"Probably."

Bright neon lights flash on Lane 6 after Sulli lands a strike. I check my phone. Tom and Eliot are still stuck in traffic, and for some reason, Jane hasn't showed. She's a new mom, so it's not so surprising.

I scan the carpeted area behind the alleys. "Is that your friend?" I ask Xander.

"Who?"

"The girl coming towards us." A short girl with chopped blonde bangs is aimed for our lane, an edginess to her stride. She's wearing red plaid pants and a beaded choker necklace. As bodyguards stare her down, she pays them zero attention, only focused on *us*. I heard Xander is attending Dalton, so maybe he made a new friend there. "Is she from school?"

"No, *no*," Xander whispers quickly to me. "I don't recognize her at all, Luna. She must be *your* friend."

My friend? From where?

College, I remember. I'm attending college. Who the hell did I invite to my birthday party?

"She looks too young to be in college, doesn't she?" I whisper back to Xander.

He shrugs, at a loss. "Maybe you met her on Fanaticon or Reddit."

"Reddit? Do I do that?"

"No, I don't know." He scrunches his face, slouching in the swivel chair. "Shit, she is coming over here."

She is, and I wonder if I met her on Fictitious. What if she's a fellow writer? Meeting up with any anonymous online persona sounds...dangerous and risky and maybe something I would consider under the right circumstances.

As she bypasses a rack of glow-in-the-dark balls and crosses into Lane 8, I'm slack-jawed as Xander stands up first and lifts a casual hand in greeting.

Is this my shy brother?

What dimension am I in?

"Xander, or Paul Atreides," he greets. "You are?"

She's holding a manila envelope, a little caught off guard by his introduction. "Harriet. Just Harriet."

Harriet?

Harriet! New memories I've recently made are surfacing. The phone call in Superheroes & Scones. Tom's disgruntlement towards her.

"Harriet?" Xander's brows pinch, turning to me but with his back to her. "Do you know a Harriet, Luna?" He's also mouthing to me, *bathroom, go pee.* Having to pee is a good escape tactic, but I might be able to wiggle my way through this interaction.

"I do know a Harriet. Lab partner Harriet."

Harriet hasn't confirmed whether that is her yet. Because a towering six-foot-five Cobalt suddenly enters our lane.

Ben Cobalt is now *eighteen*. I've always known him as the sort of boy who spends hours running barefoot through the woods and jumping into rivers. He's always been a jock, a guy's guy, yet he barely gets along with his four brothers.

I wonder if that's changed.

"Hey," Ben Cobalt smiles, a little out of breath like he jogged here from Lane 2. He's wearing a ringer tee that says *love the earth*. "We go to Penn together." He's talking to Harriet, but as Ben glances to me, I sense he's doing his best to aid me in my memory-less quest for answers. He's coming in with the save.

"Thousands of people go to Penn," Harriet says flatly. "How would you know I go there? We're not even in any classes together."

"I remember people and faces fairly easily, and I'm positive I've seen you on campus before." Ben is smiling and trying to catch her downcast gaze. "Am I wrong?"

Her squared shoulders haven't loosened. "Dude, I know who you are, and your brother hates my guts, so maybe you should stop fraternizing with the enemy."

"My brothers' enemies aren't mine."

Her brows furrow. "Aren't Cobalts all like, *we all kill and die together, hoorah?*" Her *hoorah* is dry, and she pumps an unenthused fist in the air.

Ben laughs, which takes Harriet aback even more.

Xander assesses their interaction stiffly. By the frost my brother is giving off, I assume his broken friendship with Ben hasn't been mended. Three years does not heal all.

I slip into the conversation. "You want some cake?" I ask Lab Partner Harriet.

"No thanks. I can't stay long." She leaves both guys behind and hands me the manila envelope. "I talked to our professor again, and he okayed you finishing out the course off-campus. You just have to peer-review our labs and email them back to him."

I take the envelope, not understanding this act of kindness. Did I do something to deserve it? "You didn't have to go through the trouble..."

"It's nothing," Harriet says, but it's a better gift than she realizes. I won't have to fumble my way through social interactions that Original Luna made, and possibly I can start fresh next semester on my own terms.

I can commit fully this time. Do *more* than what I did before.

"It's not nothing," I say so quietly, unsure if she hears. Louder, I say, "Thank you."

She nods once. Then on her way out, she passes between Ben and Xander and glances between them. "Bye, Cobalt boy. Bye, Paul Atreides."

"See you around, Harriet," Ben says.

Xander raises a hand in goodbye, and once she's gone, he whirls to Ben. "Why'd you come over here?"

I'm the only one sitting in the swivel chairs. The USS Enterprise is experiencing rough turbulence.

Ben motions to me. "I didn't think Luna remembered her. I was trying to help."

Xander grimaces. "No, you didn't think I could handle that situation."

"You didn't know her!"

"You didn't either! You *literally* just met her."

I spring up. "No fighting on my birthday. It's a birthday law." I spread out my arms, but they're actually several feet away from me. They're both stewing, and in one solid second, they split apart in opposite directions. Xander leaves for the bathroom, and Ben is headed for the exit.

I still have my arms spread.

That worked too well.

Back in my swivel chair, I stare at my sad plate of swirled frosting and mushy cake. The bowling alley darkens as galactic twinkle-lights explode over the ceiling. It's cool, and this party is safer than venturing to a bar alone...but being around so much family makes me feel surrounded by all the *time* I've lost.

"This seat taken?" Donnelly asks, hands on the swivel chair beside me.

My breath catches, and I check the shoe closet. My therapist has vanished. Is he allowed to be in my presence? The question drifts, thoughts stolen at the sight of his black sparkly shirt and matching pants. His purple belt kinda resembles a nebula.

Something about the outfit puzzles me, a tickle against my brain.

I shake it off. "You don't need to find Xander?" I ask since Donnelly is on-duty and wearing an earpiece and radio.

"Banks has eyes on him," Donnelly says quietly, looking me over. "Can I sit?"

I nod, my stomach in knots. "What'd my therapist say?"

He plops down beside me, arm outstretched behind my chair. He slides the mushy cake closer to himself. "To be careful with you." Using the fork, he molds the cake into a shape.

I sense there's more. "That's it?"

"Don't think I'm supposed to tell you the rest." He spins the cake to me. He formed a realistic looking alien head in two seconds. "Watcha think?"

"Needs antennas."

He grins, then draws antennas in the green frosting with his finger. Afterwards, he swipes frosting down my nose, then my cheek.

I smile back. "The blood of my people."

He licks the frosting off my face, cupping my jaw. "Tastes unearthly." He places a kiss back on my cheek, and my whole body is singing.

I have been transported to a happier place, and I really don't want to leave. *I don't want him to leave. I can't lose him.* The urge swells powerfully inside of me.

His gaze flits around the bowling alley and he tenses more. Are we drawing attention from my therapist or security? With one glance backward, I spot my therapist's pursed lips and disapproval as she grabs her purse to leave.

Why does she believe this is just a trauma bond? *Because I have no memory of Donnelly.*

I say more quietly, "My therapist doesn't want me to be with you."

"Seems like it." He angles towards me, elbow on the table. "At least while you're recovering, but we're going *S.L.O.W.* There's no pressure for you to recall anything about the past, alright?" He looks earnestly into me.

I frown more, just *aggravated* that she's against him.

"She's helping you," Donnelly says. "She's on your side, Luna."

"But she's not on *ours*." I think harder. "Maybe it's a bad idea to be public with my family and security. This would be easier if no one was involved." No opinions. No naysayers.

"It's too late now," Donnelly says casually, sucking frosting off his thumb. "We're in it to win it, sad alien."

"Winning isn't really in a Hale's DNA," I remind him in a quiet voice. I've heard it enough from my peers growing up. "You picked the wrong girl if you're hoping to win anything."

He eyes my bobbling silver antenna headband. "Good thing I'm with the right alien then."

I smile over at him, my heart lifting.

Donnelly casts a glance to the left, then to me. "I got you something for your birthday. Been rethinking it…so I don't have anything to give you right now." Pain creases his forehead. "Sorry."

"That's okay." I shrug. "I wasn't expecting anything."

He scratches the back of his head, and I can tell that's not what he hoped to hear.

My stomach tightens. "What was it?" I ask.

"A sketch for a tattoo. Thought we could match. You can't smile about it."

I am smiling. "I wanna see it."

"Maybe later," he tells me. "I hate *laters*, but it's probably better if we wait on it."

If I had memories of him, he wouldn't be saying that. Being stuck in slo-mo with Donnelly might not be my favorite setting. I'm really struggling not pushing a super speed button just to experience *more*. But that's the problem. He's ensuring I want to experience more *with him*.

I nod, understanding.

39

Paul Donnelly

I'M PISSING IN THE alleyway outside the bowling alley—thanks to Epsilon acting like they own the fucking bathroom and saying, *it's full.* It's pathetic and about the only ammunition they have. I'm not letting them get to me.

Luna's therapist, on the other hand…

My face is still hot. The interaction didn't go so well. Been playing on repeat in my head.

Dr. Raven: Luna shouldn't be worried about being in a relationship right now.

Me: She wants to be around me.

Dr. Raven: She's only attached to you because of the trauma she's experienced. She has no real memories of you.

Then she started prodding about my birthday gift. *What'd you get her, Donnelly?* I don't consider the Fanaticon Convention tickets a birthday present anymore when Luna can't remember me giving them to her, and I haven't had much time to go shopping recently. Didn't even have time to buy a new costume for her party. So I pulled out the one I wore on Halloween, which is what I wore when I kissed Luna for the first time.

Don't think she recognized it.

The birthday gift, I put a lot of thought into, but I didn't need to buy it. After me beating around the bush and her therapist digging in, I finally fessed up about sketching a matching tattoo. She said, *Absolutely not. That's too far.* Lo was also in the shoe closet with us, and he wasn't too elated either, to put it mildly.

I don't want to treat Luna like she's an alt-version. She's already insecure about it, and giving us matching tattoos is something I would've done with her before the amnesia. But they made me rethink the whole thing, and in the end, I can't even say what's right anymore.

I jostle and zip up. Not loitering outside on her birthday, I go back in, hand sanitize, and avoid the stares from Triple Shield bodyguards. Comms are *off* in my ear—that's how much I don't wanna hear them tonight.

The flashing neon lights are adding gasoline to a fire in my blood, and I try to breathe it out. When I reach the lane, Luna is collecting a bright orange ball out of the rack. Her turn to bowl. Xander is near a nacho table speaking to his dad. Safe, but I keep tabs on my little elf's whereabouts.

On the chairs at the eighth lane, Maximoff, Farrow, and Baby Ripley watch Luna, and I join them. "She still killing it?" I joke since she's been losing pretty badly.

"With a score of two," Farrow says, popping bubblegum.

"Two!" Ripley holds up two fingers.

"Uh-oh, we got a mathematician on our hands," I say.

"Uh-oh?" Ripley frowns up at Farrow, since he's on his lap.

I laugh, and Farrow shakes his head at me with a rising grin.

Maximoff smiles over at his husband and son. "You counted correctly, Rip."

Farrow tells his kid, "Your Uncle Donnelly is just teasing you."

"It's what I do," I say, holding on to one of the chairs. Not sitting down. I'm still amped, and I need better distractions. "Jane and Thatcher couldn't make it?"

Maximoff and Farrow exchange a cagey look, and I straighten off the chair. "Is it Maeve?" I ask. "Somethin' happen?"

"No," Maximoff says fast and cracks a knuckle. "It's not that."

Farrow sets Ripley on his own chair, then stands up to tell me more privately, "You'll probably hear about it tomorrow, but he failed his psych eval."

I'm off-balance. "What?"

He raises his brows. "Thatcher failed the test. He's suspended until they clear him, and Jane wanted to be with him tonight."

My head is spinning. "Thatcher?" He's the epitome of a Mack truck. A military war tank. He bulldozes. Nothing runs him over.

"Man, he got *shot* this summer," Farrow whispers. "Not to mention, he went through surgery, almost died, and missed the birth of his daughter."

I rub my forehead. This isn't the distraction I was searching for. 'Cause now I'm just thinking if Thatcher fucking Moretti failed a psych eval, what are the chances that I'm gonna pass?

I'm fine.

I will pass.

I have to.

There is a key difference between me and Thatcher. He's ethical. Moral. I'm not always those things. Not if being immoral helps me stay alive.

Farrow studies me in a sweep. "You worried?"

"No," I say with the shake of my head. "You?"

"No," he says honestly, inspecting me.

"Your son is making fart faces at you," I tell him, but Farrow is still staring right into me. I gesture to my best friend. "You're missing out, man. It's cute as fuck."

Farrow chews his gum slowly, looking me over. "Don't lie during the eval."

I'm going to.

"Doctor advice?" I ask.

"Friend advice."

"Appreciation." I sling an arm around his shoulders. *Don't worry about me.* But as soon as I think it, I'm reminded of what Loren Hale told me, and I can't say the words out loud.

"Gutter ball," Luna sing-songs on her way over. "Farrow is up."

While he heads for the lane, Luna swivels on a chair, sipping a cranberry vodka. Adorable in her alien waitress costume, and I've imagined coming inside her way too many times tonight. Hell, I've imagined picking her up and fucking her on the lane. Thank God her therapist can't read my mind.

Maximoff asks her, "Are you calling him your boyfriend now?"

Luna goes motionless in the chair. "I, uh…" She's avoiding my gaze.

My pulse picks up speed, and I'm glad I'm not sitting or else my knees would be jostling under me.

"No," Luna shakes her head very slowly. "I barely know him."

Shit.

Feels like I'm being buried alive, but the way her body reacts— chest tightening, breath shortening—I know she's dumping dirt on herself too.

"Luna?" Maximoff says, worried.

"I didn't mean it like that," Luna says, more to me than to her brother.

"I know," I nearly whisper. "It's alright." And I tell Maximoff, "Can I have a minute with her?"

"Yeah." He sends me one brotherly warning. Not as threatening as his dad's looks, but it does its job. He stands up. "Rip, you want to push that green ball?"

"Yeah!" Ripley cheers, taking his dad's hand and joining Farrow at the lane. As they squat down to help their son, I take a seat beside Luna.

She might not be my girlfriend yet. We haven't labeled anything, but she isn't someone I ever want to lose. Not in my lifetime. "It's alright," I tell her again.

She's slumped, face torn. "It doesn't feel like it is." Her amber gaze drifts around the neon-lit bowling alley, seeing the bodyguards and family members who keep their distance. "They all have the right idea, you know," she whispers. "It's dangerous to be around me. I'm not saying the right things anymore."

I tip my head towards Luna, catching her gaze. "Maybe I like a little danger."

She gives me a look. "Really? Because it didn't hurt when I said I barely knew you?"

I don't break her gaze. "Not gonna lie to you. It hurt like hell."

Her face shatters, and she blinks back tears. "I'm horrible. Horrible. *Horrible*," she mutters.

"You're not," I say so quietly, my voice aches. "You're *not*." I rest my arm against the back of her chair, but Luna bows toward me. I can't tear my eyes off her, and she's so locked into me, the bowling alley might as well be empty. Colorful lights strobe over her features, but the greens and blues soften the despair on her round face.

I barely pick up her whispered words, "It hurt me too."

"I know," I breathe.

"How?"

"It was written on your face."

Her fingers graze the rip in my jeans on my kneecap. I stop myself from holding her. *She barely knows you.* She knows me. She's looking at me like she *sees* all of me, and I can't explain how she could.

"I feel very protective over you and me," she murmurs, and I try not to tense hearing her say something she's spoken before. She blinks a few times. "I don't know why I said that to Moffy."

I tell her, "Same reason it was hard for us to tell anyone what we were the first time around." Her hand is on my thigh, and I slide my fingers against her palm. "Whatever we were or are, it's always been this fragile fucking thing. Anyone else got their hands on it, anyone else knew about it, it felt like it'd just shatter. I dunno. We're mighty, you and me, but fuck we're unlucky. And I think we always knew that."

Her breath shortens again, but her fingers curl over mine. "You think we shouldn't be together with our kind of luck?"

I open my mouth to reply.

And the shrillest voice rips into our moment. "Happy Birthday, Luna." O'Malley hovers over us with the fakest smile I've ever seen. Last we talked, it'd been in the hospital on Halloween, where he'd been unusually *nice*, but I figured that wouldn't last once he heard I'm trying to be with a Hale.

I'm not an idiot. He didn't come over here for *pleasantries* and a quick hello. But if he's starting shit with me, he rarely does it in front of Farrow. I cast a quick glance to my left. *Farrow is gone.* So is Maximoff. Their son probably needed a diaper change or something.

Luna is confused, not completely recognizing O'Malley among the neon lights. He's currently assigned to Beckett's detail, but she would know him as Audrey Cobalt's full-time bodyguard.

"He's no one," I tell her.

"O'Malley," he says, ignoring me. "Epsilon bodyguard."

"Oookaay." She squints more at him. "Are we…friends?"

"Friendly, yeah."

I glare. Fuuuuck *him*. "You're not friends." I shoot up to block him from her. Not like I have any extra inches on him.

We're the same height.

Same age.

"That's not for you to say," O'Malley glares, sizing me up. "You wouldn't know *anything* I've ever said to Luna. You weren't there." To her, he says, "I've been your bodyguard."

She frowns, "I think I remember you when I was sixteen…"

What the fuck is he trying to pull?! I sidestep so he's forced to look at me, not her. "That doesn't make you friends." I grind my teeth. "Don't *lie* to her, man."

He's an inch from my face. "Like how you've been lying to her?"

Luna freezes.

I'm boiling. "What's your fucking problem?" I sneer. "You hate me, *hate me*. Don't fuck with her."

"I wouldn't fuck with her. But you…" He skims me up and down like I'm lower than trash, worse than scum. "What'd you tell her? That you were in love? How much *bullshit* have you fed her and why the fuck is she trusting you over her own family?"

Luna is eating air, confused beyond belief.

O'Malley cocks his head to see her. "I know you better than he would—"

"Fuck you," I block him again, seething from the inside out. Does he really believe that's true? That *he* could possibly be closer to Luna than I am? Or is this just out of pure spite? Then I remember at Philly Comic-Con, Xander mentioned how O'Malley *likes* Luna, and a territorial heat blankets my whole body. What's he doing—trying to get with her?

O'Malley tries to look at her *again*. I push him back. He stumbles near the mechanical shoot of bowling balls near the lane but stays upright. If anyone watches us, I don't see. He's the only person in my field of vision, and I hate that he keeps putting Luna in his.

So I'm only a foot from him, the wooden lane beneath my feet.

"How was it being back there?" O'Malley asks, alluding to South Philly, the row house where I found Luna. I see her cuffed to the bed, and rage scrapes against my eardrums like aluminum foil. "Feel right at home? Maybe you should've *stayed*."

"You wanna see my family?" I sneer under my breath. "I can give you their number. You can get your ass handed to you again."

His chest bumps against mine. I don't back down. He's in my face as he says, "You must've told her some story to get her to fall for a piece of shit like you. But you know what I think? I think you raped her—"

I slam a fist in his jaw, wrath exploding with that one accusation. The punch should've knocked him over, but he's ready with one in my gut. Next breath, we're brawling down the bowling lane in front of the famous ones. In front of our bosses. The only thing I care about in this hot-blooded, acidic second is inflicting sheer *pain* upon O'Malley.

I bring his body to the wood and nail him in the face. As we wrestle against one another, I hear the way our bodies squeak against the lane more than I do the shouting in the background. My blood blisters, and I barely feel his knuckles slam into my mouth.

Hands suddenly pry me off him, and I'm in a haze of hatred. Can't get out.

"Donnelly. *Donnelly.*" Oscar is clutching my face.

I'm not even on the alley anymore. I'm standing on the 80s carpet by the nacho table.

"Bro?" Concern is all over him.

I taste blood in my mouth. "Where is she?" I ask, trying to see over Banks, Quinn, and Gabe.

"Let her go," Oscar advises, and hearing that nearly buckles me.

I swallow hard, about to choke out, *I can't.* I blink a ton, and crouching down, I run my fingers through my hair, just now noticing I split open my knuckles again. The chain is heavier around my neck, and I untuck the crystal from my shirt.

Oscar keeps a comforting hand on my shoulder. "For right now."

Right now. Yeah.

I don't want Luna seeing me like this anyway. She's already seen enough.

40

Luna Hale

HAS DONNELLY BEEN *deceiving me?* My head pounds with the heaviest confusions and fears. Is O'Malley someone I should trust? What if everything he said is true? Seeing them throw punches is what made me run.

I got scared, feeling like I can trust no one but myself—and Original Luna is buried too deep. I want her back.

Come back. *Please.*

Tears burn my eyes, and as family calls my name, I race past them on the carpeted area of the bowling alley. My gaze is on the squiggle and lightning bolt patterns beneath my feet.

"Luna!"

That one voice halts me in place. "Mom?" My voice squeaks, and I can hardly believe what I'm seeing. *Is she real?*

Fairy wings and a starry headband make her appear like a celestial fae. Beneath her armpits are crutches, decorated with silver tinsel.

Emotion overtakes me, and I bound towards her. "Mom!"

I catch myself before going into a hug. *What if I hurt her?*

"Surprise," she says, trying to smile but worry invades. "What happened? What's wrong? Luna?"

I shake my head, too choked to speak. People are watching.

"Let's go in here for a sec." She leads me to the nearest private party room. This one is mostly empty. Just bare tables and empty chairs.

I had my seventh birthday at this bowling alley, and I remember this room. Presents were stacked on the glittery black tablecloths. My mom bought boxes of pizza and balloons shaped like stars. Partly, I wonder if they chose *bowling* to help me hang on to a childhood memory that I do have.

For some reason, it's just a reminder that I'm not a kid anymore. I'm so much older. The party room is nostalgic in a way that aches my heart, but I don't yearn for *that* past.

I shut the door. "You really came." I didn't think she could, since she was just released from the hospital today.

She rests her crutches against the table. "I wanted it to be a birthday surprise." She tosses her hands up. "Surprise!"

It overwhelms me again. "It's the *best* surprise." Finally seeing her means the world to me. Glitter coats her cheeks, but I still spot yellow blemishes beneath the makeup. It's almost been a week, and she's still bruised.

What happened?

I was there during this attack. I saw it? My stomach flips with nausea. Do I even want those memories to return?

Her deep frown hurts me. "Oh Luna. What's going on?" She reaches out towards me.

"Can I hug you?" My voice breaks again.

She's already wrapping her bony arms around my frame. "I want to hug *you*. I've been waiting for this moment." Her hugs are magical, and I hold tighter around my mom, burying my face against her hair. Tears leak out of my eyes, but I hear her sniffling too. I don't want to let her go, and I feel that she's not ready to let me go either.

"I'm so glad you're okay," she whispers shakily. "I'msogladyou'reokay."

I breathe deeply, wrapped inside my mom's love, and I'm equally just *so glad* she's okay. After what feels like an eon, we pull apart, and we wipe our runny noses with pocket-tissues she has handy.

"How are you?" I ask in a raspy voice.

"Better now." She smiles at my Crashdown waitress outfit, but sadness glasses her green eyes. "I'm really sorry I haven't seen you sooner." Her voice chokes on the last word.

I take off my alien antennas, my temples throbbing. "No, it's okay. You shouldn't feel bad. I understand why you waited…and I was just scared…" I swallow hard. "I didn't want you to get any worse."

"You haven't heard? I'm *indestructible*. Your dad called me Colossus the other day."

I laugh softly and sniff harder. "I believe that." I ball up my snotty tissue.

My mom skims me again. "You really don't remember that night?"

I shake my head slowly, then faster. "Not a single second."

She inhales deeply, a breath of relief. Her shoulders relax like weight levitates off her. "I'm *so* glad, Luna. So, *so* glad." Tears prick her eyes.

"I'm *not*," I croak. My gaze burns. "You shouldn't have to carry that night on your own. I was *with* you, Mom."

"I want to," she whispers, touching my cheek softly. "I'm happy to. I'm your mom. That's what moms do." She nods resolutely.

I'm shaking my head, hating this reality so very much. *I can be Colossus too.* I want to tell her that, but I'm not even sure if I believe I'm as strong as my mom.

I lick my dried lips and my phone buzzes in my silver apron pocket. The number—I don't recognize. Recently, I've been answering calls to keep up appearances. Original Luna hadn't logged in all her contacts, so Caller ID can't even help me.

"Sorry, one sec," I tell my mom, stepping back to answer my phone. I see my reflection in part of the glass wall, and wet star stickers are peeling off my cheeks. I pry off a green one, my head whirling, and dazedly, I lift the phone to my ear. "Hello?"

"*Slut.*" The low, throaty voice sends a chill down my spine. He hangs up. I'd think it was a prank call, but there was no laughter in the background.

What the fuck?

I want to scream.

"Luna?" My mom senses my unease.

I gulp, lungs tight, and I rotate back to my mom. "It was a…" *What am I supposed to call it?* "I don't know, actually."

"What'd they say?" She grabs her crutches and hops closer.

"They just called me a slut and hung up."

Her brows bunch, and she goes into immediate Mom Action Mode. Asking for my phone. Screenshotting the number with her own cell. Sending a text to security. All while balancing on crutches.

She's my superhero.

Waterworks scald my eyes again, but I force down the tears.

When she returns my phone to me, she says, "You're not a slut."

"Maybe I am though," I breathe out. "I wouldn't know, would I?"

"Having a lot of sex doesn't make you a slut," she tells me, adamant.

I almost smile. "Pretty sure that's the definition of a slut, Mom."

She blushes. "You know what I mean."

She doesn't want *slut* to be a negative thing. For me to talk badly about myself. I get that. "I do," I whisper. "I do. But I guess…I don't care about being called a slut as much as I care about being called a…" I trail off, not wanting to hurt her.

"A sex addict," she finishes for me.

I wince, more pain blossoming inside me. "I keep saying the wrong things," I whisper.

"Nonono," she says quickly. "You didn't say *anything* wrong, Luna. It's okay to not want to be known as a sex addict. I don't want that for you either."

I wipe harshly at my eyes, trying to stop them from watering so much. "I'm sorry this is the second time we're having this conversation. I know it's not fun."

Her face shatters.

"What?" I whisper, more dread compounding on me.

"Luna," she says my name and it's filled with pure sorrow. "We've never had this conversation before."

No.

I don't believe that.

I stagger back a step. "If I was casually hooking up with a lot of guys, I would've *definitely* talked to you about being concerned I'd be perceived as a sex addict. No?"

"No, you didn't talk to me about that," she says, but before I break down even more, she adds fast, "and maybe that was my fault that I didn't pry more—"

"No, stop," I tell her. "It's not you. This is a fucking *theme*, Mom." I pace back and forth, hands on my forehead. "Did I even talk to you about what it felt like to have my fics leaked? Because you out of *everyone* would have understood what that felt like, right? The *shame*. The fucking *shame*." I'm clutching at the watch on my wrist, trying to keep everything together.

But I am completely unraveling.

She shakes her head and blinks, her built tears falling down her cheeks. "You didn't come to me."

I feel awful. As good as dirt.

What was Original Luna thinking? Why was she so closed off?

My mom rubs her face. "But it's *okay*. It's okay, Luna. I'm not upset at you for that."

"We're not close?" I choke out those words, my whole world tilting on its axis. I can't believe I shut her out of my life. She's my *mom*. I told her about my crush on my imaginary boyfriend and how we had invisible kisses when I was little. And I know, as I've grown older, I haven't shared *everything*, but why wouldn't I confide in her on the things that matter most?

"We're close," she defends *us*. "You wanted to get on birth control, and *I* took you."

She took me?

Okay, *okay*. I try to catch my breath. *But we don't talk as much anymore?* I scramble for memories past my eighteenth birthday, but I have none. Did having sex change things for me? Did the world viewing me as an adult make me pull away from her?

I know the media treated Jane differently the moment she turned eighteen. *Fair game.* The same thing likely happened to me.

41

Luna Hale

IN THE WEE HOURS of the night, I sift through piles of printed manuscripts on my bed, the plastic tub emptied. "Which one should I read next?" I ask Orion beside me. He's been chewing on a peanut butter filled toy, slobbering on an old fic titled *When the Earths Collide*. I wrote that one when I was fourteen, so it's already catalogued in my noggin.

I'm mainly reading the ones I can't remember ever writing.

Fairy lights cocoon my headboard, and the fan whirls with a rhythmic hum. I should bask in the solace of my space, but I find myself glancing at the bathroom.

Darkness lies beneath the crease of the door.

Donnelly. I keep picturing him flicking on the lights…and then coming in my room. But he never does.

He hasn't in a while.

It's been one week since my birthday, and we've given each other a whole lotta space. I've barely seen him, really. Both O'Malley and Donnelly were suspended for two days for fighting while on-duty. A lenient punishment, I heard. Since then, Donnelly hasn't spent much time at the penthouse. Once back on-duty, he's been busying himself protecting my younger brother, who's returned to Dalton Academy.

I've been in New York hanging out with Tom and Eliot and

reading my fics. With how much I wrote in the past three years, I'd need a solid month to catch up.

The longer I stare at the bathroom, Orion lifts his shaggy head and follows my gaze. He whines, then looks to me.

"He's not gone," I whisper to my Newfie. "He's still in his room." *He's just not with me.*

Orion lets out a longer whine, not understanding why Donnelly isn't around.

"You weren't at the party," I tell Orion. "It was…confusing. I'm still so…" *Confused.* Heat bathes my face, my throat swelling closed. But I manage to murmur, "I don't know what's real."

I've just been following my instincts, and my therapist is saying they're not to be fully trusted either. Trauma. Attachment. Obsession. I shut my eyes, then open them.

Orion paws my lap, and I scratch his furry head. "What if Dr. Raven *is* right?" I whisper. "What if I'm just latching on to Donnelly because he was one of the first people I saw when I woke up? He's just a coping mechanism—I don't really know him." It punctures me, just believing he could be bad for me.

Since I woke up, he's felt like a refuge in my mind. Why is that such an awful thing?

Then O'Malley scrambled my reality even more. I thought about asking Eliot if I know my old bodyguard really well.

Am I friends with O'Malley?

Do I like him?

But Eliot couldn't verify much about my relationship with Donnelly, so it's very likely that Original Luna could've had a secret friendship with O'Malley. Right?

It could be in the realm of possibility. A *lot* could lie in that realm, and that's why I'm going out of my mind!

I sink back against my pillows and then reach for the nearest manuscript.

Human Him, Cosmic Her: The Light.

The continuation of my Thebulan series. In the last few chapters, a human crash-landed on Thebula and Zarek, the King of Planet Demos, has cautioned Queen Solana of Thebula from intermingling with the human species. He believes Vaughn, the human, should be killed or flown out of their solar system.

"Zarek is just protecting Solana," I tell Orion, flipping a page. "He bound himself to her, so his best interests are her best interests." I read a little more.

Solana has met with the human on Thebula. A lush waterfall splashes outside the cave dwellings where the human has been residing as a visitor.

> I appraised the man on his cot. Vaughn hadn't asked for much since the crash. Only accepted what little was offered. Zarek thought humans weak but deceitful, and yet, this one hadn't tried to fool me. He sat there... cleaning his boots.
>
> "I can send you back," I told him. "We're working on finding you transportation."
>
> His eyes, the hues of the Typas waters, rose to mine. He did not fear me. Not once did he cower. Yet, he did not try to lay claim to my throne or to my people. Whatever he wanted, I could not tell, but the strength of his presence quickened my heart. "And what if I stay?" he said.
>
> "Stay?" I nearly laughed. It was so strange to hear a human speak the Thebulan tongue. When we first met, I asked him how he came to be proficient, and he said he studied many languages upon many galaxies.
>
> "I'm an explorer," he'd told me. "This isn't a bad place to land, though, is it?"
>
> "You flatter me," I'd said, still skeptical.
>
> He'd grinned, then eyed my world. "It is the truth."
>
> In the lush cave, he stood off the cot. "Yes, stay. I have nowhere else to be."
>
> "It's dangerous for humans," I cautioned.

> He came forward, a smile alight in his eyes. On his lips. Across his face. It breathed something new in me that I did not understand. Something indescribably bright.
>
> He whispered, "I have experience with danger. In fact, I think it follows me." His fingers brushed a tendril of my white hair, then slid down my arm, causing my purpled skin to radiate an iridescent green.

"Wait, wait," I say aloud, sitting upward. My heart races at the strangest turn of events. "This isn't right. This isn't supposed to happen." I keep reading. Page after page after page. I bite my thumbnail to the bed, my heart catapulting and plummeting as Solana is wooed by Vaughn, the human.

Ever since I was little, *Zarek* was always Solana's greatest love. Soulmatched. Together throughout all eternity to rule the two mightiest planets in the known solar system.

"I don't...understand," I whisper, reading more and more and more. Getting late into the night, my jaw drops as the story pulls further away from Zarek, and I hunger for the next parts to the saga. *The Hunt. The Good Fortune. The Revelry.* I lie back on my pillows. "They're kissing," I tell Orion, my eyes welling with a flood of emotion. "Vaughn and Solana are kissing."

I can't believe I'm rooting for them to kiss. I wrote their romance with a deep, cavernous longing, but it is so, so effervescent. Solana is lighter and freer with him. Her worries melt into mesmerizing moments, and I need more.

I flip a page after they kiss.

It's blank.

No. No. "It can't end there," I say, frantic. I search through the heap of manuscripts for the next part, but I labeled them in order. This is the most recent story.

It's the last one I wrote for the series.

My pulse hasn't slowed. "I don't understand," I say again, manuscripts strewn haphazardly around me on the bed. Why would I change the direction of the *entire* saga? This isn't a teeny tiny plot twist. It completely alters the trajectory of Solana's life and her future.

Fumbling through my sheets, I don't think—I just find my phone and call someone who's read my fics. It rings and rings.

He answers on the third one. "Luna," Charlie says groggily—a rare feat to catch him tired. "It's four a.m."

"Is it also four a.m. where you are?" I wonder.

"Yes, because I'm home."

Duly noted. He isn't traipsing around Paris or Montreal. "My fics, you read the entire *Human Him, Cosmic Her* portion of the Thebulan saga, right?"

"Of what you gave me," Charlie says, clearing his throat to rid the groggy rasp. "I'm almost positive I read everything or else the story wouldn't have made sense."

Okay, good. "Did she—I mean, did *I* ever explain why Solana would distance herself from Zarek?"

"We talked grammar. Your story was yours. You didn't bounce ideas off of me or brainstorm with me in the dead of the night."

I'm quiet.

He pauses, then tells me, "It's called *Human Him*, Luna. *Human.* Zarek isn't the human."

"I know, I know," I say quickly, my pulse in my throat. "I just didn't plan for her to get with the human. He was an antagonist, not the *love interest.*"

Charlie lets out a long sigh. "And why do you think you changed the story?"

I grip my phone tight, my eyes welling again. "I have to go." I hang up on him, not rationalizing what I'm doing.

I need to see Donnelly.

Bouncing off my bed, I charge through the empty bathroom and wiggle the door to his adjoining room. *Please be unlocked.* It is, *yes.* I spring inside. Orion excitedly follows at my heels, and I'm surprised to see the lights on and Donnelly wide-awake.

He's resting against his headboard. Sketchbook in hand and wearing reading glasses, he goes rigid as I barrel in. "Luna?" He canvasses the length of me, and I'm more aware I'm only wearing an oversized AC/DC tee I found in my drawer.

He's only in drawstring pants, shirtless. His chest rises in a deep breath. For the first time, I notice a stick figure tattoo by his ribs and a creepy skeleton head inked on his inner forearm. *He is new to me.*

But he wasn't so new to her.

Orion distracts him, jumping onto the bed and licking his face. He scratches and pats my puppy, but quickly, he slides off the floral comforter, concerned. "Luna—"

"Sorry, I just…" I'm out of breath, panting, overwhelmed.

Donnelly puts a hand on my back. "Lemme get you some water—"

"Nono," I slur together. "I'm okay, I'm okay." I step back from him, my breath still ragged but I manage to say, "I know we haven't talked very much lately…after my birthday."

Donnelly takes off his reading glasses, then rubs the crease of his eye. "Yeah, I've been hoping you'd want to talk to me…eventually."

It rocks me back. "You've been waiting for me to talk to you?"

"I didn't wanna push you in any direction. You've gotta figure this out on your own, Luna, and I…" He looks away, his eyes reddening. "I don't wanna hurt you. I can't hurt you." His Adam's apple bobs. "So if time away from me is what you need, then I can give you space."

He has given me that.

I open my mouth, but words are caught.

"Your therapist throwing confetti parties in my honor?" he banters with a rising smile.

"Yeah," I murmur. "She isn't sad about this break."

He nods slowly. "A break." He skims me up and down. "Is that what we're calling it?" He eases backwards in a daze, sitting on the edge of the bed. Staring at his cupped hands, he says under his breath, "Maybe I never even had you."

"That's not true," I whisper.

Donnelly looks up at me, his eyes bloodshot as he restrains raw emotion.

The truth of what I've felt flows through me. "She loved *you*. She loved you *so much* that you inspired her writing and the stories that meant the absolute most to her. No one else has ever been that for her. No one but you."

It hits him. I see that in his glassed gaze. The way he looks left, right, processing. He struggles to speak before asking in a single breath, "How do you know that?"

"*Human Him, Cosmic Her.*" I swallow a lump, my pulse on another ascent. "The human was just supposed to be a rival to Zarek. No romance plot line. Nothing like that. Then in real life, she falls for you and this entirely new character emerges that I never imagined, that I never thought of or could conceptualize—because I hadn't met you yet. And-and it's so much better than anything I could've written three years ago. It's *beautiful* and happy and hopeful. I'm almost certain she loved you."

He intakes a long breath, then rises slowly off the bed, his hand on the back of his skull. I track his movements as he paces towards the dresser.

"What's wrong?" I ask.

"I know you loved me, Luna." He spins back to me. "I just don't know if you'll ever love me again."

A tidal wave of grief surges inside my body, and I whisper, "I'm the bigger cynic and I still believe I could." I watch him unearth a package of cigarettes from a drawer. "You don't think it's possible anymore?"

"I think…" He smacks the package against his palm, choosing his words carefully. "You shouldn't be worried about being anything with me."

But…but I am afraid to lose him, and I haven't been able to explain why. Panic shortens my breath, and I try to stay calm. "Can I have one of those?" I reach for the cigarettes.

He pulls one out, comes closer, and slowly slips it behind my ear.

His touch against my skin sends a ripple down my arms. Then he whispers, "I have a lighter around here somewhere." He can't find it after a minute of searching, so I grab mine from my room.

Back in his, he's already holding his own cigarette. I put mine between my lips. He follows suit, edged close enough that our cigarette butts nearly touch. I raise the lighter between us. Our eyes stay latched while the flame licks the ends.

Donnelly sucks in, then plucks out the cigarette to blow smoke upward. My heart thumps. I could count all the many ways I'm attracted to him, and none would be because I was *told* to like him.

I take a drag, my head whirling with nicotine. We share the quiet for a calming moment, and I end up muttering, "I don't care if I shouldn't fixate on you."

He searches me, cigarette between his fingers. "I don't wanna be bad for you."

I don't look away from him. "I can't know everything you've been for her, but you've only been good to me," I whisper. "And I might not be exactly who she was, but I'm not trying to become her for you."

Donnelly almost smiles. "Good thing." He brings his cigarette to his rising lips. "'Cause I've just wanted the girl in front of me."

I smile back. "Question is, how willing are you to be with me if it means others saying it's *too soon* and *a bad idea* and *not good for me*? Because they may say that, and I'm trying to tune them out. Are you?"

He rests a hand on top of my head, bringing me closer to his chest. It's the most simple, casual form of affection I've ever slipped inside, and I burrow against the warmth of his bare skin. Quietly, he breathes, "Other people aren't gonna stop me from being with you. If this ends, it's 'cause you want it to."

He's been defaulting to my wants, my desires—and I have been flipflopping since my birthday. Uncertain and scared.

I decide to shove away the outside voices. Listening to what I feel brings more certainty, and that's the most comforting sentiment.

Pulling back, I tell him, "I don't want this to end yet."

Donnelly looks me over again, then nods. "Alright, space babe." Then he holds out his pinky.

I hook mine with his, both of us grinning. "That is one good earthly promise."

"Stamp." He smokes but keeps our pinkies hooked. Then he's twirling me in a circle, and the seamlessness of the night flows through me. Playing songs on shuffle from his phone, we smoke and dance and laugh in his bedroom while Philadelphia is sound asleep.

"The flying monkey," I say, showing him my chimp dance moves. I leap at him, and he catches me in a front piggyback. His hands on my ass, only wearing panties beneath the AC/DC tee. Arousal ignites, but next, I groom his hair.

His grin is intoxicating. I want to get drunk off his radiance and joy, and I think about telling him. Would he find me weird? *He said he wouldn't be ashamed of me.* He hasn't been embarrassed by anything I've done so far tonight.

"I want to get drunk off you," I say softly. "Your grins, your face, your being."

"You're drinking wisely," he teases.

"Uh-huh, but not responsibly. I want your face in excess." I cup his cheeks.

"Girl, you've got more than just my face." His grin is also powerful, illuminating inside me.

"Your ears," I say, touching his hooped piercing.

"Yours."

"Your eyebrows."

"Yours."

I look down. "Your lips."

He kisses me, a deeper passionate kiss that tingles and aches. I grip his hair, a whimper in my throat, and his tongue melds so perfectly against my tongue. Pleasured heat swarms me, and in one breath, I say, "My lips."

He eyes them. "*Mine.*" He goes in for another devouring kiss, and I'm such a goner in his clutch.

We make out for what could be a century. All we do is kiss, and the needy parts of me want so much *more*. I'm trying my best to resist.

Donnelly says, "I gotta…" He clears a pent-up noise out of his throat, stepping back from me. Distance is good, yeah, and he's clearly struggling too. "Smoke break?"

I nod rapidly. "Yeah, that's good."

We light another two cigarettes. He opens the window and rests his hand outside on the sill. "She's beautiful tonight." I know he's talking about the city, but I imagine he's also speaking about me. His eyes are on me as I follow him to the window.

I take another drag and walk, my eyes grazing his room, and I zone in on the floral comforter. I slow to a stop, my pulse spiking.

The pink petals—it jars me into another visual. *Floral*…wallpaper. The image resurfaces of a different room. I dizzy, my breath shortening.

"Luna?" He straightens up.

"I…" *Scuffed floorboards.* Where have I seen this place before? I don't know. I don't know! I can't catch my breath, and I must've accidentally dropped my cigarette. Donnelly snuffs it out with his *bare* foot.

I choke out, "Wait, don't…" *Don't hurt yourself for me.* I lower to the ground, gasping for breath and words. I hate this. *I hate this.*

Donnelly is behind me. "*Shit.* Luna, Luna." He's kneeling, and then we're sitting. He pulls me between his spread legs and wraps his biceps snug around me, his back against the wall while I lean on his chest and intake ragged breaths. "Luna." He whispers against my ear that he's here.

He's here.

His heart thumps, thumps, thumps rhythmically against me. I concentrate on the tempo, holding onto his strong forearms. Orion tries licking my face, then slouches his body weight against us.

Once my heart rate steadies, I whisper, "The…room."

He tenses. "What room?"

I swallow a pit. "I can't…I can't tell if I made it up. If it's not real, something I saw from a movie…"

Donnelly is silent.

I tilt my chin to look up at him.

He has the back of his head pressed to the wall, but he looks down at me. "Does it have wallpaper?"

"Yeah." My stomach sinks so low, I feel sick.

"What kind?" he breathes.

"Floral, something like your comforter only…older. From the nineties, maybe. Floorboards…but they're all worn down, scuffed."

Donnelly is even paler than usual. Then his phone rings in his pocket. I dig it out for him, and he reluctantly loosens his arm around me.

"It's your dad," I tell him.

He doesn't answer it. "I know that room."

"You do?" I twist around slowly to face him, knelt between his legs. "Where's it from?"

Donnelly stares off before meeting my eyes. "The worst night of my life."

My face falls. "The night I was kidnapped." I only know his family took me because of the internet, but the details online are slim to none. *The room is from that night.* Hope suddenly swells inside me. "This is good, Donnelly. It means I remember something."

It means I could remember so much more.

He looks gutted. "That's the one thing I didn't want you to remember."

His pain is visceral, and I want to take it away somehow. I find his hand and touch our fingertips. Our breaths slow together, and his gaze draws back to mine.

"I'm okay," I breathe. "I'm here now. I'm not there." I know he's trying to forget that past, and I'm chasing after it.

42

Paul Donnelly

SITTING ON THE FLOOR with Luna, holding her, hearing she remembers *that* room and *that* place—last thing I wanna do is let her go. But my dad called.

"Are you going to call him back?" Luna asks, seeing the phone in my fist.

"If you're still hoping to get drunk off my face, then I need to." I pick myself off the floor and extend a hand to her. She hops up with my help, and I keep an arm around her hips. The AC/DC shirt rides on her thighs, teasing my gaze towards her pussy, and thank God I've got control of my cock and these fucking impulses—or else I'd be pounding inside her.

Virgin.

She thinks she's a virgin.

Can't forget.

Luna sees me checking her out. I'm also stalling on calling my dad back, and this is a much happier place to be, I'd say.

She touches my hand that's clamped on her waist, tracing the veins spindling down my busted knuckles. "What would you do to her?" Luna asks, breathy and wanting. "Would you be slow and sweet or...?"

I drink her in. "I'd throw you on the bed for starters."

She staggers, maybe actually drunk on me.

A grin edges across my mouth, and I eye the bed, the floral

comforter. It wipes my smile away. *Buy new bedding.* Adding a shopping spree to my to-do list.

As much as I wanna get hot and heavy with her, I need to be the older, wiser one and lead this away from the promised land of our desires. *For now.* Dropping my arm from Luna, I focus back on my phone. "He's gonna want to meet up...will you be okay if I go?" I ask her. "I can do this another day if—"

"I'll be alright," she interjects. "Will you?"

I nod, but my voice is tight when I say, "Yeah."

Luna frowns, then raises a finger. "Can you hold on one sec before you go?"

I bob my head. "I can, I will."

She's already darting out of my bedroom. Orion bounds after her footsteps into the bathroom, and I have no idea what she's doing.

The past week has been brutal. Our icy streak. Thought I lost her, honestly. Thought maybe it's for the best...for her recovery. I hate thinking I could be hindering her from getting better. Then with the O'Malley shit, getting suspended, scaring her by fighting him—I fully expected Luna to pump the brakes, forget about me, and eventually play the field.

Tonight, she flipped the script, and I'm more hopeful again. Still, I've got some doubts. I'm worried she'll only see me as a good time. A temporary fix.

With so much on my plate, I'm not letting that nag me right now. Gotta see my dad for the first time after we were in the holding cell. Gotta talk to my dad. Gotta trust my dad.

I run my hand through my hair a few times. Yeah. I can do this. Piece of cake, and I love some cheesecake. I can do it.

I have to do it.

Luna returns with a purple Sharpie. "Stay *very* still." She uncaps the marker.

Just like that, the tension unwinds out of my body. I begin to grin. "I'm your wall. Have at me." I spread my arms a bit, and she edges so close, my eyes on hers before she draws on my bare chest.

The marker tip is cold, but only heat encases me as she dips the Sharpie down my sternum to my abs. She draws swirls around my butterfly tattoo on my ribs. "On my planet," she says, causing my pulse to skip, "these are markings of protection. You are *impenetrable*. No one, *no one*, can penetrate you."

I'm so fucking in love with her, it's not even funny anymore. "Worried I'm gonna be penetrated?" I ask her.

"I don't know where you're going or what you might encounter. Earth is a strange place."

"You're telling me," I breathe, and I take the capped Sharpie from her when she's done. "You stay very still now."

Luna smiles, then nods. "I am your tree." She poses, hands upright, and I feel down her body while I lower to a squat. Her breath hitches as I hold her thighs.

"Nice T-shirt," I compliment. "You like AC/DC?" I raise the hem of the tee above her hips, exposing her black panties. The galaxy tattoo on her thigh is without a doubt my best work. Think it every time I see it.

"I don't listen to them a ton," she admits, watching me with parted lips. "I didn't know I had this shirt."

"That's 'cause it's mine," I say and draw her panties down to her knees.

A whimpering noise leaves her lips, and her fingers clutch my hair for support.

"You good?" I ask since I have her completely exposed. *Virgin. Virgin. Virgin.* I'm remembering, alright.

"Uh-huh." She opens her knees for me.

"Why's my tree splitting apart?" I ask her, then uncap the Sharpie with my teeth.

"I'm a horny tree."

My lips upturn, biting on the cap, and I write alongside her hipbone and above her pussy. *Donnelly was here.* I spit out the cap, just to cup her ass and lick and suck her clit. Her moan and quivering legs are engrained in my brain, top-tier spank bank material. 'Cause unfortunately I'm not coming inside Luna tonight.

Lifting her panties back up, I rise and cap the pen. "That's so you never forget where I've been."

She mutters, "Holy shit."

I grin. Yeah, *fuck* O'Malley. Fuck anyone who tries to take her from me.

She's mine.

WHIPLASH. THAT'S WHAT IT FEELS LIKE GOING from a good night with Luna to sitting in a security SUV outside a closed Italian joint in South Philly.

Sun hasn't risen yet. It's so dark, and nobody really stirs except the early birds catchin' the worm. A little old lady sweeps outside a deli.

A recently released felon sits beside me.

Dad. He smokes a cigarette, hand hanging out of the car window. We're both smoking, actually. I picked him up on Broad and drove to a less trafficked area. Parked here.

We haven't said much yet. Small talk. *Eagles are doing good.* Yeah. *Yeah.* He takes another long drag, stares out at the deli, then asks, "You get the cops to drop my charges?"

I blow smoke out the window. "I don't think I have that kind of pull, but if I got out, I suspected you might. I saw you at the Rhino. You had an alibi."

"I was on parole," he says. "I *broke* parole."

I shrug, tapping ash outside. "I dunno what you want me to say. I didn't make that call."

He thinks this over, then nods. "Yeah, alright." After another drag, he asks, "How've you been?"

"Fine."

He inspects my face. "You sleeping?"

You care? "I sleep," is all I say, my chest tight. "How about you?"

"I'm still kicking. Beats being locked up with those fucking idiots." He flicks his cigarette angrily out the window.

"Now watch you get locked up for starting a forest fire."

"What forest?"

We share a small smile. When mine fades, I say, "Are they asking about me? Ollie and the others?"

"They're wondering why you weren't fired. I've been wondering too, honestly. I gotta say, it stinks. Somethin' isn't right." He eyes me skeptically.

My muscles try to seize. I loosen my posture and reach for a packet of cigarettes. Offering my dad another one. He takes it, still scanning me up and down. I tell him, "I didn't know the cops would show."

"You didn't lead them there?" he questions.

"No."

"You didn't turn on our family?"

What family? I shake my head to him. "No."

"Then how the hell are you still workin' for Loren fucking Hale after your cousins kidnapped his daughter and beat up his wife?" His eyes flash hot, fear in them. That I'm duping him, and I am. A wire is hot against my chest. Been wearing one under my shirt the whole time. But I need his help. I can't do this without him.

I snuff my cigarette on the lip of a Fizz can. "They don't think I'm close to you guys."

"They can't be that dumb."

I look over at him, wondering if he can see my fear too. "What I tell you has to stay between you and me, you have to promise."

"What's this about—"

"You've gotta swear, Dad."

His face falls hearing me call him *dad*. Then he says, "What'd I tell you? You can trust me and only me in our family. I won't say shit to anyone."

I nod a few times. *Here it goes.* "I'm dating his daughter—that's why they won't fire me."

Realization sobers his face. "The girl." He thinks this over, eyeing me again and his lip rises in a faraway smile. "How long have you been with her?"

"Not long enough," I mutter.

He stretches an arm out and touches the back of my head, like I'm his kid. Then he pulls away and lights a cigarette. "So you're scared your cousins are gonna pull some stupid shit if they know you're with her?"

My stomach roils. "Something like that, yeah."

"They're locked up. They're not gonna sneeze on her. You don't need to worry about 'em."

"I know how it looks though," I say to him. "I get my job back. I'm dating Luna. Like you said, it *stinks*, and I don't want them thinking I turned on them. What will happen? You tell me."

His face darkens. He sucks harder on the cigarette. He doesn't paint that picture. "Quit your job then. Don't date the girl."

I rotate more to him. "What if you tell 'em I'm using her just to keep my job? That it's not real. Me and her. That I don't even like her, really." It hurts less saying this with the worse alternatives on the table. "You can tell them that."

He considers this with a tip of his head. "Eh, maybe...they might buy it." He pauses. "Only if you prove it down the line."

This is the only way. "You'll help cover for me?" I ask him. "When Ollie and all of them start asking questions...?"

He says nothing at first.

Desperation claws at my back. "I just want them *out* of my life. Out of her life. Nowhere near us or her family."

"What about me?" he asks. "You want me out of your life too?"

I go eerily still. Before all of this, my honest answer woulda been *yeah*. Now, though, I'm questioning what a life would look like with him in it. For real. And it's terrifying that I'd even want it.

My unoiled joints loosen, and I motion to him. "You're the one I'm coming to. No one else. I *only* want to talk to you. You get that?"

He starts nodding. "Yeah, I do." One last drag, he asks, "Loren Hale isn't gonna be pissed you're hanging around me? In your fancy ass car."

"Boss's car," I say, on edge. "Is that a *yes*?"

"Yeah, I'll help you." His lips gradually rise in another smile.

"You're my son." He pats my shoulder. "This is what dads are for."

Wouldn't know. He hasn't been much of one, but he's trying now. What I'm asking isn't small, and this is the second time he's coming through for me when I really need him.

Relief eases my muscles, a sense of safety washing down me like plunging into a lagoon. Coming out clean, anew. And I know I'm going to be okay. I wonder if this is what it feels like to have a father.

43

Luna Hale

"IT'S YOUR INTERPRETATION. It's not a fact, Luna."

That's what my therapist told me after I rehashed my new findings—that I used to love Donnelly. She said, "You're assuming you wrote the human with Donnelly in mind. You could possibly just be seeing exactly what you want to see."

I reread *Human Him, Cosmic Her* five times, and there is some margin of error on my part. It's not like Original Luna ever mentioned Donnelly in the text or in a footnote.

"Why don't you concentrate on your life at the present moment and less about him?" she posed.

Dr. Raven didn't get it. Understanding the past three years isn't *just* about Donnelly. It's about who I am, the person I became and the relationships I've made, and with so many varying perspectives and voices, the only one I can really trust is Original Luna. And I. Can't. Find. Her.

I've gone from being jealous of the OG Luna to being desperate for her. I'm terrified of the next stage of grief I'm headed for. Because this one really sucks.

Next mode of action: a TV marathon. If anything will surface a memory or help piece together the missing years, it's *this*.

Only, I didn't expect half of what I've seen. In the Cobalt brothers' Hell's Kitchen apartment, a lump is lodged in my throat as I stare at the TV. A Twizzler hangs half out of my mouth, and my arms wrap around a tub of popcorn, kernels beneath my butt on the leather couch.

Wreckage of a car crash smolders on-screen, and I picture my older brother, cousins, and Farrow in the carnage. Not that any cameras caught the actual crash—but they captured the aftermath. And that's enough to knot my stomach into a figure-eight.

"Pause it," Tom says to Eliot. They've been hawk-eyeing my reaction since we started this *We Are Calloway* marathon, and now I know why.

They knew what was coming.

Eliot grabs the remote from the coffee table and looks to me in concern. "You okay, Luna?"

"Uh-huh," I mumble through my Twizzler. *How much of everyone's lives did I miss?* The answer has repeatedly been *too much*. My heart lurches with my stomach.

Focusing on the bookshelves beside the TV, I see a terracotta vase with two high-swung handles, possibly Greek pottery. Charlie might've bought it on one of his many excursions. I'm glad we're watching the docuseries in New York and not the Philly penthouse. Less people are here to see my reaction.

Right now, it's just me, Tom, and Eliot in the bachelor pad living room. I'm unsure of Charlie and Beckett's whereabouts, but I heard Beckett has this Monday off from ballet. So it's totally possible they're both holed up in their bedrooms.

Eliot is still staring at me. Tom has stopped winding new string around the guitar on his lap. I'm obviously reacting poorly if they're not restarting the show.

"You don't look fine," Tom says.

Normally, I'd brush it off with a shrug, not say much in reply. Being closed down and reserved has its drawbacks—I'm experiencing a life where I shut *so* many people out for so many years, where I didn't fully express myself, and at times, it's been maddening. Other moments, it's been excruciating—because it would've been so much easier if they *knew*.

If they knew how I felt about the things that mattered to me.

About my future. About friends. About who or what I really loved. About my fucking *fish*.

I will never, ever take the bonds I have with people for granted. I make that vow to myself. Because when the floor drops beneath my feet, they are the *only* ones there to catch me, and they need to know who they're catching.

So I bite the end of my Twizzler off and gently set the popcorn on the table. "I kinda feel guilty," I tell my best friends. "I'm eating popcorn and candy like this is some fun watch-party, but I *know* this docuseries gets deep. And I feel like such an idiot." I start sinking on the cushions, and I grab the nearest pillow to stuff my face into it. Disappear!

It doesn't count as hiding if I spilled my guts before I hid.

I peek out of the pillow.

Eliot flips the remote in his hand, a smile in his eyes. "You're not being insensitive. Of the three of us, I'm the one who wears that crown. I'd bring popcorn and candy to a funeral if I could."

"He would," Tom says, twisting the guitar string.

I wear a tender smile and unbury myself from the pillow, but my lips fall again seeing the car wreckage paused on-screen. "Paparazzi chased Ben."

Eliot says, "I think the paps were more interested in your brother than ours."

"Is Ben okay though?" *He was driving.*

Tom seesaws his hand. "He doesn't drive anymore. We keep telling him to come to New York and he doesn't do that either."

"He will one day," Eliot says more optimistically.

"Maybe if we blackmail him."

"Now there's an idea," Eliot quips.

"I was joking." Tom strums the guitar and grimaces at the high-pitched noise. "Fuck."

"And I'm staying out of any blackmail shenanigans," I say, sipping a canned vodka cocktail. They said it was Charlie's beverage and I could take it at my own risk. So I took it.

The footage is still on-screen.

"What about everyone else?" I ask them. "Are they okay after the crash?"

Tom reminds me, "You told us not to give you spoilers."

"Yeah, but I meant spoilers for romantic crushes and baby news and stuff like that. Spoilers don't extend to bodily or mental harm—" My voice tapers off as Charlie struts out of his bedroom and into the open living area, kitchen in view.

His attention beelines straight to the TV screen. A leather duffel slung over one shoulder and passport in hand, he looks ready to depart for a getaway trip. By his simple attire—white-button down and khaki slacks—I couldn't guess the climate of the destination, let alone the continent.

"Really?" Charlie swivels to shoot his brothers a look. "You're letting her watch this shit?"

"This is Emmy Award-Winning high-brow shit," Eliot rebuts.

Tom looks up from his guitar and adds to Charlie, "Shit that *your* bodyguard's husband produces."

Charlie has a blank face.

"I asked to watch it," I pipe in.

"And we complied," Eliot says, spreading out his arms dramatically.

Charlie stares hard at the footage, then says, "If you're trying to help jog her memories, this is the wrong episode." Oh, he's not referring to the show as *shit*, just this particular segment. He turns to me, then hikes his duffel strap higher on his shoulder. "You weren't in that crash."

But he was.

I already know Charlie, Maximoff, Farrow, Winona, and Ben were in the car, but I haven't learned whether anyone sustained any injuries. By the totaled state of the vehicle, I'd think there'd be carnage. Death. At least I know everyone made it out alive.

Maybe they wouldn't want me to figure out their lives through the docuseries. Is it cheating?

"Uh…" My cheeks burn as Charlie keeps staring at me. This can't be about me drinking his canned cocktail.

Off my silence, he says, "You should start writing again. It might help."

Tom grins. "You hear that Luna, Charlie misses reading your smut."

Eliot mutters something about missing my stories too.

Charlie doesn't even give Tom the satisfaction of looking his way. Instead, he says to me, "Think about it. I'll edit them again."

I've wanted to reactivate my account on Fictitious, or create a new one. Do what Original Luna was too afraid to do. But after my deep-dive reading most of what I've written, the greatest doubt monster has emerged to swallow me whole.

I could just nod to Charlie. Say nothing more. Except that's not the new path I want to head down, so with a big breath, I tell him, "I'm not sure I'm as good of a writer as her." He knows I'm referring to Original Luna.

He barely blinks. "Who cares?"

"My followers on Fictitious?" I say it like a question. "They'd care if the writing quality changed."

"Are you writing for them or for you?"

He has a point. Writing fulfills me first, and I shouldn't worry about reactions. "Okay," I say, a newfound urge to continue my saga bubbles up. "I'll write again."

"You can drop off any new chapters here at the apartment. You never trusted sending them by email."

"Thanks," I say, excited about building a closer relationship with Charlie too. I think OG Luna went halfway there, and maybe I could be better friends with him beyond just working on my fics.

Charlie is about to go.

"Off to Amsterdam again, brother?" Eliot asks casually. "Getting your dick sucked in the red-light district?"

Charlie tilts his head at him. "Since when have I ever had to pay for sex?"

Tom starts clapping. Eliot joins in.

Charlie looks pointedly at me. "Your friends."

"Your brothers," I say.

"One is a choice."

"I'd choose *me*," Eliot chimes in.

"As would I," Tom raises his hand.

I steal the remote from Eliot. "Maybe we should switch to a different season. Can we watch Moffy get married?" I'm eager to see my brother and Farrow walk down the aisle. Or...did only one walk down the aisle? Was the other standing at the end?

I frown at the thought. Didn't Farrow say I was in his procession? *I was there. I should know how it went down.*

Tom must see my dejection because he claims the remote now. "Better yet," he says. "Let's watch Beckett's interview on YouTube."

Oooh. My brows jump. "Beckett was interviewed? Wait, when did he join *We Are Calloway*?"

"He didn't," Charlie says flatly.

Tom clicks into YouTube. "Yeah, dude is still anti-being filmed. But the ballet company kind of forced him into this promotional interview."

"It's a rare golden gem," Eliot says into a grin.

Charlie wavers from leaving, as if interested in watching this too.

"Is this a popcorn moment?" I wonder.

"Most absolutely." Eliot kicks his feet up on the coffee table.

As *the* Beckett Cobalt graces the TV screen for the first time, I grab my popcorn tub. He's considered the bad boy of ballet, thanks to the tattoos along his arm and being spotted outside NYC clubs. The video begins at a studio during rehearsal. Beckett is off to the side with the rest of the dancers, watching another guy perform a solo.

Leo Valavanis—he's Beckett's longtime rival. I've known about him for a while, but this footage must be from the years I'm missing. His dirty blond hair is slightly out of his face with a bandana. He's similarly lean built like Beckett—every muscle defined.

As the music builds, Leo does the routine flawlessly and with charisma.

"Wait for it," Tom says.

The video zooms in on *Beckett* while Leo is performing.

Beckett has piercing yellow-green eyes like his mom, and typically, they're not lethal—but he clearly seems annoyed.

"There's his pissy face," Tom says in a laugh.

Eliot is far too amused as well. It is a sight to behold, and I'd be a big liar if I said I wasn't smiling.

Once Leo finishes, the chorographer makes Beckett take his place and perform the same solo.

My smile softens. Seeing him in his element is enchanting. His leaps are weightless, and every movement is grand yet smooth, as if he's silk gliding over water.

I've seen him perform before, and it always makes me smile with pride. *That's my cousin.*

And then they do a close-up of Leo while Beckett dances. His jaw muscles tic, arms threaded over his chest.

"You better be envious," Eliot says to TV Leo.

But it's truly hard to say which one is better than the other. I'm not a ballet expert, and perhaps the two of them also know they're serious competition.

Soon, Beckett falls back and the segment cuts to an actual *interview.* Beckett and Leo are standing side by side while the rest of the dancers rehearse behind them.

Eliot wasn't kidding about this being rare. I shovel popcorn in my mouth.

From off-screen behind the camera, the interviewer says, "Well, that certainly was a show you both put on." Her voice is light and airy. "Do either of you watch each other's performances on stage?"

"No," they both say at the same time. They exchange a brief, caustic glare.

I snort.

"Who would you say has the better technique?" she asks.

Leo lets out a laugh like it's a dumb question and the answer is obvious.

Eliot throws a scoop of my popcorn at the TV. I do the same.

"That would be me," Leo answers. "But he's going to say himself."

He waves Beckett on. "Go ahead, Cobalt. Give the people what they want."

"Give it to 'em, brother," Eliot says to the screen.

On the television Beckett says, "His technique is adequate."

"His technique is stale. Lifeless," Leo retorts. "People sleep at his shows. People stay awake for mine."

Ouch. I glare at his annoying, yet very striking, two-dimensional face.

"How would you know?" Beckett turns on him. "You never attend mine."

"Burn," Tom says to the television.

The interview zooms in on Leo's tensed jaw as he responds, "People talk."

Beckett makes his classic *what the fuck* face, which has me smiling again. Some things really don't change. That expression is exactly as I remember.

Leo stares Beckett down.

Beckett doesn't blink.

It's the tensest staring contest I've seen in a long while. A popcorn kernel stays motionless on my tongue like if I make a crunch, I'll break the moment.

"Viewers want to know if you're both currently seeing anyone?" the interviewer asks.

"She didn't," I whisper in shock.

"She did." Charlie is the one who speaks. His hip is leaning up against the couch as he watches the interview with us.

That personal question breaks Beckett and Leo's staring contest. Their heads swing to face the camera.

"No," Beckett says, even-tempered.

Leo forces a smile. It kinda looks fake. "Recently divorced."

I almost choke on my popcorn. "*What?* He was married?!" Did I know this in the time I lost? Probably not, considering this is likely filmed sometime in the past three years.

"Shhh," Eliot shushes me. Thankfully so. I don't want to miss any of this.

Beckett isn't shocked by that bomb drop. Maybe it's not even a bomb. It's like a sad little firecracker of information that seems so much bigger to me. Then again, these days most information seems pretty giant-sized from my point of view.

"Oh, I'm sorry to hear that," the interviewer says. "Is he still around?"

"She," Leo corrects, his glare returning. This time he's directing it to the interviewer. "And no."

"Is that question necessary?" Beckett asks the interviewer, his voice carrying an undertone of bite. "It doesn't pertain to ballet."

"It was a follow-up question," she says in defense. The camera zooms in on Leo. "What do you think of the recent text message leaks?"

Leaks?

"What leaks?" I ask Eliot and Tom.

Tom pauses the interview just to say, "Beckett hooked up with a girl and she leaked some of their texts."

I wince.

"Yeah, it was brutal," Tom says off my expression. While he rewinds a couple seconds of the video, my phone pings.

I check the text.

Getting out of my psych eval. All is good. Won't know results till later, I don't think. — Donnelly

Before I ask, he sends another message.

Think I aced it 🤘 — Donnelly

He's been so confident, but I was worried his bad sleep and nightmares would be a reason he wouldn't pass. I smile and send him a Snape and Dumbledore dance party gif, not overthinking it.

"You ready?" Tom asks me.

"Yeah, press play." I slip my phone back in my pocket as the video restarts.

The interviewer says again, "What do you think of the recent text message leaks?"

"I don't know what you're talking about," Leo snaps, hostile.

"Beckett's texts," she clarifies.

Donnelly suddenly enters the camera frame, and my whole heart jumps to my throat. Oh. My. God. He's on TV! It's so unexpected seeing him on-screen from a time *before*, and my jaw drops like my favorite movie star just entered the building.

"Stop filming," Donnelly sneers. "Or I'll call—"

The interview cuts off.

"Who was he going to call?!" I yell at the TV like my favorite show ended on the worst possible cliffhanger.

"Ghostbusters," Tom and Eliot say in unison, then share a grin.

Charlie narrows his eyes at them like they're the furthest thing from cute.

"Rewind it," I tell them. "Can you rewind back like fifteen seconds? Maybe we can figure it out."

"He threatened to call legal," Charlie deadpans. "It's obvious."

"Don't rain on our parade, Charlie." Eliot stands off the couch. "We're having fun playing guess what Donnelly said."

"Guess what Donnelly said when?" Beckett emerges with bedhead hair and sleepless circles under his eyes. Black pajama pants hang low on his waist, and he runs a hand through his thick, tousled hair. His gaze stops short on the television, and his face twists when he sees his interview frozen on-screen. "What's the point of this?"

"What's the point of living?" Eliot refutes. "To be entertained, brother."

Beckett turns to him. "Find someone else to entertain you."

"But you're so bad at it," Eliot says, picking popcorn kernels off the floor. "I have to relish in this one moment—"

"Showing Luna my interview doesn't do anything," Beckett interjects hotly. "She wasn't friends with him back then."

Him.

He's referring to Donnelly.

And if anyone knows anything about Donnelly, it's Beckett. I'd never really been close to Beckett, but did that ever change?

"How do you know I wasn't friends with him back then?" I ask Beckett.

"Because he was *my* friend," Beckett says plainly but territorially. As if there wasn't enough room for Donnelly to be friends with him *and* me at the same time.

Beckett looks away like he can't meet my eyes.

Hurt lances my throat. Unearthed tension from an unknown origin winds around the room, and then Beckett leaves for the kitchen. Which isn't out of eyeshot from the living room, so I have a superb view of Beckett's back as he opens the fridge.

Charlie looks between Tom and Eliot, then shakes his head. He walks to the front door, duffel over his shoulder, without another word.

Every new piece of information feels destructive, and I'm starting to wonder if it's safer to not go digging at all. Then again, I'm done playing it safe.

I help Eliot clean the floor, and then I say, "Let's restart the *We Are Calloway* marathon."

DONNELLY'S DAILY PLANNER

Saturday, Dec 15th

<u>Today's Focus:</u> Bass fun. Protecting the Elf comes first tho. Also, protect her. (Are you her Number Three Protector?) Make sure no nerdy types hit on my space babe with their magic swords and whatnot. It's Fanaticon Convention Day, bitch.

<u>To Do:</u>

- Ice-cold shower in the hotel room. Freezing my balls off these days. (Still trying to wait before we do the deed)

- Registration. Stay alert. Lots of ppl at these things.

- Panels? vendor halls? whatever the Hales wanna do.

- Look out for Quinnie & Frog if they need a hand.

- Late-night convention parties? Up to X & his sister.

- Wait up for the boss man's call. (He said he and Price came up with an agreement, deal, something. Just know it involves me.)

Notes: Flight to San Fran was long but got a good audiobook in ("Neuromancer" by William Gibson—Luna's rec). Quinn + Frog bickered most of the way there. Learned she's still hanging out with Scooter. WTF.

Good thing: passed my pysch eval. Knew I would. Didn't take Farrow's advice but a guy's gotta do what he has to do. Heard all of SFO passed it but Thatcher. Happy for Froggy.

Sad thing: Xander was jittery the whole flight. Not flying jitters. My Elf is nervous about being *seen* at a big con and not having his wingman Easton around. Pumped him up a bit. Xander's dad & Lily are counting on me to keep their baby birds safe. Won't let 'em down.

Also! Luna looked like she wanted me to fuck her on the plane. No cap. Then she suggested we join the mile high club. (Been there. Wish I could be there *with her*.) I'm putting on a masterclass in restraint, if I do say so. Bc no, we did not fuck.

Meals: Hotel food ftw.

Water: H2O is for hoes. And I'm the biggest hoe here.

Question of the Day: ~~Is Luna's sex drive higher? (not complaining~~ tho) why does the cobalts' private jet smell like potato chips?

44

Paul Donnelly

"THIS WAS SUCH a fucking *bad* idea," Xander says anxiously in his hotel room. He's half-dressed, sitting on the bed in acid-washed jeans and fighting with a long-sleeved *Beneath a Strong Sentiment* shirt I bought him. "Moffy couldn't come because he could have a baby any second now. Easton is grounded for doing nothing. And Kinney is mad I'm here and she's not."

I'm leaning on the dresser, letting him vent. "No one has noticed you yet. Got through the hotel unseen."

"Barely." He yanks the shirt on, then shows me his phone.

I come closer and see a very blurry pic of Xander waiting for an elevator in the hotel lobby. He has on a hoodie and a baseball cap. Someone posted it to the WAC forum on Fanaticon.

"Doesn't look like you," I tell him. "You look like this guy I knew who held up the Quickie-Mart."

Xander *almost* smiles. Damn, almost got him. "Whoever's on Fanaticon will know I'm here, Donnelly—and this is a *Fanaticon* Convention."

"You go on Fanaticon forums a lot?"

He shrugs. "More when I decided I'd go to the Con."

Yeah, about that… "You don't even like Bass," I mention.

"Luna doesn't know that anymore," he says quietly and pulls socks on his feet, fighting with those too.

"You came here for her?" I'm guessing.

Xander ditches the socks and just shoves his feet in sneakers. "Not just for her." He's having trouble meeting my gaze.

I go still. "What do you mean?"

He runs his fingers through his shaggy haircut that has all the teenagers swooning. Letting out a couple anxious breaths, he says, "I'm here for you too. Okay, look, you're *attached* to me. Where I go, you go, and if I'm stuck anywhere where Luna isn't—then you can't spend time with her."

I ruminate over this for a quick sec. "That's sweet and all, man, but you shouldn't be changing your life for me—"

"She *wanted* to be with you, and I was a complete dick about it. Now that she can't remember you, who knows what'll happen in the long run, in the endgame. She could end up with another bodyguard like"—*don't say his name*—"O'Malley." He said it.

"Would she get with him though?" I ask, only partially considering 'cause if I fully consider I might put a hole in the wall.

"Maybe." He's wide-eyed panicked at the idea, and I gotta say, I like this reality where Xander is now Team Donnelly and no longer hoping O'Malley is her OTP (one true pairing).

Xander's been a Nervous Nancy about crowd control at the Con, and he's only here to ensure I get some quality time with his sister. "You can back out of this, no worry," I tell him. "Just hang in the hotel room."

"Where will you be?"

"Outside your door or chilling in here with you."

"No." He shakes his head profusely. "*No.*"

"Xander—"

"Look, I'm doing this, and just so you know…" He stares around the room, his breath heavy like he's running even though he's standing in place. "I plan to hang around my sister a ton more, so you better get used to this."

Is this good for him or bad for him? I can't tell.

"Your decision," I say, just as comms sound in my ear. I miss Quinn's update for me, and I click my mic. "What was that?"

"Your girlfriend is ready," Quinn repeats.

I reach for my mic on my collar, about to correct him. *Not my girlfriend.* We're in the "no labels" zone. A zone I had already punt-kicked with Luna before her amnesia. Woulda been her boyfriend easily by now, but things are different. I'm in a hazy relationship land that Farrow would never step foot in, and despite me setting some boundaries, it's still murky.

I don't get the chance to respond to Quinn.

"Incoming," Frog says on comms, just as a knock sounds on the door.

"It's Luna!" Luna calls to her brother.

"Come in," Xander says, slipping me a very gentle look not to tell her shit about our conversation. He wants her to believe he's a *Beneath a Strong Sentiment* stan so she's unaware of his true intentions here. It's a bit devious for a Hufflepuff like him, but I have to roll with it.

"Heidi ho," Luna greets, springing forth in a bright orange wig that I've seen her wear when she cosplayed as Leeloo from the *Fifth Element*. With a baggie sweatshirt and glitter under her eyes, she looks cute—*beautiful*, really—and disguised enough. Being in her vicinity, my heart double-thumps, if that's a thing hearts can do.

Frog and Quinn enter the room but stay near the door. At least O'Malley is way back in Philly or New York. For once, I'm loving the West Coast.

Luna displays a blue chromed mask to Xander. "Tah-dah." She wiggles it. "For you."

He takes it. "A Riven mask?" He must've binged Bass before the Con if he recognizes the mask from the show.

"Everyone's wearing them," Luna says.

"Probably because they're dope as fuck," I chime in.

"And people always like the villains more," Luna adds.

"True that." Rivens, the chromed-mask wearers from Bass, are the antagonists. I nod to Xander. "Now you'll blend."

He releases more of his anxiety. And he puts on the mask. "What do you think?"

"Never seen him before," I tell Luna.

"Nope. He's not one of us," she says.

"Great. Let's go before I change my mind," Xander says.

Luna and I share a grin, and I make a *rock on* gesture to my bodyguard comrades. Let's do the thing.

THE VENDOR HALL. A CONGESTED HELLSCAPE I

wasn't sure Xander would ever brave. His costume is coming through, though. No one has spotted him, and I'm barely blinking while I survey the crowds around the merch booths. This isn't the sort of place I can really talk with Luna.

Making sure they're safe is all that's on the brain right now.

Xander is more interested in the hand-carved dice than any of the Bass paraphernalia, but he tears himself away and trails close to his sister.

I maneuver around him as they stop and browse. Frog and Quinn are doing the same and pretending to be Luna's besties on either side of her. We scan for potential threats. We watch our clients. No one seems to recognize us, as far as I can tell. More so, I'm worried they'll spot Quinn first. The Young Stud Casanova of SFO is a fan favorite on WAC forums.

An announcer comes on over the loudspeaker. "Reece Decker will now be signing in Hall B. Again, Reece Decker will now be signing in Hall B."

Ah, damn. That's on the other side of the conference center. Reece is the actor who plays Strider on the show. He's a main stop for Luna and her Strider fangirl heart.

Can't fault her for it. We can be on opposite teams this time.

Luna inspects a T-shirt with "The Peak" insignia and an illustration of a snowcapped mountain. *That's cute.* I can see her contemplating buying it. I lean close, just a breath away, but I'm watching Xander's back. "Lemme get that for you," I whisper.

Flush ascends her cheeks. "I got it," she whispers just as quietly back, then pays the vendor for the tee.

It hurts, not gonna lie. Feels like I took ten steps back on the Game of Life board. But I need to remind myself that I had conversations about *money* with Luna before her amnesia. Not after. It took a while for Luna to be okay with me purchasing things for her back then too.

Xander saw me get shot down, by the way.

Nothing like having your teenage client see you on your worst flirt game.

"Did they say Hall H?" a white girl with pink braids asks her brunette friend, both huddling around us.

"I don't know," her friend replies.

"This is not good," Pink Braids says anxiously, and quickly taps Quinn's shoulder, "Excuse me. Did you hear if they said Hall H?"

"Fuck," Quinn mutters. "Hall what?" He's asking Frog.

"L?" Frog whispers.

"There's no Hall L," Quinn says.

"What? Yes, there is," Frog argues.

"Oh God," Pink Braids mutters.

Xander spins around. "It was Hall B," he says casually.

"OhmyGosh Thank you!!" Pink Braids takes her friend's hand, and the girls race towards the exit for the vendor hall.

I can almost see Xander watching her—can't see his expression behind the mask—but he's faced in her direction for a long beat. Then he turns his head to Luna, and it must trigger something because he focuses on Frostie ship buttons.

"You wanna go?" I ask him, motioning to the door where Pink Braids just left.

He shrugs a shoulder. "We'll head there eventually."

Luna has been perceptive of the whole thing too. She's a watchful one. As they push away from the table and lines, Luna speaks quietly to her brother. "I've been meaning to ask; I saw this thing online about you and a girl from school."

"Delilah?" he asks.

"Yeah—"

"It's fake. A rumor. She made it up after Homecoming." He lowers his voice again. "We did *not* have sex. I would not have sex with her for so many reasons, one being she just wanted to fuck Donnelly."

Yeah, fuck me, this is not gonna help my case. Need to scout the area as people nearly bump into their shoulders, and Quinn and I take most of the impacts so our clients aren't touched. Looking at the Hales is a harder task.

"Did they…have sex?" Luna asks, drawing it out.

"No, he shot her down like every opportunity," Xander says, hushed. *Thank you for that truth bomb.* "It's gross that she was even trying to get with him. She's not eighteen, and I only heard that she wanted to sleep with Donnelly from other people at school. Winona and Vada think she was embarrassed that everyone was saying she was *desperate* for a bodyguard, so she thought she'd gain cred or whatever by sleeping with me. Which, again, *never* happened. But now it's online."

"It's buried deep," Luna says. "It took me a while to find it."

Xander eases some. "That's good."

An announcer comes on the loudspeaker and repeats Reece Decker's location. More fans are listening, and a surge of girls rushes in our direction to reach the exit.

"Jesus fuck," Xander bumps up into my shoulder to avoid being plowed down. I'm doing my best to shield him without appearing like security. Sliding to the left, I take an impact to the hip so no one shoves him. He's starting to hold onto my shirt like he's nervous he might get ripped away from me.

I clamp a hand on his shoulder and edge us closer to a Bass vendor table. "We're big Frostie fans," I tell the guy behind the table.

He beams. "We have embroidered sweaters."

"Love to see 'em," I say, keeping a hand on Xander's shoulder. Luna squeezes beside her brother, and Quinn and Frog stand behind her, creating a barrier around the Hales that alleviates Xander's panic for a second.

"Hey, are you…" the vendor squints at Luna, trying to place her.

"Leeloo," she says.

He snaps his fingers. "Luna Hale."

Shit.

Xander goes rigid.

I survey the people who may've heard. A girl to my left is slyly snapping a pic of Luna...and Quinn. *Alright.*

"Uh, maybe," Luna says absentmindedly. "How much for the sweater?"

"Forty."

"Hey, Luna Hale?" another girl tries to catch her attention. "Can I have a selfie?"

Luna side-eyes Xander, seeing how he's faring.

He's sweating profusely. I hang my arm casually over his shoulders. "You're alright, man," I tell him calmly while his sister takes a selfie with a fan.

"I'm so sorry about what happened to you and your mom," the girl says shyly.

It twists my stomach, but thankfully she's not drawing too much attention. Luna responds quietly to her, then they hug.

More people are eyeballing Luna. *She's okay.* I repeat that over and over. *She's okay.*

Quinn has pushed closer to her. I group him in with the rookies, but times like these, I can tell he's not one. He's been a bodyguard for over three years.

Under his breath, Xander says, "All the backup security is in Philly with my brother, right?" *Because of the baby.*

"Yeah, but we don't need backup," I say easily. "Don't think of the worst. That's my job."

If just a couple people recognize Xander, it would create hysteria. They're not gonna be sheepishly asking for selfies like they are with Luna.

They'll be crying and clawing at his clothes.

Still, I'm more worried about Luna since her threat level is ten times higher. But paparazzi aren't allowed in the hotel, and they'd be the ones to harass her the most. Not fans.

Luna puts some distance between her and Xander to draw the spotlight away, and he stays at this vendor booth with me. As I pretend to be Xander's BFF, I check out a lime-green sweater that says FROSTIE in embroidered neon pink. It's sick.

"Cool shirt," the vendor tells Xander.

"Oh…thanks." Xander glances down at the long-sleeved Bass tee. It says: *Control. Your. Emotion. Control. Your. Evolution.*

"I'll take this," I tell the vendor. "Actually, I'll take two." Gotta match with my space babe. Not wasting time overthinking this shit, I just do it.

While the vendor rings me up, Xander observes the congested throng of Strider fans at the double doors. "Weird…" he mutters.

"How so?" I follow his eyes, checking for anything suspicious in the masses.

"Weird being on this side of things." He breathes out some tension in his voice.

I get it now. He's used to being the Reece Decker. The object of everyone's obsession. He's rarely the one standing in the crowd.

After I purchase the sweaters, we walk a couple steps to the water fountain and wait for Luna to check-out at another table. Still in the vendor hall, but it's clearing out as everyone leaves to see the actor.

"You haven't talked to her that much since we've been here," Xander tells me.

I pull a sweater from the bag. "'Cause I'm working first and foremost."

He wafts his sweaty shirt. "I want this to be worth it for you two."

"It's worth it already." I drop the bag to my feet, then shed my shirt and pull the new Frostie sweater over my head. "I get to see her geek out over Strider—"

"You hate Strider."

"Hate is a strong word, Elf. My allegiances just lie elsewhere." I toss my old T-shirt in the bag. "I'd take seeing her geek out over anything. Seeing her at all tops the charts."

Xander bobs his head like he gets it. "Yeah, fine, okay. But you're so concerned about me that you're not paying attention to her. That sucks, man."

"It's my job," I remind him again. "I like this job. Love it, actually. And just so you know, you don't have to play matchmaker. Luna and I are already together. We're matched. It's done." Breath is knotted in my throat as I say it.

"But like…how serious is it?" Xander questions. "Because she's known you for three weeks, and I've overheard bodyguards saying you'll last like two months tops."

I try not to grimace. "Who?"

"Epsilon guys."

Shoulda known. "Have you asked Luna what she thought of me?"

"It changes all the time," Xander says. "Some days, obsessed. Some days, confused. One day, afraid."

Her birthday. I blow out a long breath. "Yeah, alright." But even with some odds against me, I pump myself up. "You don't have to worry so much, man. I'm a wooer. I woo. I've got this covered." I shake the plastic bag.

Luna departs from the vendor table. She must've bought a sweat-shirt because she's pulling it over her head as she approaches us.

My muscles flex in tensed bands. It's a STRIDER STAN embroidered sweatshirt.

Fuck.

My grip tightens on the bag, trying not to feel like a dummy. She wouldn't like a Frostie sweater. She doesn't even like Callie that much anymore. Why'd I forget that?

"Where to next?" Luna asks us, Frog and Quinn dutifully flanked on either side of her.

Xander is eyeing me, waiting for me to gift the sweater to his sister. He knows I bought it for her. Who else would I have given it to? Farrow? Oscar? Yeah, right.

"Better make our way to Hall B," I tell Luna. "It's a long walk."

She pops the map up on her phone. "Oh shit," she mutters, her brows bunching as she realizes the location. "We need to go now to make it." She skips out first, Frog leading and Quinn in the rear.

Xander lingers behind. Just to ask me, "You sure you don't need my help?"

Do I need the help of a seventeen-year-old to get his sister to fall in love with me (again)?

Yesterday, I would've said, absolutely not. Hell no. I've got this covered.

Today, I'm saying, "TBD. You're on standby."

He nods. "Just give me the signal."

45

Luna Hale

THE ENDLESS LINE to meet the actor who plays Strider curves out Hall B and into the conference center's atrium. We are in the atrium. At the back of the pack. But we didn't come to the Con with a decisive strategy. We planned to just wing it. I check the Con's schedule.

All the meet-and-greets are overlapping, and if we wait here, there's no way we'll have enough time to see Willa Holmes, the actress for Callie.

I have to choose.

Strider or Callie.

"What's up?" Xander asks me, wafting his shirt. He has sweat stains under his armpits. "Are we bailing on this guy?" He points to the long line.

"Do you wanna see him?" I ask.

"Uhh, we could?" The chrome blue mask shields his expression. I restrain from asking if *he's* okay. He's already told me *yeah* a handful of times.

When I first saw him at the hospital, I couldn't get over how physically older he appeared. But he's grown so much more than I realized. To have the kinda courage to leave the house and be at a Fan Convention with only me—the Xander I knew would've never done it.

"It's up to you, really, Luna," Xander says. "I like them all. I'm not on a specific team."

I've been getting a tingly sense Xander doesn't care about the show. I've witnessed many of his passionate nerd rants regarding *Lord of the Rings* and *Warhammer*, and vague one-sentence responses are *not* it.

"No favorites?" I ask.

"Frost is cool." He shrugs, his head still turning every which way. You'd think he was the bodyguard, but I can tell he's anticipating the rug being pulled out from under us. The chaos setting in.

I check my watch, the one that Donnelly technically gave Original Luna. I still like wearing it, but partly, it makes me miss her.

"This line is not moving," Quinn says under his breath, but close enough that I can hear. He's not so familiar to me. But I've been told Quinn Oliveira, age twenty-three, was once my bodyguard after J.P. was fired.

"Patience, *patience*," Frog says, as though channeling supreme patience.

I've *finally* met my bodyguard. Kannika Kitsuwon. She's Thai like Akara, and the only bodyguard not born and raised in Philly. She's originally from Buffalo. And I still can't believe she's younger than me. No wonder all of SFO were protecting her return to my detail. Apparently, she'd been there the night of the kidnapping. I'm shocked she didn't quit this job afterward.

She came back. I can't say why. We haven't talked too much yet, and she seems as tentative with me as I am with her.

The line inches forward, then abruptly stops.

I want my sweatshirt signed by Strider, but I was hoping to get a poster signed by Callie for Original Luna. For when I get my memories back.

What if I never do? I swallow a pit in my throat. Desperation has been gradually morphing into fragmented bits of anguish. Afraid that I never will find her.

That fear smacked me in the face at my last appointment with my neuro-doctors.

Since it's been three weeks that I've had retrograde amnesia with no progress, they told me there's a possibility it might be permanent. Or if I do get my memories back, they might not all come bursting forth in chronological order like you see in the movies. It might be more like little "islands of memory" popping up in the empty space. So far...no islands. Not even a small, tiny plot of land in the empty sea of my brain. I should be happy I don't have any other long-term side effects from my brain injury like vertigo, vision loss, insomnia (the list seems endless)—that's what my therapist harps on about— but it's hard to stay on the positive side of things after my doctors' appointments.

"You alright?" Donnelly whispers, a step ahead of me and Xander. He twists around to me.

I nod a few times, quickly, then I remember to be more forthcoming this time around. And I shake my head. "No." He meets my eyes briefly before having to scan passersby. Then I add, "I have to choose between Strider and Callie."

"Strider," he says. "The line will move faster. People are gonna drop out."

"Or we could skip the line," Frog suggests behind me.

My brows rise. Is she...rebellious? "I like this idea," I say.

"No," Quinn says, giving Frog a look.

"What?" she says like he's the weird one. "She's *famous*. We can say she needs to cut for safety reasons."

Donnelly chimes in, "Nah, that'll draw too much attention. Arguments will be had. They'll be asking who's so special. They might start shouting Luna's name. So...hard pass."

I hear Xander expel a relieved breath.

"Callie," I say, feeling this deep in my bones. "Let's leave and go see the actress who plays her."

"You sure?" Donnelly asks me.

He's a Callie stan, and I'm clinging onto the hope that one day I'll remember how I was too. This hope feels more like sand slipping between my fingers. "Yeah, I'm sure," I nod resolutely.

Because if I stay here, it feels like admitting Original Luna is gone for good. And she's not. *She's not.*

She can't be.

THE LINE FOR ACTRESS WILLA HOLMES IS MUCH,

much shorter, and I almost feel guilty for not supporting Callie sooner. She needs it more.

We'll likely reach the front in fifteen minutes tops.

While we wait, I'm doing my best to not be recognized for Xander's sake. I have my face buried in my phone, reading another writer's sci-fi romance short story on Fictitious.

My cell pings with a new text.

Hey, Luna. Miss you. You free soon? Want to meet up again? 💦 — Unknown

My pulse spikes, and I flush with anxious heat. Who is this? I scroll up in the text thread, but there aren't any preexisting messages. Did I delete them? Or is this person just texting for the first time and messing with me?

No one knows I've lost my memories. Just my family, security, and doctors. So it can't be an elaborate prank.

The wet emoji means sex. This person is likely a *he*, and he wants to hook up? Maybe he's from OG Luna's casual sex days.

I look up and see the back of Donnelly.

Why am I so drawn to him? Out of. Every. Single. Person.

Him.

Too many emotions rush into me at once, and I end up sending a quick reply: *Sry. I'm busy.*

With that, I shove my phone in my pocket and step forward. I tap Donnelly's shoulder, my heart flip-flopping.

Donnelly turns a fraction, and his blue eyes meet mine so suddenly that I'm hypnotized by their depths.

"Um," I swallow a lump. "What would she say to Callie?"

He skims me. "You'd say, 'I'm your biggest fan and those that hate your character just don't know how to love flawed things.'" He says it without hesitation and with so much admiration. I'm blown back for a second. My lips part.

He loves her.

Like *really* loves Original Luna.

I want to believe that he could also love this version of me too. He must see me processing deeper because he takes a step closer to me. "Luna—"

"Sir, you're up next," a line coordinator tells him.

"You can go up with Luna," Xander says beside him. "I'll wait with her bodyguards."

Donnelly motions to Frog and Quinn, and silently they all shift methodically around us until Donnelly takes my hand. He pulls me to Callie's table.

My heart thumps hard in my chest. The most photogenic human I've ever seen is beaming while she sits at the signing table in front of me. All thoughts zoom out of my brain.

"Hi," Willa Holmes greets with a bright smile, her lips a Marylin Monroe red. She points up at Donnelly. "You look a little familiar. Where have I seen you before?" She reaches for his travel mug he wants signed.

"Maybe TikTok," Donnelly grins more at me.

"He has a huge following," I say, which is very true. His shirtless videos have millions of views and thousands of comments. I spent one night underneath my covers scrolling through all of them. I'm betting his DMs look a lot like those comment sections—with girls asking him to fuck them.

Jealousy prickled and insecurities rose. Because it's not like I've had sex with him either—or at least I can't remember having sex with him. *Maybe he'll never want to unless I have my memories.*

It's not the first time I've thought it.

It won't be the last.

"Might be," Willa says to us.

I pass her my Bass poster, and I open my mouth to repeat what Donnelly told me. But he speaks first.

"She's not the biggest Callie fan yet, but we still love your work." Donnelly hooks a comforting arm around my shoulder, and I'm thunderstruck that he told her my opinion on the show over OG Luna's.

It's a small reminder that he's not upset I'm not her. He's okay with who I am today.

I try to hang on to that thought, even if my positivity feels a lot like dandelion seeds. One strong gust of wind towards a dandelion, and *poof* all the seeds get swept away and disappear.

I smile at Willa and tell her truthfully, "You're in some of my favorite scenes."

"I appreciate that, and thank you *so much* for watching the show. You've helped keep it alive." She signs the rest of our merch and even snaps pics with us. Even a goofy selfie where the three of us stick out our tongues.

All in all, it's a happy experience that leaves me and Donnelly grinning. His arm stays around my shoulders until we're reunited with Xander, Frog, and Quinn on the escalator.

Going up.

"She was cool," Xander tells me. "Humble. Sweet. I can see why you like her." His mask still shrouds his face and obscures his amber eyes.

"Can you really see out of that?" I ask.

"Yeah, it's better than the Iron Man helmet and spandex Spider-Man mask." He has cosplayed many fictional characters over the years. Even more than me.

We reach a hallway where attendees gather on the carpeted floor with merch bags. Looking sweaty and winded from running around the conference center all day, most either nap or eat pork bao buns from the Con's food truck.

"To the writer's panel?" I ask Xander, checking the schedule in the hallway.

"I'm down," he says.

"Wait," Donnelly interjects, extending a hand to us to stay put.

What's going on?

Frog sets a hand on my arm, silently telling me to remain here too, and Quinn has a finger to his earpiece. A look of concentration shared among the three of them, but Donnelly is the one with his phone out.

I'd say Xander and I share a glance of concern, but I can't see his face. In the hall, we're near a silver, black-and-blue balloon arch with *huge* three-dimensional cardboard letters underneath, which spell out *Beneath a Strong Sentiment.* It's the perfect Instagrammable background, but thankfully no one is trying to snap pics.

Xander whispers to me, "What do you think's going on?" His breath has quickened.

"Maybe a famous actor showed up." Just as I say it, my phone rings, and my heart lurches to my throat. Oh no.

It's Moffy.

Donnelly being on his phone is making more sense. We're in San Francisco. I think they might be out of comms range, and if something *bad* is happening in Philly, our bodyguards wouldn't hear through the radio.

I put the phone to my ear. "Moffy?"

"Luna," Moffy says a little out of breath.

"It's Moffy?" Xander whispers, worried. "What's he saying?"

I can't exactly put our older brother on speakerphone in public. I just ask him, "What's up?"

"I just wanted to let you both know…" Moffy starts telling us.

"What is it?" Xander asks, and without thinking, he flips the mask to the top of his damp hair. Flushed and sweaty faced, he instantly becomes a beacon to every young girl in the hallway.

A girl gasps, "That's Xander Hale."

"XANDER HALE!" another screams.

His expressive amber eyes grow wide. "Fuck."

"Oh my God, I think that's Luna Hale too!"

I take his hand, ready to fight off the crowds. But our bodyguards are so incredibly quick. No time to think or move on my own accord. Frog and Quinn are ushering me to the nearest exit, and Donnelly leads Xander in the same path. My brother quickly slides the mask back on, even if it's too late.

"Wait, Xander!"

"XANDER!"

I glance back to see overwhelmed attendees shedding tears and snapping photos of my brother.

Frog thrusts open the double doors of the emergency exit. "Luna?"

"I have her," Quinn says, his hand on my shoulder, easing me forward. I just now notice how Donnelly twists back to check on me. I wonder how much he's been doing that this trip.

My heart flutters in a strange pattern. How often did he check on Original Luna? Was he always attentive? Was he always here, looking out for her?

I want to know *so badly*, but not from anyone but her. *Accio, my memories!* I've already tried every conjuring spell from multiple fictional works, and my mediocre magical abilities aren't saving the day.

Would Mom be sad knowing she birthed a muggle?

Xander and I are led to a security SUV in the parking lot. We're fast enough that no one chases us, and I hurriedly climb into the backseat beside my brother. Our bodyguards remain outside the vehicle, talking between themselves in a serious conversation.

Xander rips off his mask, eyeing me consolingly. "I'm sorry I fucked it up," he whispers sadly.

My brows bunch. "You could never fuck it up."

He slams his head back against the headrest. "I fucking hate my life."

My heart clenches. Sometimes I felt suffocated from the fame, from needing bodyguards, from being a teenager and not on my own yet—but I never felt as trapped as my brother.

Silently, I place my hand on his hand, which rests on the leather seat. Xander looks down, his breath slowing. There could've been an alternate universe in which I woke up, and my brother wasn't alive. It was plausible. I know that. I feared that.

His gaze lifts to mine.

"I'm just happy you're here," I whisper.

Xander's eyes glass with tears as he nods. "I'm happy you are too, Luna." I reach over, and my brother hugs me the same time I hug him.

My phone falls between us.

Shit! Moffy...

I hurry and put the call on speakerphone. "Moffy? Are you still there?"

"Yeah, is everything okay?" Worry is tattooed to his voice. "Farrow says you guys got spotted."

Huh, the bodyguard hotline works in mysterious *quick* ways.

"Summers?" Moffy asks.

"All good," Xander says, wiping his watery eyes with the back of his hand. "What's up with you? Why the call?"

"MK is in labor," Moffy announces. "Farrow and I are at the hospital with her."

Oh wow, it's happening. "Is everything going okay?" I ask.

He assures she's doing great. He just wanted to let us know before the news inevitably leaked to the media. Xander and I start calculating the time it'd take to fly to Philly from San Francisco. But Moffy doesn't want us to cut our trip short.

"Take a ton of pics. I want to see all of them," Moffy tells us, a smile in his voice like he's imagining the dorky photos we'll send him. Which I already have a few of Xander and I posing like action stars in the hotel hallway. "Your niece will be here when you get back. Just be careful. We'll FaceTime later."

My heart is torn. I want to be there, but I like this time I'm spending with Xander.

"Okay," I whisper. "We're sending our good energies towards the baby and MK."

"Me too," Xander breathes.

Moffy says, "I love you both more than Dad loves Hellion, Cyclops, and Quicksilver all rolled in one."

"Bullshit," Xander nearly smiles.

"My love is that big, Summers. Better believe it."

I begin to smile now. "I believe," I whisper. The love of my family is the easiest thing to have belief in.

"WELL, AT LEAST KINNEY WILL BE HAPPY SHE gets to hold the baby before us," Xander says, lying on a queen-sized hotel bed and flipping through the TV channels. After attending *one* Fanaticon late-night party, which awesomely included foam and 3D sunglasses and EDM music, we're chilling in my brother's room and waiting for news on the baby.

"Yep," I say. I've been writing a little on my laptop, lying on the other queen-sized bed. Which is actually Donnelly's bed. Xander requested security to stay in his room. It's not that unusual, but it *is* unusual when said bodyguard is a guy that I have feelings for.

Feelings that've been difficult to make sense of.

Right now, Donnelly has an arm bent against the wall, gazing out the window at views of the bay. He's been checking his phone every couple of minutes.

I'm not stalking him. I'm just observing. I can do that without it being obsessive. Can't I?

Cheeks hot, I go back to writing *Human Him, Cosmic Her* where I last left off. Not even five minutes later and my phone rings.

"Is that them?" Xander nearly leaps off his bed.

I set aside my laptop while he dives onto my mattress and collects my phone first. "It's him!" Xander clicks into the FaceTime, and I scoot closer to him.

I glance up, and Donnelly is so far away still, just watching us. Isn't Farrow his best friend? "Do you wanna come see?" I ask him.

His chest rises, then he nods. Sitting beside me, Donnelly joins our video frame.

"Moffy?" Xander calls. "We can't see you, man."

We hear Farrow tell our brother, "Click the video button."

"Yeah, I got it, thank you for that helpful instruction," Maximoff says.

"Anytime, wolf scout." Hearing the smile inside Farrow's voice instantly calms me. *All must be well.*

They suddenly appear, Farrow and Maximoff—and my brother is cradling a swaddled rosy-cheeked baby with the cutest little pout. They angle the camera to show MK in the background, still in her hospital gown but sitting up on the bed. She looks swoony watching the new dads, and she gives us two thumbs up.

"Everyone's healthy," Farrow tells us.

Donnelly makes a hand gesture, one that I think means *love.*

Xander can't stop smiling, and I feel more overwhelmed.

Moffy's eyes are bloodshot like he's been crying, I hope only happy tears, and Farrow touches the back of his skull in affection. To us, Moffy says, "Xander. Luna. You have a niece. Her name is Cassidy Keene Hale."

Cassidy? If they told me about this name before, I've forgotten it. Sadness envelops me, and I try to banish every last bit of it. But it's starting to feel insurmountable.

I want to hang on to the amazing pieces of life. Seeing my niece for the first time. This is spectacular, a singular moment in the timeline that I'm witnessing. I might not have the past just yet, but I have this.

Tears build. "It's cosmic," I suddenly realize.

"What is?" Moffy asks.

"Cassidy's birth. Maeve's birth. Ripley's birth," I tell everyone. "They were all born on the 15th. One in November, one in December, and the last in January. Cosmic happenings bring good fortune, I've always believed."

"The lucky few," Donnelly grins, but as our eyes briefly meet, we acknowledge that we're not so fortunate. And I hope they won't ever be unlucky like us.

I HAVE AN ADJOINING HOTEL ROOM TO MY

brother's, and I lean in the doorway between our rooms, about to let my brother go to sleep. Donnelly is saying goodnight to me, his hand perched high above my head.

I vacillate between wanting to talk to him longer and to go write more.

Laptop in my hands, I ask him quietly, "Why'd they name her Cassidy? Do you know?"

He nods. "Cassidy Walsh."

I frown. "Who's that?"

"Farrow's mom," Donnelly says, just as hushed. "She passed away when he was four. Breast cancer."

"I never knew that," I murmur.

"He might've told you."

And I just don't remember. Donnelly was trying to comfort me with the fact, but it sinks heavier. "Yeah." I glance up at him. "Time feels so strange to me. All these babies are being born and announced and just yesterday it felt like all my cousins were single." I stare far away. "I'm just waiting for everything to slow down, but it's not. It won't."

"Everyone else might feel like they're moving at warp speed, but I'm at your pace, space babe. We're in the slo-mo zone together." He's trying to make the slo-mo setting sound fun. For me, I think, but with him, I haven't wanted to go slow.

"Are you usually snail-paced with girls?" I ask him.

"Not usually, no," Donnelly admits, trying to read my expression. "But I've gotta be with you, you know that..."

I know. My gaze is downcast, mixed emotions torpedoing me. The only way for him to speed up is if I remember.

He takes my hand in his and rubs his thumb over my mood ring. It's grayer than purple today. Donnelly says, "I'd be frozen in a cryochamber pod with you, if that's what it took."

I brush some stray tears at the creases of my eyes. "Shit," I curse, lifting the collar of my shirt to wipe my face.

"Luna." He draws me closer, but I pull my hand out of his, then step further into my room.

"I'm okay." I lift my laptop. "I'm just gonna go write."

Donnelly shifts so he's facing my room. "Can I get you anything?"

Her. "No," I breathe.

"Alright." He checks over his shoulder, possibly at my brother. "But I'm a call or knock away if you need anything."

"Thanks, Donnelly," I whisper, fighting tears. I reach for the door handle. He inches back into Xander's room. And our grief-ridden eyes catch as I slowly shut the door on him.

FANATICON FORUM

We Are Calloway

Posted by @Omega4Ever

LunaQuinn should be taken seriously! Here's why (see pic)
The most underrated ship needs to sail ya'll. Stop sleeping on Luna & Quinn. I'm telling you these two are the ones secretly together. I've been through all the Fanaticon Con pics posted of Xander & Luna + SFO, and the pics from the foam party are epic. She loves him. And he's back on her detail after the kidnapping? How motherfucking CUTE. He's there to support her and help her. It is the *only* thing that makes total sense.

@BeetleJuice23: I can't see Luna with anyone.

@ConnorsEggpant: LunaQuinn is cute. I like it. But I def need to see more foam party pics. Someone should try to toy with the contrast. They're all so dark and grainy.

@LionsTigers_andHales: Of all the dating theories for Luna, this is the most plausible for sure. He's legit behind her ass in the pic. If you zoom in, his hand is on her hip. I bet she was grinding on him.

@Iheart_ryke_meadows: Awwwww they would be soooooo freaking cuuuuute!! Imagine how sweet he prob was to her after her fics leaked?

@beckett_is_mine: I love the LunaQuinn theories and all, but I think Quinn can do a lot better.

@StaleBread89: Never heard of a LunaQuinn. Luna and Donnelly are the better match. No contest. #Lunnelly

@dragons_breakfast15: Luna and the ass-wiper? Fuck no.

46

Paul Donnelly

XANDER IS CONKED OUT in the other bed, but I can't sleep. I sit up against the mound of pillows propped on the headboard. Hotel room is pitch-black, except for the blue glow of my cellphone. It's not what's keeping me wide awake though.

For one, Luna is sad, and that makes me really fucking sad. Giving her space is what I think she wants, so that's what I'm trying to do.

For another, I got stuck scrolling through the WAC forum on Fanaticon. I thought I blacked out seeing the LunaQuinn thread. I literally had to *blink* to read beyond the title of the post.

The "epic" foam party picture is so dark that I had to fiddle with the brightness and contrast for fifteen minutes to see anything worth seeing. Which isn't much. Luna bent over to grab the 3D glasses she dropped, and Quinn had been behind her. Hands off her. That's the truth of the non-romantic matter.

Yeah, it looks like he's up against her ass…but he wasn't. *I* was there. Right there. You just can't see me in the pic. I'm obscured in the dark background.

I pinch my eyes, aggravated, and I rub at them. Exhaling, I pop open Twitter and tweet about my favorite triad. Akara, Banks, and Sulli announced their marriage and pregnancy today. Finally. Lots of joyous things happening this December 15th. *Love. Commitment. Babies.*

My gaze burns, and I close out of Twitter, not sure how to release a heaviness off my chest this time. I think it's mostly stemming from not knowing if Luna is alright. I keep glancing over at the adjoining door.

I'd send her a text, but I also don't want to wake her.

Stop thinking about her. Impossible. Don't wanna do it. Don't wanna be in that hellscape.

I'm gonna keep thinking about her, but I can't spend another hour torturing myself with social media and bad thoughts.

As quietly as I can, I slip out of bed and sneak into the bathroom. Shutting the door softly, I flip on the lights. Pristinely clean as hotel bathrooms should be, I hop up on the counter and push aside Xander's dopp kit.

I dial a number. He might be awake.

"Bro," Oscar answers on the second ring. "You've been missing the fuck out."

I smile. "Nah, I like where I am." *Just wish I was in her room tonight.*

"Did San Francisco hijack my best friend? Last time you were on the West Coast, you said it smelled like snot and sad dreams."

"That hasn't changed much," I say casually and pick up a complimentary mini bottle of hand lotion. "Where are you?"

"Hospital. All hands on deck for when Redford leaves with the Husband and Baby Number Two. Get this, Gabe and MK."

I start to grin. "Our Gabe?"

"Gabe Montgomery," Oscar confirms. "Our big rookie buffoon. He was feeding her *ice chips*, Donnelly. While she was in labor and delivery. Redford saw it with his own two eyes."

"They're together?" I ask, opening the lotion bottle and sniffing. Smells good, like citrus. *Luna smells better.*

"Dating. Early stages is the rumor. They didn't know how to tell Maximoff and Farrow, so they've kept it to themselves."

"He was dating her while she was nine-months pregnant," I realize.

"It's juicy. I love it."

"Stamp." I grin more, no judgment from me. "That's the big thing I'm missing out on?" I pick up a mini bottle of bath wash.

"Besides holding Cassidy, there's not much else. Just miss you, bro. I'm surrounded by way too many temp guards. SFO is *down* for the count around here. Akara and Banks are in Costa Rica. Thatcher's suspended. You took my baby bro and Frog to California. Gabe is throwing heart eyes in MK Land. Redford is all I've got, and I love that motherfucker but he's not you."

"Knew I was your favorite," I smirk. "You gonna let me tattoo you now? Been perfecting the cock and balls since elementary school."

"You ever try tattooing a dick on me, I'll have my husband dig up the ugliest footage of you from background clips of WAC and spam-post them."

"He'll be digging forever."

"You wish you were that pretty," he slings back.

"Luna thinks so," I say more softly.

Oscar goes quiet for a beat. I glance out at the shiny glass shower stall. These hotel rooms don't have the bathtub combo with flimsy plastic shower curtains. Just snazzy black tiles and premium soaps. After the pause, he asks, "How are you two?"

I've replayed our last conversation a dozen times. Can't figure out where I went wrong. Seeing her cry is a knife slowly sinking in my gut, and the raw sorrow in her eyes before the door closed on me—I can't shake that. Her pain is my pain, and I've never been fastened to another person's emotions this way.

"She's going through a lot so…" I pop the mini bottle top. "I just wanna be there for her."

"You are there. No one is expecting you to be a motherfucking magician and summon her memories."

"Yeah, I know," I breathe. "Just wish I could make it easier on her in the meantime."

"Highly doubt you're making it harder on her. She's like your cling wrap, suctioned to you."

I see her shut the door on me, and the bathroom seems emptier. Lonelier. "Makes sense. I'd fuck the whole Saran wrap box."

"Fuck you for that visual."

We're both laughing, but the sound fades out with the distance. He's back in the city that has my heart, but I'm here with the girl who has my heart and soul. Easy which one wins out.

I sniff the bath wash. Citrus again. "You see the Kitsulletti announcement?"

"Oh yeah, they dropped it today to help us here. Press is trying to hunt them down rather than mob the hospital. It's a stroke of genius. Wish I could claim it as my own, but that one is Kitsuwon—or really, Meadows." Akara and Banks took Sulli's last name after they got married. They're all Meadows now.

Their fitness app went live not too long ago too. Haven't had much time to check it out, but it's been buzzing online and hyped up.

Oscar asks, "You hear back from Akara about the deal he's making with Price?"

"Nah, he said he'd call, but I figured the signal must be bad where they are." The Meadows' Costa Rican treehouse is remote. "Been thinking I'll hear from him another day, maybe when he's back in PA."

"Check your email," Oscar says. "He sent me one this morning. It might be how he's communicating while he's out there."

I lower the phone from my ear, putting him on speaker, then I pop open my inbox. Sure enough, I have an email from my boss. "Yeah, I've got one."

"Call me a fucking mastermind."

I'm about to joke back, but I start reading the email and my face just plummets. The bottom of my stomach falls out. My brain goes woozy, and I lean further back until my head hits the mirror.

"Don't leave me hanging," Oscar says. "What's the prognosis? They make you Epsilon's errand boy for a month?"

I can't speak, thoughts evacuate, and I'm burning up. I grip the plain black tee I'm wearing, but I don't take it off.

"Donnelly?"

"I am Epsilon," I say.

"What the fuck do you mean? You're fucking with me?" Oscar says, worried. "Ha-ha. Okay, now tell me what it really says."

I scrape a hand down my face, nauseous. "I'm Epsilon. I don't work for Kitsuwon Securities anymore—"

"They can't do that," Oscar cuts in. "They legitimately do *not* have the power to transfer you from one company to the other."

I swallow a rock. "They do if I want to continue working in private security."

"The client hires the firm. Your client is turning eighteen in two weeks, so *Xander* chooses who to pay, either Triple Shield or Kitsuwon Securities."

"And if he wants me as a bodyguard, I'll be employed by Triple Shield," I tell him. "It says it right here."

"Send me the email."

"No."

"Donnelly—"

"I can fucking read," I shoot back.

"I'm not saying you can't. This isn't right. Why would Price even want you on his firm if he's putting up a fit about you being with a client?"

I have these answers. Akara explained everything in the email, not leaving me in the dark.

"'Cause he wants to keep an eye on me—that's what Price told Akara, but Akara thinks he just wants a bodyguard who's closer to the families on his firm." The bodyguards that are dating clients have been known to have special privileges, and it'd be useful. Before Oscar speaks, I add, "He gave Akara a choice. It was me or Quinn, Frog, and Gabe all together on the table. He let me go."

I'm not worth three bodyguards. Even the three *youngest*, greenest ones, and I'm trying not to let that get to me 'cause I'd rather go instead of them. But I know—*I know* I'm worth more than that, and it's ripping into my skin. Digging under the surface.

I could scream, but when I'm this upset, I usually crank down the volume.

Holding the phone loosely in my palm, I tell Oscar quietly, "Akara apologized over a dozen times in the email."

"Love the guy," Oscar says, "but he shouldn't have to *bend* to Triple Shield…" He trails off 'cause he knows why Akara *needs* to keep the peace with Price's firm. We work so closely with them, it'd be detrimental to our daily operations if we couldn't communicate effectively with Alpha and Epsilon. There might be bad blood and rivalry, but we've never let that compromise the safety of our clients.

If Price really felt offended or slapped in the face by *another* bodyguard getting with a client and not getting fired, then Akara needed to smooth things over the best he could.

I run my fingers through my hair. "At least I still have a job."

"There has to be a way to combat this."

Akara has done so much for me already. His hands were tied. I can't even fault him for how this went down. "I'm not combatting it," I say quietly.

Oscar lets out the heaviest sigh. "I can't get Redford right now, but I'll tell you exactly what he'd say. *You don't deserve this.* Epsilon will try to make your life hell until you quit—"

"I know what they're gonna do." I hop off the sink counter. They're the same pricks who think hazing is cute. At one point, they threw my luggage out of security's house in the gated neighborhood. Just 'cause they didn't want me living with them.

Being Omega means I was protected, always, by Akara. Now he won't be my boss.

I clutch the sink counter, staring at myself in the mirror. The persistence in my eyes, the determined lines etched in my forehead, I'm twenty-nine *beautiful* years old and I know what it took to see each one. I'm not easily defeated, and they're gonna have to really work to get to me.

"Donnelly—"

"I'll be alright. Gotta go."

Oscar lets out another breath. "Yeah, text me when you're in PA."

After we hang up, I inspect the stubble along my jaw. Need a good shave, and so I dig through my dopp kit for my stainless-steel straight razor. I can't…find it. Dumping the contents on the sink counter, I sift through floss, toothpaste, shaving cream—I know I brought my razor. I check underneath the counter. I didn't drop it.

So I look through Xander's dopp kit, thinking maybe there was a mix-up and he took mine thinking it was his. He has a Gillette with disposable heads. No straight razor among his toiletries.

"Where the fuck...?" I breathe out, wondering if Xander might've taken it and stashed it. *No.* No. Tension in my neck, I rest a hand against the searing muscle. *Could he have?* I shouldn't have brought that razor, knowing we'd be sharing a bathroom.

Then another jarring thought—*Luna.*

Didn't she use this bathroom today?

Panic punches me, and I immediately call her. It rings and rings and *rings.* Then I hear, "Howdy ho, don't you know that you've reached the voice inbox of a very peculiar specimen. If you meant to contact her, she shall review your message once she's returned from her interplanetary voyage. Can't say how long it will take, as the universe is a fickle place, but be patient with her. She hopes she won't let you down." Her voicemail ends, and a ball is in my throat.

I call again.

She doesn't answer.

I call a third time. *Pick up, Luna.*

No answer.

Instead of leaving a message, I leave the bathroom.

Careful not to wake Xander, I sneak over to the adjoining door. My side isn't locked, but as soon as I try to push her door open, I realize hers is. More hurriedly, I swipe a keycard off the dresser and exit the hotel room.

Since Luna doesn't know Frog that well anymore, she just wanted to room alone. So Quinn and Frog are sharing a hotel room, but right now, he's posted outside Luna's door, sitting and scrolling on his phone. We're taking extra precautions after the kidnapping and all. I'm positive no one has broken into her room, since her two bodyguards have been swapping late-night duty.

Quinn sees me, then glances back at Luna's door.

"Just checking on her," I tell him, nearing with the keycard to her room. I withhold alarm, trying not to alert Oscar's brother of anything wrong. It might be all in my head.

He stays seated. "Just say you're taking a three a.m. booty call. I might be six years younger than you, but I've been around the block."

Not her block. Territorial, possessive feelings flex my muscles. I could quip back, *tell your block I say hi*, with a grin, but I can barely muster one right now. So I just mutter an, "Alright, Quinnie," and swipe the keycard. Lock flashes green, and I push inside, closing the door behind me.

It's dark.

"Luna, it's me," I whisper, my pulse gradually ascending.

The sheets of her king-sized bed are rumpled. A laptop is folded open on a pillow, but Luna isn't on the bed. I flip on a light. Her room is empty, but I hear the shower running.

Adrenaline overrides fear, and I sprint to the bathroom. Not even wasting time calling her name, I go for the handle. It's unlocked, and as soon as I charge inside, the single thought in my head is *please be alive.*

I won't survive if she dies; in this second, I feel that truth radiate through me.

"Luna?" I bolt for the glass shower stall. She's sitting on the black tile, her head tucked against her knees and thin arms wrapped around her bent legs. Hot water pelts her naked body, steam billowing to the ceiling, and with my heart shredded in my throat, I snag a towel and quickly rush into the shower.

"Luna?" I call out, her head just barely lifting. Her eyes are puffy and bloodshot, and I swivel the faucet, shutting off the cascade of water.

Bending down to her, I wrap the towel around her shoulders, cocooning her, but I'm checking the wet tile for my razor. Blood, is there blood? No—what if it washed down the drain? I see her watching me search, and so I end up sitting in front of Luna, slowing my movements. I edge closer to her, spreading my legs open so she's between them. She hardly stirs.

Then I gently touch her left arm, checking for cuts. Right arm. Her legs. Insides of her thighs. When I lift my gaze to hers, knowing she's not harmed, an onslaught of emotion slams against me. My eyes sear, my nose runs, and I wipe it with the back of my hand before I hold her splotchy, flushed cheek, my fingers nestling in her wet hair.

She hasn't torn away from my gaze, but hers is so wrecked.

"What's going on, Luna?" I whisper.

She opens her mouth, but she's choked for words. It takes her a long time to speak, but when she does, her voice quakes. "I just really want my memories back." She breaks into a gutted noise, sobbing against her knees. "They're not coming back like I hoped they would."

I touch the back of her head and kiss her forehead. I weave my arms around her small frame.

Grief rattles her body, but she manages to look up again. "I know it was wishful thinking," she says in the smallest voice, "but I started believing writing would bring her back. I've written and written and written, and *nothing*, Donnelly. I remember nothing. It's lost—it's really lost, or she would've come back by now."

I hold her face while her tears slip.

She's mourning the forgotten past, and I can't pretend to know what it feels like to lose three years of my life. I can't pretend to understand that pain, but I feel hers excavating a space inside me. "I know you expected to remember more," I murmur, brushing her wet cheek with my thumb, "but what's the rush, Luna? The past isn't a place I ever want to live inside."

It's where I've had to be. It's what she lost.

"Memories are all we have," Luna whispers tearfully. "When I'm gone, when you're gone, that's all that's left of us, and I want to remember you. I want you to remember me. I don't want to leave an invisible footprint on the world."

My nose flares, talk of invisibility hurtling me to the past and our present and towards the future. I dip my head closer to hers. "You won't," I breathe. "We aren't invisible—you and me. Everyone can see us now, and I see you." I look into her while she's looking into me.

"I've seen you, and even if you don't have all of the past to hold on to, you can still make new memories. You can live *now*, Luna. You can live the life that you get to choose. The universe is yours, space babe, and you're going to do and experience amazing things on my planet—I just know it."

Her eyes well up again. "Dancing in your bedroom at four a.m. Eating homemade turkey sandwiches," she says, recalling the new memories she's been creating. "Kissing that makes my whole body sing. Talking so late into the night, I wished morning never came."

I start getting choked up.

"Loving when I should be grieving. Smiling when I believed I couldn't be happy. Hopeful when I only knew to doubt," she whispers. "I've experienced plenty of amazing things already on Earth, and they're all because of you."

I pinch my watering eyes. Fuck me. Then I cup her cheeks again, this time with both hands. She finally releases her death-clutch on her legs, and she hugs onto me.

I look at her lips, then at her eyes while she's searching mine, and I breathe, "My heart is a chasm of everything I know and love, and it will always be filled with you." I can't look away from her. "I love you, Luna. I love you so bad, not having you just hurts."

Her breath shortens, more tears cascading.

"Luna?" I try to catch her drifting gaze. Is she sad? Distressed? Can't tell.

She swallows hard to ask, "If I told you I loved you too, would you even believe me?" It comes out tiny and feeble.

"Why wouldn't I?"

"Because I'm obsessed." She rubs at her eyes, frustrated. "Because it hasn't been long enough. Because I don't have her memories."

Maybe that's partly why she feels like she needs them sooner rather than later. She thinks I won't believe in her love for me if she can't remember the years we had together.

"I'd believe you," I tell her. "Truth be told, it's harder for me to doubt you, space babe."

She holds onto my gaze, and I hope she believes *me* and what I'm saying. Then she whispers, "Will you spend the night? Just to sleep."

"I was about to ask if I could," I tell her, then I press a gentle kiss to her lips before I stand. She watches me rise, then she brings the two ends of the towel tighter around her body and follows suit. Back in her room, I mention how I need to speak to her brother for a quick sec.

She might think it's about how I'm leaving his room and how I'll have Quinn post up outside his door, but it's more than that.

I TURN ON THE BRIGHTEST LIGHTS OF THE HOTEL

room, and Xander groans into a squint. He shields his eyes. "Everything okay?" he asks tiredly.

"I'm getting Quinn to stay outside your door. I'm gonna be in your sister's room."

Xander cringes. Can't be a pleasant feeling being reminded I've banged his sister, even if we're not doing anything now. Surprisingly though, he asks, "Things are better between you two then?"

"I think so." *I hope so.* I take a seat on the edge of my mattress, facing his bed.

Xander rolls onto his back and starts pulling himself up. "If all she wants is your dick, maybe you should be playing hard to get."

Who says I don't also want her pussy? He's not the audience for that comment, so I'm keeping my mouth shut. I wanna say I have enough experience to overturn a teenager's relationship advice, but I don't. I have as much as Xander does in this realm.

"Don't think that's all she wants," I tell him casually, then nod to him. "Need to ask you somethin'."

"Yeah?" He sits on the edge of his bed, facing me too. "What's up?"

I grip my knees, trying to figure out how to pose this. I usually don't press people too hard, but I should've with Beckett when he was using drugs. I'm not making that mistake again.

I try to remember what it's like being Xander's age, but his two-weeks-from-eighteen doesn't look like mine. I was already on my own by then. I could only rely on myself and the new friends I made.

"I'm not your mom," I tell him. "Not your dad."

"Yeah, I know," he says with very little bite to his voice. He's soft. It fucking reminds me of his sister, and that screws me up for a second.

"You're not gonna get in trouble with me, alright? I won't talk about this to anyone. Just please don't lie. You can even tell me to fuck off if you really want to."

Xander tenses. "Okay."

"I can't find my straight razor," I breathe. "And I'm not saying you took it, but I'm not saying you didn't take it 'cause I don't know where it is. You get me?"

He runs his palm over his forehead a couple times, then looks over at me. The expression in his eyes is one of confliction. I say nothing. Do nothing. Then he rises, goes to his backpack on the floor, and returns to me with my stainless-steel razor.

Xander hands it to me.

I fold it up. "Were you going to use it?" I ask, and I wonder if maybe I shouldn't have asked. Too late now.

"I don't think so," he answers truthfully. "I thought about it. One time." When he sits back down, I come over and take a seat right beside him. He turns to look at me. "I'm sorry, Donnelly."

I turn to look at him. "Thanks for being honest with me." We chat for a while longer, until I know he's not stressed or anxious. We're cool, and I sense trust. Hope he feels like he can come to me, if need be.

Back in Luna's room, I find her already beneath the covers. Lights off, and I shed my damp pants and my tee before crawling into bed with her. I think I'm quiet enough, but as soon as I roll towards her, she scoots into my chest. Holding her, I feel her heart beating against my pulse. Alive. Slumber and something more content ease my eyes closed.

It feels like my first sleep in weeks.

47

Luna Hale

EVER SINCE THE Fanaticon Convention five days ago, I've tried to put Original Luna to rest. I suppose this is the final stage of grief.

Acceptance.

And with the new year on the horizon, I have greater plans for my future. Back in Philly at the penthouse, morning light shines through the curtains of my window, and I sit cross-legged on my bed, scrolling on my laptop.

I'm enrolling as a full-time student at Penn next semester. English major, I've decided, but maybe I'll double major in Business too. On the laptop screen, the red and blue University of Pennsylvania logo stares back at me while I choose my college courses.

I pick my last one and click into *Television and New Media*. It sounds fun to dive deeper into the mediums that I use often and love so much, and I want to learn more about digital media and the history of television, which the course says it covers.

It fits into my class schedule too. Mondays, Wednesdays, Fridays. Professor: *Wyatt Rochester*.

Done.

I shut the laptop, and Orion leaps off the bed, wagging his tail like we're about to adventure the Philly streets for a morning walk and hydrant sniffs. I just took him out to pee. "We can go exploring soon, I promise," I say, and he flops happily on his doggie bed. "I need to clean my room first."

I start with the heap of manuscripts on my bed. Gathering them, I put each one gingerly into my plastic tub, only storing the ones I've read. So I check each title carefully. I'm not back on Fictitious yet, but I've given Charlie more of my stories to edit.

When I reach for a thinner stack of papers, my brain whirls and dizzies at the typed font. "The Chasm of Elsewhere," I read out loud, pulling the story closer.

More slowly, I sink back on my butt and flip the page. I haven't read this one yet, but my heart speeds like I know it's important somehow. Like a string to a memory is tickling my mind, and I just need to pull…

So I read.

And as soon as I reach *the* line, tears flood my eyes. "He didn't," I whisper to myself, and with my finger, I trace the printed words that Donnelly spoke to me.

> My heart is a chasm of everything I know and love, and it
> will always be filled with you.

My chin trembles, realizing he quoted my story, and I didn't know until now. I clutch the papers tighter, treasuring them a thousand times more. Memories are threads sewn into a magnificent tapestry of life, and following this one teeny string led me back to him.

They all keep leading me back to him.

Donnelly loves me. This me. The Luna of Today. The Luna of Yesterday. And I hope he'll continue to love the Luna of Tomorrow and each version of me thereafter.

Silently, I read more.

> "In time, everything could be destroyed, and your
> knowledge and love could be strewn elsewhere," Jocoby
> feared.
> "You will be with me for eternity." She squeezed harder.
> He held her cheek, stared into her depth, feeling her
> chasm of everything. "Eternity is not long enough."

I wipe the last of my tears. Those lines mean more to me after losing love and time, but Original Luna couldn't have known she'd have amnesia. "I wish I knew what you were telling me," I say to myself. "I have so many questions still."

Was he your first love?

Was it love at first sight?

Do you think you were star-crossed to end tragically?

Were you hopeful that you'd be together for eternity?

Did you feel like eternity was not long enough?

If I don't ever get my memories back, I'll never really know, and the weight of despair tries to bear on me again. I blow out a long, long breath and try to concentrate on what I can control now. Clean my room. Fresh start. Original Luna decorated this space, and though it's still full of everything I love, I figured it might be good to have my own touches too.

So I declutter my desk, chucking dried out markers, and I feed Moondragon fish flakes. I unspool a string of multicolored fairy lights, and using a rinky-dink ladder, I carefully staplegun them to the molding of my walls. When I reach the Sagittarius tapestry, I hop onto the ground, and I thumb the sketches Donnelly drew for OG Luna that are still tacked up.

I'll leave those.

The tapestry can go. Maybe I'll draw on the walls instead. I unfasten the tapestry, and as soon as the fabric cascades to a pool at my feet and I see what it was hiding, my heart begins to race.

"Luna," I say to myself. "What is this…?"

It looks an awful lot like a vault. A steel safe. Nothing wildly large, just a small nook in the wall. The weirdest thing of all, there is no code. No lock. Just a button.

It's as though I intended for this to be found.

Goosebumps pimple my skin, and I press the green circle, hearing the spring mechanism before the vault easily swings open.

The cubby is small, and only one thing is shelved. Stepping forward, I seize the *nicest* bound manuscript among all my printed stories. The pages aren't stapled together or in a three-ring binder. I must've glued the edges in the spine of a hardcase book, but it has no title. Still, I can tell this is my handiwork. Shimmery silver, green, pink, and purple glitter decorate the hardcover.

My heartbeat hasn't slowed, and with a deep breath, I flip the cover and see the title page, more like a preface.

"Dear Unearthly Reader..." I begin to read the typed font. "One day, possibly millenniums from now when you discover this planet, I imagine you'll find this story entombed beneath centuries of rubble and heartache." My voice starts to shake a little. "If it's buried with my fragile bones, likely you'll think I'm the strangest creature you've ever seen. With my human arms and legs and feet. This story is not just so you'll understand how often I've thought of you—that I've wondered what you'd be like..." Tears prick my eyes. "...and if your planet is far better than the one I've lived on."

I choke up, but I push myself to keep reading out loud. "I want you to know who I am. Even if I'm gone." Silent waterworks stream, but I read more strongly, "This is my story that I hope you'll find and be able to read. And it's his."

I cover my mouth, my hand trembling.

"I couldn't exclude him," I read. "You'll find out why soon enough. The story does not begin with my first breath on Earth. I've started at the part that matters the most to me. May you discover something of worth in this text; I hope it finds you well." I rub at my wet cheeks, my voice cracking. "Somewhere far, far away...Luna Hale." I squeak out my name.

I turn the next page, but I already know what this is.

I wrote a diary.

Staggering back into my globe chair, I sit and try not to sob on the pages. *I wrote a diary.* My body heaves in tearful, overcome waves. Before I even devour it whole, I hug the hardcase binding against my chest. It feels like I'm hugging her.

"Thankyouthankyouthankyou," I hiccup out.

I've searched for her. I've cried for her. I've needed her. And now

I've found a piece of her. Even if I don't have my memories now, I have *this*. Her words. Her heart.

When I gather my breath, I inspect the diary more, and I realize it has *one* violet ribbon folded through the pages. I open it up on that bookmark.

It's another preface to the Unearthly Reader. I start reading, "...I wasn't sure I should continue, not after all that's happened. But he's a big reason why I'm not stopping."

I wonder if this is the place in time where her fics leaked, and maybe she thought about stopping the diary like she stopped writing her stories.

I read, "If you ever find this, you should know there are *good* people on Earth. He's worth knowing. He's worth remembering." I know she must be referring to Donnelly. "And when the world has decayed and all I've ever known has disappeared in time, you should know the very best of humankind is him."

Tears brim again.

I didn't have premonition, but I did want to leave my story behind. My story with Donnelly. Because I closed myself off to others and never shared as much as I wanted, but I felt safe enough to leave it behind for a future.

I just couldn't have known it'd be left for my future. For me to find.

I read in a shaky voice, "Please, keep him alive."

I will.

"I promise," I say to myself. "I will." With another breath, I read, "It's always been easier to believe in you than anything else."

It hits me hard, and I repeat it again, "It's always been easier to believe in you than anything else."

I've been hard on Original Luna. On myself. Frustrated and angry for not remembering the past in enough time, for being so mysterious and secretive and shut off, and my self-belief shrunk more than grew.

It's always been easier to believe in you than anything else.

I want to always believe in myself.

Because writing this and finding this feels so, so unbelievable, and no sentient creature descended from an unknown galaxy to gift me the knowledge I craved.

This, all along, was just me.

Before I read too much, I rush into the bathroom. Does Donnelly know about the vault? This diary? I want to tell him about it, and without knocking, I push into his room.

"Donnelly!" I exclaim excitedly, but his bed is made, a new white comforter replacing the floral one. He's taken down most of the grannie décor in favor of his own style. A Van Halen tour poster is tacked to the wall, along with the signed Bass poster from the convention.

The only thing he left was Jane's oil painting.

I'll find him.

It's a desire, a need, an obsession, possibly, but mostly, it's a yearning to simply exist with him. And I really want to exist with Paul Donnelly.

48

Paul Donnelly

ON THIS HAZY, chilly winter morning, I stand on the shingles of a very well-built roof. Sturdy. Robust. "You beautiful shingled bastard, don't let me down on the ground," I say and squat to grab a heap of colorful Christmas lights I brought up here.

Goal: *Don't slip. Don't fall.*

I balance well enough.

Shingles still beneath my boots, I smile. "Good, roof. I knew we were friends."

Been on many roofs, even helped a friend of a friend with a roofing project back at Yale for a free meatball sub and case of beer. So I feel equipped for this task at the Hale House.

I look out at the still, quiet neighborhood. The road is empty of cars, and only a few birds are chirping. It's really early. I came here to sign contracts at security's mansion, which is on the other street. I'm in a transitionary period between both companies at the moment while paperwork gets filled and filed.

Since I'd been in the literal neighborhood, I wanted to see if Lily needed any help around her house. Thought it'd be a nice thing to do since she's still on crutches.

I didn't account for her being at her sister Rose's house this morning.

I also didn't account for Xander's dad answering the door. Still, show must go on, and so I asked Lo if there was anything that needed to be done.

He gave me a ladder and a cardboard box of badly twisted lights, then sent me outside.

Think maybe he believed I'd fight with the ensnared strands and quit, but these tedious tasks are calming to me. It took me less than an hour to check all the bulbs, replace the busted ones, and detangle the lights.

The Hales deserve a happy holiday, after all they've been through. They've been so preoccupied the past month, they haven't put up any decorations, and it's five days till Christmas. Even the fir tree in the front yard looks barren and pitiful.

Gonna fix that too. There might be ornaments and ribbons in their attic.

Going to the lake house is a typical Cobalt, Meadows, Hale family tradition this time of year. But plans for the holidays have been up in the air. I've heard they're leaving on Christmas Eve, then it changed to the week after New Year's, then the week before. Don't know what it'll land on yet or if the trip will get scrapped altogether.

The roof clips are in place, and I've already plugged in the multicolored lights, so they're lit in the detangled spool at my feet.

I start systematically hanging the strands, and midway into my work, Xander's dad emerges to check on me.

He stands on the front lawn and hoists a coffee mug to his lips, one that says *World's Mightiest Dad* beside a caped superhero.

I ask him, "How's she look?" I gesture to the lit dangling lights.

"Crooked," he says dryly.

I survey my work. "You need your glasses?"

"Where's your coat?" Lo suddenly asks, his brows pinched like I'm nuts. He looks warm in a red fleece jacket, whereas the long sleeves of my thin T-shirt are rolled up to my elbows.

"I like the cold," I say. "Makes my nipples hard."

He glares, then touches his chest. "Luna's dad."

"Change your name for me again?" I say with a grin, walking over to another section of the roof. Smells like progress, with the lights and my relationship with Lo. Sure, I'm not his best friend (yet), and he hasn't invited me over for a bagel and cream cheese.

But in his eyes, I'm no longer just his son's bodyguard.

It's something, someone, more.

Lo drinks his coffee. "I'd tell you not to fall, but I'm actually hoping it happens. Imagine that." He feigns surprise.

"Imagine," I smirk and focus on *not* slipping. Steady on my feet, I hang another strand, framing the house, one that I've always thought resembles Kevin McCallister's from the Christmas flick *Home Alone*. It's built for holidays and loving families.

As Lo watches me, I'm gonna pretend he's pleased. The sharper lines of his cheekbones say otherwise, but that could just be his morning *I hate the world* face.

He begins to retreat inside the house.

"See ya, Luna's dad!" I shout to him.

"Bye, Paul."

Win some, lose some. I glance at the tattoo on my wrist. Things could've been so much worse by now, and the fact that I'm still even thirty feet from Loren Hale and on his property is a success worth celebrating.

No achievement is too small in my eyes. Seeing Luna sleeping this morning, *celebratory.* Girl sleeps hard too. Didn't want to wake her on my way out, but now I'm wishing I left a note or something.

Not sure how much time passes while I string up the lights, and I'm not wearing a watch. Gave mine to Luna, and I'm glad she's kept it. My phone is on the front porch with my radio. And right as I start getting antsy to contact her, a car rumbles down the road.

The black security SUV rolls up the Hale driveway, and a big fluffy Newfie the size of a mini-pony springs out first.

"Orion!" Luna calls, chasing after his leash. Once she grabs it, he tugs her towards the house, and I'm just standing here on the roof, grinning at the cutest sight in my universe. As long as she's with me, I don't really care which planet we're on: hers or mine. I just still hope it can become ours.

"Your horse is trying to get loose!" I call to her.

Luna looks up, entranced by the sheer sight of me. On her parents' roof and next to a bundle of lit Christmas lights. A grin spreads across my face. Then she jerks forward as Orion pulls harder, and she falls on her knees in the dewy grass.

"Shit," I say and descend the ladder quickly.

The security SUV has already begun backing out of the driveway. Looks like Quinn and Frog dropped off Luna, and her bodyguards don't need to stay at the house while she's here.

As they leave, my boots reach the earth, and I go to help Luna. She's picking herself up, so I collect Orion's leash. It's not just puppy pep, considering his littermates don't have the same energy. Out of the Hale's four Newfies, only Luna's dog is this excitable and lively.

The furry guy tries jumping up on me, and he's practically my height. "Down, down, down. Sit for your mom." I scratch his head while he complies, and I kiss his fur. "That's my good boy." He slobbers all over my hand, and I wipe my palm against my jeans before I turn to Luna.

She's here, and the sight inflates my lungs, lifts my chest. I try to read her overwhelmed expression, but I can't decipher the entirety of it.

"You looking for me?" I ask her.

She nods. "I want to show you something." Her cheeks look rosy from the cold, but she's wearing a cozy white puffer jacket. Then she unburies a manuscript from beneath it.

I think it's a manuscript at least. It's bigger than a book, but the binding is different from her others.

"Have you seen this before?" Luna asks, handing me the hardcase, the cover glittery. No title. I search for one on the spine. Still none.

I frown. "No. It's from…?"

"Original Luna," she confirms. "I found a bank safe in my bedroom."

"Where?"

So she tells me in the wall behind the Sagittarius tapestry. I never even noticed that part of the wall felt different. Luna also explains the safe had no lock.

"You work in mysterious ways, space babe," I tell her and flip the cover. Reading the preface silently, overpowering emotion of disbelief and awe and love swells like a full-body rush.

"I found a piece of her," Luna says softly. "It's a diary."

I intake a staggered breath, and she's waiting a long minute for me to reply. Luna left this without realizing she was the one who'd need it.

It's nothing short of amazing, but I can't even be completely surprised. Because amazing is what she's always been to me.

I catch her gaze. "You're the Unearthly Reader." I wipe a tear that falls down her cheek. "Always knew you were too extraordinary to be only human."

"Humans aren't so ordinary," she says quietly, staring into me. "You are extra-spectacular." She glances at the diary in my hands. "Even though I can finally get some answers from myself about the past and my feelings for you, I know it's not the same as living it."

I hold in a breath, on an edge. I shut her diary, tucking it beneath my arm. "Yeah?"

She nods. "But I have enough of her and *all* of me to know what I feel today, and I don't want to keep fretting over a past I lost. I just want to move forward into the future I have. One where I get to experience so many more things than I ever did. New things, weird things, wishful things, daunting things, romantic things."

"All the things," I start to grin, my heart pounding. "You'll get that, Luna."

"Will you give me that?" Luna suddenly asks, her voice pitching a little with nerves. She's hanging onto my belt loops. "And I know it's a big thing to give. Yourself. But I just really want to experience every possible thing with you." She adds more strongly, "I choose you, Donnelly. I want you. I'm falling in love with you."

With me.

Luna continues, "And you might think it's too soon—"

"It's not too soon," I say, releasing a breath. "I'm just happy it's not too late." I cup her flushed cheek. "I can keep giving you who I am, and just so you know, the weirdest, strangest, most beautiful Luna will always be the one you are. Not the Luna you think I want." Her body bows closer, and I say, "You've got me. I promise. And I know how promises are made on your planet."

Her eyes sparkle. "Tell me. Show me."

I explain, and in seconds, we collide. The tips of our tongues touch and toy, and pure affection reflects in our gazes. My grin has never felt this bright, and effortlessly I bring her mouth nearer and close my lips over hers, turning our promise into a kiss.

Her hands fist the back of my shirt. Clinging. This isn't a quick two-second peck. We make out on her parents' front lawn in an endless, hot, heart-pumping moment. I don't want time to stop with Luna. I want to live each second, each minute, each perfect hour—so we're all over each other's timelines.

I've lifted her up in a front piggyback, my hands on her ass, and her legs are wrapped around me. Deep, hungry kisses.

"Do not desecrate my lawn!"

Our heads turn, but the voice came through a window. *Her dad.*

Luna laughs, and I set her on the ground before Lo finds a hose to spray us. She bends down to pick up the diary. Orion is lounging at our feet.

I dig in my pocket. "I've been meaning to give you this," I say. "It's an early Christmas gift." After fucking up her birthday present, I wanted to be better prepared. So I did some online shopping, and I could wait until the 25th to give it to Luna. But the moment is now, and I'm capturing it.

I keep it hidden in my fist, and while she comes closer, I explain, "You once told me all about the balance in the Force. How light and dark exist together, but it's up to us to choose the light." I open my hand, a pool of silver chain in my palm.

Luna sees, and I lift the necklace over her head.

She touches the new green kyber crystal at the end of the chain.

"In dark times, you found the light side, Luna Hale," I say. "Think that means you need one of these."

Tears crest her eyes, and she skims the crystal, pinched between her fingers. "I haven't always thought I could be a Jedi, but you know… today, I've started to really believe I can."

I wrap my arms around Luna, and she tucks herself against me. I'm proud of Luna, and I'm about to tell her, but she asks, "Where's yours?"

I pull mine out from under my shirt. I haven't taken it off. She touches the tips of the crystals together like it's a power-up move.

I start grinning. "Is this where we self-combust together?"

"And merge into our final forms."

"Bet my final form is me inside your pu…" I trail off at the sound of a car. Our heads turn as a red Audi SUV slows into the driveway.

Maximoff and Farrow. I recognize their new car, and soon enough, my best friend is unloading his brood. Arkham hops out first, but the brown Newfie waits dutifully for an almost two-year-old boy. Farrow lifts Ripley out of his car seat, and once the little boy is on the ground, he hangs onto Farrow's pant leg, looking tentatively over at me and Luna.

"Sometimes I think he's scared of me," Luna says to me under her breath. She hasn't been around Ripley too much recently. "Like he knows I'm not all the same."

"Nah, he's timid around everyone at times. Except for his dads."

Maximoff hasn't left the car for some reason. Not even as Farrow comes over with their daughter in a carrier, and Ripley walks off-kilter with tiny baby steps beside them, picking up speed when he sees Orion.

"Loonie's Doggie!"

Orion bounds for the baby, and I grab air instead of the leash. The dog barrels into Ripley, a full-on suplex, and the boy goes down in the grass.

"Shit," I curse.

"Orion, no!" Luna yells.

We all spring forward.

Farrow is at his son in seconds, carrier set down. He helps Ripley to his feet, speaking quietly with his son, who nods in reply. Farrow's head swings to the car like he knows Maximoff would be freaked seeing their kid take that impact.

Sure enough, the car door is cracked open. Maximoff is halfway out, about to come rushing to the rescue—literally one sole on the driveway. But a phone is to his ear.

"He's fine, wolf scout!" Farrow calls out.

"All good, Papa," Ripley says, brushing imaginary dirt off his kneecaps (he fell on his back), then looks to Orion with these toughened blue eyes and hugs onto the puppy's black fur in an embrace. Arkham greets his littermate with a wagging tail.

I'm smiling. Farrow would be smiling too if his concern wasn't beelined to his husband. "We're good!" Farrow calls out to Maximoff, who finally relents and returns fully to the car.

He must be on an important call, I realize. Through the windshield, I spot distress in his eyes.

Farrow's gaze finds mine, and he just shakes his head like *don't bring it up*.

I won't.

"Looks like your kid wants to be a pro-wrestler," I tell him instead.

Farrow's smile stretches while chewing gum. "And just yesterday he cried over a goldfish cracker."

Luna chimes in, "Goldfish crackers are kinda sad. They're dried up like they've washed ashore and crusted in the sun."

His smile grows fonder on her. "Hey, Luna."

She waves in a rainbow pattern, then eyes the newborn. "Can I hold her?"

"You don't even have to ask," Farrow says. He bends down and picks up Cassidy out of the carrier, cradling her. She looks fast asleep, her little lips puffing out air every couple of seconds.

Luna scoops Cassidy into her arms, stroking her soft cheek and whispering *hellos*. She really loves babies, and my stomach tries to clench.

Farrow is keeping an eye on Ripley, but I ask him, "You home for the holidays?"

"Yeah. We're staying here or going to the lake house. Whatever the families decide." He chews his gum slower, looking me over. "What about you?"

I run a hand against the back of my neck. "I'll go wherever Xander goes."

"Okay, but if he doesn't need a bodyguard here, where are you going?" Farrow asks.

I glance at her. "Wherever Luna goes, unless her dad—"

"He won't," Farrow says, "and if he does say you can't spend the holidays with us, then my family will be spending them with you."

It slams into me. He's choosing me over the Hales. Farrow has always put action to his words, and if there's any proof that I am his brother, his family, then this is it.

But I can't accept that offer.

"Don't do that," I whisper to him, shifting on my feet and getting nearer so Luna can't hear. "I'm not tearing apart any families. Not on Christmas."

Farrow has a look like his mind is made up.

"Lo will want me to stay anyway, I'm betting," I tell him, then motion to the lights on the roof. "He let me do that."

"It's pretty," Luna muses.

"See, I made their house pretty."

Farrow pops his gum, shaking his head but smiling.

The car door opens, stealing our attention. Maximoff walks over to us, shoulders squared, and Luna whispers, "Something's wrong." She's observing his grave expression.

I reach for her hand, and she holds it tight.

Maximoff joins us, pocketing his phone. And he looks at his sister as he says, "There's been a death in the family."

ABOUT THE AUTHORS

Krista & Becca Ritchie are *New York Times* bestselling authors and identical twins—one a science nerd, the other a comic book geek—but with their shared passion for writing, they combined their mental powers as kids and have never stopped telling stories. They love superheroes, flawed characters, and soul mate love.

CONNECT WITH KRISTA & BECCA

www.kbritchie.com
www.facebook.com/KBRitchie
www.instagram.com/kbmritchie

Milton Keynes UK
Ingram Content Group UK Ltd.
UKHW040730010823
426141UK00004B/315